THE
MŒNQUEST ™

A True Fantasy

To Yasmin
Inspired
journeys

2009

THE MOONQUEST™

A True Fantasy

MARK DAVID GERSON

Published by LightLines Media
223 N. Guadalupe St., Unit 171
Santa Fe, NM 87501
www.LightLinesMedia.com
www.TheMoonQuest.com

First LightLines Edition: January 2008

Interior book design: Bob Spear
Cover design: Angela Farley

ISBN: 978-0-9795475-8-4
Library of Congress Control Number: 2007902665

10 9 8 7 6 5 4 3 2 1

To the bard in all of us

May the stories, songs and dreams
flow forever

Acknowledgements

To all those whose aid, encouragement and guidance helped midwife *The MoonQuest*, sometimes unwittingly, I offer my deepest, heartfelt gratitude: among them, Bruce Barnes, who offered me the key to my dreams; Carole H. Leckner, who helped me claim my bardship; Ron and Carole MacInnes, who opened their hearts and home to me and the second draft of *The MoonQuest*; the monks of the sadly now-shuttered Nova Nada monastery, whose devotion to the silence inspired me to allow *The MoonQuest* to emerge from my own; the Emissaries of Divine Light at Sunrise Ranch, who created a space into which my words could flow freely; my readers, clients and writing students, whose support has always recharged my passion and creativity; Marisha Diaz, Courtney Eves, Sander Dov Freedman, a'Alia Golden, Fred Henderson, Geri and Art O'Hare, Rebecca Michaels, Francene Shoop, Kent Spies, and Karen and Larry Weaver, whose unwavering belief in me and my work has kept me on track; and a single card, pulled from *The Celtic Tarot* in 1994, that started it all.

Places and the embracing spirits that inhabit them have played a singular role in *The MoonQuest*'s genesis and creation: in particular, the trees and trails of Toronto's High Park; the mystical cliffs, salt marshes and oceanscapes of Nova Scotia; the numinous waters of Ontario's Georgian Bay; the Castle Rose-like majesty of Sedona's Courthouse Butte; the pulsing surf of San Diego's Pacific Beach; the enfolding refuge of California's Ojai Valley; and the enchanted mountains and high deserts of New Mexico.

This book is also a child of a cafe culture that, for the price of a cup, let me occupy a table for hours of uninterrupted literary flow. My hosts over the years have included The Coffee Merchant in Wolfville, Nova Scotia; The Daily Perk in Midland, Ontario; Desert Flour, Ravenheart Coffee and Wildflower Bakery in Sedona, Arizona; Java Jones in San Diego, California; and Seattle's Best Coffee at Borders Books in Broomfield, Colorado and Santa Fe and Albuquerque, New Mexico..

Special acknowledgments, too, to Bob Spear and Angela Farley, the creative team whose design magic has wrapped my words in this magnificent package.

Finally, to my daughter, Guinevere: Thank you for your voice and your light, which always reignite mine, and for the gift of your loving presence in my life.

Prologue

Na'an came to me in a dream this night. It was early. I had not been in bed long and the night was newly dark.

"It is time," she said, "time to fix The MoonQuest on parchment."

I was gladdened to see her after so many seasons, but I was not cheered by the message she bore. I tried to engage her in other discourse, but she was single-minded as only a Tikkan dreamwalker can be.

"It is not for me to boast of my exploits," I argued. "Others have sung them. Let them continue."

"No," she said, and her silver tresses shimmered as she shook her head. "It is your story to tell. It is for you to fix it in ink, to set the truth down for all to read."

I tried to resist, to shut Na'an's words from my heart, to return to the dreamless sleep that preceded her appearance. But Tikkan speak only what we know in our hearts to be true, and my heart would not close to her even as my mind longed to. Only by forcing my eyes open and my body to this table was I able to banish her milk-white face from my mind's eye. Only by letting my quill rasp across the blank parchment have I stilled her voice.

But my quill hovers over oceans of emptiness. I don't know what to write, where to begin. The story has so many beginnings and no clear ending. As a bard, as Elderbard, I am trained to know how to weave disparate elements into a tapestry of word and song that brings light and meaning to life. When recounting others' stories, I have no difficulty. The tales unfurl from my tongue as if by magic, as if M'nor herself were singing through me.

Na'an says it is my story. Perhaps she is right. Is that why the words come so reluctantly? So many seasons of storytelling and still I hesitate. Of all the stories to stick in my throat, how ironic that it should be The MoonQuest, a tale of the freeing of story itself.

You see how confused I am? I have not even introduced myself. My truth name is Toshar and I am old, so old that most who knew me by that name have passed on to other worlds.

Toshar... Even I have forgotten the boy who was Toshar, the youth who embarked on The MoonQuest all those seasons ago.

They call me Ko'lar now, the ancient word for Elderbard. It is a sign of honor and respect, but it separates me from the youth I was.

Perhaps Na'an is right. Perhaps it is time to bring back Toshar, to allow the boy I was to touch the man I have become, the man I will soon cease to be. Soon it will be time to release the ageless spirit from this aged body and move on to other realms, set off on other journeys. I have seen it and I welcome it. But it cannot be mine until I have told this story. Na'an insists.

She speaks, even as I sit here in full wakefulness, staring at the shadows cast by my flickering taper. Now, they loom, large and menacing. Now, they flit and flutter in delicate dance. I see it all now, in the leap of light against dark. The shadows will tell me the story and I will write what I see. I will write until my fingers and beard are black with ink. I will write until the story is told.

Only then will I be free to continue my journey. Only then will my daughter, Q'nta, be free to continue hers. She is nearly ready. Ryolan Ò Garan taught her well, taught her the lessons of The MoonQuest. Soon she will live them through my words and will be free to assume the mantle of her birthright, according to the ancient orders of succession:

From father to daughter, mother to son
The mantle passes, the Balance is done

I was an exception to the Law of Balance, a law as old as the land itself. But those were exceptional times, the darkest of ages, in a land where "once upon a time" was a forbidden phrase and fact the only legal tender.

That was the land I was born into, a land of slaughtered bards, a land dulled and divided by fear. That was Q'ntana, and this is its story, and mine... a story that begins once upon a time.

Pre Tena'aa: The Beginning

One

The day Yhoshi and O'ric arrived in Pre Tena'aa began much like all the other days that had passed since our Circle of Bards straggled into this remote land. Rising before dawn, we slipped silently through the labyrinth of underground passageways and out into the gray, timeless time between night and day. We gathered in a circle, all twelve of us around Eulisha, following the line of her oak staff as it traced a north-south arc through the sky and then paused. It lingered there, on a spot just above the horizon, where a faint shadow-streaked orb fluttered into view then dissolved.

"We send the strength of our hearts to M'nor that she may return to light in joy and truth," Eulisha said. We touched our right hands from heart to mouth and repeated the refrain. No other sound broke the early morning still. Only when spikes of pink and white speared the gloom did we break circle and file back inside.

Danger rose with the suns. Little traveled though Pre Tena'aa was, we were outlaws. Though we didn't officially exist, there was a price on our heads — heads King Fvorag craved as the crowning display on his Wall of Traitors.

No one knew we were here and had been for seven years. No one, save the Tena'aa themselves, and their fabled ferocity kept visitors, including the King's Men, at bay. Legend proclaimed them man-eaters, asserted that the suns-bleached bones heaped along the highway and picked clean of all flesh were all that remained of any who strayed from the road that pierced this barren land like an arrow.

In truth, the Tena'aa ate no flesh, only the roots and herbs that flourished in their darkened tunnels and the scratchy grains that swept out across their treeless prairie. Yet their culinary magic transformed these into such incomparable flavors that I was always first inside their cavernous dining hall at mealtime.

This day was no exception. I raced down the familiar route and took my place at our table just as a Tena'aa server set a steaming bowl of puna porridge in front of me. Often, Gwill'm, the Tena'aa chief, or his brother Heraff joined us for meals. This morning, however, we thirteen bards sat alone, freeing Zakk to resound a familiar theme.

"You must be tired, mother. Let me work with the boy today." My father's younger brother forced his thin lips into a smile of forced charm that fluttered between sneer and servility. His eyes squeezed into colorless slits that flicked from Eulisha's face to mine. Eulisha and Zakk had taken over my bard-teaching from my father and tutor, both missing these nine years and believed dead.

Eulisha shook her head. She was my grandmother and Elderbard, a title that once ranked alongside the king in importance. At least four score and ten, she smiled with the face of a dried apple, the heart of a child and the laugh of a wind chime rippling in a summer breeze. She laughed now, good-naturedly. But her mien was firm.

"No, son. Your work with Toshar is done."

The solicitous shading faded from Zakk's voice. "I am Am'dar's brother. I am to be Elderbard when you—" Catching himself, he reshaped his scowl into something almost genial. "I am to be next Elderbard. It is right that I take over *all* the boy's education." He silently canvassed the table for support, but only his wife, Myrrym, acknowledged him.

"The boy is no longer a boy," Eulisha chided gently. "He's a young man. A young man with a name. Why do you never call him by it?" Zakk glowered at me.

"A young man?" he spat. "Look at him." Zakk's gray eyes bore into me with unprecedented malice and I flinched as though I had been struck. "You see why I call him 'boy'? A man wouldn't cower like a wounded fahriya. If he is ever to *be* a man, he needs a man to teach him what that means. He needs—"

"*Zakk.*" Eulisha's voice was chill as ice. "I am still Elderbard. *I* will decide who teaches him and when."

Zakk's eyes flared. He opened his mouth, then shut it again. Clenching his fists, he jerked his shoulders back and stormed from the hall.

And so another breakfast and another quarrel made way for another morning's lessons with Eulisha. If one day in Pre Tena'aa was much the same as the last, my time with Eulisha was always magically unique, alive with storytelling and song as I absorbed the history and lore that all bards must learn and pass on.

"As the youngest surviving bard, you have a special responsibility to learn and remember," she said as I prepared to leave her chamber at midday.

I hesitated at the door.

"What is it, Toshar? What have you been waiting to ask?"

"Are there other stories, Grandmother? Ones you and Zakk haven't taught me? Ones not yet written?"

It was a question Zakk had answered the previous day — with his usual cuff to the back of my head.

"What does your heart tell you?" Eulisha asked in turn.

I started to shrug, my customary response to this question, but then sensed an unusual stirring, the faintest glimmer of an inner knowing. It seemed as though a butterfly had landed in my chest, its wings beating in time with my heart. It unsettled me, igniting a spark of fear. But I wanted to please Eulisha, so I listened and pushed and probed, my face contorted with purpose.

"Don't impose your will on it, Toshar. Let it come as it comes. Free your breath."

I exhaled — more sigh than surrender — then shook my head in defeat. I felt nothing, saw nothing, knew nothing.

"You will know what is yours to know when it is time to know it," Eulisha whispered. She stood so close I could smell her sweet-scented soap, the one that always reminded me of my mother. I swallowed hard, trying to hold back the tears, trying to be the man Zakk demanded I be.

"You will know the stories that are yours to know at the same time," she added. "Until then, be still and have patience."

Patience: always difficult counsel for one on the cusp of manhood. I left Eulisha's chamber and wandered blindly through dark tunnels eerily lit greenish gold by the phosphorescent maya weed that climbed their earthen walls. I walked, ignoring the call to lunch, ignoring the call to chores. I walked until my legs ached and I no longer knew where I was. All the while I sought the return of that butterfly, only to push it away whenever it approached.

Day and night are much the same beneath the earth, where time has no meaning and the shadowy glow of maya never alters. Only when a commotion erupted around me did I discover how long I had wandered. From all directions, Tena'aa scurried past and up a ramped shaft to the surface. Curious, I followed. To my surprise, daylight had fled and Aris blazed defiantly in the northern sky. With lesser stars it formed a web of twinkling diamond chips that glinted off the luminous fangs of the Tena'aa.

It was easy to give credence to the legends of their ferocity. It was said, Gwill'm had told me, giggling, that the play of starlight on their giant teeth lured travelers off the road to what seemed to be a settlement, only to be eaten alive, their bones heaped by the road. It was a myth the Tena'aa encouraged, he said. It kept them safe in perilous times.

So I was surprised to see two travelers emerge from the shadows, following a snaking, tooth-lit course through the scrub. It could be a treacherous route, even in daylight, because of the camouflaged air shafts and entryways that pocked the landscape. One traveler rode a dappled mount, the other sat atop a wooden coach drawn by two horses. These were not King's Men. Though that fact alone didn't mark them as friends, I knew them to be such.

I knew and saw much, even as the dim starlight revealed little: the curious rune-like markings on the coach...the even curiouser horses that drew it, whose names I knew (without knowing how) to be Rykka and Ta'ar, the ancient words for dawn and dusk. But for the white bolts that flashed from forehead to muzzle, Rykka's coloring was the pale blue of morning sky, Ta'ar's the smoky plum of twilight.

Neither bridle nor reins secured them to the coach or to the most curious piece of all: the driver, who sat upon a three-legged stool perched at the front of the coach's flat roof, clawed hands folded on his lap. He was clad in a hooded robe of deep forest green that hid all but his eyes. Yellow and unblinking, they ignored his horses' progress. Instead, they scanned our wonderstruck group until they found me. Only then did he pull back his cowl to reveal his face. Bald and clean-shaven, his skin was neither smooth nor wrinkled, neither light nor dark. It had a translucent scaliness, as though it could flake off at the touch. Ancient, yet ageless and ethereal: That's how O'ric seemed in those first moments.

His companion, who I would soon know as Yhoshi, was near to my age and wore dun-colored garments that hung loosely on a muscular frame. He had bristly blond hair and a brush of platinum on his upper lip and chin that had the opposite of its intended effect on a face that was resolutely cherubic. Sea-blue eyes, hooded with suspicion, darted warily as he passed me.

It was strange to see so clearly in so little light, but I didn't question it. I just watched. And listened to the faint strains of music that wafted toward me from O'ric's coach.

At last they stopped, only to be instantly surrounded by a circle of flinting, glinting teeth. Panicked, Yhoshi heel-kicked his horse. It turned and turned again as he sought a way through the ring of tightly linked arms. All the while O'ric gazed calmly in my direction. Despite the dark, I knew he saw me as clearly as I saw him.

Finally, shoulders slumped, Yhoshi brought his horse to O'ric's side. Nothing stirred, Yhoshi's fidgeting the only movement in the stone-like tableau. Even Rykka and Ta'ar, their necks bent over the grass, suspended their chewing.

Then, as if acting on a signal from O'ric that only he could detect, Gwill'm stepped forward, the circle closing in behind him. He stood motionless for some minutes more and even I, who knew his gentleness, was struck by the savage aspect he presented. Little taller than a child, his tiny head was a mountain range of warts and moles dominated by a glistening glacier of teeth and two lakes of fiery, unlidded eyes. His right arm, three times the length of his left, belted his waist in a snakelike coil that culminated in three crooked fingers that themselves ended in a hook of claws. In place of a nose and ears, forked, twig-like antennae protruded from dark holes in his skull, their tips quivering.

"Welcome," he said at last, bowing first to O'ric then to Yhoshi. "Welcome to the land of the Tena'aa. And to you, my friend—" he uncoiled his preternaturally long arm and extended it upward to O'ric "— most special greetings. It has been too many dark moons since we have seen you."

O'ric nodded in reply, finally turning his gaze from me. He grasped Gwill'm's claw and stepped down as Gwill'm wrapped his lengthy arm around O'ric in a Tena'aa embrace.

"M'nor has called," he said to Gwill'm, even as one yellow eye wandered back to me. "The time is now."

Two

Dinner was always a special time in Pre Tena'aa — served in the largest, grandest and deepest of the subterranean chambers, its lofty ceiling hung with thousands of starry tapers. Yet this night was more special still. Instead of random clusters scattered through the hall, the low, wooden tables were set in paired concentric semicircles that enclosed a small, central inner circle: the ring of honor, where we bards were joined by O'ric and Yhoshi, and by Gwill'm, his mate Minda'aa and their son Bold'ar.

Yhoshi said little at first and ate less. He picked guardedly at the strange stew that filled his bowl, wrinkling his nose at the curls of aromatic steam that rose lazily from it. I devoured mine greedily. Served only on rare occasions, the lustrous orange-yellow concoction was one of my favorites, its naturally sweet broth an ideal base for the red bela nuts, green zanga fruit and elegantly thin strips of purple gela'aa that floated within.

"Aren't you hungry, young man?" Myrrym asked. "After all your travels?"

Yhoshi's gaze shifted nervously from Bold'ar, cleaning his second bowl of stew with a long black tongue, to the two massive cooking fires that danced at the far end of the hall. Loud crackling pops exploded from one, where a sapphire oval of oil-brushed p'yan root sizzled. A man-size cauldron bubbled into the second.

"H-hungry? No, I mean yes. But I can't." He shuddered as Bold'ar held his bowl up for a refill. "How can *you*?" he asked Myrrym. "You know. The bones."

"It isn't true, you know," O'ric interjected, his first words since the start of the meal. Until that moment, he had stared silently into the middle distance, eating nothing. Now, he dipped a spoon into his bowl and ate distractedly.

"What isn't?" Yhoshi asked.

"The bones. "

Gwill'm bugged his eyes, bared his teeth and lunged. All color drained from Yhoshi's face.

"Stop it. You're frightening him." Minda'aa's long arm caught Gwill'm in mid-charge. She turned to Yhoshi. "Forgive him, Yhoshi. He thinks he's playing. Someone," she glared at Gwill'm, "should have told you about the food. Tell him, Toshar."

Once I did, Yhoshi's face grew as red as the untouched bela nuts on his plate.

"I-I thought...," he stammered. "People say..."

"Ha!" Gwill'm exclaimed. "Let them say it. It keeps 'em away."

"The King's Men," Minda'aa explained. "They never come through here anymore."

"That's a good thing," Yhoshi said, his mouth full and bowl nearly empty. A Tena'aa server hurried over to refill it.

"It is," Eulisha said. "Our Tena'aa friends are as kindly as they are feared. That has made these caverns an ideal sanctuary for us. Until The Return, may it come soon."

"It will," said Zakk, clearing his scowl as his voice rose above the mealtime clatter and din. "I have seen it."

"Zakk has seen it." Myrrym nodded. "He also—"

"*You* will lead it, Mother. I have seen that too."

"Thank you, Zakk. And you too, Myrrym. But no. I'm too old for that."

"But Mother —" Zakk began.

Eulisha raised her hand to silence him. "My traveling days have passed, Zakk. They ended when Gwill'm took us in." She paused, as if to gather her vision as well as her thoughts.

"No, one of you—," she regarded each bard in turn, her gaze advancing from Zakk to Myrrym to Plenath, from Mord'c to Polit to Kayn, from Komr'a to Sitha'aa to Ghônn, and all the way around the circle to me. I felt her eyes on me and looked down, to my plate.

"One of you," she continued, "will lead The Return, will lead the great journey that will restore the truth of the tale to Q'ntana. I pray only to live long enough to know that The Return has been joined, that The MoonQuest has begun." She shook her head. "No, Zakk. It will not be me."

Clenching his jaw, Zakk returned to his meal. Myrrym patted his hand as an uneasy silence fell over the table.

"What of you, young traveler," Minda'aa asked at last, "what brings you here? And in such fine company." She tilted her head toward O'ric.

"I'm not sure I know," Yhoshi said between hungry mouthfuls. "I was riding toward the capital. I'm a Messenger, you see. I had taken the road, something I never do. But this time I counted on the King's Men being even more frightened of those stories about you than I am." He smiled at Minda'aa. "Than I *was*." He held up his bowl for a refill.

"One moment the road was empty. The next, this strange coach appeared right in front of me. Out of nowhere. So did he." Yhoshi looked expectantly at O'ric. But O'ric, lost in a world of his own, said nothing.

Yhoshi continued. "He looked me, O'ric did, and said, 'Right on time, Yhoshi son of Yhosha.'"

"'For what?' I asked. But he wouldn't say. And he wouldn't move. I tried to ride away. But wherever I turned, the coach was still in front of me." Again, he turned to O'ric, who continued to ignore the conversation.

"Then there were King's Men. Suddenly. I tried to get away, past the coach, but it wouldn't let me. The coach, I mean. It kept blocking me."

"'Come close,' O'ric said. I didn't want to but I still couldn't get by. So I did."

"'Closer,' he said. 'Touch my hand.' As soon as I did, it was as though the King's Men rode right through us. It was the oddest feeling." Yhoshi shook his head as if he still couldn't believe what had happened.

"After that, I wanted to ride off even more, I can tell you. I'm still not sure why I didn't. There's something about him..."

"There surely is," Gwill'm said. He stretched his arm to the next table and retrieved an ale pitcher from which he refilled O'ric's tankard. O'ric paid it no heed.

"Where do you go next?" I asked.

Yhoshi shrugged, turning again to O'ric, whose yellow eyes suddenly snapped into focus.

"Along the road you must take," he said, one eye fixed on Yhoshi, the other on me. Once again, I sensed that he knew me, more fully than I knew myself. The sensation lasted an instant and was gone, as was his focus.

"What about you?" Yhoshi asked. "I never thought I'd meet a bard. I've heard rumors of living bards, of a community of bards that had fled Q'ntana, but I didn't believe. And here you are, inside Q'ntana."

Plenath rose and raised his arms in a prophetic stance. He looked the role with his white hair, beard and robe and glassy stare. "The long arm of the Tena'aa extended itself to us in hospitality and security," he intoned.

"What my brother means," explained Myrrym, "is that Gwill'm's brother, Heraff, found us, starved and half-dead, in the mountains of Pinq'an." She leaned across the table toward Yhoshi. "But tell us, Messenger, what news do you carry from the outside world? We hear little, though Eulisha sees much."

Zakk glared at Myrrym.

"And Zakk," she added quickly.

Yhoshi's face darkened. "Nothing good," he said. "The king's built a second Wall of Traitors in the capital. There wasn't any more room on the first," he added bitterly.

"The King's Men kill more Believers every day. They don't just kill. They rape. They torture. They're...they're evil ." He clenched his fists knuckle-white. "I've seen Believers take their own lives to avoid being discovered." His eyes blazed. "No place is safe anymore, not even this one. Spies are everywhere. Even the rocks and trees—"

"Yes, yes," Zakk interrupted, "we know all this. Haven't I seen it? Haven't I told of it?" He drummed his fingers irritably on the tabletop until Myrrym gently took his hand. He shook it free.

"Pinq'an," I repeated softly, stung by a sharp memory.

"Over by the eastern frontier?" Yhoshi asked.

Zakk jerked his hand free of Myrrym's. "That was our destination," he growled. "But with an old woman and young children —" A sharp glance from Eulisha silenced him.

Still standing, Plenath again raised his arms and declaimed, "And the blinding snows of the q'eenah blowing clouds of drenched cotton in our paths —"

"Yes, Plenath," Myrrym broke in, "and the blinding snows of the q'eenah blowing clouds of drenched cotton in our paths... And no food, warm clothes or shelter, we had settled in to die."

"Better to die in the q'eenah's company than the king's," snapped Zakk.

"Better not to die at all." Eulisha's gentian eyes burned into Zakk's until he looked away. She turned to Yhoshi. "My son would not trust Heraff," she said.

"I was prepared to die, Mother. That is all."

"You were ready to die, Zakk. That is not the same. Heraff's eyes told me he was no enemy. Heraff's heart sang of friendship."

"But the bones, Mother. The stories."

"You are a bard, Zakk. You are trained to know when stories sing true or speak false." This last sentence she uttered sternly, the lines in her face fixed as in stone. But as quickly as they set, they melted back into an ever-changing maze of folds and wrinkles. She clasped Zakk's smooth hands in her own, spotted and quivering.

"We must stop our bickering, son. We must wait. Patiently." She released Zakk's hands and cupped hers firmly around her goblet, staring into it as though seeking M'nor there. "We must wait for The Return."

"For how long?" Yhoshi asked.

"As long as we must," she replied, looking at O'ric. As their unblinking eyes locked, a filament of fire raced between them. All at our table fell into expectant silence. When the fiery energy linking them had dimmed, Eulisha smiled and sighed.

"The wait is nearly over," she said. It was the saddest smile I had ever seen.

Three

Morning broke slowly over Pre Tena'aa, ignored by the refugee bards for the first time since our arrival in this land. Pale fingers of light reached up toward each other across the inky darkness. Black faded to gray then to the softest of blues, dimming then extinguishing the sparkling diadem of constellations. Then the dance of fire began as Aygra and B'na crept over the far hills, faint smudges on the eastern and western horizons. Pale orbs now, the two suns would gradually brighten as they climbed into the sky, gaining in brilliance until they merged for a single moment at midday. Separating, they would continue their individual journeys across the sky until, balls of spent fire, they would finally sink into the earth to replenish themselves.

The only vigil to greet this dawn was shared by Yhoshi and me. The other bards huddled in council with O'ric. Still. Their meeting had begun after dinner, continuing through the night. I was disappointed to be excluded. I too was a bard. But one look from Eulisha told me not to argue.

Instead, I led Yhoshi up and out into the moonless dark. Senses alert to the night's perils, we felt our way along the one path I knew well. It snaked through tall grasses that brushed our arms and tickled our chins, and then through a dense thicket that concealed a narrow, earthen ramp into a hidden gully. Steep and ringed with coarse brush, the gully penned O'ric's and Yhoshi's horses and the Tena'aa's diminutive korée mares, protecting them from the nayla and other wild night-beasts that roamed the veld.

Horse, human or Tena'aa: it was all the same to marauding nayla — black as pitch, swift as hawks, always hungry, never sated. So stealthy were they that the first sign of a nayla's presence was the flash of incisors and sour smell of spittle as it leapt for your neck.

As dangerous as were the nayla, the King's Men were even more so. At least death by nayla was quick. The King's Men, dark as nayla with their black pants, shirts, masks and mounts, held out the threat of a lengthier, grislier end. Fortunately, they rarely passed this way, even if Pre Tena'aa was the quickest route to the capital.

"We're only thirteen," I told Yhoshi from the safety of the gully. "We were thirty-nine when I was a boy, when my grandfather was still alive..."

I thought of my grandfather often, now that Eulisha was preparing to join him. She mentioned her readiness often, weaving it into her stories and lessons. "I don't know what will happen when she does die...to me...to any of us."

"Who will be Elderbard?" Yhoshi's voice was barely audible.

"You needn't whisper," I replied in full voice. "For some reason, sounds never escape this place. We can hear what's happening up there...listen." A nightmarish howl curdled the air, rising and falling with bloodthirsty intensity. Before it could dissolve into the night, another cry picked up in response, then another. Yhoshi jerked his head toward each addition to the hungry chorus.

"Can't they smell us, and the horses?" he asked.

I pointed to the low wall of shadowy thicket that crowned the perimeter of the gully. "That's porii," I explained. "Its scent is so strong it masks all others."

Who would be the next Elderbard? I looked up at the stars, where Ky'nar, the constellation of the ancient bard, shone brightly.

"I've never heard it called Ky'nar," Yhoshi said. "Everyone calls it Fvorag, constellation of kings."

This was new to me, but no surprise. How could King Fvorag accept a bard in the sky when he outlawed bards on earth? "From thirty-nine to thirteen," I repeated. "Soon there will be none. Then there will be no need of an Elderbard...so perhaps Zakk is well-suited to the job."

"*Zakk!?*"

It was an incredible thought, but Zakk would have to be Elderbard. That was the law.

"'From father to daughter, mother to son. The mantle passes, the Balance is done,'" I quoted. "There has never been an exception. My father should have been Elderbard after Eulisha. And my sister Tamar after him. Now it can only be my uncle and, after that, his daughter, if Myrrym gives him another." Ky'nar passed behind a giant cloud bank. "If there's a Q'ntana after that."

We sat in silence, each lost in our memories. Mine returned to my mother and then further back to my father. Everyone assumed him to be dead, but no one knew for certain. I was nine when he disappeared. We had heard that other bards might be hiding in Briyna, and despite the danger he knew he must find out for himself.

He never reached Briyna.

Within days, Ryolan Ò Garan had also vanished. Zakk blamed it all on Garan, but I knew my tutor could never betray us.

We waited for them as long as we could. When we could wait no longer, we fled — from Kemet to Sannjay to Mann'wa — the King's Men never far behind.

Soon, no place in Q'ntana was safe, and exile the only solution. That's when we turned toward Pinq'an and the eastern border. It was there the winds and snow of the q'eenah found us. It was there the q'eenah took my mother and Tamar. It was there the q'eenah took Zakk's daughter, Imbla. It was there we met Heraff and, through him, found our way to Pre Tena'aa.

I flinched as I remembered the sting of the ice pellets that had flung themselves at us, at the misstep that had killed my mother, sister and cousin.

"My family too," Yhoshi said after a long silence. "All of them. The whole village. A cell of Believers. Betrayed. Dead."

"What happened?"

"I was out walking. When I got back, I found nothing, no one. Only blood. The next time I saw them was weeks later, in the capital," his voice began to shake, "flies buzzing around their heads, staked on top of the Wall of Traitors." Yhoshi stood unsteadily and walked into the darkness, toward his horse. His voice still quavered when he returned a few minutes later. "I should have been up there with them," he said.

I too knew how it felt to be condemned to life. Imbla died because I had quarreled with my mother, because she had taken my place at my mother's side.

"I still feel it should have been me some days," I said, clutching the ivory moon disc that hung from a leather thong around my neck. "Zakk feels the same — most days."

I released the pendant from my grip and showed it Yhoshi. "This was hers, my mother's. It was my father's and Eulisha's before that. My mother gave it to me just before we started up the mountain...as if she knew..."

Tears ran down my cheeks. I wiped them with the back of my hand, grateful that it was too dark for Yhoshi to see. "Eulisha tells me again and again that it happened as it needed to," I said. "She would say the same to you."

"Perhaps." Yhoshi pulled a stem of brittle grass from the hard-packed earth and peeled its layers of protective coating until he reached the thin strand of moist green hiding inside.

"Is that when you became a Messenger?"

Yhoshi nodded.

The men and women who carried news from cell to cell of Believers were favored targets of the king and his men. Rare was the Messenger who survived more than a few journeys. Rare was the day when a Messenger's head did not sit atop the Wall of Traitors.

"It's a miracle you're still alive."

Yhoshi shrugged.

Night was fading, but day had not yet arrived. Even though I sensed there would be no predawn Moon Ritual, I clambered back to the entry tunnel — just to be certain. When I returned, Yhoshi was feeding and nuzzling his horse.

At the far side of the gully, Rykka and Ta'ar stood motionless, each in a pool of faint light that matched its coloring. Unblinking, they stared at me, drawing me toward them. My hands tingled. My mouth went dry. My mind raced, then stopped. I knew nothing of Yhoshi and the other horses. All I knew were Rykka, Ta'ar and a soft, velvety mist. I stroked first one then the other along the bolt of white that flashed down from between their eyes. The tingling spread...up my arms and down my back and chest...into my shoulders...my throat...my eyes...my ears...

The tingling in my ears grows stronger...louder. It has words but no voice... music but no words.

The sounds separate from the tingling and vibrate within me...from somewhere deep inside. Too deep. I try to block the sound of my heartbeat, to listen...to grasp. I struggle and strain, but to no avail.

Now it's almost clear.

Now it's muffled.

I hear but don't hear, absorb but don't understand.

Like the tide, it breathes toward me then withdraws, breathes toward me then withdraws, never quite touching the place of perception.

Finally, it exhales one last time and the spell washes away...

"Where were you?" Yhoshi's voice dissolved its final echoes. "Your eyes had that same queer look O'ric's had at dinner last night."

"I-I don't know." I didn't, and wasn't ready to share what I had sensed. A chill shuddered through me. I started to shake and couldn't stop.

Yhoshi looked at me curiously then shrugged. "You need a fire." Even deep in this gully, a night fire had been too risky. Who knew what might have been attracted by its glow?

"A small one," I said, hoping telltale smoke would melt into the twilit haze of dawn.

I huddled close to the feeble flames. Slowly, their meager warmth seeped into my body and stilled my shivering. As the fire died, a streaked, grayish sphere wavered, barely discernible, above the southern horizon.

"M'nor?" Yhoshi asked.

I nodded. "It's not often that she makes herself known, even like this. The streaks," I traced them with my fingers, "are her tears."

The shadow-circle emitted a weak glimmer and then disintegrated — just as Aygra crested a low hill in the east.

"Each time I want to cry with her." My fingers still caressed that piece of now-empty sky.

"Have you ever seen M'nor's smile?" Yhoshi asked.

I shook my head. "Not even in my dreams. I wonder if anyone ever will again."

B'na followed Aygra into the sky, rising from behind a higher, western peak and helping to burn off the few strands of mist that still clung to the mountains.

"Do you know M'nor's story?" I asked, still watching that patch of southern sky, now a blank palette of deepening blue. Without waiting for Yhoshi's reply, I began to speak the tale I had heard from infancy.

"Once," I began, stopped, then began again.

"Once upon a time," I said defiantly, "M'nor rose every night, full and bright and luminous. She journeyed through the heavens, from north to south, deriving strength and sustenance from the words and songs of the bards...of the people. For all people were bards once upon a time.

"From dusk to dawn, the light of her joy illuminated Q'ntana and neighboring realms, even unto unknown lands far distant. Such was the power of the story.

"Then one day a new king conquered Q'ntana. Swayed by Bo'Rá K'n, the Lord of Darkness, this king silenced the stories and slaughtered those who spoke them.

"Instead of voices raised in song, M'nor heard the keening of mourners. Instead of bearing the gentle notes of the harp, the wind sent her the crack of shattered bones. Instead of harmonies wafting up into the heavens, M'nor tasted anguish, felt silence, smelled fear.

"So saddened was she that her tears doused the fires that had lit up the night sky — first from time to time, then many nights, then most nights. Now her tears flow without cease and her light is visible only in dreams...to those who still know they dream.

"Only when songs and stories return will M'nor dry her tears and return with them, sharing her gentle light of the night with all."

I looked again to the spot where M'nor's shadow had vanished and felt the power of the story vanish with it. For all the times I had heard and repeated this story, I rarely even saw her tears anymore. Would I ever see her smile? I shook my head. The stories...the hiding...the life we lived: What was it for? What could we do? What could anyone do? Was all life this futile?

"Your despair feeds Bo'Rá K'n and starves M'nor, Toshar son of Am'dar," O'ric said severely, appearing suddenly from Prithi knew where.

"And you, Yhoshi son of Yhosha: Your guilt, shame and self-pity do the same."

"But M'nor—"

"M'nor waits for *you*, Toshar. For you as well, Yhoshi. When you are ready to see her, she will be ready to be seen." One yellow eye focused on me, the other on Yhoshi. "Are you ready?"

"But—"

"Yes or no."

I nodded.

"Yhoshi?"

Yhoshi looked down, saying nothing.

"Are you ready, Yhoshi? Are you ready to live?"

Still studying the ground, he twitched his head in reluctant assent.

"Then M'nor will show herself. To you both. Soon."

He raised his eyes to the sky, his gaze arcing from north to south. "We come to the end of the beginning and the beginning of the end," he announced to the heavens. "Soon." He nodded as if in reply to a silent question. "Very soon."

Four

"Will you take some tea, grandson?" I nodded. Eulisha filled each of two bowls with steaming brew from the earthenware pot at her side. The teapot was the color of mud, a double chevron set in each side — one sapphire, the other maize. The bowls matched the teapot in all but a single detail: one bore the sign only in blue, the other in yellow. Eulisha lifted the pot by its rush handle.

"Which cup?"

My eyes flicked from one bowl to the other and back. My grandmother never asked casual questions. If I was to choose, there was a reason for the choosing.

There is a reason for everything, even if the reason remains unknowable. Some mysteries lie close to the surface. The rift between Zakk and Eulisha was one such. Did anyone in Pre Tena'aa not know by now of Zakk's impatience to assume the Elderbard's mantle? That morning the taut wire linking them had been stretched to within a hair of snapping. When breakfast was done — foaming tankards of black, ale-like g'nda and bread fried in leftover stew gravy — Zakk stood and grasped my arm. Firmly.

"You had best come with me," he said. He was trying to sound kindly, but loving words rarely spoke true from his lips.

"No, Zakk," Eulisha said. "He will stay here with Yhoshi until you and I have spoken. Then he will come to me." She rose slowly and shuffled to Zakk's side, towering over him. She towered over us all by at least a head, even with the stoop of advancing years. Zakk reached down for her staff, a thick branch of mirror-polished ebony topped with an oak burl.

"No," she said, "give me your arm. Toshar will bring me the stick later."

A shadow left the hall with them. It wasn't long gone. Within moments, Zakk burst back, his eyes dark with fury.

"Your grandmother wants you, boy. *Now*." His words lashed at me and I recoiled. Yhoshi placed a steadying hand on my shoulder, steering me toward my uncle, the only way out of the dining chamber. As I passed Zakk, he grabbed the ivory pendant at my neck and pulled me toward him.

"Not a word to her, *boy*," he spat.

I shook myself free and hurried out.

"Boy!" he called after me. I stopped, not looking back. "The stick."

It lay at Eulisha's place in the circle, the slight bow of its length forming a frown directed at Zakk.

Yes, some mysteries lie close to the surface. Others, like Eulisha's tea bowls are buried deeper. I disliked those mysteries. I wanted to know, to understand, before choosing. I sought a clue to the tea bowls from Eulisha, but found none.

I reached for the one with the blue markings and froze, my hand hovering in midair as my eyes shifted to the yellow. I breathed in the heady, spiced steam, inhaling deeply, willing one cup to call out to me over the other. Then, as the subtle blend of herbs and spices tickled up my nose, a forgotten memory flickered before me — short, sharp and as sweet as the honey brewed in with the tea...

I'm a child, no more than five, entranced by the kaleidoscope of fabric and stitching hanging on the wall, its cloth shimmering in suns-light that filters through gauze-veiled windows. My mother sits on one side of me, Eulisha on the other.

It's my birthday and there is tea. There is always tea, seasoned with extra honey for young taste buds that crave sweet over spice.

"Choose a cup," my grandmother says. "Choose a cup and it will be yours for all time...if you let it." Without hesitation, I reach for the bowl at Eulisha's place.

"Toshar!" my mother exclaims. "That's your grandmother's. Choose another."

"No, T'yanna." Eulisha pushes my mother's hand away. "He has chosen wisely. This shall *be his cup." She fills it with tea and presses it into my hands. "For all time, my boy, if you let it."*

If I let it...

One wash of eyelids over time-journeyed eyes clears the memory, leaving only the scent of tea to link me to the past.

I withdrew my hand, still poised over the blue cup. "Isn't there a third cup, a green one?" I asked.

Eulisha exhaled and smiled. Had she been holding her breath all this time?

"Look again and choose, Toshar."

Where there had been two cups on the low, three-legged table were now three. Without thinking, I reached for the new one. It was identical to the others, but its chevrons blazed green, growing brighter as my hand drew nearer, until its light streaked through the chamber. My hands cupped the space around the bowl but wouldn't touch it. Part of me wanted to shield my eyes from the painful brightness — better yet, to flee. I sat there, suspended in time. For how long?

A soft, whispering whoosh... "Yours for all time," it echoes again and again, around and through me. "Yours for all time, if you let."

For all time.

I touch the bowl and pull it toward me. The light burns through my hands, through my skin. It sings...music my heart recognizes, words my mind does not.

Mir M'nor m'ranna

M'ranna ma Mir

Then they're gone. Light, music, magic, mystery.

The chamber is as it was when I walked in, as it has been these seven years: dim, ordinary.

Grandmotherly.

The look of a grandmother. The sound of a grandmother. The sound of a grandmother...

She is speaking to me. Is she speaking to me? What is she saying?

"...some tea?"

"Oh. Oh, yes. Please."

"I've brewed it with extra honey, the way you like it."

"Yes, of course. I mean, thanks." I looked hard at Eulisha, but if she had seen any of what I had, she betrayed nothing. Had there always been three mugs on the table? I shook my head sharply, trying to clear it back to reality — whatever that was.

"A piece of kolmah?"

I lifted a triangle of buttered toast from the gold-rimmed platter Eulisha held toward me and dunked one corner in the tea. Waiting. I waited for something. For what?

Eulisha smiled at me with teeth white and strong. "Have another piece of kolmah," she said.

I had finished the first without knowing it. I took a second, dunked it and nibbled away at one corner after the next until my hand was empty. Then, for the first time, I raised the tea bowl to my face, letting the steam bathe it in wet, aromatic warmth before taking a sip. I swished the sweet, spicy heat in my mouth and felt it charge down my throat, into my stomach.

I swallowed fire, not a fierce inferno but a single, embracing flame, its gentle power surging through me.

"Now we can talk."

Eulisha set down the cup she had cradled through our silence. It was also green.

"You have chosen wisely, son of my son. You have chosen wisely and drunk well." She refilled my bowl.

"Now, I will tell you a story."

I took another sip of tea, wrapped my arms around my knees and waited. This was my favorite part of our time together. Most of her stories I had heard before, but it didn't matter. Eulisha's way made them all new.

She closed her eyes for a silent moment as she always did, gathering the story to her.

"Once upon a time," she began, "when this land was deep in forest and man but a babe, the world was alive with song. Whatever lived, sang. Whatever was, sang.

"Trees trilled in harmony as each bough and leaf took its part in a magnificent chorale. Rocks and flowers added their own voices, their own colors, to the symphony that flowed from valley to valley and hill to hill, carried by wind, by birds, even by the tiniest of insects. Everywhere, the sound of nature's music fluted and fluttered.

"The people of that time, the Gwna, inhaled the music. It was the breath that gave them life, that gave life to the Lady Gwna, daughter of Prithi, the One who created all.

"Led by their Lady, the Gwna sang of rising suns to setting suns. They sang of summer to winter, of autumn to spring. They sang what they heard. They listened and sang. They opened their hearts to the music of the world, made it their own and sent it back out into the world. They hummed and whistled and chanted, each in a unique way. They sang separately and together, in harmony and unison. They sang instead of speaking — sharing their melodies among themselves and scattering them far into distant lands.

"As they sang, the years slipped into the sea. Many hundreds of years. Saplings soared into mighty pillars then fell. Oceans swallowed mountains then receded. The song of the soul rose from the earth, filled the earth, was the earth, its palette of textures and hues spiraling into the heavens with passion and joy.

"And the years slipped into the sea. And life continued in this way."

Eulisha sipped her tea.

"You know this story, Toshar, do you not?"

"Yes, Grandmother. From Zakk."

"Then finish it for me."

Finish it? I fidgeted. It was easier to listen then recount. Safer, too. I knew Eulisha would not correct me as Zakk did, would not smack the back of my head when I altered a word or phrase in the stories that, like this one, had passed through so many generations of telling.

Still, I hesitated. "Finish it, Grandmother?"

Eulisha nodded. I stared into my cup, turning it absentmindedly.

"And the years slipped into the sea and life continued in this way," I said, closing my eyes as I picked up the narrative.

"For many hundreds of years this continued, generation after generation. And the land grew in beauty and swelled in luxuriance, and the heavens radiated with celestial light. And the Lady Gwna lived still, not on earth, but in the night sky, within M'nor, fed by the song of the soul. Until one generation came into the land, a generation with ears of stone and hearts of steel.

"'If we cannot hear,' they said, 'there is nothing to be heard. If we cannot sing, there is nothing to be sung. If music is not in our hearts, there is no music.'

"If music was not in their hearts, music would not be in any heart. And so they ordered the bards to still their singing. But the bards would not. Or could not.

"'We sing what we hear,' they sang. And so the king, the first to take the name Fvorag, sliced off the singers' ears.

"Yet still they sang.

"'We hear not with our ears, but with our hearts,' they sang. And so the king sliced out their hearts.

"Yet still they sang.

"'The music leaps from the trees to our tongues,' they sang. And so tongues followed ears followed hearts.

"And their music was finally stilled.

"Yet Fvorag and those he gathered around him so many generations ago feared the music of the earth, though they heard it not.

"So they felled all the trees and plowed all the flowers and took their bows to all the wild creatures until the land stood silent. Until the land stood barren. And then they perished, in a wasteland of their own creation.

"They breathed and spoke and walked and worked, yet not as living men. They were ghosts that dwelt in the desert that was Q'ntana, as do their children and their children's children, even to this day."

I stopped, the story complete, shifting my eyes from the patterns in my tea bowl to the folds of Eulisha's face.

"And then what?" she asked.

"What do you mean?"

"There's more to every story," she replied. "Tell me how it continues."

"I-I don't know. That's all Zakk taught me." The bile-taste of panic surged up my throat. Cold sweat iced my palms. I didn't want to disappoint Eulisha, but how could I take the story beyond its end?

Eulisha took my hands in hers, warm as suns-baked stone.

"You must find your own continuing," she said softly. "Look for it in the swirl of steam that rises from your tea, in the glow of the maya, in the grain of the wood." She pulled her hands free and caressed the table's polished surface, following the whorl of grain with her finger.

"Taste it in the crunch of kolmah, smell it on the breath of your horse, touch it in the pattern of your cup." She stood now, her arms outstretched, her voice full and strong.

"Listen for it in the hiss of the kettle, in the howl of the nayla, in the pounding of your heart." Her voice softened again.

"Close your eyes, Toshar, and see it. The story is there. The story is always there."

I closed my eyes as Eulisha bade me, but all I saw was blackness, thick and impenetrable. *There's nothing there*, I longed to cry out. Ashamed, I didn't dare open my eyes to meet hers, didn't dare admit that I, grandson of an Elderbard, saw nothing.

The blind silence continued, growing deeper, enveloping me in infinite shadow. "I'll count back from ten then open my eyes," I said to myself. "Ten.... nine....eight.... "

A pulsing, whisper drives through the dark, through the void. Eulisha's voice, though she speaks not. Eulisha's voice, though I hear it less than I feel it.

"Yours for all time, if you let it...let it...let it..."

LET IT!

The two words explode then echo softly until they melt into the silence from which they emerged. And then I see a light. A tiny pinprick in the darkest distance, approaching steadily, purposefully.

Moving toward me.

Or do I move toward it? On horseback?

Yes, I'm on horseback...feeling the rhythmic beat of a canter...hearing the click-click-click of hooves on stone...hearing a second set of hooves, tapping in counterpoint.

Is someone following me? Chasing me?

Terror clutches at me, and the light ahead begins to recede.

"No." A voice. Calm. Steadying. "Breathe. Breathe deeply."

I close my inner eye against the light, against the sounds, against my fear, and let the horse carry me where it will.

I know this horse. But how? Her strides are too long for a korée, her mane not coarse enough. How do I even know she's a mare? Yet I do. Something about her feel, her scent, her...

Slowly, I surrender back into the vision, back into the sound and sense of my surroundings.

No one pursues me. Someone rides next to me. And my horse...

Wait. These are O'ric's horses. I ride Rykka. But who rides Ta'ar? It must be O'ric.

If only it weren't so dark. If only the light...

I do know. That pinprick in the distance is M'nor. I ride toward M'nor. Yhoshi is at my side.

We ride... I know where we ride and why. I know it but can't touch it.

What is this journey?

Where do we ride?

Why do we ride?

"It is best not to know too much too soon." O'ric's voice startled me into full consciousness.

My eyes opened with a start and shut as quickly. Even the dim maya-glow of Eulisha's chamber was bright after my shadowy vision. When I reopened them, O'ric sat with us, drinking tea.

"Your vision is powerful, Toshar," Eulisha said softly, "despite what Zakk has done."

"He-he's done nothing," I lied.

"I know all about Zakk and his lessons, Toshar." She shook her head sadly. "I'm sorry it had to be that way, but it did. Without Zakk you would have been ready too soon."

"Too soon? For what?"

"For what you have seen," O'ric replied. "For what you have chosen. For what has chosen you."

"I-I don't understand."

O'ric stood and circled the table three times, the four claws of his right hand clasping the six of his left. He stopped behind me.

"The moment has come when M'nor's tears will either cease for all time or flow for all time."

"What does that mean?" I asked, even as I knew that I knew.

"It is said," Eulisha continued, "that only the youngest of the old, who is also the oldest of the young, can initiate The MoonQuest, can lead The Return."

"What's that have to do with me?"

O'ric pressed his hands into my shoulders. He said nothing, but the voice in my heart was his: "You, Toshar, son of Am'dar and T'yanna, are that one."

Panic tightened its grip on me, squeezing me of water and air. I lurched forward to grab at my bowl of tea, but its green marking glowed more brilliantly than before, emitting a searing, scorching heat. I felt heat as well where O'ric's hands had been, even though he now stood by Eulisha. From her eyes, I knew she too had heard his words.

"Every choice you have ever made, Toshar, has led to this moment," she said. "Your moment. Still, the power to make a different choice remains yours."

I said nothing. What could I say? I looked into Eulisha's purple-blue eyes and saw only love. I didn't dare look at O'ric, but felt the intensity of his gaze.

"How can it be me? I've never seen M'nor smile." I paused. "I've never heard her sing."

"Are you so sure?" O'ric asked.

The music of O'ric's coach and the tea bowls teased at me. Part of me wanted to banish it. Part of me yearned to hear more.

"I wouldn't know what to do, where to go."

"It is best not to know too much too soon," O'ric repeated. "It is best to know only that the story continues and to follow where it takes you."

Confusion and panic battled for my attention. Panic won.

"Must I?" I asked O'ric.

I would happily see the back of Zakk. But Eulisha? Pre Tena'aa? This was my only home. Here was my only family, my life. Of the world beyond, I knew little. Of the road to M'nor, nothing.

"I don't want to leave you," I said to Eulisha.

"No one can force you," replied Eulisha. "But if you don't..."

O'ric's yellow eyes drilled into mine. "There will be no more bards, no more stories, no more M'nor."

"What if I fail?" I whispered.

"What if you don't?" O'ric replied.

I gripped the table, fearing I would fall over. I squeezed my eyes shut to dispel the dizziness then opened them again when rapid-fire visions of nayla and M'nor, Yhoshi and the King's Men, shot through my inner vision.

"Do I have to decide now?" I asked. "In this moment?"

Eulisha glanced questioningly at O'ric. He nodded slightly.

"Go now and rest," she said. She unscrewed the oak burl from her staff and emptied its contents into my palm. "Place this under your pillow and sleep on what we have asked you. We will be here when you return."

I slept. Fitfully at first, tossing from side to side, back to front. First I was hot and flung my covers into a corner. Then, chilled, I crawled over to retrieve them, my teeth clamped to stop them from chattering. As I burrowed my hands deep into my pockets for warmth, I touched metal. Hot metal. I pulled out Eulisha's talisman.

I had barely glanced at the gold disc in Eulisha's chamber, instinctively thrusting it into my pocket in case I passed Zakk.

Now I examined it. On one side, Aygra and B'na approached the moment of perfect union, their light radiating up into the heavens and down to softly rolling countryside. Atop the highest of the low hills stood a man, woman and child, hand in hand in hand, gazing up at the midday suns. On the reverse, the landscape was the same, but it was night. M'nor hung in midheaven, one eye smiling as the other wept. In place of the humans, a pack of nayla howled up at her. Around the edges on both sides were runic markings, not unlike those on O'ric's coach.

I traced the images and letters with my fingers, as a blind man might, trying to feel out their meaning, but felt only fatigue. Slipping the disc under my pillow, I closed my eyes. Within moments, I slept and Na'an was guiding me to the scene on the suns side of the disc.

I know this place, this land of undulating fields and slopes. And I know these people, even as I see them from a great height.

Now, I'm with them.

Now, I am the child. The child is me and I feel my father's strong, comforting grip in one hand, my mother's — gentler but equally firm — in the other. They point to Aygra and B'na, telling me the suns' story. As they speak, I watch the suns melt together into a single, fiery ball and feel embraced by the love and light of the two-suns-as-one.

I squeeze my parents' hands. They don't squeeze back.

I squeeze again. Again, no response.

I tear my eyes from the now-separating suns. I'm alone. No longer a child. Eulisha's staff lies at my feet, its oak burl pointing out a distant road to the north. I kneel to pick up the stick and when I rise, day has fled.

"Yow-oool. YOW-OOOL." The cry of approaching nayla sends spikes of terror through my spine.

"You mustn't wait." I hear the voice before seeing the face, see the face before perceiving the rest of the body.

"Father?" I reach out to touch him but feel only a current of moist, warm air.

"I'm here, son."

"I'm afraid."

"Of course you are. All are afraid, no one more so than the king."

"The king?"

"Yes, the king. And you can do what he cannot, Toshar."

"What's that?"

"Feel your fear. Then pass through it to the other side, where your destiny awaits."

"Is it safe?"

"As safe as life, my son, which is not safe at all." He laughs an air-filled, whispery laugh.

"I'm afraid." I step toward him. *"Can you hold me?"*

He shakes his head. *"Not hand-to-hand as I did once, but heart to heart. Know that as you travel, wherever you travel, my heart holds yours. Draw courage from that, Toshar, and from the hearts of all the bards and Elderbards who have ever lived and died in Q'ntana. We all watch you. We all stand with you."*

I try to hold back the pressure behind my eyes, to be as strong as my father. But the pain is too great.

"Be your strength, not mine, my son."

Great gashes of sobs rip through me. *"But what do I do?"* I cry out through the storm of tears.

"Do what you must. Listen and know — not to my heart but to yours." A distant howl chills my blood. *"The nayla are nearing. They are hungry. You mustn't wait..."*

Voice and image fade and, just as a clutch of blood-red eyes leaps toward me, the dream fades too.

The Highest of the High...

To the Top of the World

Five

The northbound trail carried us through a dry, treeless plain that stretched far beyond the underground warrens of the Tena'aa and into the distant heat haze. Only the sky added color to this landscape of relentless brown, its deep cobalt pocked by puffs of cottony white that offered brief respites from the intense suns-light. I rode Rykka, Yhoshi rode Ta'ar, and the hypnotic clop-clip-clop of iron shoes on hard-packed earth half-drew me back to my shadowed reverie. But for daylight, here I was: living my vision.

The dream of my father hadn't banished my fear, but when I awoke from it I knew I had no choice but to leave Pre Tena'aa. Eulisha and O'ric must have known too, for when I returned to them, they wordlessly led me through a long, dark passage and out to a camouflaged enclosure I had never seen. There, Rykka and Ta'ar awaited, already packed with foodstuffs and supplies. Yhoshi fed them clumps of sweetgrass while Gwill'm secured their saddlebags.

"Can't I even stay for midday meal?" I asked. "Then I could say goodbye to everyone at once."

Eulisha shook her head. "It is best that you be off quickly and quietly."

Doubts tugged at me with tiny crab claws. "I still don't know where I'm going, or what to do when I get there."

O'ric raised his hands over my head in benediction. "Ride north one league at a time. Aris will guide you at night. A path between the suns will guide you in the day. Your heart will guide you always."

He touched his left hand to my heart. "Listen for its stories, Toshar. Share them with M'nor. She waits for them. She waits for you."

From the infinite folds of his cloak, he pulled out a dagger, its blade whiter than silver, its hilt inlaid with emeralds patterned into a double chevron. "Take Oriccan, Toshar."

"Is it...?"

"Yes, Toshar, there is only one Oriccan." According to legend, Prithi had forged Oriccan and the Arms of K'varr and given them to the dragon Kumba for safekeeping until the time of Q'ntana's greatest need. No other being had seen them. Until now.

"But—"

"Take it, Toshar. You are worthy."

Awestruck and feeling anything but worthy, I took the dagger from O'ric, feeling the sharpness of its edge, the solidity of its grip...noting the play of suns-light on its tip, seeing my boyish reflection in its mirrored surface.

"Remember, Toshar," O'ric said, "all flows from The MoonQuest. Dreams flow from it. Impossible dreams. And once the people of Q'ntana again let themselves dream the impossible, the impossible will come to pass. Only then will Fvorag's time be past."

As O'ric stepped back, Gwill'm unfurled his long arm and wrapped it around my waist, pulling me toward him in a tight embrace. "Travel safe, young friend. Travel safe." Standing on tiptoe, the tiny chieftain buried his face in my neck, and the hot salt of his tears mingled with my own. "You are as dear to me as my son," he sputtered, wiping his eyes and nose, then mine, with his free arm.

Once disentangled from Gwill'm, I turned to Eulisha. She stood by Rykka, leaning heavily on her staff, her knuckles white as she clutched the oak burl. For the first time I sensed her age, her fatigue, not in the wrinkled folds and flaps that layered her face but in her eyes. They still sparkled, but their indigo was fading and their lids hung heavy, as though only a supreme effort kept them open. She was going to die. Her dying wavered in front me, the image fading before it could gel. I knew I would never see her again.

"Grandmother," I cried.

"Hush, child." Eulisha eased her weight from the staff and opened her arms to me. "So you saw," she said, as much to herself as to me. "Soon your vision will exceed mine." She brushed her hand through my hair. "It is time for you to leave," she said softly. "We must all go when we are called, I to my place no less than you to yours." She pushed me an arm's length away and touched my cheek. "The road awaits you, as does M'nor. Go, son of my son. Go."

Yhoshi pulled a ripe piila from his pack and bit into it. Purple-red juice squirted in all directions, staining his mouth, lips and mustache bright scarlet.

"Why did you decide to come?" I asked. We sat by a riverbed that had dried to the slowest and meanest of trickles, having abandoned the highway for a more direct cross-country route north. "Hadn't you planned to travel on with O'ric?"

"Yes," he replied between bites, "just as I planned to ride to the capital before that." He popped the rest of the piila into his mouth and spat out the pit. "What are plans?"

"Plans are plans," I said. "You set out to do something and you do it."

Yhoshi laughed. "I thought that too. But not O'ric." He devoured another piila then dunked his hands in the water and wiped the juice from his face. "'Yhoshi, son of Yhosha,' he said to me" — so perfectly mimicking O'ric's voice that I laughed — "'a forced change in plan is opportunity disguised as irritation.'" Yhoshi laughed with me. "It didn't make sense to me then, but now... It still doesn't! Here, have a piila." I shook my head and reached instead for the water skin, draining it thirstily then refilling it from the meager stream.

"Besides, he didn't give me much choice."

"What do you mean?"

"He said I couldn't go with him, that *this* was my opportunity, whatever that means."

"So here you are."

"So here *we* are."

"Going Prithi knows where."

"Going Prithi knows where."

By late afternoon, empty flatlands had blossomed into the lush abundance of the Forest of Marrh. Ancient mountains encircled us, their age-softened summits ringed by clouds that by nightfall had puffed up into a thick, fog-like shroud that obliterated Aris, Ky'nar and all the stars. With no constellations to guide us, Yhoshi wanted to stop for the night. I wanted to continue. For someone who had spent seven years in underground caverns, I felt strangely confined by the deep, dense woods. I sought a clearing, with a view to the sky. We pressed ahead, but passed no openings in the weave of tree limbs, which grew tighter and tighter, closer and closer, until we could ride no farther. Dismounting, we led Rykka and Ta'ar on foot through the thickening foliage. At last we came to a gap where the trees stood just apart enough for two young men to huddle together in the dampening night, just apart enough for two horses to wedge between a pair of scratchy trunks.

When we awoke, weak light filtered halfheartedly through a crosshatch of limbs and leaves so dense we could barely see the fog that wafted in and around the treetops. Sky did not exist. Nor did a way out. A solid tangle of trees and scrub entombed us, offering no clue as to how we had entered this clearing. Shivering with cold, we searched for dry wood for a fire. But the fog that had dampened us dampened all. When finally lit, our miserly fire offered little but smoke, which hovered in the heavy air, reluctant to dissipate through the veil of trees. As efficiently as the forest cover prevented light and air from entering and smoke from escaping, it offered no protection when the rain started: intermittent drops at first — but thick and heavy enough to squelch the struggling fire. Then a torrent.

Slashes of lightning fired overhead, illuminating our small, soaked prison in bursts of ghostly white. Rykka and Ta'ar slapped their tails, whipping beads of water at us. The rain lashed through the trees and beat down on us with merciless intensity.

"I'm s-sorry," I stammered through chattering teeth. "How many times do I have to say it? We should have stopped when you wanted to. I'm sorry. But even if we'd stopped earlier, we'd still be soaked."

"Yeah, but we wouldn't be trapped," Yhoshi snapped, his face an angry cascade of rushing water.

"I'm sorry. What do you want me to do?"

"You're a bard. Do *something*."

"I'm a bard not a wizard. All I can do is tell stories. And I don't know that I'm even very good at that."

Yhoshi looked at me irritably. "Do you know one that can make me believe I'm warm and dry? How about one that gets us out of here?"

My mind wandered through its repertoire of bardic tales. "Kanta and the Desert Maiden. How does that sound?"

"Whatever." Yhoshi shrugged.

I stared off into the rain, off into the forest, then closed my eyes.

"Once, in a land far from Q'ntana, the rains came."

Yhoshi groaned and turned away.

"For forty days and forty nights they came. Then for another forty and another forty, until it had rained four hundred forty days and nights without cease. A steady drumroll of rain that never varied rhythm, never varied pulse.

"First crops washed away, then cattle, then homes.

"Then people.

"Each day brought tales of new drownings. Young and old, lord and commoner. It mattered not to the rising waters. They devoured land as greedily as they devoured all that stood upon it. The king issued proclamations. The priests prayed and fasted. It mattered not to the rising waters. Still the rains continued."

"Still the rains continue," muttered Yhoshi.

"Still the rains continued. There were no shipwrights in this landlocked land, so attempts at boat-making failed, inspired as they were by the shapes, sizes and proportions mandated by the priests. Some boats had tall, twisted towers at one end. Others, golden spires. Nearly all sank within hours of their launch, taking only nobles and priests with them, for nobles and priests claimed to be the only classes worthy of deliverance.

"It was the morning of a new day. Another boat had broken apart in the previous night. This one, crafted of finest birch and bearing the high altar and other temple treasures, had been fit for a king...and high priest. Thus, had the king and his retinue — and the high priest and his — perished in the swirling, bottomless waters. On this first morning with neither king nor high priest above him, the carpenter Elphan made his way through the remains of his village, skirting pools and lagoons.

"What would become of his wife, Sarra, and of his neighbors, he wondered, if the floodwaters continued their relentless journey. Yet another new river surged across his path, and as he searched for a safe crossing, he spotted a plank floating toward him. That it was a piece of royal wreckage was clear from the golden lamb at its prow. As though piloting this vessel from its regal figurehead, a large, black kyrrel stared fixedly ahead, whiskers twitching, its white-tipped tail erect as a sail. The plank docked where Elphan stood and the kyrrel hurried off, never once looking back. Without thinking, Elphan followed — across narrow bottlenecks, over logs that spanned eddying streams, and up into the hills.

"Finally, they came to a forest high atop a mountain peak, thick, lush and green, echoing with birdsong. Elphan had little time to take in this paradise, for still the kyrrel scurried on. When at last it stopped, it turned and stared at Elphan. It stared with piercing yellow eyes and Elphan found he could hear its thoughts. It was an odd, uncomfortable feeling, as though the kyrrel had lodged inside his head. What he heard came not in words, but in sensings that described this as a sacred place unknown even to the priests, as a mystical place normally invisible to humans.

"Why am I here, then? he wondered, looking to the kyrrel for an answer. But the kyrrel was gone.

"Just then an earsplitting screech sliced through the air next to him. He ducked as a jymra whizzed by, clinging to a vine. Then another, screeching more loudly than the first. And another. Elphan had never seen jymra, not living ones. How different these looked from their crude temple likenesses, still and unsmiling. Here, they laughed and teased like furry children, pulling and playing as they swung, several to a vine. He tugged on a vine then hoisted himself up, swinging jymra-like through the glade, feeling the weight of worry lift among these childlike creatures. He climbed as high as he could and saw an infinite curtain of vines extending deep into the forest. Then he remembered the plank, that single piece of wood that had borne the kyrrel to him, and a vision formed in his mind's eye of planks lashed together with vine — floating platforms that could outlast the rains. Clutching his vine with one hand, he reached for his knife with the other, to cut off an adjacent vine.

"'I can't,' he said. 'This is a sacred place.' And then the vine fell into his hand, bitten free by a grinning, chattering jymra. Maneuvering himself into position, he cut as many vines as he could carry and returned to his village."

Rykka whinnied. I heard her, but only as through a mist.

"The rain is stopping," I said.

"Slowing down, maybe...but stopping?" Yhoshi asked. He was barely present for me.

"'The rain is stopping,' Elphan told Sarra one morning many months later. Theirs was one of a flotilla of raft-homes drifting aimlessly through a vast, gray ocean.

"'How can you know?' she asked. 'The beat of rain upon wood has not altered once in all this time.'

"'The rain is stopping. We must prepare.' Elphan paused, squinting in concentration. 'We must prepare for dryness. We must collect rainwater before the rains stop.'

"Within two days the rhythm of the rain did change, and soon there were long stretches of daylight when no rain fell. Elphan and Sarra set out every ewer, pot and crucible, filling them with precious rainwater. Their neighbors mocked them and rejoiced at the rain's lessening power. They forgot that Elphan's wisdom had saved them once. Only when the rains ceased and the suns' glare soaked up the ocean water did they remember. For many it was too late. Elphan and Sarra shared their rations, but many rafters still died from fevers brought on by the dank and fetid receding waters.

"Soon these too disappeared and one morning the rafts came to rest on muddy ground that through the day dried to rich, loamy soil. The next morning awoke to trees and flowering meadows, all in the first blush of a spring that by nightfall had bloomed into the rich luxuriance of summer. Buds unfurled and blossomed in a kaleidoscope of color. Willows, bare at dawn, were by noon laden with golden tresses that had opened into thick, green strands by day's end.

"As Elphan drifted off to sleep that first night in this new land, Sarra enfolded in his arms, he saw the flash of a white-tipped tail dart across his line of vision. Mind's eye or open eye? To his dying day he was never certain. And there were many, many happy days until that one."

"Toshar, look!" Yhoshi jabbed me and I hurtled from the paradise of my story to the teeming rain of reality. "*Look!*" He pointed to a spark of white — like the tip of a paintbrush — that flashed through the underbrush at the clearing's edge. Yes, there it was: a white-tipped black tail, flicking nervously from a tiny opening in the thicket.

"Is it a kyrrel?" Yhoshi asked.

That would be too strange, I thought, stranger even than the story, which had come from I knew not where. As I had opened my mouth, my mind set for a happy, almost dull tale of warmth and contentment, the words that emerged were of peril and cataclysm. It was as though I was the mouthpiece for some powerful instrument beyond my control. As its music sang through me, carrying me where it would, I felt nothing but its rhythms, saw nothing but its revelation. I was the story. The story was me. Only when Yhoshi jabbed me did that other world dissolve into the rains of this one. Or were they different worlds at all? It was a kyrrel, and it looked to be the same kyrrel I had just seen, just been.

It picked up a bela nut and began to gnaw on the shell, ignoring us as it focused all its attention on breaking through the woody barrier to the fruit hidden inside. Only then, nut lodged between its teeth, did it take note of us. It stood for a moment on its hind legs, its nose aquiver, then scampered toward me, dropping the nut into my palm.

"Eat it," it said in a silent heart-link no different than that experienced by Elphan. Its yellow eyes bore into mine as I placed the red kernel on my tongue, barely hearing Yhoshi's attempts to stop me. It was the sweetest, most tender bela I ever tasted, melting into a thick, nutty syrup. As I swallowed it, I knew what I needed to know, what I needed to do. I was to follow Mishak — for that was his name. Alone.

Of course, Yhoshi argued. Even when I repeated Mishak's reassurance that the rains would end and underbrush melt away soon after our departure, he was reluctant to let me go.

"I have to do this," I said, not entirely convinced. Was this wrenching, queasy, uncertain certainty what it meant to follow my heart? I didn't want to leave Yhoshi behind but felt I had no choice. "Besides," I said as much to persuade myself as him, "look around you." The forest loomed up, dark and impregnable. "There's no other way."

"Come, you," I heard. "It is time and there is no more time." Mishak turned, sniffed the ground, followed a scent to the edge of the clearing and stopped, the white tip of his tail twitching impatiently. I threw my arms around Yhoshi in a hurried embrace, quickly nuzzled Rykka and Ta'ar, and fell to my hands and knees behind Mishak. One moment I was crawling through an opening that seemed to expand just enough for me to squeeze through; the next, forest and rain were gone, Yhoshi's farewell barely a whisper on a warm, summery breeze in a field of golden lilies.

Mishak was nowhere to be seen.

Six

M ishak," I called out. "Mishak." The only reply was my own voice, carried back on the wind.

"Misha-a-a-k," it sighed. "Misha-a-a-a-a-k."

Waves of gold rippled around and past me, emitting a scent of subtle sweetness. Lilies. A sea of lilies. Golden lilies in all directions. Where was I? How did I get here? Questions floated aimlessly through my mind. Answers didn't matter. Nothing mattered. I lay back on the bed of lilies and, taking deep breaths of perfumed air, watched Aygra and B'na fire long wisps of angel-hair cloud as they met overhead. My eyelids grew heavy. I let them slip shut as a languid lethargy washed over me and drew me into dozy nothingness.

The sensation of a cool hand caressing my face woke me. I opened my eyes to a velvet blackness studded with pinpricks of twinkling light. Another rush of air brushed by. Clean air. Unscented. I inhaled deeply and tried to see where I was. But the glow was too feeble. I felt the ground around me. I still lay among the flowers. Beyond that, I saw nothing. I searched out Ky'nar to get my bearings, but the stars and constellations resembled nothing I had ever seen. And then I spotted it: a gleam on the northern horizon. It formed into an iridescent disc that floated gracefully up into the sky, flooding the landscape with soft, silvery light. M'nor! I stared up into her luminous face, at the smile forming in the creases and folds of her creamy surface, and felt her calling to me. Her gentle, rippling song was so distant I feared my ears teased me. Did M'nor sing...to me? She glided higher into the sky, growing larger and fuller, her joyful song gaining in force until my body and everything around it resonated with celestial music. "Come to me," she seemed to be singing. I sat motionless, unwilling to move, as M'nor climbed to the midheaven. "Come to me," she sang, more clearly now, but what had begun in delight became a heartbreaking lament. I knew if I didn't begin my journey she would be overcome with sorrow. Reluctantly, I stood and began to walk north. All around me, the lilies slept, pressing against each other, against the night air.

That first night filled me with terror. Although M'nor's light never faltered, it was too subtle to ease the uncertainties of the dark. Was that black patch ahead a harmless plot of earth? Or would I sink into a deadly bog of disappearing sands? Were the disembodied shrieks that pierced the night near or far? Venomous or benign? By moonset I had determined to travel only by day, when the direct light of two suns delineated everything. A boulder was a boulder, to be climbed or skirted, its footholds and jagged edges clear to the eye. Moonlight was tricky, a constant play of light and shadow under which nothing was ever as it seemed. But if the morning glow of Aygra and B'na lifted my spirits, it did the same for the never ending sea of gold, which opened to the new day, soaking the air with its opiate.

Within moments of sitting down, I was asleep. I woke to the rising moon, but still reluctant to embrace the dark, I shut my eyes to M'nor, trying to store enough rest for the next day's journey. But even a full night's sleep couldn't keep me awake past morning's unfurling of those delicate blossoms. It wasn't until the fresh, unscented air of the third night woke me that I realized that the lilies' perfume would hold me back forever if I didn't walk through the night. If I didn't walk through the night, I would never cross this sea of deadly beauty. For four more nights, with M'nor as my guide, I moved forward through fields of slumbering flowers, encountering nothing but the sounds of the dark and my own fear. The fourth night M'nor set early. She sank lower and lower, her lengthening shadows swallowing more and more, even the stars, until all was inky blackness. I wanted to continue but could barely see the soil beneath my feet. Nor could I be certain of maintaining my northward course. I dropped to the ground and slept.

Something snuffling at my face woke me. A lion? Or had I dreamed the lion? The memory was vague — a gauzy film. I touched my cheek where I had felt the wet nose and sandpaper tongue. It was dry. I lay under a broad, ancient oak at the center of a circular plateau, alone in a sea of flowers. Wildflowers this time. Deep purple with yellow centers. The only hint of lilies was a wavering line of distant gold. Or was that a trick of the light? Strong yet suffuse, the light came from everywhere and nowhere. No suns lit the sky, which possessed an almost greenish cast to its cloudless blue.

I stood. I counted two hundred paces to the plateau's edge, a sheer wall of shimmering stone that plunged past a scattering of fluff and into a hazy ocean of colors and shapes. Far in the distance, a pair of tiny lights blinked up at me.

"Oh," I whispered in a voice as small as the faraway suns. My knees gave way. For an instant, I pictured myself slipping over the precipice and hurtling down, down, down, into...into what? I crawled shakily back to the safety of the tree and closed my eyes.

"You don't remember, do you?" The voice, squeaky and guttural at the same time, came from deep within the oak. I opened my eyes to tongues of fire that leaped and flashed around two eyes and a beak.

"I do remember! You're...you're...you're..."

"Tashek, bird of fire, at your service." Eyes and beak bobbed in the slightest of bows and the flames stilled, revealing a fiery-plumed bird, its head crowned with upright feathers of brilliant orange, yellow and crimson.

"I'm here for your story. Tell me your story. I love a good story."

"I don't understand. What story?"

"I'm here for your story. Tell me your story. I love a good story."

"Where am I? And Yhoshi. Is he okay? And the horses? Where are they?"

"All safe. All sound. All down." Tashek swooped to the rim of the plateau, dipped below the edge, then swept back, circling me and the tree trunk so rapidly all I could see was a ring of fire. "Tell me your story. I love a good story."

"What story?"

Tashek slowed to a hovering halt in front of my face. "Your dream, bard. Your dream! Don't say you don't remember. Of course you remember. Of course you do."

"Let's see... One moment I'm alone among the lilies," I said slowly, "the next, I see a lion...in a cage." I screwed my eyes shut, trying to make solid the wisps of my dream.

"Don't force it! Never force. Never force."

"The lion is enormous, larger than any creature I've ever seen. But the cage is small, so small the lion can't move. It can only sit and roar, its thunder shaking the ground beneath me. I remember thinking, 'Thank Prithi the lion is locked away and I'm safe, with the key in my hand.' And as I think it, I find myself holding a gold key in my right hand and I know that I can't leave the lion there to suffer, whatever my fear. And my fear is great, swelling as I near the cage and feel the heat of its breath.

"Suddenly, I notice the quiet. Everything has stilled. The world itself holds its breath. All I hear is the clamor of my heart and the clinking, clicking clunk of metal on metal as I turn the key in its lock. As I pull open the door and back away, I hear again the sounds of the world: a trilling choir of birds, the chattering squeak of field mice, the wind whistling through the lilies. Nothing from the lion. He squeezes out of the cage and pads toward me, his green eyes averted."

The image faded and I opened my eyes. "It was a dream," I said to Tashek. "But it seemed so real. What's strange is that I only remember it as I tell it." Tashek hopped onto my shoulder. "I don't even know yet how you fit in," I said. "But I know you do."

"It is best not to know too much too soon." It was O'ric's voice, with a bit of a throaty squeak. "It is best to know only that the story continues, and to follow where it takes you."

"How do you know about that?" I asked.

"Never mind. Continue your story. I love a good story."

I picked a flower and held it to my nose. It smelled of lemons and spring.

"Where is this place?" I asked.

Tashek hopped onto my head. His claws pinched my scalp. "Never mind. Continue your story. I love a good story." He flapped his wings impatiently, sparking two small plumes of fire in front of my face. I flinched, expecting to be burned. Instead, I felt a warm, gentle caress. He fluttered to the ground and looked up expectantly.

"Where was I?" I asked.

"Door open. Lion meek."

I closed my eyes again and willed the dream memory back. Slowly, images reformed.

"All of a sudden, the lion leaps up at me. I don't have time to move out of the way and now I'm cradling this huge bundle of tawny fur. It's purring, a deep, rumbling vibration. I feel it in *my* stomach, in *my* heart...

"Now the lion is on my back, its great furry paws slung around my neck. And then...then..." I looked down at Tashek in amazement. He was fussily preening himself.

"You!" I cried out. "The next thing I remember, the lion is gone and you're perched on my shoulder."

"I am the lion," said Tashek, with a guttural, purring growl too big for his tiny frame.

Memories cascaded into my consciousness, almost too quickly to speak.

"I was flying? No, *we* were flying."

"Yes...yes...?"

Tashek grips me in his claws and lifts me up and away, toward Aygra and B'na. Higher and higher we soar. I'm no longer dangling from iron claws but riding on Tashek's back, enfolded in light and fire, clutching the now-giant bird's neck feathers to keep from slipping off.

"Where are we going?" I shout, barely able to hear myself over the thunder of the wind in my ears.

"Into the light," he roars.

"We'll burn!"

"Burned, maybe. Consumed, never." The air is warmer and I see spurts of flame spiraling on the surface of the merging suns. My body is awash with sweat, my hands so slippery I can barely hold on. The heat is unbearable. The light sears through my eyes to the back of my head. I squeeze my eyelids shut. Burning light still cascades in. I raise my left hand to screen my eyes and clutch at Tashek even more tightly with my right.

"Careful or you'll pluck me clean!" Tashek jerks his head around. "You're covering your eyes," he roars. "Keep them open. Shield them now and you'll never see again."

"It's so bright," I cry.

"Keep them open! Open! Open! Open!

"It hurts."

"Hurt but never harm. Hurt but never harm."

The suns are directly ahead. Columns of dazzling orange flute and twist, flicking out toward us. Tashek picks up speed and aims for the center of this giant expanse of flame. Fingers of fire beckon, draw us in. Flames slap across my face, rip through my clothing, lash my back, legs, chest. Burning. Burning. Burning. I'm naked, clothed only in sweat.

Tashek is gone. I'm suspended in an orb of light. Images flash before me. Faces. Old. Young. Some I know. Most I don't. They smile. Light and reassurance radiate from them. Fire burns around me but I feel no heat, no pain. No fear. Only love. Peace. Courage.

It all happens in an instant and then I'm again riding Tashek, clothed in a new tunic and leggings, green as the lion's eyes. A scarlet cloak hangs from my shoulder, the crest of a full moon emblazoned over my heart.

Aygra and B'na are separating. Yet Tashek continues upward, higher and higher, leaving suns far behind, until they shrink to the size of tiny golden lights.

"Next I remember," I said to Tashek, "something was tickling my face. The lion's tongue on my cheek. It woke me up."

"And? And? And?"

"And what? It was a dream."

"Dream?" Tashek fluttered his wings in my face, then pecked at my chest — not at the ragged shirt I had been wearing since leaving Yhoshi but at the full moon crest decorating the cloak of my dream. Under the cloak, tunic and leggings were just as I had recalled them moments ago.

"It *was* a dream. I was sleeping and I woke up." I fingered the rich fabric. "How—?"

"Dream and not dream. Real and imagined," squawked Tashek from atop my head.

"All one." He hopped to the ground and flapped his wings. Fireworks sparked into the sky. "All one. All one. All one."

I shook my head. "I don't know what's real and what's dream anymore."

Tashek, now smaller than a hummingbird and shrinking rapidly, fluttered past my right ear. "Good!" he whispered. I turned my head to reply, but Tashek had vanished.

I stood and paced out the perimeter of the plateau. The cliff was as sheer and smooth as ever. Would I have to dream my way down? I returned to the shade of the oak and closed my eyes, but sleep eluded me. The caged lion roared through my head each time I dozed off. Sitting up, I thought of Yhoshi and the horses. Had they escaped the clearing? I wondered where they were and if I would ever see them again. I hugged my cloak tightly around me as if its nearness could ease my sudden loneliness. As I did, I felt something solid under the moon crest. An inside pocket. I hadn't noticed it before. Reaching in, I pulled out a tiny volume, barely larger than my hand and slender as my finger.

Bound in rich, crimson leather, its front cover bore the same golden moon crest as did my cloak. *The Journeys of Toshar, Son of Am'dar and T'yanna* flowed across the top of the title page in elegant script. Beneath it in smaller type: "Being the Chronicles of a Young Bard in Quest of the Moon." Other than a heading atop each page, no text graced the creamy vellum, only handsomely drawn maps that continued from page to page to page. The maps traced my life through the hideaway villages of early childhood, through the attempted climb of Pinq'an, into Pre Tena'aa and along the route Yhoshi and I rode that first day out. As I focused on any particular event, that drawing came to life and grew to fill the page. There I was sipping tea with Eulisha, drinking from the green bowl. I could smell the brew and see steam rising from the page. And there we were, Yhoshi and I, huddled and soaking in the Forest of Marrh, with Mishak in the right-hand corner, seeming to turn the damp page.

I flipped ahead to the present, to a page titled "Highest of the High: At the Top of the World." It showed me sitting with my book under the oak.

Was this how I now looked? I touched my hand to my face in disbelief — as did the young man in the book — and felt the coarse stubble of a beard-in-formation. I had neither shaved nor seen my reflection since I left with Mishak. How long had I been gone? My hair had grown longer and wavy, framing my suns-tanned face with loose curls. My eyes, which had always seemed hooded, now possessed a vibrancy I barely recognized. Who was this Toshar? Where was he?

As I studied the map, a broad, curving road formed at the cliff edge and descended through the clouds and off the edge of the parchment. Eagerly, I turned the page. No map greeted me, only abstract swirls that grew fainter with each succeeding page until, by the end of the book, all pages were blank. Baffled, I turned back to the map of the present, which only confounded me more. The road on the page had no real-life equivalent. Or did it? Slowly, I looked up.

A crystalline, almost translucent road fell away from the precipice in a spiraling sweep then vanished in the distance. I edged toward it and tentatively touched my right foot to it. It was solid. I pressed down. It seemed to support my weight. Taking a last look at oak and flowers, I stepped firmly onto its surface and began to walk. The road coiled down the cliff face, closely enough that I could touch the sleek stone. Soon, though, the sheer wall melted away, leaving only me, endless sky — and a dizzying queasiness. I quickly learned to train my eyes to look no more than a few paces ahead. At that distance, a faint, silvery glow marked out my path. It was almost opaque. Yet if I looked back or farther ahead, I saw no sign of road. No sign of anything.

Downward and downward I continued. Down and around. Around and down. The road pushed and I followed. I grew hungry and tired, but stopping would ease neither complaint. There was no food up here. Even the birds flew far below. And to lie down on a road no wider than my shoulders...well, I might roll over — and off. So I urged my reluctant feet forward and did my best to ignore my stomach's insistent rumbles.

A cloud drifted onto the road, forcing me to slow my pace. When I emerged from the thick, vaporous fog I could see the ground below, clearly for the first time, though still from a great height. In the farthest distance, toy-size black horses charged forward. I shuddered. Nearer, a gently meandering river sparkled through a great swathe of forest and then out past rolls of fertile farmland, promising food and rest. Yet still such a long way off.

I hurried forward then nearly tripped over my feet in my haste to stop. The road ahead had ended. No silvery glow. No gossamer strand. Nothing. Nothing ahead or behind. Even the road beneath me had lost its opacity. Suspended in midair and supported by nothing, my dizzy nausea returned. As I wrapped my arms tightly across my chest, I felt the book. I had forgotten the book. Quickly, I pulled it from my cloak and riffled through the pages until I found where I was. I didn't like what I saw.

On the map I was stepping off my tiny patch of skyway...into nothing. Once again I flipped to the next page. Once again an abstract whorl greeted me. I closed the book and shuffled forward. The patch of road moved with me. I shuffled forward again. Again it moved with me. I took a larger step. Still it supported me. As my steps again grew more confident, the road began to reform and within minutes was dropping steeply toward the ground, following the course of the river.

I tried to moderate my gait but, drawn by the road's plunging momentum, I broke into a run. I could almost touch the tops of the tallest trees. They were pyynch'n, giants among trees, said to be as old as Prithi. In some places they grew so high that their topmost branches were hidden in cloud. Their distinctive bouquet rushed up to greet me in a burst of wind — sweet and fresh. The smell of early morning, of wakefulness, of life. I wanted to reach down and pluck one of its juicy, fan-shaped leaves, but I was still too high — and running too fast.

Running too fast.

Following the river course...winding in and out...snaking this way and that...but dropping, dropping, closer and closer to the ground...my feet almost floating. Flying. Floating. Flying. Floating...

I no longer saw the road.

My feet still ran, but I felt nothing beneath them. Just a rush of air. Panic.

Still, my feet carried me. Down. Down. Down.

Now I was falling. My feet pedaled but nothing supported them. Falling. Hurtling. Plummeting.

"Jump," a voice deep within me urged. "Jump. Now." My mind rebelled. In the space of a lightning flash, I argued.

"Now, Toshar. Now!"

On their own, my knees bent.

I leapt.

The free fall slowed, slowed, slowed to a gentle, feathery descent. Drifting. Drifting. Lazy, sleepy, floating. An autumn leaf cradled by the wind.

Just beyond the stand of pyynch'n, where the river swelled into a pond before narrowing again to continue its course, a tiny cluster of buildings took shape. The buildings grew larger and more distinct as I floated nearer. There were six of them, haphazardly set down to form an irregular courtyard.

As I glided silently onto a thatched roof, a young woman led two horses through the courtyard and into a stable. The woman's gait was weary and pained, as though life itself weighed sorrowfully on her shoulders.

Just before they passed from sight, one of the horses looked up, snorted and tossed her head, her pale blue mane shaking out glistening drops of light before settling back like a cloud of feathers.

The Heart of the Maze

Seven

"Of course, I believe you," said Yhoshi. We sat alone in the inn's dim dining room. Its low ceiling and dark paneling gave it a cave-like aspect, brightened only by the shaft of sun that pushed through the small leaded pane at our side. Across the room, a fire threw dancing shadows onto a smoky wall. Dishes clattered in the kitchen, where a low murmur of voices rose and fell like waves on the sea. I sopped up the last of my soup with a crusty hunk of dry bread and moved on hungrily to the stew.

"But your hair...your beard...?" he asked incredulously. "How could that happen in one morning?"

One morning? My spoon stopped midway between bowl and mouth then clattered to the worn, wooden table. "What do you mean? It's been days...weeks..."

"Hours." Yhoshi reached across the table. "Feel my clothes. I'm still wet from this morning."

"But—"

"As soon as you were gone, the rain opened a path through the thicket to the river. Just like you said it would. I followed the river here." He stared out the window and into the sky. "The same way you followed it from up there." Cottony filaments drifted wispily across a pristine sea of sapphire. I followed his gaze, straining for a glimpse of the skyway, of the towering plateau. Nothing.

A thunder of hooves pulled us back to earth and eddied a cloud of dust that obscured everything through the window but a forest of black-and-orange pennants. The king's colors.

Yhoshi drew two daggers, sliding one across the table to me. "I found this on the ground," he said, "after you followed the kyrrel."

Oriccan. My hand dropped to my belt. How could I have been so careless? I hadn't even noticed its absence. I picked up Oriccan gratefully and stroked its hilt. The suns burst through the dust and sparked off the mirrored brilliance of its blade.

"Those toys won't help if it's you they're after," a female voice whispered from a shadowy corner. We had thought the room empty. "If it's not you they're after, they'll change their minds when they hear your talk of bards and M'nor." The young woman I had seen leading Rykka and Ta'ar to the stable emerged into the light, her waist-length hair as fiery as the flames dancing in the grate. She wore a white pinafore over a coarse, ankle-length robe and appeared younger than I had first believed — somewhere in the vicinity of Yhoshi's years and close to his height. Her face bore a determined hardness that spoke to seasons of hardship and sorrow.

"Who—"

She touched her finger to her lips. "Say nothing," she hissed. "You've already said too much too freely. If you value your M'nor, you'll come with me. Now." Yhoshi and I exchanged anxious glances, our fingers tightening around our daggers. "Now. You're wasting time."

"But who—" I tried again.

"Follow me." She was already gliding back into the shadows. "Come," she urged. She led us through a side door and deserted pantry, then along a dark passage to another door. It stuck, then squeaked as, wincing, she forced it open. We stepped into an overgrown, garbage-strewn garden and down an embankment to where river met pond. Her eyes, white orbs afloat in a sea of green, darted along the shore, up to the inn and back to us.

"I know my fath— Crozon too well." She touched one of the greenish purple bruises that scarred her ghostly complexion. "He would betray you for less than this." She snapped her fingers.

"Wait here. I'll bring you your horses." She flew up the embankment before we could say anything and disappeared into the inn.

"Do we trust her?" Yhoshi asked.

"Do we have a choice?" From the moment her innkeeper father had groveled up to me, I sensed something menacing about him that belied his servility. It was clearest in his questioning, which was more penetrating than his manner suggested. His daughter was right. We should have been more discreet.

Raised voices crackled through the air. From the courtyard. Yhoshi started to crawl up the embankment toward them. He motioned me to follow.

"It's the soldiers," he whispered. "We need to know what they know." We crept into a shadowy break between two buildings and peered into the courtyard.

A squadron was arrayed behind Holgg, its captain, imposing though shorter than any of his men. All wore tunics and jodhpurs, masks over their eyes and peaked caps over shaved heads. Only an orange crest on each left arm and a light flour-coating of dust softened the unremitting black of their uniform. In front of Holgg stood Crozon, stooped to appear shorter than his inquisitor.

"Two traitors have passed this way. Young men. Traveling together." His eyes swept the courtyard, settling for a moment on the spot where we hid. I clutched Yhoshi's arm so tightly he gasped. "Have you seen them?"

I released Yhoshi's arm and began to edge back toward the river then stopped, my curiosity greater than my fear.

"I'm not saying as they have. I'm not saying as they haven't," Crozon wheedled. He drew closer to Holgg. "Would there be a reward for my coop-e-rayshun?"

Holgg recoiled, wrinkling his nose. "What's your name, innkeeper?"

"Crozon, your majesty sire. Crozon at your service. Always at your service. Ever at your service."

"Well, Crozon," Holgg began in a friendly tone that deepened into an angry roar, "this is my reward...if there's no *coop-e-rayshun*!" A barely perceptible jerk of Holgg's head signaled two men to grab hold of the innkeeper and press knife points against Crozon's bloated belly.

"Have you seen them? Yes or no?"

"P-please, your holiness, sire. There 'uz two fellas all right, but they came apart-like."

"And? You try my patience, innkeeper."

"One with two horses, a-sopping wet they was, though we'd had no rain here since midday last. Right queer it was. And then this other, dressed like a prince, but with no horses, no coach, no nothing. We found him on the roof. Right queer, I tell you."

"You're drunk," Holgg spat. "You," he ordered Kor, the nearest soldier, "smell his breath." Half-holding his breath, Kor put his nose to Crozon's matted, food-spattered beard.

"Ale," he coughed, "and rotten teeth."

"Rotten, indeed," Holgg muttered. "Anything else before I have you sliced into a thousand pieces?" He nodded and Kor delivered a sharp, fierce blow to Crozon's stomach then drew his saber. "Where are they now?"

"In there," he gasped, pointing to the window. "They came separate-like, but they ate together."

"Show me." Kor prodded Crozon with the point of his curved blade. Holgg strode toward the door and kicked it in. Then he spun around. "Prak," he barked to his lieutenant, "check the stable. Keep two in the yard. The rest with us." He stepped into the gloom and merged with the dark.

"What's this?" Yhoshi asked. He pointed to a sleek black mount standing next to Rykka and Ta'ar. Crozon's daughter held the reins of all three. Pinafore and robe were gone. In their place were black tights, a purple jacket and a gray shoulder pack.

"It's Holgg's horse...*was* Holgg's horse. He's mine now. I ride with you."

"Do what you want with the horse," Yhoshi replied brusquely, "You're not riding with us." Yhoshi reached for our horses' reins. She pulled them close to her body.

"Not until you agree to take me with you."

Yhoshi reached for his knife.

"A boy and his toy," she taunted. "Act as one, soon undone." She flicked her wrist dismissively then gripped the reins more tightly, her knuckles pale against chapped, work-red hands. "You'll have to use that blade," she said. "You'll have to kill me for these horses."

"No one is killing anyone," I said, gently pushing Yhoshi's hand away. "What's your name?"

"Fynda." Her mouth was set in stubborn defiance. I smiled at her. She didn't smile back. "Yhoshi's right," I said, "you can't come with us. Why would you even want to when you can see how dangerous it is?"

Fynda tossed her head, her hair cascading like Rykka's mane, her eyes burning with fury. With her free hand, she touched the angry bruises that ringed her mouth and mottled her cheeks. "More dangerous than these?"

"You know nothing of our journey," I said quietly. "You aren't part of it."

"Are you so sure?" The words issued from Fynda's mouth. But the voice? It was hers yet not hers...as though it echoed from another time.

"Time is wasting," Yhoshi hissed.

"Your knife-friend is right." Fynda's voice hardened. "While we argue, King's Men draw closer. Listen." Angry voices pushed toward us. "I'll make it simple. Take me or I scream."

Yhoshi thrust forward, wresting the reins from Fynda and grabbing her wrist. She flinched. He tossed the reins toward me, spun her around and covered her mouth with his other hand. "Ride off, Toshar. I'll hold her. Ride off and save yourself. I'll catch up if I can."

I jerked forward, set to leap onto Rykka, then stopped when I saw Fynda's face.

Something tugged at me. Not pity. Not compassion. Not even the fear lurking beneath her bluster. Something else. Something deeper. I sighed. "I can't see it, but... Let her go, Yhoshi. She rides with us."

Yhoshi opened his mouth then snapped it shut and shook his head. As he released her, her sleeves rode up to reveal a forearm and wrist blotched with bruises. She jerked the fabric down again.

"Your arms," I said. "Can you ride?"

"As well as any," she retorted, leaping onto Holgg's horse but unable to mask the pain. The shouts drew nearer.

"Where have you hidden them, innkeeper? In that fat belly of yours? Let's cut it open and see if they fall out."

Yhoshi jumped onto Ta'ar. "Whether she comes or stays," he said, "we have to leave now."

"She comes, but not on Holgg's horse."

"But —"

"No, Fynda. No horse is as fast as these. Come down. You'll ride with me."

Crozon's scream sliced through the air. Fynda blanched. She hesitated for an instant then climbed up behind me.

In a moment we were off, a bluish purple blur racing over the river, across a stretch of open country and toward the protection of the pyynch'n grove. Rykka and Ta'ar wove a knowing course through the stand of sky-scraping trees, then carried us over meadows and fields, through creeks and bogs, and along scrubby trails — always northward. Not until we reached the hilly, forested core that lay within the crescent of the Horusha Mountains did the horses slow their pace.

Aygra dipped behind the mountains, leaving a fiery corona pierced by a jagged, snow-crested crag. We continued for some leagues more as B'na dipped behind the lower mountains to the east and the sky darkened.

"I think we'd best stop here," I said. We had reached the edge of a wooded incline. A shallow stream gurgled playful somersaults over its rock-strewn bed as it tumbled down from the mountain. The light failed rapidly now and, slipping down from the saddle, I strained to gain a fuller sense of our whereabouts.

"I'm sorry, Yhoshi. I rode us too long again," I said. "We should have stopped while we could see. Still, what's blind to us is also blind to the King's Men."

"What's blind to *you*," Fynda said. She scanned the darkness and nodded. "Excellent. Wood for a fire, berry bushes for food, fish in the brook, and a path up through the forest."

All I saw were shadowy outlines. "How—?"

"Night-seeing," she replied simply. "What's shadow to you is clear as day to me." She slipped into the dark. "Come. I'll show you." Neither of us followed.

When she returned a short time later, she bore an armful of piila and tokku, plucked from trees only she could see. We ate the fruit silently by the light of the small fire Yhoshi had reluctantly kindled. Suddenly, Fynda tossed her tokku core into the flames and leapt up, her face radiant with firelight.

"I'm free!" She pirouetted around the fire pit, ruffling her hands through Yhoshi's hair then tugging playfully at mine. "Free-ee-ee-ee," she shouted, and the sounds wove through the trees and in and out of the branches.

"Stop that," Yhoshi swatted Fynda's hand away, "and keep your voice down." He glanced around nervously. "Soldiers and spies could be anywhere."

"I don't care," Fynda sang out. She leapt over the fire then back again, squealing in mock pain as the flames licked up at her. "I don't care. I'm free, free, free, free, free! No more Crozon. No more inn. No more loathsome guests. Guests. Ha! They'd be no guests of mine in any household I ran. An uglier bunch I've never seen." She paused thoughtfully. "Well, not all of them..." Her voice rang out again as she resumed her euphoric dance. "But most of them. Imagine scores of Crozons, year in, year out. That's what I saw. That's what I served. Year in, year out. And now I'm free of them, free of him. Free! Free! Free-ee-ee-ee!" She tore round and round the circle, her hair streaming behind her like a mad, fiery cascade.

Yhoshi grabbed her arm and jerked her to the ground. "If you want to stay free," he hissed," you'll keep still. The fire is risky enough without you shrieking for all the King's Men to hear. Do you want to get us killed?"

Fynda's cheeks reddened. "I'm sorry," she panted, "but you can't understand what it's like to be free of that place, of that man. You can't know what it was like with those greedy eyes ogling me every day, every day...for as far back as I can remember."

"Crozon's?" I asked.

"And others'." Fynda shuddered.

"Did any of them...?" I left the unaskable unfinished.

"Once," she began after a moment's silence, then stopped, shaking her head.

"Once what?" I asked.

"Almost," she whispered.

"Why that—" Yhoshi sputtered.

"It was worse than that, or might have been." She gathered her thoughts, marshaled her memories. "I was twelve. My father... No, Crozon. I can't bear to call him 'father,' to think of him as my father. I used to pretend, you know, that he wasn't my father, that he had kidnapped me and that my true father would charge into the inn on a white stallion and rescue me. He never did. And when my brave knights finally appeared," she looked from me to

Yhoshi and giggled, "I had to force them to rescue me." The giggle gurgled and choked as the story she had begun pushed its way through.

"A man stopped at the inn. A wealthy man, if clothes could tell. He was dressed in finery the likes of which I had never seen, not at our miserable inn: a crimson cape, a white tunic and silver sash, and a feather in his cap — brilliant green with slashes of scarlet. Imagine that: a feather in his cap." She shook her head in wonder. "You saw how Crozon acted with the soldiers, how he can be when he sees power. He's even worse around gold. I didn't know that then. All I knew was that for the first time in as long as I could remember, Crozon treated me well, treated me like a daughter not a slave. He spoke softly, offered me the same meal as the guests, not the usual dinner scraps, and tucked me into a real bed in a real guest-room. Normally, I slept on a pallet in the kitchen. He was sweet and gentle and kind, and I believed him." She spat. Her saliva struck a faintly glowing ember, sizzling as it extinguished both itself and the coal. "It was as though he really cared...really cared... It was nice. For those few minutes until I fell asleep, it was so nice. Then the mattress creaked and shifted. It woke me. Someone was lying down next to me. I woke but I didn't open my eyes. I didn't dare."

"It wasn't —"

"No, not Crozon. I knew his smell and this one was different...clean, powdery, pleasant. But I was still afraid. More afraid. It was a stranger, a man. I couldn't be certain without opening my eyes, but I sensed it. A man in my bed. What did he want? Why was he there? I was innocent, but I knew enough to be frightened. I knew enough to scream. I screamed and screamed and screamed, praying for someone to come. Even Crozon. At my screams, the man leapt up. I heard a flint strike and saw candle-glow through my eyelids."

"'Hush, little one. Who are you? Why are you in my bed?' A man's voice, but gentle. I opened my eyes a crack and saw the wealthy guest, the one Crozon had fawned over earlier. His bed? Not mine? And then I knew. He knew too. We knew together. I was Crozon's gift to this man, this stranger. A bribe, a tribute." She began to shake. "His own daughter!" But the anger within could find no outlet and the shaking ebbed into a sigh. "What did I do to him that he should treat me so, that he should hate me so? I want to understand. I want to know how I could have changed things, made them different...made them better..."

"He was evil," Yhoshi said. "He *is* evil."

"It's that simple?"

"What happened then?" I asked.

"Nothing."

"Nothing?"

"Larán — that was his name... Larán fell into a fury. At first I thought he was angry with me, for being afraid, for not...for not... But it was Crozon he was raging at. He nearly exploded when I told him I was Crozon's daughter. He threw his clothes on, tucked his dagger in his belt and roared toward the door. I leapt out of bed and hurled myself at the door. I begged him not to go after Crozon. I begged him to stay."

"Why ever for?" Yhoshi asked incredulously.

"I don't know. I should have let him go. He would have killed Crozon, I think. Or maybe he would have tried and failed. I was afraid. I was afraid that if he didn't kill Crozon, Crozon would kill me — or worse — for spoiling his plan. I was afraid that if he did kill Crozon...what would become of me?"

"Things couldn't have gotten worse," I said.

"I couldn't know that. How could I know that? I was only twelve...barely twelve. This was all I knew. Crozon was all I knew. So I begged Larán to say nothing and, reluctantly, he agreed. He laid a blanket on the floor for himself, tucked me back into bed and left a candle burning for me. He didn't know about my night-seeing, and although I trusted him, I didn't trust him enough to say. So he left the candle burning and I felt safe, safer than I had felt in a long time, safer than I felt until this minute — far from Crozon, far from the inn." She sipped from the water skin and absentmindedly caressed its leathery hide. "I think Larán must have spoken to Crozon in the morning. I don't know what he said, but Crozon never tried to gift me to a guest again. But he did punish me. For months I prayed for Larán to return, to take me away. I imagined he was my real father, my knight. But I never saw him again. Crozon never spoke of Larán, but his eyes were angrier after that night, and his words even more cruel."

"What about your mother? Where was she in all this?" A trace of gentleness crept into Yhoshi's voice. Startled, Fynda turned to him. He looked away.

"Dead," she said. "A long time ago. So long that my memories of her come only in flashes — with me one instant, gone the next. I know she rocked me in her arms, sang to me — wordless songs that she hummed and whistled by an open window overlooking the pyynch'n grove. I think I remember that, but maybe I imagine it because it makes me feel better to believe it was real."

"It doesn't matter whether it happened at the inn or only in your heart," I said. "It happened. That's all that matters."

"I hope so. It was so reassuring. I was so frightened so much of the time."

"Of what?"

"Of life. Of him. He beat her, I never saw it. I never heard it. But I know it. I saw into his darkness just as I see into the night. I'm sure he killed her.

Not outright, but bit by bit he beat the life out of her. Not the love, but the life and the light. They dimmed bit by bit, until they were gone. Until she was gone." She grabbed a stick and beat at the flame. It flared back at first, but as she struck out at it again and again, it weakened and finally died. She looked at the stick with horror than flung it into the pit. "Like that," she said. "Just like that."

Yhoshi raised his eyes. In the dark he couldn't see her face, didn't realize how well she could see his. "I'm sorry," he murmured. Fynda nodded a silent, invisible acknowledgment.

"Then what happened?" I asked.

"I don't know when it began, because I don't know when my mother died." She paused. "He began to beat me. First he slapped me — across the face when I displeased him, which was often, across the buttocks when I pleased him, which was too often. Then the slaps turned into smacks and smacks into whippings. All the while he groped, grabbed and pinched. You've seen the bruises...some of them..." She stared into the blackness, then gazed beyond it, back along the route we had traveled that day, back toward the inn. She shivered. "It excited him," she said at last. "I didn't see it until now. But when I see his eyes in my mind's eye, I know." She blinked out the tears that gathered under her lids. "And I know now that I always knew."

Yhoshi half-rose, but she turned from him, from us, wiping her face clear of the tears that had softened it. When she turned back the same look of defiance I remembered from the inn greeted us.

"Do you want to see where we are?" she asked. "I'm going into the woods."

"I think it would be better if you stayed here with us," I said.

"Follow if you choose," she retorted and stalked off.

Yhoshi hesitated then leapt up after her.

"Aren't you coming?" he called back to me.

Their voices faded into the dark, leaving me alone with the night, with only the tinkle-plash of the brook as company. Even Rykka and Ta'ar had wandered off. I looked up, trying to catch the reassuring blink of the stars — Prithi's all-seeing eyes — but a crosshatch of boughs kept even that light from me. All was blackness.

"Where are you, M'nor?" I called up through the trees. "How do I find you?" The stillness deafened me with unanswerable questions. I reached into my cloak. The book was still there. I stroked the leather, but left it where it was and dropped my hands back into my lap. If the book had an answer, it was too dark to see it. Too dark. Too still. Even the brook seemed muffled and distant. Too dark. Too still. I shivered then stiffened at a crackling noise.

"Yhoshi? Fynda?" No reply. I hugged my knees, trying to roll my body into an impenetrable ball, impermeable to the black, blank emptiness that enveloped me. Then I heard it again. A burrowing, crunching noise...drawing nearer, the only sound in that suffocating veil.

"Rykka?" I pulled my knees closer to my chest, trying to squeeze into invisibility.

It's louder now. Closer. It sounds like snapping twigs, but it's not. It sounds like shuffling footsteps, but it's not.

A single tap on my right arm startles me. I turn my head. Nothing is there.

Another tap. Gentle but insistent.

And another.

I open my mouth to scream. I feel the strain in my throat but hear nothing. The tapping continues.

With my left hand I reach over to grab it, whatever "it" is. Nothing is there. I try to push myself up from the ground, but I'm rooted.

"Who are you?" I shout, though I don't hear my own words. "Where are you? What are you?"

"The night is full of questions." The reply comes as a heart-link, but with what? "The night is full of questions. I have one for you."

A bell-like soprano ripples through the night in cascades of colored light.

"What is truer than true and stronger than strong?

"What is brighter than bright when sung sweetly as song?

"What rises within and must call out or die?

"Why is darkness so dark?

"Why do tears streak the sky?"

I see the music slide away like raindrops down a windowpane. Silence. Again.

"Why is darkness so dark? Why do tears streak the sky?" The lines repeat with insistent urgency.

"Stories," I say slowly, as though spelling out the word. "There are no more stories?"

"But there are, young bard-in-becoming." The heart-link again. "You know them all, even those you do not yet know. Complete the song, Toshar. Complete the song." Again the words whisper through the air: "Why is darkness so dark? Why do tears streak the sky?"

I don't know what to say. I've never heard this song before. Or have I? I feel music swell up inside, a delicate carillon that spills effortlessly from me.

"Stories are truer than fact, stronger than fear

"They rise from the soul, bursting forth in song clear

"Our tales feed the moon, her tears they do dry

"There's but one that can save her, and that one is —"

I'm coughing, choking, even as the music continues expectantly.

"How does it end, Toshar? How does it end?" The tapping jabs at each word. "How. Does. It. End?"

"I-I don't know."

"Do not lie to me." I feel a growling rage in the pit of my stomach. "You cannot lie to me. FINISH THE SONG."

"I-I can't." I'm crying, shaking uncontrollably. "I can't. I can't. I can't." Each "I can't" wracks through my body with a violent shudder.

"I daren't," I whisper.

"I'll sing it with you." The heart-link softens to a reassuring purr. "We'll sing it together.

"Stories are truer than fact, stronger than fear

"They rise from the soul, bursting forth in song clear

"Our tales feed the moon, her tears they do dry

"There's but one that can save her, and that one —

"And that one, Toshar? And that one?"

"Is I," I whisper hoarsely.

Eight

Dawn broke through the night with a rush of brightness, as though day was eager to begin its new life. Shafts of rosy light arced overhead, burning away the night in a fiery, celestial pyre.

"Good morning, sleepybones." Fynda smiled a relaxed, toothy grin. Her face had lost some of its pallor. "I was right," she said. "There were fish in the brook." She knelt in front of a fire, waving a skewered tosti at me. "For me, I would eat it raw. Fish is fish. But for you...here. Be careful. It's very hot."

I blew a perfunctory cooling breath and devoured the speckled fish in three gulps.

"That's the nice thing about tosti," she said. "Small bones. Easy to digest. No fuss." She skewered another from the slithery pile at her side. "Here, have a second. It may not be as cooked as the last, but it will swim down just as easily."

I bit into the hot, crunchy skin and grimaced. The flesh was slimy and raw.

"Ah," she laughed, "a bard of delicate tastes." She handed me a stick. "Cook it to your own liking."

When I had cooked and eaten the rest of it, I pierced and grilled another and then a third. I hadn't eaten tosti since I was a child. I had forgotten how succulent they were. I had forgotten how hungry I was. "How did you catch them?" I asked. "And so many?"

Fynda popped a raw tosti into her mouth, whole, and held up her hands. "They may be bruised, but they're quick. Tosti rush to them like a babe to its mother's breast." She tossed another to me. "Have another. I'll pack the rest for the road."

She nodded toward Yhoshi. He lay on his back, snoring softly. "Is it time to wake your friend?"

"Let him sleep a few minutes longer. We have a long day ahead. Somehow we must cross those." Hulking mountains loomed large and dark on three sides, their jagged peaks thrusting bony witches' fingers into the sky.

"What's this quest you're on? We're on?" she corrected herself, stealing a shy glance at me. I said nothing. "I'm now part of this," she added quietly. "Aren't I?"

"You were meant to travel with us," I said, not sure what else to say.

"Wait," she said shyly. "I haven't thanked you yet for letting me come. We both know you could have left me behind, for all my threats. I'm sorry for those." Her voice rose. "No, I'm not. I'm not sorry for anything that took me away from that place." She shivered and inched closer to the fire.

I left her to her thoughts for a moment then asked, "Has Yhoshi told you anything about this...this quest?"

"Of course not." She looked up expectantly. I said nothing. "I only know what I saw and heard at the inn. I know you're a bard and that there's something magical about you. How else could you have walked through the sky? I also know you're human." She paused, then continued so softly I could barely hear her over the fire's crackle. "Gods don't cry themselves to sleep."

The night memory returned with a hot-knife stab.

"It felt as though I had much to cry for," I whispered, more to myself than to Fynda. "It feels less so now." I stared into the fire and thought I heard "*It is I*" in the popping of the twigs. "It is I," I said aloud.

"You repeated that often in your sleep. What does it mean?"

"You're full of questions, Fynda-of-the-night-eyes," I replied. "I know little and understand less. Together, we're to travel north to find M'nor and restore her power to smile and sing for all. This MoonQuest initiates The Return. From it there is no return, not for any of us. There's only one way, and that's forward."

"Then let's get going," said Yhoshi, stretching and distending his mouth in a gaping, smiling yawn. "Do I smell fish?"

Nine

The late afternoon suns gilded the lush valley below in honeyed light. Above us, blinding eddies of snow obscured Horusha's summit. We had climbed quickly that morning along the forest trail Fynda had sighted in the dark. Once the trees had thinned then disappeared, we inched along a narrow, rock-rubble path — ragged cliffs and boulders to one side, a precipitous drop to the other.

Now, we rested. Yhoshi and I sat on a ledge of cushiony moss, our feet dangling over the darkening forest. Behind us, Fynda paced angrily, her shoes clicking a brittle tattoo on the stony path.

"I didn't trade a slow death at home for a quick one here," she said. "Why can't we take the horses?"

"It *will* take longer without them," Yhoshi conceded, averting his eyes from mine. I could tell he took Fynda's part reluctantly.

"Perhaps," I said, "but it will be impossible with them."

Fynda stopped, but her staccato beat echoed on. "You make no sense," she snapped.

"There's none to be made," I replied. I rose and gazed up the rocky slope. Reason told me that the horses would carry us over the top and part way down the other side before the worst of the night's freeze. Yet I knew we had to leave Rykka and Ta'ar behind.

"I can't explain it," I said. "I wish I could but I can't." I stroked Rykka's blaze and read my truth in her eyes. "Ride on if you want," I said. "I must continue on foot."

Yhoshi stepped toward me. "I'm going with you, whatever you decide. But the horses... We can't just leave them."

"I'll ride one and the other can follow," Fynda said. She hoisted herself onto Rykka. "I won't die tonight, as you will if you spend a night up there." The swirling, blinding snows of the mountaintop seemed suddenly nearer, fiercer. Fynda tugged gently on Rykka's reins. "Come," she crooned. Rykka didn't budge. "Come, Rykka," she repeated. Rykka stood statue-still. "Come *on.*" She dug her heels into the horse's flanks. At that, the blue mare reared and Fynda tumbled to the ground. Rykka snuffled insouciantly at the moss around Fynda's body. Fynda struggled up, her hand raised to strike the horse.

"Why that —"

"No," I said quietly. Poised between rage and despair, Fynda dropped her arm and sank back down. I stripped Rykka and Ta'ar of their gear and stood back. With one leap, they blended into the bluish-purple stone and were gone. "They brought us here," I said. "They'll find their way back. And they'll find us again when we need them."

Fynda said nothing as we climbed higher, dancing delicately around loose rocks on the narrowing ledge-trail. Above us, a blizzard squalled savagely, gusting closer and closer, lashing stray whips of ice across our faces. We would soon need shelter. The solid rock-face offered none.

"I was sure there would be caves up here," I said.

Yhoshi brushed feathers of snow from his jersey. "It's probably best to just keep going," he said doubtfully.

Fynda shrugged and kept walking, trancelike, the wind rippling her hair in wild streamers. "We shall die up here," she chanted, each word matching a step. She paid little heed to the shifting rubble, tripping first into Yhoshi then into me. "We. Shall. Die. Up. Here. We. Shall. Die. Up —"

Suddenly, the rock beneath her foot gave way. She slipped and rolled with it, over the edge, her shrieking cry merging with the wind's.

Shock jerked the breath from my lungs and I stumbled. For an instant I expected to join her, wherever she was. But Yhoshi's strong hand steadied me. I clutched at his shoulder, afraid to look down. Slowly, I let my eyes slide along the rock to the trail, to the edge, over the edge. Nothing. I shivered. Yhoshi's face matched the thickening snow. The wind howled. The wind wailed. "I don't want to die," it cried, echoing through the mountains. "To die...to die...to die..."

We dropped to our knees and looked over the rim. Shaking uncontrollably, Fynda huddled on a half-hidden ledge barely large enough for one. "I don't want to die," she whispered.

"You won't," I said. My eyes turned to meet Yhoshi's." Will she?" they asked.

"Are you hurt?"

"I-I don't think so. I landed in some brush. I don't want to die."

"Can you climb back up?" I asked.

"I don't know. Everything's so slick from the snow."

Yhoshi leaned down toward her. "Can you reach my hand?"

She shook her head. "I can't move. I'll fall." She pressed against the cliff wall, nearly out of view. Yhoshi struggled to contain his impatience.

"If you won't take my hand," he said, "then you *will* die. There's no other way to get you up."

Fynda looked up me pleadingly.

"Yhoshi's right," I said. I leaned over and reached toward her. She stretched. We stretched. But our fingers couldn't bridge the gap. She shrank back down again.

Yhoshi inhaled deeply through clenched teeth. He pointed to a rocky finger jutting out from the cliff-face above Fynda's ledge. "If you climb onto that," he said, "you'll be able to grab onto the edge of the cliff."

Fynda swallowed, stood and grimly followed Yhoshi's instructions. As we grasped her bruised wrists, her foothold crumbled. She shrieked. Legs flailed in desperate quest for support. Fear-bleached fingers clung to the cliff edge.

"It's all right, Fynda," I said, "we've got you. Try to relax into our grip." Her legs went slack but her fingers tightened on the stone.

"Let go," Yhoshi said.

"I-I can't. I'll fall. I don't want to die." She swiveled her head to look down. Her jaw muscles tensed. She shut her eyes.

"Look at me Fynda," I said. "Look into my face. Look at nothing but my face." Her eyes opened a crack and a white slit stared back at me. "Now, let go. First one hand..." She released the pressure and cried in pain. "Now, the other." She shook her head. "We won't let you fall. Let go and we'll pull you right up. I promise." I hoped I sounded more confident than I felt. The snow was heavier, the wind more frenzied, our hands wet and slippery.

Slowly, Fynda opened her other hand, gritting her teeth to stifle another cry as we pulled her up next to us. She collapsed into my arms, a sobbing heap.

"I don't want to die," she whispered.

"Silly fool," Yhoshi muttered. "She'll get us all killed." He walked away.

"I don't want to die."

"Of course you don't. None of us does."

"Come, Toshar. Come quick," Yhoshi shouted. "I've found something."

Next to him, a fold in the rock masked a narrow fissure that opened into a dark, dank cave. We crawled in, grateful for the shelter and watched snow sheet past the small aperture.

"She could have killed us all," Yhoshi mumbled.

"Instead of only me, you mean." Fynda glared at him. "I've apologized and apologized and apologized again. I've thanked you and thanked you and thanked you again. What more do you want?"

Yhoshi said nothing. He and Fynda sat on either side of me, two stone columns of angry silence. Outside, raging swirls of white howled past on a wind that never paused for breath, choking off the light long before nightfall did. I shut my eyes to the storm, but sleep came reluctantly. When it did, it seemed to last but an instant before Fynda's panicked voice shattered the dreamless void.

"Wake up! Wake up!"

"What is it?" Yhoshi asked drowsily.

My eyes opened to a gray half-light.

"We're trapped. I've been digging and digging but all I find is more snow. We shall die up here."

Yhoshi elbowed her aside and felt his way to the icy wall that blocked the entrance. "Don't start that again," he said. He clawed through the fissure and tunneled out onto the trail, but no light broke through the dense, packed snow.

"Stop," I said. "If you keep going, you'll go over the edge."

Yhoshi continued to scrabble at the snow, aided now by Fynda.

"If we don't get some air, we'll suffocate," she said.

I inhaled deeply and felt musty coolness fill my lungs. "There must be air coming from somewhere," I said. "Maybe it's a way out. Can you see anything, Fynda?"

Fynda stopped digging and moved slowly around the cave. We all did, vainly poking and probing for the air source. Frustrated, we huddled in hungry, impotent silence, waiting for the drip of melting snow, for a needle of suns-light. But the silent darkness remained whole, and whatever snow vanished did so because it was our only sustenance.

Time hung motionless, draping us in its empty shroud. After a while, even my stomach stopped calling for food and all was silent but for Yhoshi's sleep-heavy breathing.

"You two are like nayla fighting over the same mate," I said to Fynda.

"He doesn't want me here. I can't help that."

I looked down at him. "He says he doesn't dream, but look at his eyes."

"Twitching eyes means a dream?"

"Often." I watched Yhoshi for a few minutes. He mumbled something incomprehensible and his eyes darted wildly under fluttering lids.

"I hope he's dreaming a way for us to get out of here," I said. "Otherwise..."

Fynda groped for words, but none came.

"What is it?" I asked.

"Do my eyes twitch?" she asked at last.

"I've never noticed."

"I'm sure they don't." Fynda shook her head, then added with absolute conviction, "They can't."

"We all dream, Fynda. Even Yhoshi, who is so sure he doesn't."

"No, really I don't. Anyhow, it's forbidden."

"The king would like you to think that."

"You mean, it's not forbidden? I don't understand."

I pointed to Yhoshi, whose mumbles had graduated to moans. Tears coursed down his cheeks, even as his eyes and lids still jerked rapidly.

"You can't forbid something like that, any more than you can outlaw breathing...or stories."

"But—"

I recalled Eulisha's words, repeated to me when my dreams eluded me. "Those who aren't frightened to remember have forgotten how to remember," I said. "Those who haven't forgotten are frightened."

"Except for bards?"

"Bards are also afraid," I said.

"Of what?" I shook my head. "Of what?" she asked again.

"Of the dark. Of dreams with no message." I paused. "Of stories with no end. Of stories that come from nowhere."

"I envy you your stories," she said. "I don't have any."

"None that you remember, like your dreams." I closed my eyes and opened them again. There was little difference in the light. "Right now, I'd trade my stories for your night-seeing," I said.

Fynda's gaze warmed my face. "I'll be your eyes if you'll be my story," she said. "Tell me one?"

"What do you see in my face?" I asked.

"Light."

"I wish I could see that. I wish I could feel it."

Fynda squeezed my hand. "It's there," she said, "and it doesn't take night-vision to see it."

"Then I'll tell you a story about light." I thought for a moment, then began.

"Once, the land was darkness. No suns shone through the day. No moon lightened the night. The land was as this cave. The land was a cave. A child lived in this cave-land. The child was called Manu.

"The child Manu lived alone with nothing, not even the memory of arriving in this place. He lived on a mossy rock by a stream. Moss was his food, water his drink. There was no need to move, so he remained by his rock. He ate when he was hungry, drank when he was thirsty. And thus time passed. He bathed when he was dirty and slept when he was tired. Thus time passed. Time passed in its own way, for there was no way of measuring it.

Manu grew older, but there was no way of measuring that either. He was neither content nor discontent. He just was.

"Then one day, if day it was, Manu woke to a shadowy form standing before him. He thought he dreamt, for he had often dreamed this hooded, faceless figure. It carried a lantern in one cloak-shielded hand and a gnarled staff in the other. Manu covered his eyes, which were unaccustomed to even the weak light cast by the lantern.

"'Who are you?' Manu asked, startled at the sound of his long-silent voice. The figure began to walk away. Soon, all the child saw was a slowly swaying lantern flame receding into the dark. He closed his eyes to return to sleep, but they opened again of their own volition. Of its own volition, Manu's body lifted itself from the rock and began to follow the light. Perhaps it was the distance. Perhaps Manu's eyes had adjusted to the light. But when a gray brightness began to form on the far horizon, Manu no longer felt the need to shield his eyes.

"The light triggered a faint memory that grew stronger as the glow turned silvery peach. He ran toward it, toward the hooded figure. The figure stopped. As it raised its arms to the light, a brilliant sun burst from the ground beneath him. Staff and lantern vanished. In their place, both hands held a luminous grail.

"Manu heard a whooshing roar overhead and looked up. A dragon so massive it turned the sky from blue to scaly green hovered over the figure, breathing fire into the grail, which glowed even more brightly. The dragon then scooped up the figure, flew into the rising sun and vanished, leaving the grail suspended in midair. After a moment, the grail dissolved into the light.

"'I have been waiting for you,' the sun sang. 'I could not come to you until you came to me.'

"Manu did not know what to say. He looked around. What had been closed and colorless exploded into an endless symphony of vibrant green.

"'Who are you?' he asked.

"'I am Aygra, the father,' it answered. 'I am your brother in light.'

"'Where am I?' Manu asked.

"'In the promised land.'

"'Where is that?'

"'Where you are.'

"Where Manu's world had once been silent, it now echoed with joy. Animals squeaked and chattered. Birds sang fearlessly. From the green beneath his feet erupted a kaleidoscope of flowers: white, violet, wine-dark red, burnished orange. And from the tree limbs hung a cornucopia of succulent fruit, ripe and ready to eat."

I paused. Yhoshi had awakened and listened as raptly as did Fynda — as did I, for this telling was as new to me as to them. I waited for the story's ending to come to me, to identify Manu and describe his fate. I waited in long silence. At last I spoke the words the story demanded of me, words that answered none of my questions.

"As the sun hovered overhead, Manu woke from his dream to know it was no dream, to know the truth of creation. Thus did Prithi raise Aygra and form our world. Thus was Q'ntana born from darkness. Thus did Manu witness the return of all that was lost."

Lucky Manu. What I wouldn't have given at that moment for a slice of his sky, for a taste of the light and life that had sprung up around him. Instead, we sat entombed in darkness. First Fynda then Yhoshi fell asleep, breathing in a single rhythm they never shared while awake. I slowed my breath until it melded with theirs and sat, awake and alert, feeling our breath as one. Finally, the darkness itself answered my question with a whisper of coolness that tickled the base of my neck.

"I feel it too," Fynda said when I woke them.

"Can you see anything?" I asked. "It's blowing down from somewhere over our heads."

Fynda shuffled from wall to wall, her shoes rasping against the stone floor. "No, but the higher I reach the more air I feel. Hoist me up and I'll try for a closer look."

Yhoshi and I stumbled into position and Fynda stepped into our cupped hands. "A little higher. No, wait. Down a bit...over to the right....a bit more... There *is* something... Push me up."

Free of her weight, I stood on tiptoe and peered into the dark. "Where are you?" I called up. "What do you see?"

"I'm on a ledge." Her voice rang back, amplified by the stone. "There's an opening here, a tunnel. I'm going to see where it goes."

We heard an eerily scraping echo, then nothing. Nothing, for the longest time. Too long. Then the scraping sound returned, faintly at first.

"Is it a way out?" I asked.

"I don't know, but it's a way somewhere."

We groped and grabbled up to the ledge then slithered after her through a black, snaking crawl space, my hand clutching her foot, Yhoshi's clutching mine.

After a time we emerged into a spacious cavern hung with torches whose infinite reflections flickered in glass-enclosed cabinets. Bookcases. They rose from a slate floor in unbroken panels and disappeared into shadowy heights. Thirteen archways, including the one through which we had just passed, punched through the perimeter and descended into blackness.

A way somewhere. Into the Maze of Horusha? I remembered an old rhyme and shuddered:

The Maze of Horusha, where evil dwells
There's but one way out, where the death bell knells

The rhyme said nothing about books. So many books. I yearned to touch them, to feel their supple leather, to read their glass-distorted titles and flip through their gold-edged pages.

"Do all these books have stories in them? Like the ones you tell?" Fynda asked, wonder suffusing her voice.

"There's only one way to find out." I studied the ebony-framed cabinets but could find neither latches nor hinges that might open them. Frustrated, I pressed my palm against the glass. A shock sparked through me and flashed through the cavern. Its force flung me limply toward the massive fireplace.

When I could stand unsupported, I edged as close as I dared to the wall of books. "The king would kill anyone with a library like this," I said.

"Then he would have to kill himself." A voice echoed around us, bouncing off the glass, hissing through the fire. We drew our daggers, moving slowly from archway to archway, but saw no one.

"Find me if you can," the voice teased. It was a man's voice, a deep, growling rumble. "Here I am." A quick flicker flashed far down one of the tunnels. "And here." Another light in another tunnel, then thirteen flashes all at once.

"Something moved in that one," Fynda whispered. Yhoshi started toward it.

"Wait," I said. "We have no reason to come after you," I called into the tunnel. "You have done us no harm and we wish you none. We seek a way out. Will you guide us?"

Cruel laughter crackled through the cavern, gaining in volume until even the glass rattled in distress. Suddenly it stopped. All was silence.

"Do what you will," it said finally. "It matters not. This is the Maze of Horusha. Death is your only way out."

"If we are to die anyway," I called back, "show us your face. Why do you hide?"

"Why do you seek?"

"I'm called to seek."

"He thinks he is chosen." A hideous cackle again filled the cavern. "Chosen to perish, and his friends alongside him. Foolish friends that would choose such a path. For such friends, I offer one chance and one chance only. Depart now the way you came, but leave the 'chosen one' to me. Go, but go now. My mercy will not show itself again."

Fynda looked at Yhoshi and shook her head. He stepped forward.

"We go as we came," he said. "Together." As we linked arms defiantly, a roar of outrage rumbled through the mountain. Nine of the torches fell to the ground and extinguished, as did the fire in the giant grate when an avalanche of earth, sand and stone tumbled into it, casting the cavern in a strange, uneven light. Shattering rock clattered deafeningly around us.

"There is no more cave," the voice said serenely once the noise had abated. I pulled the book of maps from my cloak, but before I could open it, a light flickered in one of the tunnels. "Follow me if you dare." The light vanished to the left.

"I follow no one whose face I have not seen," I called into the tunnel.

"Yet you follow a moon whose face is but stone in the sky," it snarled.

"I have seen her face. I have yet to see yours."

"You will see it when I choose to show it. Meantime..." A burst of wind bellowed from the tunnel and into the cavern, dimming the remaining torches and blowing a black and gray tumbleweed at us. When the wind ceased and lights brightened, the tumbleweed had straightened into a gray-skinned creature, its creased, bloated head crowned with a single tuft of coarse, black hair. Baggy black overalls hung over its spindly frame, emphasizing the disproportionate size of its head. Its hand pressed a scimitar to Yhoshi's throat. A bead of blood appeared on its blade.

"See to them, Rog," echoed the disembodied voice.

"You heard what he said," Rog said amicably. "I must see to you. First off," he said to Yhoshi, "I suggest you stand *very* still. Any movement and, well, who knows what might happen... Now, drop your knives." We did and he kicked them into the tunnel. "That book of yours," he said to me, though his eyes remained fixed on Yhoshi. He took it from me and pressed it against the nearest pane. The glass softened to accept the volume, which slipped neatly into a vacant slot on the shelf.

"I won't gag you," he said, still pleasantly, as he tied us up with rope from his bib pocket. "But I warn you: The first one to speak will speak for the last time. My friend will see to that." He brandished the scimitar then sheathed it in a scabbard tooled with ancient characters and hung it over the fireplace. Then humming absentmindedly, he began to tidy the cavern, restoring fallen torches to their brackets, digging out the fireplace and sweeping up the stones and dust that had settled on the slate floor. All the while he kept his distance, never looking directly at me. His tidying complete, he stood in the center of the cavern and turned slowly, inspecting his handiwork. He nodded, satisfied, then pulled a lit torch from its bracket and moved toward the fireplace.

"No," he mumbled shaking his head before the logs caught. From there, he walked to the extinguished torch farthest from us. Once again with flame poised, he hesitated, shook his head and moved away — back to the center of the cavern. He stood indecisively, scrutinizing everything but us, then scurried off into one of the tunnels. Light and footsteps receded, then disappeared.

"That was almost too easy," Yhoshi said moments later as he slipped free of the rope that bound his wrists behind his back. He had been working at it surreptitiously through Rog's cave-cleaning.

"It's almost as though he wanted us to escape," I said thoughtfully.

"I thought that too, and I don't like it," said Yhoshi. He prowled from archway to archway, peering into the dark. "It could be a trap."

"I don't think so," I said. There was something familiar about this Rog, a quality, a spirit, I was sure I had encountered before. "I know him. I'm certain of it. I just don't know how."

"How could you forget that face?" asked Yhoshi.

"It's not his face I know." I stared off into the tunnel then shrugged. "It'll come when it comes."

"What do we do now?" Fynda asked.

"We're free to leave," Yhoshi replied.

"To lose ourselves in the maze, you mean." Fynda stepped cautiously into one tunnel, returned and looked into three more. "Each tunnel is its own labyrinth," she said. "We'll never find our way through."

"Well, we can't stay here," Yhoshi countered, "and we can't go back the way we came. Toshar?"

The answer came not from me but in the tap-tap of boots on stone that echoed toward us from one of the tunnels.

Ten

"hat's your name?"

"You know already," Rog replied, refusing to meet my gaze. "They call me Rog."

"What do you call yourself?" I asked.

"Rog is fine."

"You didn't always look this way, did you, Rog?" I pressed.

"People change," he replied, still looking away.

I sat next to him and watched him in silence, searching for the face behind his face. We had ambushed him as he passed back into the cavern armed only with his torch. He didn't struggle as we bound him, nor would he speak, ignoring both Yhoshi's interrogations and Fynda's more gentle questioning.

"You've seen me before, haven't you?" I asked. He shrugged.

"Answer him." Yhoshi pressed his blade closer to Rog's throat. Rog didn't flinch nor did he strain against his bonds.

"Let him be," I said. I studied the strange man a few minutes longer, seeking the truth from the deep pools of anguish-scarred compassion that shone sky blue through that grotesque face.

Those eyes. I knew those eyes.

"He won't harm us," I said. "Will you, Ryolan Ò Garan?"

He shook his head, still refusing to look at me. "You're mistaken."

"Am I? I've seen your eyes. They haven't changed."

Rog said nothing, but his eyes pooled with tears. He turned to me at last. "If you know who I am," he sighed, "you know I couldn't hurt you. It would have been better if you hadn't recognize me, but..." He sniffed the air as I untied him.

"What is it, old friend?"

"He's gone, I think."

"Who?" Yhoshi spun around, dagger at the ready.

"Bo'Rá K'n?" I asked.

Rog nodded. "There's a faint odor of decay when he's here. It's subtle, but I've learned to detect it. I've had lots of time for that. I'm as much a prisoner here as you are. Bo'Rá K'n is my jailer."

"He's Q'ntana's jailer," I said.

"True, true." Rog stood and held out his hand to Fynda and Yhoshi. "I am Ryolan Ò Garan, minor magician and onetime tutor to a young bard." He threw me a lopsided grin. "When I had friends, they called me Garan."

"You have friends again, Garan," I said. "In all of us."

Garan's grin faded as he picked up the rope and wound it around his arm. When he was done he turned to me. "I hoped you wouldn't know me," he said." I've changed...in too many ways."

"Not your eyes," I said.

"No, not my eyes." He took my hands in his. Though crabbed and bony, they still looked human. "I never betrayed your family," he said. "You must believe that."

"I always have." I squeezed his hands. "But what happened? I thought you were dead."

"And I, you." He walked to the grate and stared into it. "It's not long to tell. Would that it were, for we will be here long time. A very long time." Stooping for some kindling from the brass barrel next to him, he relit the fire and started to pace.

"My feeble wizardly disguises may have fooled some, but they didn't fool the King's Men. They tried to make me talk." He shuddered. "I refused. I never said anything to give you away. I never *said* anything. But Bo'Rá K'n taught the king's inquisitors how to read a man's thoughts. Crude ways that deliver crude results." He stopped, his grotesque form silhouetted by the fire. "They learned all they needed." He resumed his pacing, stopping every few words to poke at the flames.

"I'm still alive, Garan. So is Eulisha."

"Your parents?"

I shook my head. Garan shook his sadly.

"Zakk?" he asked.

I nodded.

"Too bad." Garan stared into the fire. It blazed angrily, throwing dancing shadows of his misshapen body across the rough stone floor. Finally, he turned to face us again.

"By the time the King's Men were through with me, I was so eager to die they thought it crueler to keep me alive and exile me here, to live out my misery as guardian of all that was forbidden but not destroyed. Roshan, the previous guardian, was dying. I was to kill him once I'd learned the maze from him, but I didn't. In gratitude, he shared secrets of this place only Bo'Rá K'n knows, secrets that go back to when this was sacred ground."

"If you knew the secret of the maze, why didn't you just leave?" Fynda asked.

Garan turned to face us. "Look at me. I would have been recaptured in an instant. And tortured... I couldn't face that...again. No. It was safer to stay here. I leave only for food, but I don't go far. Never far."

"You said you knew no way out," Yhoshi said.

"I knew the way once. I don't any more."

"The tremors that shook through here?" I asked.

Garan nodded. "One of Horusha's secrets is that there are always three paths out. Roshan showed me the way you came in and the way I went while you were freeing yourselves. Both are now blocked."

"What about this?" Yhoshi asked, tapping the chimney excitedly.

"Only smoke can find its way through. Even it sometimes returns in confusion."

"You said there are *always* three ways out," Yhoshi pressed.

"Where one path closes, Horusha opens another. Somewhere. We might find it today or tomorrow...or never."

"What about the third way? You only mentioned two."

"It lies across disappearing sands," Garan replied. "It's undamaged but it's no way out. There is no way out."

Disappearing sands. Those unyielding, glutinous pools sucked in and devoured whatever brushed their sandy skin, from the feather touch of a hummingbird to the lumbering charge of a mandopleth. According to Garan, a bottomless pool of disappearing sands not only filled the exit tunnel from one slick wall to the other but broadened outward beyond the threshold. He knew no way over, through or around it. Yet it was the only way. Or was it? I walked to the bookcase.

"That book you took from me —"

"Bo'Rá K'n... I'm sorry."

"I understand, but can you retrieve it?" I described its contents.

"The glass accepts hungrily but does not yield readily. I'm sorry. You can't imagine how hard it is to be here among all these books without ever being able to open one." He shook his head sadly. "Do you remember me teaching you about the ancient temple-libraries, Toshar?"

I nodded. It was a vast network of storehouses where bards recorded history — past, present and future — in song, fable, prophecy and parable. Although they were secured, anyone with a thirst for story could find the way and would be welcomed by the scribes and keepers of The Word.

"'The Word as temple, voice of the people,'" I quoted.

"Precisely. These were holy places, places of power. It was that power that Bo'Rá K'n and the Fvorags he has served — no, the Fvorags who have served him — sought to crush and control. They could destroy the bards, or thought they could, but they couldn't destroy The Word. In olden days, getting a book through the glass was harder than getting it out. Now, it's the reverse. Try as I might, I have never been able to retrieve a single volume from behind its glass curtain. You already know what happens if you touch your hand to it."

I peered through the glass but couldn't even find my book, so well had it blended with its mates. "There's only one way, then," I said.

Garan shook his head. "That way lies death."

"Which way doesn't?"

Torches in hand, we followed a reluctant Garan into the tunnel. We moved slowly, through clammy, winding passages and over slippery surfaces, squeezing past knife-sharp shards that could slice through flesh, yawning crevices hungry to be fed and black craters of stagnant slime. At times, the ceiling dropped without warning, forcing us into a backbreaking slouch. At others, the floor gave way and we slid or tumbled down a rocky ramp. Often, the tunnel narrowed to little more than a crack, forcing us to slither sideways, backs to one wall, noses scraping the other. At every turning, Garan insisted I score a mark on the wall. "If something happens to me, you'll be able to find your way back." I knew there would be no going back. I also knew it was pointless to argue.

"We're here," he said at last. "Don't step beyond this point." We had reached a crossing. To the right, daylight seeped through from the end of a broad, sandy passage. It looked so easy. It was so deadly. To the left, the tunnel plunged back into the dark. I picked up a loose stone and tossed it toward the light. A slurping, sucking sound filled me with nausea. Yhoshi tossed another. The same hungry sound, the same queasy sensation. At first, we tried to gauge the extent of the quagmire, but soon we were all throwing whatever loose rocks the tunnel would surrender. A grim, ghoulish fascination had overtaken us. I felt sicker and sicker but couldn't stop. It was as though we were trying to fill the pool, to make it solid. But there was no satisfying it. It consumed greedily all we offered — until there were no more stones to dislodge, no more rocks to pry loose. Exhausted, we collapsed to the ground.

I had known it was futile. Yet I had come, hoping to be proven wrong.

Garan was right. There was no way through to the arch of light that beckoned so teasingly. I closed my eyes. An afterimage of light remained, clinging cruelly to my consciousness. I tried to shake my head clear of it. For once, I yearned for darkness. Still, the light lingered. Eyes open or shut, there it was. It broadened now, rippling out into waves of amorphous radiance.

It shimmered, deepening into gold. Slowly, it took form: a key, giant and glimmering — still beckoning. I opened my eyes. I saw it still, not in the midst of the disappearing sands but hovering in the other tunnel, and still beckoning.

I prodded Yhoshi. "Do you see that?" I asked.

"What?"

"There." I pointed. "A giant gold key."

Yhoshi peered into the tunnel and shook his head. "There's nothing there. Your eyes are playing tricks in the dark."

I turned to Fynda.

"I see tunnel and more tunnel," she said.

"Garan?"

"Nothing. It must be a reflection from the torch light."

I stood and edged into the tunnel, moving my torch up and down, left to right, but the image didn't change. I took a few more steps. The key remained the same distance away.

Alarmed, Garan grabbed my arm. "Where are you going," he asked.

I shook him off and moved deeper into the tunnel, but no nearer. "We must go this way," I said. "We must follow the key."

"No!" Garan exclaimed. "That's the heart of the maze. Even Roshan never dared explore that tunnel." He tried to pull me back. "Let's go back the way we came."

Yhoshi moved to join me. "That way is no way," he said to Garan.

Fynda looked from us to Garan and back. "Come," she said to him, "if Toshar trusts this vision, we should too."

"Even if it's Horusha's cruel joke?"

"Even so," I replied.

Garan shrugged and sighed.

We walked for a long while, yet for all we walked, the key grew no closer. We walked past walls of sameness, our torch light casting eerie shadows on rough, wet stone. Soon the stone smoothed, dried and began to lighten from black to charcoal to gray. Its surface grew increasingly hard, until a knife could no longer score it. I said nothing and kept walking. We would not be returning this way.

Straight and level for a long time, the tunnel began to slope downward, spiraling into the heart of Horusha, toward the heart of the maze. The walls were almost white now, clean, milky and bright with reflected torch light. Yet the key shone even more brightly.

I ran my fingers along the smooth, warm stone. It felt as though untold eons of tides had polished its rough edges then receded one last time, leaving the suns to bake its glassy surface. Deeper and deeper it bored, the incline steepening so quickly it was hard to keep from running. And so we ran, tripping over our feet in the rush to the bottom, propelled by an unstoppable momentum.

And then it stopped. With no warning. A cold, blank wall forced itself into our path. Instinctively, I thrust my arms out. My torch fell. I knelt to pick it up. When I rose, the key was gone. I stared and stared, but the image wouldn't return.

It took me only a moment to see that all we faced was a sharp jog in the tunnel. Saying nothing, I relit my torch from Yhoshi's and continued around the bend, hoping to find the key on the other side.

No key.

I stopped after a few paces and counted thirty-two branches forking out from where I stood. I counted again. Still thirty-two. Where was the key? The others stood a few paces back, believing me deep in thought. I was deep in panic.

Finally, Fynda came up behind me. "Is everything all right?" she asked. I didn't know what to say. When she saw my face, she gasped. She knew.

No one blamed me. They didn't have to. I blamed myself. Paralyzed, we stared into the thirty-two arms and back into the thirty-third behind us, our faces as blank as the stone, each hoping another would offer a solution to the impasse. Fynda spoke first.

"We still have some of Garan's food," she said, forcing brightness into her voice. "We might as well eat." She reached into Garan's pack, withdrew the remains of a roasted k'nrah and carved the meat into four portions. "I don't know about you, but I'm ravenous."

"I'm not hungry," I said. "Take my share and divide it up."

"What's this?" cried Garan. "Is this the brave young bard ready to follow his story into any peril? Who is this person?"

"Fine words, Garan, but you were right from the start. We should have stayed in the cavern. There's no way out. I've let you down." I averted my eyes. "I've let M'nor down," I whispered. I turned and began counting the tunnels again, this time out loud.

Yhoshi interrupted. "You haven't let anyone down." He draped his arm around my shoulder and led me to the meager spread Fynda had laid out.

"This is worse than awful," he said with a grimace, "but it's food. Take some, Toshar. Whatever else we do, we don't have to starve."

I bit at the meat. It was so tough I had to tug at it with all my strength to rip a piece free. In spite of myself, I smiled. "I see your cooking hasn't improved with time, Garan. Should I tell them about the last time you cooked for me?"

"It was a fine meal," Garan countered.

"Oh, yes," I said. "So fine that it found its way back from my stomach by the same route it had traveled in, only quicker."

Fynda and Yhoshi stopped mid-chew.

"Eat, eat," urged Garan. "I've been roasting meat for myself for many years, and I'm still alive."

Only when I took another bite did Yhoshi and Fynda resume chewing. "Are you sure it was the king's work that changed you and not your cooking?" I winked and we all laughed. It felt good to laugh. Garan laughed so hard he began to choke and cry. He almost looked his old self as the creases in his convulsing face shifted and smoothed.

"Tell us again about this key," Yhoshi said.

"Yes, Toshar," Garan added. "Maybe we'll learn something more in the retelling."

"I don't know anything more than I've said." Once again I described the key and how I had come to see and follow it. "It was leading me," I insisted. "I'm even more certain of it now. How did I lose it? How do I get it back?" I paused as I tried again to conjure it up. It wouldn't come. I shook my head in defeat.

Garan paced anxiously. "I knew this was a bad idea," he said. "I don't know why I let you talk me into it. Let's go back."

"I'm not going back," Fynda said.

"None of us is," I said, "even if we could find our way back."

"The markings?" Garan asked.

I shook my head.

"There has to be a way out," Yhoshi insisted.

"I keep telling you," Garan said. "There is none."

No one spoke for a few minutes, each of us lost in the futility of our situation.

"Tell us a story, Toshar," Fynda said at last.

"What? A story? Why?"

"Your stories are like magic. You tell a story and something fantastic always happens."

"Like with Mishak," Yhoshi said.

"I don't know a story that will make quicksand go away." I shrugged. "Okay."

I closed my eyes and waited.

"There was a king," I began after a few moments.

"There's always a king," giggled Garan.

"There was a king," I repeated, "a young king named Coriann who had lost his kingdom. It happened suddenly. One morning he woke and his bed was all he had. His bedchamber was gone, and with it the elegant tapestries, finely wrought swords and horned heads of noble beasts that had hung there. Gone too was the impregnable fortress that had housed it. Not a single foundation stone remained of the mighty hilltop redoubt that had taken seven years and hundreds of men to construct, that had repelled fearsome armies more powerful than his own. Nothing remained of his world save his bed, and even that dissolved into dust the moment he stepped from it. He was alone, with nothing, in the midst of a silence deafeningly loud in its vast, noiseless emptiness.

"'I must be dreaming,' Coriann said, 'for even my most powerful sorcerer could not perform such a feat.' So he poked himself, thinking to reawaken to his lady wife's snores and to find all his subjects and possessions back where they belonged. He poked himself not once, not twice, not thrice, but many multiple times, until his arms and legs were blotched with bruises. But the dream did not fade. The nightmare did not end.

"'It's true, then,' he said. And for all his legendary courage, he knelt and wept. He wept and wept, his tears gathering in a salty stream that trickled down into the grasses, gaining force until they formed a sparkling brook and Coriann found himself sitting on its bank.

"'I was not a cruel king,' he cried to the gods. 'I did not pillage and plunder. I defended my people and tried to rule wisely. Why have you taken everything from me? Why have you punished me?' There was no answer. The gods themselves had vanished. Only land and sky remained. Even his royal silk nightclothes were gone. His skin itched instead with the rough trousers and jerkin of his poorest subjects.

"At last Coriann rose and followed the river of his tears down the hill. Around it wound, deepening as it followed the contours of the land, slithering and sliding through meadows until it pooled in a great lake formed by a mighty stone dam that rose so high he could not see past it. When his thirst grew insistent, Coriann cupped his hands to the water and raised them to his lips. He expected the bitter salt of hot tears. He tasted cool, sweet nectar. As he pulled his gaze from the water, his eye caught the glint of something shiny at the bottom of the river. A gold coin?

"'What good is coin to me?' he asked. 'There is nothing to spend it on. I have not even a pocket to put it in.' Half of him was annoyed at finding something so useless in this empty world. The other half was amused at the absurdity of it. He began to walk away but, with his first steps, felt an inner nudge and stopped. 'I have nowhere to go and nothing else to do,' he said as he removed his clothes and lowered himself into the water. The cold, so refreshing in his mouth, was numbing to his body and he came close to abandoning the endeavor. But his body soon adjusted and he dove to the bottom in search of the gold. Coriann had to swim to the surface several times for air before he was able to dislodge it from its hiding place beneath sand and rock.

"It was not a coin at all. It was a key.

"As he waited for the suns to dry him, Coriann studied the key. It had three jagged teeth and a diamond-shaped hole at its head, around which spelled out the words YOU ARE THE KEY.

"'You are the key,' he read aloud. And as he spoke it the key vanished and the river spoke. 'You are the key,' it said in a rippling, gurgling voice.

"'I am the key,' he said. He repeated it again and again. 'I am the key. I am the key.' As he spoke the words, a loud crack ripped open the dam, revealing to him a new life and a new way forward.

"'I am the key,' he said, and the sterile past, though never forgotten, receded into the distance, little more than a bump on the far horizon."

The story had ended, but I remained deep within it. "I am the key," I said and moved, trancelike, back toward the blank wall where I had dropped the torch. "I am the key," I repeated as a loud crack ripped an arched opening into the wall. I stepped across the threshold and into a small, round chamber, barely aware of Yhoshi, Fynda and Garan behind me. When the last of them had passed through, the opening vanished.

Eleven

A thick, marble-slab table and four high-back oak chairs dominated the tiny circular enclosure. Not even a crack marred its white, luminous walls. Fynda glanced anxiously at the doorless wall then at me.

"I knew this was a mistake," Garan said. "I don't care for myself. I can never leave. But now Horusha has swallowed you too."

"There was no way in until Toshar found one," Fynda said. "He'll find a way out." She turned to me. "Won't you?"

Would I? I saw the same solid walls they did. Nothing more.

Settling into one of the chairs, I touched my palms to the marble, shiny, black and cool, except where blood-red veins sliced through it. They felt warm and alive, as though real blood throbbed through them and into my veins, mixing with my blood. As Fynda, Garan and Yhoshi joined me at the table, the marble faded to white and walls dimmed to black, until all we saw was a floating disc whose halo illuminated our faces.

Then I heard it. A gentle trill that gained in volume and clarity until a bell-like soprano echoed through the chamber.

"Welcome, Toshar and friends of Toshar," it sang. "Welcome to the heart of Horusha. I am the Lady Gwna and I thank you for your story, for the story that has brought me to you as it brought you to me."

"The Lady Gwna," I gasped as slowly a face took shape in the moonlike orb of the tabletop: midnight eyes set above high cheekbones in a creamy complexion framed by a waterfall of silky red. "The Lady Gwna," I repeated. "Do you see her?"

Garan looked around. "Where?"

"In the table."

All three looked down then up, shaking their heads.

"You don't hear her? You don't hear the music?" It was so clear, so real, so present.

"When they are ready, they will," the Lady Gwna said.

"If you are here, my lady, then M'nor must be here too. Does this mean we have come to the end of our MoonQuest?"

The Lady laughed a bittersweet chime. "Though you see and hear me, it is this table, the Table of Prophecy, the Kol Kolai, that brings me to you — not in substance but in spirit. No, this is not the end of your journey but the beginning, as every step is a beginning and every beginning a step."

"I am afraid, my lady. I have brought my friends into this place and see no way out. What do I do? What do we do?"

She smiled, and her smile flooded my heart with warmth. "Trust," she said. "Trust that what guided you in here will guide you out. Close your eyes and trust. Close your eyes and see. See from your heart."

"What's happening?" Garan asked. "What's she saying?"

An explosion of color greeted my closed eyes, a kaleidoscope of shifting, swirling hues. In the center, framed in black, was the gold key.

"Now," she said, "let the key unlock the secrets of the Table."

My jaw tightened. "How?"

"Just let it."

I inhaled deeply, dropped my shoulders and tried to relax. The key grew larger and brighter until it eclipsed the colors around it, until it expanded beyond my field of vision, until all I could see was the hole at the top, a circle of black that slowly faded to white and became the table.

"Now," she said, "look into the table, Toshar. Look into the Kol Kolai and see."

Somehow, without me being aware of it, my eyes had opened. I was looking into the table. In place of the Lady Gwna, I saw a tapestry of colored light whose abstract shapes glided into an image.

"I see an army," I said, "of black-shirts. They thunder along the road to a village near Kemet. Legions and legions of them. In a huge chariot of dirt and dust. Thundering. Thundering. The noise is so loud it hurts my ears...

"I can't see now, the dust is too thick.

"Wait, it's clearing... I see...

"*No!* Sabers slice down the villagers. All of them. One after another, one after another. Old and young. Women and children. I can't look!"

I tried to close my eyes but they wouldn't cooperate. I could only stare at the table and watch the carnage.

"Arms and legs and heads and hands litter the ground, drenched in blood. Soldiers pick up the heads and toss them back and forth. Like balls. Like toys. They're laughing. *Laughing!*

"It's over."

I swallowed hard as that image faded to make way for another.

"It's night now. There's no light, no one about. Clouds hide the stars. I see shadowy forms. Two. Two men huddle together. It's too dark to see who they are... No, I do see. One is Zakk. I can't make out the other one. They're talking. Whispering. Mouths move but I can't hear what they say...

"Now Zakk is alone. He looks at me. Right at me. As though he knows I watch. His eyes are blocks of ice. He grins. It's a cruel smile. Why is he happy?

"He knows I see him. He knows I know... Something... What? About this massacre? About him? What is it? He knows and doesn't care. He wants me to know he doesn't care. What is it I know? What is it?

"The image is fading...fading... It's gone."

I couldn't lift my eyes from the blank tabletop. What was that about? Had Zakk betrayed those villagers? It wasn't possible. For all his callousness, he couldn't do that. Could he? If he could, had he also betrayed my father? And Garan? I looked up at the tragic deformity across the table. A strange, ethereal light washed over Garan, erasing the damaging years and restoring the face I remembered from childhood: smooth, placid, untroubled... Foolish too, but gentle and compassionate in infinite measure. The table's halo also embraced Fynda and Yhoshi, extending a childlike innocence to their features.

"I see her!" Fynda cried. "Do you see her, Garan?"

"Yes, yes. Is that the Lady Gwna? Is that what you saw, Toshar?"

"I hear her too," Yhoshi shouted. "I hear the music."

I looked back into the table. The Lady Gwna had returned. She sang.

Beneath Horusha, buried deep
The marble sits, fast in sleep

When The Return is joined in heaven's ring
When moonchild laughs and moonbeams sing
When bards restore the storied king
The Table's secrets to the world she'll fling

Until that day, her prophecy
Is heard alone by The Four Who See

One with eyes that pierce the dark
One whose loyalty is true to mark
One whose learning will sing this song
One whose heart ne'er leads him wrong

The music faded and she spoke. "You are The Four Who See."

"The Four Who See?" I asked.

"It means you see with your heart. That's how you are able to see me in this table. That's the only way to see anything in this table.

"You have come together as The Four Who See, not only to see what you see here, but to see your way on this MoonQuest. Together. For together you are the key that unlocks The Return." She paused. Her face grew larger, her expression more serious.

"The prophets speak of it, but prophets are fallible and the future is not fixed. Time is not fixed, is it Garan?" Once again the music swelled. "Sing, Garan. Sing the song you forgot you knew."

Garan opened his mouth and for an instant, the light in his eyes wavered and his face hovered between the Garan of old and the tortured soul we had found in the library. The light won out and his full, rich baritone echoed around us.

When the Table's light is yours to see
Its visions come to set you free
Time is present, time is past
Time is future not yet cast

The Table speaks, the Table shows
Of time's true face, only the Table knows

"Kolai Kol Kolai," Garan whispered. "I had forgotten."

"Does that mean that what I saw has yet to happen?" I asked hopefully. "That it can be averted?"

"Time is not fixed," the Lady Gwna repeated. She looked up, past me, as though through the roof, beyond Horusha and into the sky. "Yet the hourglass empties and there is much to be done in its limited span. You know of Bo'Rá K'n?" I nodded. "Beware Bo'Rá K'n. He appears in many guises and will try to stop you. He must try to stop you. That is his part. Stay together — that is yours. Stay together and your power will rival his. Break the chain and..." One final time, music flooded the chamber, a minor-key lament that tore at my heart. This time she and Garan sang together:

Break the chain, the Table cracks
And nayla rule in howling packs

Break the chain, you Four Who See
And story's might will never be

Break the chain, the future's lost
Break the chain and bear the cost

"All Bo'Rá K'n's power emanates from a single source, from a single weapon," she said.

"What is it?" Yhoshi asked.

"Your fear. Stay together, refuse your fear its power and your mastery will rival his. Break the chain and..." Gwna's voice began to waver.

"Don't go," I cried.

"Your story gave me strength," she said, "but one story in a silent land is not strength enough." Streaks of black and gray began to weave through the image.

"What do we do? How do we get out of here?"

"The Table, it..." Voice and image faded, and with them the table's creamy glow. The marble blackened to match the walls. Only swirling veins of blood-red glowed in the silent darkness.

Drip...drip...drip... Drops of water, faint but steady, sliced through the silence.

Drip...drip...drip...

It grew louder. More insistent.

Drip-drip...drip-drip...drip-drip...

Where did it come from? I heard it overhead. I heard it under the table. I heard it behind the walls. I heard it everywhere at once, not as an echo but as the same omnipresent drip. Louder and louder, like rain — a single, urgent drop at a time.

Drip-drip-drip...drip-drip-drip...drip-drip-drip...

Each drop drilled deeper and deeper into my skull, drowning my thoughts, flooding my head with pain.

DRIP-DRIP-DRIP-DRIP-DRIP-DRIP...

Faster and louder it fell until there was no longer an audible gap between the drops, only an unremitting, unrelenting, rushing boom.

And then, even louder than the water, came a rapid-fire sequence of searing explosions. Fiery lightning bolts branded themselves into the floor, walls and ceiling. As the final, thunderous blast thrust through the stone, a mighty torrent of watery rage spewed at us from all sides.

The marble's dim red glow revealed no way out through the roiling deluge. The chamber filled rapidly. Water covered our ankles, our thighs, lapped at our knees, boiled onto our laps.

The marble's veins brightened and throbbed, pulsing more rapidly like a quickening heartbeat. Like my heartbeat.

I saw my panic in the glowing blush that lit Fynda's face. Yhoshi's face. Garan's face.

"Onto the table," I shouted. It made no sense. The marble could hold us, but how could it hold back the water?

The water wouldn't be held back. It licked thirstily at the rim as we clambered onto the table, began to surge after us as we huddled together, our eyes darting in search of an escape. I grabbed Fynda's hand. I grabbed Yhoshi's. They in turn reached for Garan's. A spark flashed. The table began to rise with the water. A moment later it began to spin, slowly at first then with increasing speed until, still spinning, it bored through the stone and into the blackened, flooding maze.

Horusha itself erupted in a volcanic spew of racing water and shattering stone. We clung desperately to each other as the spinning disc whipped us through a serpentine labyrinth then hurled itself out into daylight, still supported by a foaming fury. Water and light — that's all we knew, all we could distinguish in the shapes, shadows and colors that melted into each other as we sped forward, Prithi knew where.

Moments later we were hurtling down a waterfall. Frothy streamers cascaded all around us. Down we tumbled, enclosed by a shimmering curtain that seemed never to end.

But it did. We splashed into a pool, raising a cloud of flying spray, every drop of which contained a prism of refracted light. As we spun through this living rainbow, I could almost taste the colors. Zanga green...plum...bela red...mandarin...lemon...p'yan blue...claret...maya... Rather than piquing our hunger, which had been gnawing at the edges of our consciousness, they satisfied it. Then, as our hunger faded so did the rainbow, until once more the view was a mesmerizing, froth-framed blur.

Next I knew a lurching thud had flung the four of us onto a mossy beach. Steam rose from the now-stilled disc, which emitted a single, heaving crack then crumbled into ash, burning a scorched crater in the springy verdure.

The Lost Land of the Tasheen

Twelve

I opened my eyes a slit to a flash of color in dawn's gray half-light. The others still slept. Perhaps I did too. Nothing seemed real anymore.

The bird was back. Parika, I called him. We had first seen him the previous day, moments after the table turned to ash. He seemed to appear from nowhere, a green-and-scarlet streak that swerved toward us, circled three times then disappeared into the cerulean of a cloudless sky.

"Caaa-ooo-eee," he shrieked now. "Pa-REE-ka, caaa-ooo-eee!" I opened my eyes wider. Parika hopped purposefully around the blackened crater, pausing every few skips to claw at the ground, step back, then poke his beak into the sooty residue. His dance — two hops forward, claw-claw-claw, one hop back, poke about, repeat — took him all around the perimeter, then inside. As he spiraled inward, he picked a stone from the debris and dropped it in the center, soon adding a second, third and fourth to the first. Then, carrying two stones in his beak and one in each claw, Parika launched himself into the air in a whispering flutter of flapping wings and once again disappeared.

Without rousing the others I inspected the crater but found nothing, only a fine, gray talc, which I sifted through my fingers. The only evidence of Parika's visit was a stray feather, like none I had ever seen. Bristly fronds branched off a silver pinpoint whose tip drew blood at the touch. Gingerly, I placed the feather in my pocket and joined the others.

We camped where the table had deposited us: on the only accessible stretch of shoreline within view. The carpet that rolled in under us in a soft crescent of emerald sponge halted abruptly at a jagged cliff crowned with thick forest. Except for our tiny cove and a steep trail up from it to the summit, the craggy palisade soared forbiddingly from the water on both banks.

"I'm not going with you," Garan announced as we readied to leave. It was an overcast morning, the day having brightened little since Parika's dawn dance.

"How can you stay?" Yhoshi asked. "There's nothing here."

"I'd go back to Horusha if I could," Garan replied. "I didn't want to leave." He looked back along the river, straining in vain for a glimpse of Horusha's peaks.

"You were afraid to leave," I said softly.

Garan picked up a raw tosti from the slithery pile Fynda had amassed. Nibbling tentatively, he grimaced and raised his arm to throw the fish back. He stopped mid-toss and dropped it into his mouth.

"Some things are more frightening than others," he said. He walked to the water and studied his reflection in the liquid crystal. "Yes, I was afraid to leave," he said to the face that greeted him. "How can I go looking like this? It's not safe for me out there. Better to stay here, where no one will see me. Better to have stayed buried in Horusha's darkness."

He smashed a rock into his watery reflection and waded out to where Fynda, with flicks of her wrist, flipped tosti onto shore. "Will you show me how you do that? That's all there is to eat around here."

"Garan..." she said.

Garan shook his head. "My mind's made up. Will you show me, yes or no?"

I walked to the water's edge. "Have you forgotten already?" I asked.

"Forgotten what?"

"The words you sang with the Lady Gwna. Don't you remember? 'Break the chain and—'"

"The Table's already broken," he said defiantly. "It's dust. Not a single stone remains. It's either too late or it doesn't matter." He knelt and tried to mimic Fynda's motions. "Or it never mattered."

"Four stones remain," I said. There was silence. "Four stones," I repeated. Yhoshi moved toward the crater and began to sift through the ash.

"Where are they?" he asked.

Fynda waded to shore, but Garan stayed and stared into the water. After a minute, he picked up another rock and heaved in into the water with all his force. A thousand distorted rings rippled out into the river. When the water was smooth again, I told Yhoshi and Fynda of Parika's visit and showed them the feather.

"That's— That's—" Fynda took it from me and turned it over incredulously.

"What is it?" I asked.

"Larán's feather. It's just like it!" She stroked the fronds lightly, taking care not to cut herself. "What does it mean?"

"I don't know? That Parika is a friend?"

"No, you keep it," I said as she passed the feather back to me. Fynda smiled and tucked it into her waistband.

Yhoshi looked from feather to sky, a worried look knotting his face. "Nothing against your Larán," he said to Fynda, "but I still don't trust that bird."

Through all this, Garan said nothing. I waded out to him, took his hand and led him back to dry land. "'Break the chain, the future's lost. Break the chain and bear the cost.' There's more to this than the table, Garan. You know that, don't you?"

"Your safety, what about that?" he asked weakly.

"We're in greater danger without you. We're safer if we stay together. The Lady Gwna said so. Please come."

Fynda took his other hand. "Please?"

Yhoshi completed the circle and I thought I detected a trace of that same embracing halo I had seen in the chamber at the heart of Horusha.

"I'm scared," he whispered.

"We're all scared. Bo'Rá K'n is counting on that."

"We're The Four Who See," Yhoshi said, "not the Three Who See and a Fourth who stayed behind. Please, Garan."

From the narrow, rocky lip at the top of the cliff, we saw the river, a fortified, silver highway, curve elegantly into the distance. On either side of us, vaults of loose rubble cut us off from adjacent cliffs. There was only one way: through the forest, which greeted us with an impenetrable weave of greenery.

So we pushed inward, trying to maintain a northerly course. Yhoshi led, using his dagger to hack away at the worst of the brambles. I followed, trying to hold the position of the suns in my mind, for little light penetrated through the thick canopy. Behind me, Fynda and Garan talked quietly.

"Which way?" Yhoshi asked every few steps. At first I knew. Then I guessed. Now I shrugged. The forest had thinned but not enough to see the sky. Whichever way I looked, the view was the same, the choices the same. I reached for a crimson berry from the cluster that burst through the infinite greens, grays and browns of leaves, limbs and earth.

"No!" Yhoshi knocked the berry from my hand. "That's cuna. If you even touch your lips with the hand that touched it..." He mimed a slit throat. "Spit on your fingers and rub them into the ground, like this." He burrowed his hand into the earth where it had touched the berry. Chastened, I followed suit.

"Which way?" he asked again.

"You know more woodlore than I do," I pouted. "You decide." It was well he did. By skill or luck he found a stream that led us to an overgrown footpath.

"I don't know if this goes north," he said, "but it should carry us out of the forest. What do you say?"

I shrugged again. "It's a path."

The frenzied drone of bloodthirsty insects buzzed around my head. I smacked and swatted, to no effect. Pinpricks of blood began to spot my flesh wherever it was exposed. The only other sound was the crackle of dry timber underfoot and the occasional scolding screech of a shrike offended by our presence. It was hard to keep to the path. When upturned trees, their exposed roots like ossified tentacles, didn't block the way, a swampy morass did. At other times the path petered out, forcing us to retrace our steps. Most of the time, it seemed we were creating a path, not following one.

We stopped to rest. We stopped to eat. We stopped to sleep. We continued. The forest continued.

The path did not.

I lost count of the days. Mercifully, it never rained, but few other mercies marked this endless, aimless trek through a forest that grew increasingly venal with each day not free of it. Roots maliciously tripped my listless feet. Jagged, calcified fingers poked, pricked and cut. Yhoshi, stalwart that he was, forged ahead without complaint. Garan and Fynda giggled and chattered, thriving on the adventure. The teacher in Garan began to reemerge as he shared his knowledge of the natural world with his eager acolyte.

My reality differed from theirs. With every jab, stumble and scrape, my discomfort deepened into a despair that blinded me to any potential beauty. I longed for the simple comforts of Pre Tena'aa. But there was no going back, any more than I could return to the concealed colony of my childhood — now laid bare like the rotting trees around me, their exposed bellies crawling with slimy g'goma bugs. There was no going back and I could no longer bear to go forward. For all I knew we walked in endless circles and would continue until the end of time. Or until the g'gomas got us too. Had I been alone, I would have planted myself on the nearest log. For good. Instead, a brave front pasted on my face, I followed Yhoshi.

We stopped to lunch on weeds and berries. We stopped by a brook to drink and wash. We camped by a fire, roasting the pair of plump flyks Yhoshi had captured in a crude trap. The others chatted, leaving me to my moody silence. We slept. I saw Na'an at the edge of disturbing dreams, but when I awoke I remembered nothing. We breakfasted on more weeds and berries and set off again, as the dance repeated itself that day and the next, and the day after that. It was like Parika's dance, only less purposeful.

Parika... Fynda thought she heard the bird's shrill cry as she woke before us each dawn. I tried to take comfort in that, but couldn't.

I walked in a trance, barely aware where my legs carried me. All I knew was that I had to keep going. I repeated it like a mantra. "I have to keep going. I have to keep going. I have to —"

Something jabbed my arm. Knifelike, a dead branch had slashed through my sleeve. I stopped and swore, lunging for the offending tree. I beat my arms against its brittle trunk, and when it collapsed, I collapsed with it.

"I can't go on," I cried. My head ached. My chest heaved. My nose ran. But tears wouldn't come. I sobbed, dry, wracking sighs. Yhoshi handed me his jacket. I pushed him away.

"It's not the tunic," I cried. "I don't care about the tunic." I clawed at the gash, making it worse. "It's everything else. Us. Here. Lost. Everything." I wiped my nose. "Everything. Zakk. Eulisha. Gwill'm. *Everything*. Everyone's dead. Everything's lost. We're lost. It's hopeless. Garan was right. We have to hide." I wrapped my arms around my knees and dropped my head into my lap, rocking back and forth, back and forth.

"I don't want to be Elderbard," I whimpered. Elderbard? Where did that come from?

Someone touched a hand to my shoulder. I shook it off and buried my head deeper.

"What do you mean?" Yhoshi asked. "I thought you said Zakk—"

I shook my head and looked up. "I don't understand how it can be so. I don't want it to be so. I don't—" I shook my head again and traced the lines of my left palm with my little finger.

"Leave him be," Garan said. "It will pass."

"I don't want it to pass," I longed to cry, but said nothing, staring at my hand.

"Let's stop here for the night," Yhoshi said. "We can all use the rest."

Yhoshi, Fynda and Garan set up camp around me, gathering wood for a fire and food for a meager meal. I barely moved, eating and saying nothing and ignoring the worried glances they cast in my direction. Finally, Garan knelt next to me and touched his hand to my forehead. He stroked my face until I opened my eyes.

"So you are to be Elderbard. What an honor! For me too. After all, I was your tutor." I said nothing. "It's good news, isn't it?"

I shifted uneasily and studied my palm again, seeking a different answer in its lines. Instead, I saw Eulisha's face.

We sit together in a light-filled place removed from time. "I don't want it. I won't have it," I shout at her. I claw my right hand along my left palm, vainly trying to alter the lines of destiny. Then I clench my fist, digging my fingernails into my palm, and press it against my lips. Slowly, rhythmically, I shake my head back and forth, left to right, right to left. Eulisha stills my head and pulls me toward her. Only then, my head buried in her breast, do the tears come. She strokes my hair as I heave in her arms.

"You don't even know why you cry, do you, son of my son?"

I swallow back a sob, hiccup and pull back my face to look into hers. "I can't be Elderbard," I say. "What about the Law of Balance?"

"Nothing is ever written in stone, child. There is always a choice." She fades into the light, leaving only a smile that becomes a line running along my palm, the line of destiny.

"I don't want to be Elderbard," I whispered.

"Why not?" Fynda asked. "To tell stories, to dream dreams, to be the wisest one in the kingdom. Who wouldn't want that?"

I clenched my fist to hide my palm. "Would you?" I snapped.

"I-I-I don't know enough," Fynda stuttered, her confidence drained. "I don't dream. I wouldn't know what to say, what to do, how to be. No," she shuddered, "it's not a life for me. What if I saw wrong? What if I spoke wrong?"

"What if I did?" I countered.

"No, Toshar. It's different for you. You're a bard. You come from a line of bards, of Elderbards."

"I don't want to be different."

Garan took my fist in his hands and massaged it. "You forced me to remember my words. Now I ask you to remember yours," he said gently. "We're all afraid at times. That's what you said. All of us. Even Yhoshi." Yhoshi fixed his attention on a millipede's single-minded march from his left foot to his right. "Our fear," Garan continued, "that's what Bo'Rá K'n counts on. That's what the Lady Gwna said. That's why I'm here."

I shook my head and turned away.

"Look at me. Look what fear has done to me."

"No, Garan. Torture deformed you. The fruits of your courage deformed you. If you'd given in to your fear, if you'd agreed to betray us, there wouldn't have been any torture."

"Then what courage created, fear has fixed for all time. Look into my eyes, Toshar. Look into the one part of this miserable body that hasn't changed since you last saw me all those seasons ago in Kemet." I raised my eyes to meet the gentle, luminous blue of the Kemet sky. "I've known you longer than nearly anyone," Garan went on, "and I know when you're not telling all there is to tell. Answer Fynda's question, Toshar. Answer it for all of us. Answer it for Q'ntana. Answer it for you."

The Kemet sky in his eyes grayed then blackened as thunderclouds rumbled across my line of vision. For an instant, I saw Zakk, felt his lashing laugh slice through me. "I want to hide," I breathed. "I don't want to be seen." And then in a smaller voice still: "It's not safe." The black clouds split open and gashes of salt rain scored my face. I sat still as stone until the storm passed. The muscles in my face loosened, my posture relaxed. But I didn't move. I didn't smile. I didn't speak. I rose in a single, fluid movement and turned my face to the fire. Its warmth baked the salt into my skin, into my clothes.

"I know what I know," I murmured, "but it's not enough." I opened my mouth wide and felt the salt crack on my face. "It's not enough," I shouted into the sky, and then again: "It's not enough!"

Thirteen

Slender fingers, three on each webbed hand, pull back an indigo hood to reveal long, silver tresses flecked with gold framing an ageless face. "Why do you ignore me?"

"Na'an..."

"I have tried to come to you every night, but every night you push me away." She glides toward me, her feet invisible under a gown that shimmers with starlight. I try to move forward to greet her, but my feet pull me back. I want to reach out my hand to meet hers, but my arm won't obey. "What are you so afraid of, Toshar, that you run from me so?"

I am afraid. She's right. This new awareness frees me from the prison of my body. I leave it behind and float toward her.

"You have left your fear for the moment," she says, "but you will have to rejoin it presently unless..." Her eyes — one silver, the other blue — capture me in a gaze of alarming intensity.

"Unless what?" I whisper.

"Unless you are ready to leave your body behind for all time. You are young, but age need not be a factor. It would be a pity, but the choice is yours. The choice is always yours."

I don't have to wake up. I don't have to continue. Relief floods through me, lightens me further, as the dark blotch that is my body recedes into the mist.

"Would I stay with you?" I ask eagerly. "Would I join the Tikkan? Would I become a dreamwalker?"

"That would be for others to decide...once you decide. There are many possibilities, but there is no ultimate escape. There never is." Her eyes release me into the space between two worlds. I imagine a free-floating bliss far removed from endless forest treks and futile MoonQuests. Eulisha's face glimmers in front of mine. I try to become one with it, but it collapses into wisps of light that reform into the sleeping faces of Yhoshi, Fynda and Garan.

"What will happen to them?" I ask.

"That will no longer be your concern."

"What will happen to Q'ntana, to M'nor?"

Silence greets this question. Other faces take shape in the light. Bodies and faces with blank eye sockets, black mouths. They cluster on the left. On the right a dark, faceless figure emerges — a giant shadow in the light. With a single, sweeping motion he spreads open his cloak. There's nothing there. One by one the people file into the void and disappear.

The last to pass through is a young woman. Unlike the others, she has eyes and a mouth. Her eyes are open and her mouth is set. She lays down her quill and a piece of parchment. I catch a glimpse of script but make out only one word: Toshar. She turns toward me for an instant then strides into the cloak's black nothingness and is gone.

The light, too, is gone. Giant and cape have swallowed it all. Only Na'an is left, and she is smaller, dimmer, her voice fainter.

"The choice is yours," she repeats.

I feel the grip of returning panic as I move closer to my body.

"Is there no one else, no other way?" No response. I hover over my body, pushing toward it and pulling away from it with each rushed breath. "All right," I exhale, and I no longer float. A lead weight presses on my chest, but the cloaked figure is gone. The light has returned. Na'an again stands before me in full radiance.

"What do you fear, Toshar?"

The answer comes without thought. "Everything," I say. "I fear the uncertainty of the path to M'nor. I fear its perils. I fear failure and the darkness it will bring. I fear success and the weight of the Elderbard's mantle. I fear Fvorag and his men. I fear Bo'Rá K'n." I pause and swallow hard. "I fear myself."

"It is not cowardly to fear," Na'an says gently. "You live in fearful times. But fear need not exclude courage. Fear need not exclude action. When fear stops you, Bo'Rá K'n has won."

I shake my head in defeat. "He's already won. Look at me."

Reassuring love fills Na'an's gaze. "I do," she says. "I see a young man who will grow into a wise, courageous and compassionate Elderbard. You already direct wisdom, courage and compassion toward others. Whatever you have for them, you have also for yourself."

"Will I always feel this fear clutching at my throat?"

"Just as fear has not stopped you from reaching this point in your journey, it will not stop you from continuing, unless you submit to it. Don't submit to it, Toshar. When you do, Bo'Rá K'n grows stronger." She looks away, into the distance. "Don't give him any more victories in this silenced land."

"What do I do now, Na'an? Help me."

"I cannot. You are all the help you need. You are the solution. You are the key. Either to Bo'Rá K'n's victory or M'nor's. It's your choice." She offers me a key. A gold key. The gold key. As I take it and feel its warm solidity in my palm, Na'an evaporates into the dream and is gone.

"Caaa-ooo-eee!" Parika's call sliced through the morning air and I glimpsed a flash of scarlet through the woody latticework. Fynda smiled triumphantly.

"I told you I didn't imagine it," she snapped at Yhoshi. Then, her features softened and she reached for his hand. "I'm sorry." She caught my mystified glance and blushed.

"We talked last night," she said, "after you fell asleep, and we decided, Yhoshi and I decided..." She looked at Yhoshi until he met her glance. "We agreed to try to get along. Didn't we?" Yhoshi mumbled an incoherent assent and looked away.

Fynda bit her lip and portioned out the morning's gugu berries and sascha weed — the same meal we had breakfasted and supped on for...for how many days? I let the sugary fruit melt on my tongue. "Garan also made a decision," she said. "Tell him, Garan."

Garan gazed deep into the forest before speaking. "I wasn't going to come with you," he said. "I was going to stay behind when we reached the end of the forest. For all I said before last night, I'm still afraid to go on."

"Then we can be afraid together," I said. "It's only when fear stops us, Na'an says, that Bo'Rá K'n wins." I told them about the dream.

"You are the key," Yhoshi repeated when I had finished.

"No," I said. "We are the key." I smiled. "Even if at least one of us is always bound to doubt it."

By midday the trees had begun to thin and by late afternoon they had given way to a wide greensward bisected by a broad, stately river. A fiery column of light bridged the shores as Aygra and B'na slipped to the horizon. On the opposite bank, smoke spiraled from a clutch of chimneys huddled around a brown ribbon of riverside road.

"A village," Yhoshi said.

Garan inhaled sharply and shrank back.

"Do we know where we are?" Fynda asked.

"I don't even know if we're still in Q'ntana," I said. "But it's best to assume it's not safe and to stay on this side of the river." Garan expelled a relieved breath. "The river flows north and we can just as easily follow it here as on the other side."

Fynda craned her neck for a better view. "You're right, of course. Still, I wonder what the people are like, what their village is like. I've seen no faces but yours since I left home."

Standing next to her, I tried to see through the dazzling suns-set and into the village. "I wish we could go across for a look," I said, "but it's too dangerous — for all of us."

Yhoshi nodded. "Where there's a road there may well be King's Men." Fynda said nothing, but her eyes sparked a familiar willfulness.

Fearing the villagers would notice us, we lay in the grass until after dark, then crept down to the water's edge. The river was too wide for voices to reach us, but we took comfort from the patchwork of flickering yellow squares, watching them in silence until the last one went black.

"Wake up, Toshar." Cold water dribbled onto my face as Fynda's breath warmed my ear. "Wake up."

Yhoshi and Garan snored softly. Pale fingers of light poked into the night sky. "What is it? Is it raining? Why are you soaking?" I jerked up. "Fynda, you didn't!"

I caught a glint of white as she flashed a quick grin. "You knew I'd swim across, didn't you?" I nodded. "I'm sorry. I had to. No, I'm not sorry. Nor will you be." She paused and looked across at the village, now glowing with the first reflected light of dawn. "What do you see?" she asked.

"Nothing." The village still slept.

"Wouldn't you expect chimney smoke? Wouldn't you expect to see *something* by now?"

"I suppose."

"Do you see anything? Anybody?"

I shook my head impatiently. "What are you trying to tell me?"

"There's no one there," she whispered.

"They're still sleeping," I countered.

"No, there's no one there. I swam across in the dark, expecting to find most villagers in their beds. Don't worry, I was careful, not that it mattered. I knew some farmers might be up and some women might have begun the day's baking." She paused. "Some farmers had been up. I saw cows standing over pails half-filled with steaming milk. Some women had begun their day's baking. I saw handprints in half-kneaded dough. I saw flies buzzing around half-eaten food. I saw tools dropped in mid-task." She looked back across the river. "But I saw no one. No people and no lamps. No lamps and no light. I looked in every room, in every bed, in every shop, in every shed. There was no one."

It was as Fynda said. There was no one, only a whimpering k'nrah that bolted when it saw us.

We stood in the last room of the last silence-shrouded house. On a simple wooden table lay a newly sharpened quill, surrounded by curled shavings and a small knife. An uncapped inkpot lay between it and a single sheet of parchment, which bore the heading "The Lost Land of the Tasheen" in a neat, feminine script. A ring of black burned into the table where an oil lamp must have stood. Defeat hung heavy in the air.

"It's as though a sorcerer cast a spell and everyone vanished," Yhoshi whispered. We all spoke in whispers.

A familiar scene flashed through my head: a long line of people filing impassively into the black void of a giant's cloak. I remembered the young woman of my dream and saw my name hovering over the parchment. This was her house, her writing. Her message. I shuddered. Yhoshi opened a traveling pack that had been flung across the chair and pulled out a tin mug, an ivory comb, a loaf of bread and a hunk of cheese. He looked at me questioningly.

"No," I said. "Leave everything as you found it. We've seen what we came to see."

Outside, leaden air pressed into us, stooping our shoulders. Clouds obscured the suns. The k'nrah watched us warily from a distance, silver-black ears glued to the sides of a drooping head. We tried calling her, but she backed off, whining, only to edge toward us again once we turned away. Suddenly, her ears pricked, her striped tail stiffened and she let out a sharp bark.

"Look!" Fynda pointed to the sky.

Parika glided toward us in a slow circle, his wings outstretched and still. The k'nrah barked again and Parika swooped into a steep dive, so low that he raised dust from the road. He soared up again, shrinking to a speck against the overcast sky. He dove again. "Pa-REE-ka," he shrilled and spiraled back up into the clouds. The third time down, he aborted his dive, whirled around each of us in turn, then lit on my left shoulder. He sat there for a moment, picking bits of fluff from his coat with a hooked, golden beak. When he'd finished, he glanced around, cocked his head and in a lighting, fluttering flap of green and red took off, north along the river.

"He dropped another feather," Fynda said. She knelt to pick it up. It was as sharp and bristly as the first. The k'nrah barked once more at the vanishing bird, then her head fell, her tail drooped and she began to whine. She crawled behind us, belly dragging along the ground, as we walked out of the village and onto the river road.

I don't know why we kept to the road instead of returning to the opposite shore. We never discussed it. We just pressed forward, eager to leave behind the ghosts of the abandoned village. One ghost, though, continued to haunt me. Waking or dreaming, I saw her again and again, that instant just before the darkness drew her in. What had happened?

Na'an would know, but Na'an did not return.

"I'm cold," Fynda said through chattering teeth. The air wasn't cold but we'd all felt chilled since passing through the abandoned village. I pulled her toward me as my eyes darted around for a sign of Yhoshi and Garan.

Fynda snuggled next to me. "What is this place? Where are we?"

"I wish I knew. Maybe Yhoshi and Garan will know when they come back."

"If they come back."

"Of course they'll come back. Why wouldn't they?"

Fynda said nothing but I knew she feared they had met the villagers' fate, whatever it was. I hadn't tried to stop Yhoshi and Garan when they set off to explore after our midday meal. Now, with the suns on the final leg of their downward journey, I wished I had. I wanted to go after them but didn't know where to begin looking. So we waited.

"Tell me a story," Fynda said. "It will move the time along."

"I don't know one to tell."

"You always know one."

"I do, don't I…" I closed my eyes, but nothing came. I thought back to Eulisha, to the stories she had told me, to the stories I had told her. But none would come. "I need a new story," I said, half to myself.

"What's that?"

"I said I need a new story. The old one isn't good anymore."

"What do you mean? What old one?"

"I don't know, Fynda. I don't know what I mean." Fatigue washed over me, fatigue and impotence. "I don't know why I said that and I don't know what it means. I don't know what to do." I shivered and my heartbeat sped up until it raced like a frenzied flot.

"What is it?" Fynda asked. "What's wrong?"

"I don't know. Everything is changing. Or maybe it already has." I shook my head. "I don't know. I don't know the story anymore."

"Did you ever?" a voice within, Eulisha's, asks.

"I thought I did," I sigh.

"Let it go, son of my son. Let it go so the true story can emerge. Let go and live your story as it yearns to be lived. Let it take your hand and lead you along new roads, across new rivers, over new mountains…into new realms. Let go and M'nor will find you. Tell the story, Toshar. Speak it as it demands to be spoken. Speak

the truth so you can live it, so you can be it. Speak it as the bard you are, as the Elderbard you are becoming."

"I'm frightened," I whisper.

"You are in awe. That is good. Your awe will keep you in touch with the earth as you soar toward the stars, as you fly like an eagle and reach out for M'nor."

"Toshar?" Fynda shook my shoulders lightly. "Toshar?"

"I'm sorry, Fynda. I was elsewhere...with Eulisha."

"Did you ask her where we are? Did you ask her where Yhoshi and Garan are?"

"Those weren't the questions to ask."

"Why not?" Fynda pouted. "What could be more important than that?"

I said nothing. Filaments of fire shot through the sky as Aygra and B'na bid their final farewell to another day. Only when darkness had enveloped the last of the light did I reply. "You look out into the dark, Fynda, and see everything as if it were day — trees, leaves, waters rushing down from the mountains, eagles circling high. I look out and see nothing...only a story, if I'm lucky."

"Are you lucky tonight?"

"I think so....maybe." I watched the stars blink alive in the sable sky. "They tell stories," I said. "Every night they tell stories, stories of gods and goddesses, stories from deep in Q'ntana's past, Prithi's stories... Do you know the constellations?"

Fynda gazed heavenward, tracing lines from star to star with her eyes. "Only in my imaginings," she whispered.

"That's the best place for them."

"Will you tell me about the constellations? Will you tell me one of Prithi's stories?"

I didn't answer right away. I too looked from star to star, from constellation to constellation. "No," I said firmly. "I will tell you one of mine." I pointed to the brightest star. "That's Aris, the north star. It lies at the center of the constellation known in these times as The Hunter. It's the tip of the hunter's spear."

Fynda studied the stars surrounding Aris. "That's no hunter," she said. "That's an eagle, an eagle with a single eye in the center of its forehead."

I touched Fynda's face, outlining her eyes with my finger. "Your eyes see more than you think they do. In ancient times it was called Thyra, the eagle, and Aris was his golden eye, his sun-eye." I paused, my eye focused on the eagle's, waiting for him to speak.

"The story I will tell is one you already know, just as you knew Thyra, just as you know all stories, even those not yet written. You do. I do. We all do. For we are all bards in Q'ntana. We are all bards when we let the stories fly free as the eagle."

I crossed my legs and rested my hands on my knees, palms up. "Once, there was a lotus that lived in the heart of a little boy. The boy was called Raffi. When I say 'lived,' I exaggerate, for the lotus was, but it did not live. No one suspected its presence, not even Raffi, for a wall had grown up around it, a wall of thistles and thorns, of burrs, briars and brambles so thick that not even a whisper of breath could penetrate. Yes, it was pale, the faintest blush of pink. And it paled more with each passing year bereft of air, light and warmth. It cried out, the lotus did. It cried and cried. But each day's cry was weaker than the last until one day, with a whimper of impotence, it fell silent. It was, but it lived not.

"Raffi, too, was but lived not. He grew, as boys do. He grew even as a tree continues to grow for a time when its insides dry out and hollow. He grew into adolescence and young manhood, but like the tree that dies from the inside out, he at last fell visibly ill. His parents fussed and worried over him. They called in the finest physicians, who also fussed and worried over him but could not discover the source of his illness. So the physicians left. They called in sorcerers and wizards, but they could not discover the source of his illness. And they left. Nor could the combined wisdom of all the wise men and crone elders of his village aid him. Potions, tonics, salves, prayers, incantations — none had any effect, no more than did leeches, spells, midnight animal sacrifices or ritual immersions. Through them all, Raffi lay in the same sightless coma. No one could reach him. Nothing could touch him. Suns rose and fell, rose and fell. Time passed. His affliction did not.

"Then one morning, the suns rose to reveal an old man garbed in feathers perched at the entrance to Raffi's village. So old was he that he appeared ageless to the wary villagers, who became warier still when he refused all offers of hospitality with a firm shake of his head. He spoke no words but proceeded directly to Raffi's hut, to the bed where he lay lost in his ailment.

"With a single sweep of his feather-clad sleeve, he swept Raffi into his arms and strode out into the sun. Ignoring the villagers' shouted protests, impervious to their threats, he ascended the sacred rock that stood at the village center. With flaming eyes as golden as the suns, he stared down any who approached too near. Then from his beak-like lips burst a trumpet cry that exploded into the morning air and shattered the tumult into a million pieces. The villagers' mouths still opened and closed, but no sounds issued forth.

"As they watched in silent agitation, he touched the tip of his beak to Raffi's heart, then to his throat and lips and finally to the center of his forehead, just above his eyebrows. He touched it gently at first, then pecked at it, stabbing deeper and deeper until he drew blood. The blood spread, forming a perfect circle of scarlet just as Aygra and B'na merged overhead. They cast a single beam onto the rock, onto Raffi, onto that perfect circle of blood, turning it golden yellow.

"When the suns moved apart to once again travel their separate ways, the yellow circle between his eyes glowed more brilliantly than any sun and a brilliant lotus, redder than blood, grew from his heart. He sounded but one sound, but in that single sound lived all the stories he had been unable to speak before he fell ill, all the stories locked away in his coma and all the stories he would yet tell in all the lives he would yet live. And as he sounded it, the old man dissolved, the suns vanished, the heavens darkened and he leapt into the sky on feathers that sprouted from his body. He leapt into the sky with the yellow glow still radiating from his forehead. He leapt into the sky and became one with the stars, the brightest of which shines down to us still as Aris, the golden-eye."

My gaze returned from the sky. "I didn't know that story until I spoke it."

Fynda smiled. "You didn't know you knew it."

"My own words come back at me, again!" I laughed.

"Can I ask a question?"

"Of course."

"What was the sound he sounded?"

I turned my face to the sky, opened my mouth and called into the night. "Aiiiiiieeee." The night shivered with the thrill of the sound. "For many years the villagers would look up into the night sky at Raffi and argue whether the sound had been 'I' or 'EYE.'"

"Which was it?"

"Neither and both. It was what it was: the cry of the eagle."

Fynda watched Aris beam down on them, a beacon of reassurance in the empty darkness. She stood and stepped away, no longer chilled.

"They're safe," she said. "Garan and Yhoshi are safe. I know it."

"So are we," I said, looking up. "So are we."

Fourteen

What do you say, Nya?" I asked the k'nrah. She nuzzled closer. I stroked her head and she began to suck on my arm feverishly. She slurped noisily and purred a deep throaty growl. "Hush," I whispered, "you'll wake the others." She stopped, kneaded my skin with her front paws, then resumed, no more quietly than before.

For two days Nya had followed at a distance, devouring whatever scraps we left her, but backing off when any of us tried to approach. "Nya," I called out on the third morning, and she ran to me, leaping into my arms with a joyous grunt. I don't know where the name came from. It just did. That moment transformed her. Fear drained away and she romped around, behind and ahead of us — tail flicking, nose twitching, ears tuned to every sound.

"What do you say, Nya?" She stopped purring and stared up at me. Her eyes shone, red as the embers of the dying fire. There were answers in those eyes, but I couldn't read them.

Even before we saw the first house of the next village, Nya's tail flopped to the ground and she began to tremble. She dragged her belly through the dirt, whimpering, then stopped. She wouldn't budge. When I picked her up and continued walking, she struggled to jump from my arms. I held her tight, cooing reassuringly. As we approached that first house, she stiffened and buried her claws into my flesh, clinging tenaciously until the last of the village was well out of sight. Only then would she let me set her down.

We passed through four more villages in the days that followed, each as empty as the last. Doors swung with eerie, forlorn creaks and tattered, dirt-streaked curtains flapped from shattered windows. After the fifth village, the road widened then split. One fork continued long the river, the other climbed into hills that rose in the west. Nya sniffed each fork in turn then stood at the junction of the two and barked.

"What is it, girl?" I knelt and she snapped at my face then tore around me, still barking. I tried to pick her up, but she wriggled away and sped around me in the opposite direction.

"She's trying to tell you something," Fynda said.

Yhoshi peered ahead. "It's probably just another village," he said.

I tentatively stepped onto the river road. Barking, Nya wove in and out of my legs.

"She must want us to take the other road," Fynda said. "Is that what you want, Nya?" Together, we stepped onto the hill road. Nya's barking grew even more frenzied.

"What are you trying to tell us?" I asked. She replied in a staccato of high-pitched yaps. Whenever we tried to move forward, she tangled herself in our legs. Suddenly, she stopped and fell silent. Ears and tail erect, she angled her pointy snout into the air. Her nose twitched feverishly. Then, without looking back, she raced down the short grassy bank and leapt into the river, paddling furiously toward the opposite shore.

"Nya," I called. "Come back." But the k'nrah paddled faster, her head skimming noiselessly across the water.

A distant rumble filtered through the air. It rolled nearer, with the inevitability of approaching thunder. I looked up. The sky was clear.

"Horses," Yhoshi said.

Garan paled. "King's Men," he whispered.

The hoofbeats grew louder. The clattering roar surrounded us. Across the river, Nya slid from the water, fired a muffled bark at us and scurried out of sight. As one, we dove in after her.

"There they are! After them!"

I didn't dare look anywhere but forward.

"Toshar!" Garan's voice gurgled weakly at me. I let Yhoshi and Fynda surge ahead and slowed so Garan could catch up.

"Don't — stop — for — me," he gasped. "I'm — not — going — to — make — it." He breathed heavily, gulping as much water as air.

"I'm coming back for you," I yelled over the approaching din. Slipping one arm under his neck and shoulders, I paddled forward. But Garan's fear-stiffened weight pulled me back and the hot breath of the lead horses burned into my neck.

Garan struggled to free himself. "Let me go," he cried. "Save yourself." It was too late for that. Even without Garan, I would never outswim the horses.

"Take a deep breath and hold it," I said. Tightening my grip on Garan, I dove — down and back under the horses. Above us, the water churned. Below, tall, mottled plants swayed sinuously as schools of rainbow ovals parted to let us pass. We glided back until the water above was as still as the water below, then, praying that no King's Men remained on shore behind us, charged to the surface. Heaving and rasping, Garan swallowed great gulps of air. I scanned the river. Ahead, a dozen soldiers urged their mounts forward in pursuit of Yhoshi and Fynda. As long as none glanced back, we were safe.

"Are you okay?" I asked when I could spare breath to speak. "Can I let you go?" He nodded. Freed of the extra weight, my aching arms and shoulders relaxed into a gentle tread. Garan tried to ape my movements, but his fear-tautened body began to sink. Panicked, he flapped his arms, thrashing noisily. His head dropped beneath the surface and bobbed back up again.

"Relax," I said. "Hold on to me." He lunged at me. "Gently," I added, wondering where I would find the strength to keep us both afloat. I started to swim back to shore, but the current tugged at me, pulling me from both soldiers and shore and down the center of the channel...and then just down, down, back among the dancing weeds, the rainbow fish, the smooth, contoured dunes. Pinpricks of light waltzed around my head. I longed to open my mouth and breathe them in.

"Let go," an inner voice crooned. "It's finally over."

A conflicting impulse thrust my arm up, as if pulling me back to the surface. I let it pull me, pull us. Us? There was no us. Where was Garan? My arm went limp. My eyes darted left and right. I sank back down.

"Garan!" I called. A rush of water surged into my mouth. I clamped it shut and shot back up, breaking through the water line in a fit of choking. Again, I began to sink, then stopped. Something supported me. Something supported Garan. He sat on the water next to me. He had already coughed his lungs clear.

"Look," he said, pointing to the furry head and tail that swam circles around us. Nya paddled over and licked my face reassuringly. Only then did I peer into the water. Holding us aloft were two river ottafins, flanked by inverted pyramids of oval fish. Garan grinned.

Ahead, the first soldiers rode onto shore. Any minute, they would turn and spot us. Nya's ruby eyes gazed at me with all the intelligence I knew was there, then she pointed her snout downward and disappeared into the water. We hung on to the ottafins as, guided by the fish and Nya, they dove beneath the surface and toward the far shore. Within seconds, the river bottom sped up to meet us. Then, just as suddenly, it plummeted again. Nya pointed her snout and dove deeper into an underwater cove. Stunted bristles crowned with purple coneflowers poked out of cracks in the stone walls and floor. A pillar of light pierced the water ahead. Following Nya and the light, we burst out of a bubbling spring and into an ancient grove. The ottafins shook us off, silently slid back into the water and were gone.

"In here," Fynda hissed.

I saw no one, only caiio trees layered in concentric rings around the pool. Thick, green fronds draped from a tangle of limbs, hiding massive trunks furrowed with venerable ridges.

"They can't have gone far," I heard from beyond the grove. A horse snorted and stamped impatiently.

"Spread out and find them," another, familiar voice ordered.

I felt a tap on my shoulder and spun around, ready to strike.

"Whoa," Yhoshi whispered. "It's only me."

Nya leapt into his arms, licked his nose and jumped down again. Following her, we threaded through delicate tracery to a shaded caiio trunk. Nya bolted halfway up and disappeared. Yhoshi, climbing behind her, disappeared too.

"Where are you?" I called.

A hand reached out from a camouflaged hollow and drew me in, just as soldiers crashed into the grove.

"They didn't just vanish."

"Maybe they drowned."

"Then we'd better find bodies to prove it. Holgg won't settle for less."

"Captain Holgg, Kor."

"Yes, sir.

"I *won't* settle for less. I want bodies. Or I'll have yours in their place. Understood?"

"No, sir. I-I mean yes, sir."

A splash, then the voices faded. Nya scampered from my arms and out of the hollow. Her claws skittered against the bark as she shimmied down the trunk.

We huddled in silence, waiting for Nya, afraid to move, afraid the soldiers would return.

When they did, we didn't dare breathe.

"Where are they?" Holgg barked. "Did you find them?"

"N-no, sir, captain."

"You know what that means, don't you?"

"B-but—"

One terrified scream then a second sliced through the air. Then the splash of one body and a second falling into the river. Hoofbeats drummed into the distance.

For the longest time, none of us spoke, or could.

Finally, an excited chirping broke the uneasy stillness.

"Nya," I whispered. "Is it safe now?"

She barked softly, found my arm and settled into another round of sucking. She purred quietly.

"Thank Prithi for that k'nrah," Yhoshi said, burying his hand in her thick, silver-black coat.

"She swam out to meet us —" Fynda began.

Yhoshi interrupted. "And just in time. Another few minutes and we would have been lance bait." Fynda glared at him. He touched Fynda's hand and smiled apologetically.

She smiled back but pulled her hand away. "Nya led us to the river bottom, through a spring and into this hideaway, just as she did with you."

"Not quite," Garan said. "We had ovals and ottafins to help us." He touched his hand to his heart. "I will starve before I eat fish or ottafin again... or a k'nrah. I swear it."

Nya grunted and we all laughed.

"How do they keep finding us?" Fynda asked. "We don't even know where we are. How do they?"

"Zakk," I replied. "It must be."

"He can't track you unless you carry something of his," said Garan.

"What?" I asked. "My clothes are all new, though you wouldn't know it." I fingered the sopping rags that barely covered me, all that remained of the finery I had acquired on Tashek's back. I drew O'ric's dagger. Even in the dim light of our den, its jeweled hilt and silver blade sparkled. "I have nothing else."

"There must be something," Garan said.

Yhoshi looked up. "The pendant," he said. "Do you still have the pendant?"

My hand flew to my throat. The ivory moon disc still hung under my shirt. I pulled it out. "What does Zakk have to do with this?" I asked. Its warmth surged through my hand, along my arm and through my body as faces flashed before me. Eulisha. My mother. My father. Each had worn it. Now I did.

"What does Zakk have to do with this?" I repeated.

"It's probably nothing," Yhoshi said.

"What?"

"He touched it. Don't you remember?" He turned to Garan. "Would that be enough?"

"Touched it?" I asked. "When?" Then I remembered: the dining chamber in Pre Tena'aa. I let the pendant drop. Suddenly it felt dirty.

"That might have been enough," Garan said, "but it wouldn't be very powerful."

Powerful enough. King's Men had come upon us twice — twice too often. I slipped the pendant from my neck and placed it next to me.

We slept as we sat, Nya curled in my arms. When morning came I returned alone to the river. Dew glinted from the bloodstained grasses. Overhead, swallows swooped and swung around the rising suns. I opened my fist. The moon disc rested in the center of my palm, its thong looped around my hand. For an instant I saw my father gaze back at me from the water. Then a gentle gust whistled over the river, skimming ripples across the image and through to the other side. I hesitated. This keepsake was all that remained of my parents, my family.

"Not all," Eulisha's voice whispered. "Everything you need is still in your heart."

I spun the thong over my head and let it go. The pendant flew halfway across the river, then dropped into the water with a quiet splash, sending band after band of wavelets back to me. When the last one smoothed, I left. In the sky, another bird joined the swallows. "Caaa-ooo-eee," it shrilled. "Pa-REE-ka, caaa-ooo-*eee*!"

Healing Waters of Alanda

Fifteen

For three nights we followed the river's northerly course with the stars and Fynda as our eyes. We took what daytime shelter we could in copses and gullies, one of us always alert to the waves of shouts and hoofbeats that rolled toward us across the plain. Halfway through the fourth night, the river looped sharply eastward, but we continued north with Aris as our guide. Firm meadowland soon softened into damp, spongy soil dense with tall, wet grasses that soaked our shoes and leggings. After a while a heavy fog veiled both constellations and Fynda's vision. We sloshed on blindly through the dank, stale night and over sodden ground that could no longer absorb the water that flooded over it. When it rose past our ankles to lap at our shins, we stopped and waited for light.

Dawn brought discouraging news. We stood in a fetid marsh. Gray, calcified limbs jutted from the brackish swamp, stabbing angry, accusing fingers at the lifeless sky. In every direction, only rare clumps of turf broke through stagnant waters that assaulted our nostrils with death and decay.

Wrinkling my nose, I stepped forward charting a northward course between the two whispers of rising suns-light. Nya barked, a single sharp *brahwk* that startled the deadened air.

"What is it, Nya?" Fynda asked.

The k'nrah pointed her snout to the sky, sniffed, then began to swim back toward the river.

"This way, Nya," I called. Reluctantly, she turned to follow me only to repeat the performance a few minutes later.

"No," I said firmly. "The true way lies north."

"Maybe she knows a dry route," Garan said.

"This is the way," I repeated. "I know it. M'nor sleeps in the north and north is the way we must go. I know there's a land bridge ahead. I'm sure of it."

There wasn't. We dredged waist-deep through rank waters, with no place even to sit, pushing through tangles of slippery weed. The smell of rot nauseated me. The damp chilled me. But the leeches were worse. Fleshy hunks of black slime, they dug into any exposed flesh with viselike grip. We tugged them off ourselves and each other, but the dotted lines of blood they left in their wake attracted two for every one removed. Finally, we let them be, trying to ignore their jabbing pinpricks on our skin.

Morning dredged into afternoon, afternoon into evening.

"Where will we sleep?" Garan asked.

"This marsh can't go on forever," I replied.

Nya whimpered in Fynda's arms. "Are you so sure?" she asked.

Didn't they trust me? Hadn't my dreams and stories brought us this far in safety? O'ric had said to journey north to M'nor, so north we would travel. This was a test. We would see it through.

"If this is your heart talking," Garan grumbled. "I wish it would be still for a while."

I spun around. "This is the right way," I exploded, trying to ignore the fatigue in his mud-splattered face. They all looked worn. Well, I was tired too. "I know it, so I will continue. Do as you please." I turned my back on him and swashed forward.

"Know it or feel it?" Fynda asked gently. "Which is speaking, your head or your heart?"

I didn't stop. "They're one now," I said, "Each supports the other."

Yhoshi took my arm. "Even I can't believe that anymore," he said. "I thought I would follow you anywhere, Toshar, but my loyalty isn't blind. I'm turning back while there's still light. I'm going back toward the river to find dry land, to build a fire, to rest until morning, when we'll all see things more clearly. We can always come back this way tomorrow. What about it, Toshar?"

I jerked my arm free. First Garan, then Fynda splashed forward. Each touched my shoulder before turning to follow Yhoshi. Nya jumped from Fynda's arms and paddled toward me.

"Nya knows I'm right," I said.

She shinnied up my shirt, barking loudly. But when I picked her up she slithered out of my grasp and swam toward the others, stopping every few strokes to turn and bark at me.

Then, all was silent.

I wanted to turn and follow. It was too late.

"I am the bard," I said. "I must be right." With my first step forward, my foot hooked into a knotted root. It pulled me face-first into a pool of smelly muck. Black slime oozed into my mouth. I picked myself up and tried to clear the foul taste.

"I am the bard," I breathed. "I must be right." Evening mist gathered around me, shrouding the sky. Daylight, already enfeebled, slowly dissolved. Which way was north? The insistent voice that had urged me on fell silent. I was alone.

"I am the bard. I must be right." Had Yhoshi, Fynda and Garan made it back? I swiveled slowly, straining my eyes for fire glow, for voices.

Nothing.

"I am the bard. I must be right." It would soon be too dark to continue and there was no place to sit, let alone sleep. If I didn't act soon I would have to spend a second night standing, waiting for morning light. If I didn't act... I turned full circle again, but every direction looked the same: equally hopeless in the dying day. A cacophonous inner chorus pelted me with conflicting directions.

"That tree stump ahead, that's north."
"No, that's west. Over there, by that clump of grass, that's north."
"North doesn't matter. You'll never make it, so why bother?"
"You should have followed Nya's nose."
"That was west."
"The k'nrah knows."
"The k'nrah knows nothing. You know nothing. It's all futile."
"You should have gone back with Yhoshi."
"You should have stayed by the river."
"You should... you should... you should... you should... you —"

"Stop!" I cried, my voice instantly muffled by the misting damp. I clamped my hands over my ears, but that only amplified the rebukes.

"You're a fool."
"You're a fool and a coward."
"Elderbard? Why you're not even a true bard. A true bard would know the way. A true bard would—"

"I will not listen to you," I shouted. "I will not." With all my power, I pushed them away, stilled them one by one, until once more all was silent.

I welcomed this silence, absorbing it, refusing whatever stray thoughts and fears clamored for my attention. Eyes closed, I stood in the velvet stillness and waited. I would wait like this all night if need be. It was all right. I was all right.

The quiet wrapped itself around me, clothing me in a mantle of tranquility. Through it, I noticed sounds I had missed in the babel.

"Chirrup-crowk, chirrup-crowk," a swamp groh called to its mate.

"Ca'rook-cheep, ca'rook-cheep," echoed the response.

Then from somewhere overhead: "Cheep-wah. Cheep-wah." Yhoshi and Garan would know that bird just from its call. I smiled. A breeze brushed against my face. It carried a trace of freshness through the reeking rot. I sniffed. It carried something else. I opened my eyes to darkness. Night had fallen. Sensing a flicker in the corner of my eye, I turned to see a hazy reddish glow smudging the veil of black. It was fire I had smelled. I pushed a few soggy steps toward it, then stopped. What if it was soldiers' fire?

"No," I said firmly. "That's the way."

It was a long, sloppy slog, farther than it had seemed. At last I reached dry land, though by then I was so wet and filthy it made little difference. Wafts of clean air blew the rank, weedy odor back into the marsh, carrying the comforting smell of wood smoke past me as they went. They bore a familiar sound too.

"Caaa-ooo-eee! Pa-REE-ka, caaa-ooo-*EEE*!" Parika shrilled past, his call fading into the night. I thought I felt his wings fan by me. Or was it the wind?

"I was so sure," I said. "I'm sorry."

"You weren't sure at all," Garan growled. "You were reckless and arrogant. You could have drowned. You could have drowned us all."

I edged nearer to the fire. I was dry but chilled. We all were. Our clothes hung from tree limbs, dribbling beads of water that popped and sizzled when they hit the flame.

Fynda took my hand and rubbed some warmth into it. "Don't listen to him," she said. "He was more worried than any of us. He kept pulling me to the edge of the marsh and asking if I could see you."

Yhoshi threw a handful of dried leaves into the fire. It flared for an instant, thrusting a starburst into the sky. "I'm sorry about the mutiny," he said.

"No," I said. "You were right. So were you, Garan. I was reckless." I watched the sparks extinguish one by one. "I don't know what it was. There were just so many voices..." I looked around. "Where's Nya?"

"I don't know," Fynda said. "One minute she was here, the next she was gone. I looked everywhere. I hope she's all right."

"Caaa-ooo-eee! caaa-ooo-eee! CAAA-OOO-EEE!"

"Maybe that bird got her," said Yhoshi. "What do you call it, Toshar?"

"Parika."

"Parika follows us everywhere. We heard it as you came back. I don't like it. It's as though it's always watching us."

"He is." A disembodied face floated into the circle of firelight. "Come down," she called, extending a gossamer arm from the folds of a cloak that merged with the night. The bird swooped down and landed on her hand.

"Who are you?" Yhoshi called out. He leapt up, then, realizing he was naked, crouched down again, pulling at the nearest garment. It ripped.

With her free hand, the visitor threw back her hood. Gold-flecked silver tresses rippled down her back as Nya, draped around her neck like a scarf, jumped into my lap. Firelight bathed her eyes, which bore into mine.

"You know me, Toshar, do you not?" The words rustled like autumn leaves on a gentle breeze.

"Yes, Na'an, but I never thought to see you here, in this world. You are here, aren't you? Or am I dreaming?"

"Touch me if you need proof." She extended her hand. I kissed it. The texture was one I had never experienced — soft as moss, delicate and translucent as onion skin. She was solid, yet it felt as though she might vanish in a single gust of wind.

"Don't Tikkan live only in dreams?" I asked.

"As a rule," she replied, "but when the times demand it, we step into the waking world. The dreams I carry into your sleep are no longer powerful enough on their own. So here I am. Here we are. Aren't we, Parika."

The bird squawked.

"That's really its name?" I asked, at last diverting my eyes from Na'an's to the bird. It hopped up to Na'an's shoulder, over to her other shoulder then back again.

"Pa-REE-ka!" he cried.

"His truth name, yes. He has many names. All do. But his power is linked to his truth name."

"Truth name?" Fynda asked.

"The name many keep hidden to protect their power," Na'an replied. She turned to me. "You have the Elderbard's gift of naming, Toshar."

Nya licked my hand and purred.

"What does that mean?"

"It means you see the truth names others cannot. It means you speak the truth names others dare not. It's a rare gift and potent weapon. It will aid you when you least expect it."

Parika issued another shriek.

"Hush, Parika. You have spoken enough for one day. And you," Na'an said to Yhoshi, "do you think I have never seen human nakedness before? I see through clothing, through flesh, through bone — to the essence within. Cover yourself up if you wish. It's the same to me." She returned her hand to her cloak and withdrew a golden needle. It glittered in the firelight. "Ryolan

Ò Garan will find he needs this," she said, "once he reclaims his trousers from Yhoshi son of Yhosha."

As Garan wrenched his overalls from Yhoshi's grip, we all heard another rip. Fynda giggled. "Let me," she said. She reached for the needle.

"I can manage just fine," Garan snapped. He pushed Fynda's hand away. "Excuse me, ma'am. Have you any thread?"

Na'an sighed. "You have no imagination left, little man. This needle takes no thread." She released the needle into his hand. "May I sit? I have need of a warm fire too."

I cleared a place for her on a flat stone next to the fire." Forgive me, Na'an. I didn't think."

"It seems to me you have been thinking altogether too much. Is that not why your clothes drip into the fire?" She smoothed her cloak and sat down.

"I wish you had come earlier," I said.

She held her hands to the fire and watched the dancing flames in silence. At last she turned to me. "I cannot teach you what you will not learn. I come not when I am ready but when you are." Her gaze moved to each of us in turn, resting finally on Garan, stooped over his mending.

"Yow!" he cried, shaking his hand in pain.

Needle and overalls fell to the ground. Na'an picked them up before the fire could. She sat quietly for several minutes, running the threadless needle through the torn fabric, which fused seamlessly as the needle did its work. When she was done, she handed the trousers to Garan and pocketed the needle.

"I have watched you," she said, her gaze embracing us all. "Through Parika's eyes I have watched you throughout your long journey. You have come far. Continue your travels and the land may yet heal."

"Is there much farther to go?" I asked.

"That depends."

"On what?"

"On you."

I averted my eyes. "My folly in the marsh has kept us back," I said.

"Folly is only folly if its lessons go unheeded," she said. "Remember that, Toshar...all of you."

Fynda poked at the fire. It crackled and spit in protest. She looked up at Na'an shyly. "You have followed us?" Na'an nodded. "You have seen everything?" Na'an nodded again.

"Something troubles you, child."

"What happened in those villages? What happened to the people? Every time I think back to what I saw, I want to cry."

"You are right to weep, child. Tragedy lives in the Valley of the Tasheen." She shook her head. "It is not time. The answers will come, child. But first we must eat. I have no need of food when I walk through your dreams. But your waking world always sparks a great hunger in me." She burrowed into the folds of her cloak. "I think I can dream us up some sustenance. Eh, Parika?" When she pulled out her hand, she held a tray with four tins of steaming broth.

Yhoshi, Fynda and Garan each took the mug she offered. I reached out, then pulled back. "What about you?" I asked.

"I don't like soup," she replied. After more rummaging she retrieved a hunk of warm bread and a slab of cheese. She fed a few tidbits to Parika and Nya before taking her first taste, a small, dainty bite, which she chewed and chewed and chewed, then chewed some more, before swallowing.

"Sixty-seven times," she explained before taking a second bite. "I have delicate digestion. Most Tikkan do. It comes from eating so rarely." After that, she spoke no more until bread and cheese were consumed and she had wiped her mouth with a cloth napkin, also pulled from the recesses of her cloak.

"Now," she said. "Now is the time to talk."

Sixteen

Na'an folded her hands on her lap and gazed into the flames. We waited, watching her watch the flickering light. After a while, she leaned toward the fire and passed her hands over the flames. Her hands still glowed as she moved them to her eyes and held them there, before letting them slide down first to her mouth then past her throat to her breast. It was as though she carried the light of the fire into her soul.

"The fire tells me it is not my dream to weave," she said at last. "Toshar will say what needs to be said."

Startled, I shook my head. What did she mean? I didn't know what to say.

Once more, Na'an passed her hands over the flame. This time, she stood, walked behind me and placed her hands over my face. The light seeped through my closed eyes, swirled around my skull and down into my body. I felt its warmth and could almost see it driving through me.

"Open your eyes, Toshar," she said. Her hands were gone. "Look into the fire and see. Look into the fire and hear."

I looked but saw nothing, heard nothing.

"Don't strain for facts. Find the truth and speak it."

The truth. Which truth? Golden plumes shot with red and orange thrust up into the sky. Fiery plumes. I remembered Tashek and again felt the brilliant intensity of merging suns sear through me. For a moment I was with him, soaring into the light. Then I was back, seeing images dance within the flames, images that slowly gained clarity.

I see a hill, a green hill dressed in the colors of spring. Atop this hill stands a single pyynch'n that soars into the heavens. Two handsome young Tikkan dreamwalkers, a boy and girl, dance around the pyynch'n, laughing and singing.

Now they're older. The girl I know to be Na'an sits under the tree at a loom, weaving stories that travel up its stout trunk, shoot off into its limbs and branches and then fly into people's hearts as dreams.

The young man paces impatiently, ignoring his loom. He tries to argue with Na'an, but she smiles a smile of purest love and continues to weave. Finally, he throws himself at his loom and produces not a dream but a nightmare: an angry, faceless demon dressed in a cape of darkest pitch. The demon steps into the young man's body, disfiguring it horribly. Even as Na'an continues to weave, the demon grows larger and larger, spreading his cloak wider and wider, until its blackness engulfs all.

Now, the same evil, mocking laugh that rumbled through Horusha's cave echoes here too. Louder and louder. I clap my hands to my ears, but that only amplifies it.

"NO!" I scream, trying to overpower the chilling shrieks. "No..."

"No," I whispered. "He can't be." I jerked my head around to look at Na'an.

"Yes," she said, "Bo'Rá K'n is my brother."

"But how...?"

Na'an returned to her seat by the dying fire, little more than a cluster of embers cooling as the night cooled. Nya climbed onto her lap and disappeared into the folds of her cloak.

"Dreams guide man but do not control him," she said slowly. "That did not satisfy my brother. He sought a power that dreamwalking could never bring him. He sought it and found it. In your kings. In your people. They gave it to him. Readily." Her gaze fell on each of us in turn. "With M'nor's help you can reclaim it."

"He must be destroyed," growled Yhoshi.

"He can be stilled but not destroyed. That is the way of your world in these times."

"You say we know where to go and what to do," I said, "but we don't. At least, I don't. Didn't I prove that today?"

Na'an smiled. "You also proved that your sight has not left you," she said. "You will find the way." She turned to Fynda. "In the morning give Parika back his feathers. Then he will guide you all through the marsh. After that, you must follow your heart to M'nor. She waits for you."

Na'an rose, reached into her cloak and pulled out four smooth, black stones, each with an eye of red in its center that glowed like the last of the embers. "Here," she said, placing one in my palm and closing my fist over it. Eyes closed, she held my fist for a moment, whispering an invocation I could barely hear. "Kol kolai, para'a koh ny'hh hama."

A charge pulsed through me, the same energy I had felt in the heart of Horusha. She moved to each of us in turn, repeating the ritual. When she was done, she had us link hands around the fire pit, each stone sandwiched between two palms.

"The power of The Four As One," she said. "Feel it." The charge quickened as the circle closed. A rosy halo formed around us. Dim at first, it brightened until all we could see was its fierce red light. "The Table of Prophecy lives with you and in you," we heard through the light. "Kol Kolai will become one again through you, if you let it."

When the halo faded, Na'an had gone, taking Nya and Parika with her.

It was still dark when a piercing CAAA-OOO-EEE startled us awake.

"Caaa-ooo-eee! Pa-REE-ka, caaa-ooo-eee!" Parika buzzed so near we could feel his wings fan the air around us. "Caaa-ooo-*EEE*!"

"I'll gather berries and herbs for tea, if you'll stir up the fire," Yhoshi said to Garan. Garan stretched his mouth into a capacious yawn. He rubbed his eyes and began to poke at the fire. Yhoshi turned to Fynda. "Will you come with me, Fynda? I'll need your eyes in this dark."

Fynda nodded.

"Wait," I said. "Leave Parika his feathers."

Fynda had barcly pulled them from her waistband when Parika dropped from the sky and snatched them from her."

"Caaa-ooo-*EEE*!" Parika shrieked. He swooped in front of Yhoshi's face, a steely feather scraping his nose. Yhoshi swatted the bird angrily.

"Maybe he'll join us for breakfast," I said.

"Maybe he'll join us as breakfast," Yhoshi muttered.

Parika screeched and dove again for Yhoshi's nose.

"It was a joke," he said and ducked out of the way just in time. Parika shot back up into the fading dark, only to swoop down again, weaving in and out among us until it was impossible to move. Not a single flick of a wrist went unchecked as he screamed ever-tightening circles around us, then began to shepherd us toward the marsh.

He flew low over a chain of narrow, linked islets that looped and threaded through the swampy morass, and we followed. Every deadened stump seemed to watch us from blackened knotholes and every tangle of roots seemed eager to twist around our feet and pull us off our dry path and into a stagnant pool. I thought back to my attempt to force my way through in the dark and shuddered, quickening my pace.

Parika guided us forward, along a path half-hidden among chest-high marsh grasses and barely wide enough for one. Circling back with increasing frequency, he urged us on.

"Caaa-ooo-*EEE!*"

"We're walking as fast as we can," I called back.

In reply, he swooped onto my shoulder and cooed insistently into my ear.

"I wish we could fly like you," I said, stroking his feathers. Parika bobbed his head, snapped his beak, fluttered his wings and took off. He zoomed straight up, hovered for a moment, then dove down again, continuing this up-and-down rhythm as he led us through the marsh.

Overhead, Aygra and B'na moved toward each other and then apart. On we walked. Still, nothing but swamp lay ahead. My stomach rumbled and I looked around. Even the slimy weeds floating on the water began to look appetizing.

"Is any of this edible, Yhoshi?" I asked. "We've eaten nothing since Na'an's broth."

"True," he said, "but I'm not hungry enough for that. Soon, maybe, but not yet."

"Can we at least stop for a few minutes?" Fynda asked.

Even with no food, I welcomed the idea. I looked to Parika for permission. His wings beat frantically as if battling a great wind. Suddenly, the sky darkened under the veil of four massive, ribbed wings, one pair on either side of a black-scaled serpent. Its two single-eyed heads completed the arms of a giant crescent. In unison, its mouths yawned open and tongues of green flame spurted out.

"CAAA-OOO-*EEE!*" Parika cried, trying to dodge the beast.

"Watch out!," I shouted to Parika as the serpent snapped at him from behind.

The serpent paused mid-flight to glare down at me, then returned its attention to Parika. One head chased the bird from the rear while the other looped around to block him from the front. Frozen in horror, we watched the two gaping mouths close in, roasting him in twin bursts of green flame.

"Pa-REE-ka, caaa-ooo—"

He was gone. The serpent trained its eyes earthward.

"Down!" shouted Yhoshi as it streaked toward us. We huddled in the dirt and marsh grass. With a roar and a gust of wind, the serpent flew up again. Black steam spewed from both mouths, an acrid mist that rained down from the sky, coating us in damp soot. Within minutes, we couldn't see. We could barely breathe, so thick and noxious were the fumes.

"Here." Yhoshi's hand reached toward me, as black as the mist that cloaked the rest of him. He held a swatch of fabric, ripped from his shirt and dipped in water. "Breathe through this," he said.

I put the cloth to my face. For all the unpleasant memories its taste and smell triggered, at least I could breathe. A green flash shot through the blackness over my head, then a second. Flames singed away the top of the grasses. Now, those grasses barely concealed us. With my free hand I felt beyond them to a tangle of weeds pushing out of a pool of mucky ooze. I rolled toward it.

"Into the water," I called and let myself fall in. Three splashes echoed after me. I sank into the slime then forced myself to the surface and began to tread water. My heart pounded against my ribcage. Another pair of green flames blazed through the spot we had just left.

"Can you see anything, Fynda?" I asked. "Can you see through this?"

"This isn't dark. It's dirt," she coughed. "I'm as blind as you,"

A rush of wind ruffled the water and, for a moment, cleared the air. In that moment I saw two yawning mouths, teeth jagged peaks of charcoal, coming toward me.

"Duck," I cried and dropped back underwater. It made no difference. With a hissing, sucking slurp, I felt myself pulled in. I tumbled into a darkened pool, turning slow-motion somersaults in the fetid water. Weeds and branches caught in my hair, twined around my arms and legs. The current swept me along and then slowed, discarding me in a wet, slimy heap next to Yhoshi, Garan and Fynda. Steam rose from the puddles around us. It wafted up in clouds of white iridescence that lit the dank clamminess of the serpent's belly.

"This serpent..." I said when I gained some semblance of equilibrium. "I know its truth name. Just like Na'an said."

"How do you know?" Fynda asked.

"I don't know. I just do."

"What will happen if you say it?" Garan asked worriedly.

The serpent roared and shook with fury.

I inhaled deeply. "I know you," I said. "You are S'kala."

S'kala shuddered, lost altitude and then belched a fiery inferno that propelled it back upward.

"You dare call me by name!" S'kala's rage rumbled through us.

"I do, S'kala. I do more than that. I demand that you release us."

"Oh, I will releas-s-s-s-e you," it hissed. "To Fvorag, True King of all Q'ntana."

The puddles sloshed one way then the other as the ground beneath us slid a slow, slithering curve to the left, then a slow, slithering curve to the right.

"We have to get out of here," Yhoshi whispered. He stood and drew his knife. "We'll cut our way through." But push as he might, his blade couldn't pierce the fleshy wall.

"Ss-ss-ss-ss," S'kala laughed. "Scratch a little more to the left. I have s-s-s-such an itch. Ss-ss-ss-ss-ss."

Yhoshi turned away in disgust. "The only other way out is the way we came in," he whispered. He looked from left to right and back again, trying to gauge which mouth lay closer.

"Why do you whis-s-s-s-per? Why even s-s-s-speak when I can hear your every thought, when I can plant any thought I like in your human minds? Human minds? Ss-ss-ss-ss."

The steam blackened, plunging us into darkness. Traces of acrid sootiness floated up my nose and into my mouth. I began to choke. Remembering Yhoshi's strategy, I tore a wet strip from my shirt and held it to my face.

There, that's better. I can't see, but at least I can breathe.

Wait. I can see.

I see a light. A torch.

Is someone coming? It's a soldier. No, two... No, two groups of two. Marching.

A hooded prisoner, head erect, limps between then. He wears a bardic robe, slashed to expose bloody, pussy welts. The soldiers push, prod and drag him, kicking him when he falls, jeering as he struggles up. A soldier steps forward. He raises a black scimitar to the prisoner's throat.

"No," I shriek.

The prisoner's head rolls toward me, through brambles that slice away his hood, through puddles that clean the dried blood caking his face.

The head rolls toward me.

Nearer and nearer.

It rolls to a stop, its face horrifyingly familiar, blank eyes staring into mine.

Its eyes. My eyes.

They are the same.

"No!"

My no was Yhoshi's no, and Garan's and Fynda's too — all sobbed out at the same moment. None of us spoke. Though the smoke had cleared, the nightmare vision still clung to us.

"Did you like that?" the serpent asked. "I have more where that came from, an endless s-s-supply." S'kala paused. "Here's another, especially for the bard. You'll like it. I know you will."

I screwed my eyes shut and covered my ears. "I will not hear, I will not see," I shouted, then shouted it again.

It makes no difference. Once more I see a distant light. It grows larger, rounder. My shouting dies as its glow infuses me. M'nor. She has come to me. She is alive and more powerful than S'kala. I smile with relief. I laugh. The higher M'nor rises and broader her smile, the more joyous my laugh.

Ahead, his face awash in moonlight, stands a young, red-haired man. He wears a white robe that reflects M'nor's glow into an aura that shimmers around him and glints off the gold circlet crowning his head. He walks toward me, smiling in friendship.

I reach out my hand, move toward him, then stop. My hand snaps back. It leaps to my mouth in horror.

The two ends of his gold torque slither toward and past each other, coiling around his neck, tighter and tighter. Tighter and tighter

He pales. He fades.

He is gone.

All that remains is the circlet and the snake, which weaves its black body through the crown, obliterating the gold.

I look up to M'nor. Fingers of black mist slowly strangle her, dimming her light and then, as the snake's blackness merges with the surrounding dark, blotting her out of the sky altogether. Only black smoke remains.

"So you s-s-s-see, last of the doomed bards, there is no M'nor. It's over."

S'kala's voice softened. "The struggle is over," it crooned. "Accept it, Toshar. Feel the relief of it."

"Yes," I said. S'kala spoke sense. We had fought well, but we had lost. It was over. It felt good to acknowledge that. Why resist the inevitable? I shrugged and sat with the others. They too had seen reason.

"There's nothing we can do," Fynda said dully.

"Nothing," said Garan.

"You see how easy it is, how much better you feel?" S'kala spoke in the same languid, hypnotic rhythms as the sliding movement of its body. "There's no need to struggle. I'll take care of you. Here—" A soft gust of warm, sweet air embraced us. "Let me dry your clothes."

Yhoshi's face relaxed into a smile.

"You're safe now. All of you. Safe...safe...safe..."

Yes, I thought. We're safe. This is a good place, a comfortable place.

We sat on plush, green carpets in a palatial pink chamber hung with a galaxy of dancing tapers. Atop a sideboard, silver platters steamed with savory meats and vegetables. As we helped ourselves, the platters replenished themselves. It felt *so* good to eat.

Everything was fine, more than fine. With amazement, I patted my shirt. It was dry and whole, as though mended by Na'an's golden needle.

Na'an. What would she say? What could she say? We did our best. It was over. I patted my trousers. They too were like new. Wait. What was this? I slipped my hand into my pocket and touched throbbing heat.

My heartbeat quickened. I closed my fist around the stone, clutching it tightly. Shards of light slashed in front of me. Through them, I caught flashes of scaly flesh, of ashy particles suspended in drenching mist.

"The kolai," I cried. I grabbed Yhoshi's hand, slipping the stone between our palms. "Quick. Join hands."

They gazed at me blankly. Then Yhoshi's puzzled expression vanished as the power of my stone began to flow through him.

"No!" S'kala roared. But it was too late. As our circle closed, jagged tears ripped through the illusion. Layer after layer peeled away with the sound of shredding canvas, peeled away with such speed it made me dizzy. Fearing I would faint, I squeezed my eyes shut.

When I opened them again, we sat, still holding hands, on an arid plain, empty but for a hazy silhouette, quivering in the heat. A curl of smoke rose from the midpoint between its two giant heads.

"What happened?" Fynda gasped.

We all struggled to catch our breath. "The kolai," I said. "The power of The Four As One. Na'an said it would protect us." I gazed at the broad expanse of scrubby desert, burnished gold in the late afternoon suns. "I wonder where we are…"

Yhoshi looked off at the serpent, smoldering on the horizon. "Is it dead?" His eyes remained fixed on S'kala. "If it's not, it may come after us."

Garan pulled his hand free and studied his kolai. The red eye in its center throbbed. "Can't we use this to kill it?" he asked.

"Or to bring us food and drink?" asked Fynda.

"I don't know," I said doubtfully. I remembered a vague warning about things of power like the kolai. Too vague. Whatever Eulisha's admonition, it had come long ago, when the possibility of me wielding anything this potent seemed remote.

"If these give us power, why not use it?" Fynda asked impatiently. She reached for Yhoshi's hand and mine. I hesitated.

"Would you have us swallowed up again while we're sleeping? I don't want to die."

"Who knows what we'll unleash if we misuse it," I replied.

"How can we misuse it by trying to stay alive?"

There was truth in her words. But was it whole truth? Reluctantly, I closed the circle.

"Now what?" Garan asked.

"I don't know," I said. "Concentrate." The kolai felt cold against my palm. Inert. No energy. No pulse.

"Concentrate on what?" Fynda asked.

"On safety," Garan replied. "That will cover us whether S'kala is alive or not."

I detected a weak pulse from the still cool stone. It stuck damply to my palm, felt as clammy as S'kala's belly.

Suddenly, a rumbling shook through us, throwing up a veil of dusty earth. Lightning zagged through the dust. Another flash, this one longer, but still too quick to recognize what lay on the other side.

Whatever it was, we teetered on the cusp between this place and that. Another flash exposed a split second of rosy haze. A knot formed in my stomach. Familiar smells steamed toward me and the knot tightened.

With a cry of recognition, I jerked my hands free. Two kolai thudded to the ground. The rumbling ceased. The dust settled. The serpent smoldered as though nothing had happened. Yet something had.

I took a few steps toward S'kala, trying to see through the haze, now bruised purple with dusk. "You aren't dead, are you?" I expected no reply and received none, only lazy puffs that rose to merge with smoky trails of cloud.

Knowing I wouldn't sleep, I took first watch. The haze cleared as evening's chill chased away the heat. Stars poked through the inky blackness and familiar constellations winked down at us like old friends. The Traveler. The Harpist. The Bard. Through them all, Aris shone brightest, pointing the way north, toward M'nor.

"Go back to sleep," I said when Fynda wakened. "I'm not tired."

"No," she said. "You need sleep too. Go ahead. I'll be all right."

Reluctantly, I stretched out on the scratchy ground. The cold leached through my ragged clothes and I quickly curled against Yhoshi for warmth. He grunted as my body molded against his.

All is blackness. I'm floating in a vast, velvet emptiness, aware of nothing, feeling nothing. Out of the dark emerge two white globes, one brilliantly luminous, the other wavering dimly. The first sucks in all other light, hoarding it for itself. The second casts a frail, anemic glow, enough for me to recognize the treeless plain and to see Fynda twenty paces ahead. Unaware of my presence, she walks toward the brighter of the lights. I follow behind.

Now, I see the scene as though from a great height. Are there three of me? One dreaming, one walking, one floating? I'm aware of each, not as part of me but as all of me. From above, I see that the lights belong to S'kala. They are its eyes. S'kala stretches out, wall-like, in front of me, one gape-mouthed head at either end. As the last of its light seeps away, the dim eye blinks out and that mouth crumples shut.

Fynda continues toward the other eye. It pulls her to it. She walks easily but blindly, tranced, losing light and will the nearer she draws. I want to stop her, but my arms can't reach. The walker in me becomes a runner. Fynda runs too, her legs in step with mine. When she stops in front of S'kala's mouth, I stop, still twenty paces behind, unable to move.

Steam rises from S'kala's scales, up to my floating aerie. Cold and lifeless as a dead fish, it slaps my face and I recoil. The steam wraps around me, obscuring my eagle's-eye perspective. On the ground, the view is clear. Black scales sweat hot ooze that hisses as it touches cool earth. Jagged, coal-shard teeth glisten. An orange tongue flicks eagerly as small jets of green phosphorous streak from a trio of cavernous nostrils. From where I stand rooted, the flame's heat singes the hair on my arms. Yet an icy chill creeps over me and I shiver.

Fynda steps forward. My steps match hers. A snort of flame sketches her in a lightning flash of green. Its fire bathes me in a thin layer of perspiration that hardens into lacy ice on my arm.

Suddenly, the steam clears. At that same moment, all three of me see Fynda lift her right foot toward S'kala's open mouth.

"No," I shout. She doesn't respond. I call out again, louder. She hesitates. "No!" And then a trio of voices, all mine: "FYNDA!"

I woke to misty darkness. For a moment, I didn't know where I was or where I had been. Then I remembered.

"Fynda?" I whispered.

No response.

"Fynda!"

Silence.

A faraway beacon flickered through the haze. Just below it, a green flash, like heat lightning, split the night. I saw S'kala, its remaining eye focused into the dark. I called out again, but the mist swallowed her name before it left my mouth.

Garan sat up with a start. "What is it?" he asked. He screwed his fists into his eyes and rubbed. "Is it time for my watch?"

"Fynda. Where's Fynda?" I danced around him, pointing to the distant light, then knelt and shook Yhoshi. "Fynda," I panted. "S'kala." I pointed again and started to run.

I raced toward the light, Yhoshi and Garan trailing behind. It burned through the night with a gaze so cold and cruel I cried in anguish. I saw nothing else, felt nothing else, save the pull of that eye, the sting of its force. Slowly, dawn paled the sky. I strained for a glimpse of Fynda. Nothing.

"Faster," I huffed and hurled myself toward the undulating line of steaming darkness that scarred the horizon. I tried to imagine myself in the sky again, but the eagle view belonged to Na'an, and I no longer dreamed.

The crisp morning air turned clammy, that same amalgam of heat and ice I had dreamed. S'kala loomed ahead. Where was Fynda? I scanned the length of its body. At the far end head and trunk had collapsed into a volcanic heap, while a gash half-severed an outspread wing from the scale-littered mountain of ash. The nearer wing was tucked tightly against S'kala's torso, largely intact at our end. Directly in front of us a gargantuan head rose up in scaly profile, its oval eye bearing down on us in white-hot fury. A trident of green flame shot from its nostrils and its eye bulged as it strained to slide toward us.

Then I saw Fynda. She climbed the side of S'kala's head, all her attention focused on the ascent. As she shifted her grip from one scale to the next, water slopped from a silver ewer tucked into her belt, hissing when it splashed onto a scale.

"Fynda!" I called.

No response. Up another scale, over another scale. She climbed higher, aiming for S'kala's eye, which seemed to absorb her and all of us, taking in every thought and feeling.

"I'm going after her," I announced.

"No," Yhoshi said, pulling me back. "You stay here. It's too dangerous. I'll go."

I shook my head and drew Oriccan. "I can't let you do this for me."

S'kala's mouth opened then fell shut. Its jellied eye looked ready to explode from the effort. Another flash of flame, this one weaker than the last. Fynda stopped and cocked her head. Her lips moved. I stepped closer and into a cloud of hot-cold air. Gingerly, I reached out and touched S'kala, expecting to recoil from the heat. Instead, S'kala recoiled. To my surprise, its scales were no warmer than suns-baked rock and just as dry. I wrapped one fist around Oriccan's hilt and the other around the kolai. A flood of confidence surged through me. I returned the stone to my pocket and dagger to my belt and began to climb — more quickly than Fynda, who calculated every movement to avoid spilling water from the ewer. Again and again I called up to her, but she paid me no heed.

One more scale and I could touch her foot. I clambered up. She stopped, tilted her head again, then tightened her grip. As I reached for her foot, a violent spasm shuddered through the serpent, knocking me off balance. Jagged scale-edges slashed at my hands as I slid and groped for support. I caught a glimpse of Yhoshi and Garan rushing together a bed of sand and grasses to break my fall. I would fall. I was falling. Falling...

Suddenly, I jerked to a stop. My belt had snagged on a scale. I braced myself and looked up. Fynda had resumed her ascent. Within seconds, so had I. I pulled myself up scale by scale, my palms greased with blood, my eyes tearing with pain. Fynda still moved slowly, pausing every few scales to check the water. Once again, I reached for her foot. I grabbed onto it this time, holding fast.

"Listen, Fynda," I said urgently. "I know you can hear me. Deep down. You know my voice. You know I'm a friend. Listen to me. Speak to me. It's me. Toshar."

She hesitated, then with an angry jerk she shook her foot free. The impact sloshed water from the ewer onto my hand. Its soothing coolness massaged away the bloody cuts. Amazed, I flexed my hand. No pain.

Seizing the nearest scale, I climbed after her. She stopped, her head level with S'kala's eye.

Four more scales and I could reach her. Steadying herself with her left hand, she reached for her belt with her right.

Three more scales. Gently she released the ewer.

Two more scales. She raised her arm.

One more. As she tilted the spout, I came up under her outstretched arm and knocked the ewer free. Water splashed into S'kala's eye and over both of us. Startled, Fynda looked at me, gasped and released her grip, tumbling to the ground after the ewer.

S'kala shuddered and heaved with renewed strength. "You," it hissed. "I will kill you."

Steam issued from the gaps between the scales, scalding my hands and face and drenching my clothes. I didn't know how much longer I could hold on. I looked down after Fynda but dense black clouds billowed up to meet me. Gagging, I climbed higher. They chased up, skirling around me, obscuring everything but the piercing light of that unblinking eye. A vast network of red and orange veins thrust through the snowy whiteness, crisscrossing it like the leafless limbs of a winter forest.

S'kala roared, and a sulfurous flash scarred the acrid smoke with green. I couldn't breathe. Should I jump? Should I climb higher? I couldn't climb higher. My numbed hands could barely grip the burning scales. My stomach heaved at the smell cooking flesh. Was it mine or S'kala's?

I felt myself slipping. Sliding. Knife-edge scales scraped my arms and hands. One chance. Slim, but a chance. Gritting my teeth against the pain, I pulled O'ric's dagger from my belt and plunged it into the serpent's eye.

A thunderous explosion ripped through the half-light of dawn.

Next I knew I was gliding gently earthward as a giant fireball spewed into the sky, more brilliant than the suns. It thrust higher and higher, firing the clouds it pierced until, little more than a pinprick, it vanished into the heavens.

A heavy, black gash scorched the earth in front of us. Fynda stared at it then looked around stupidly, trying to connect pieces that refused to come together in her mind. "I remember…" she began. "I remember…" She shook her head helplessly. "I don't remember anything. What happened?"

"What's the last thing you do remember?" I asked. We sat where we had touched down, she and I, miraculously unscathed.

Fynda shrugged. "I don't know. I remember taking the watch from you then regretting it because I couldn't keep my eyes open. I kept dozing and waking, dozing and waking. The last time I woke I felt sure someone was watching me. But all I saw was a haze even my eyes couldn't penetrate. Then this white light cut through the night. It seemed to call me. I don't know what it was but I must have gone to it. After that…" She shrugged again.

I picked up the ewer, unscratched despite its fall. "What about this?"

"What is it?"

"What do you mean, 'What is it?'" Yhoshi asked angrily.

"I-I-"

"Maybe if you hold it again," I said.

Fynda took it from me, even as her eyes asked, *Do I have to?* She ran her hands over it searchingly.

"I found it," she said finally, "on a sheltered ledge by the brook. Yes, by the brook."

"What brook?" Yhoshi asked.

Fynda pointed beyond S'kala's charred remains to a crease in the landscape, a narrow dip where the plain dropped then rose again in a slender ravine. "The light directed me there," she said. "It had a voice…a hissing, raspy voice that spoke directly into my mind. It wasn't unpleasant, though. It was almost comforting." She half-smiled at the memory. "After that…"

Yhoshi turned flaming eyes on her. "After that, you nearly got Toshar killed. All of us killed. Again."

Fynda's smile dissolved. "What happened? Did I do something bad? I don't remember anything else until the fall. Toshar?"

I recounted the dream and my ascent up S'kala. She winced.

"Oh, Toshar, I'm sorry. Did I hurt you badly?"

"Nothing the water couldn't cure," I said. "Do you remember anything more about the water?"

"I'm sorry, no." She stared toward the ravine. "Wait, yes. 'The healing waters of Alanda.' That's what the voice called it."

"'The healing waters of Alanda flow through the Plains of Akiann,'" Garan recited.

"What's that?" Yhoshi asked.

"A line from an old story."

"Is that where we are?" Fynda asked.

"You should know," Yhoshi snapped.

"That's enough, Yhoshi," I said. "I'm fine. We're all fine. That's all that matters now."

"But—"

"Garan, do you know anything more about this Alanda?"

"No. Why?"

"That's where we must go." I rose and crossed the blackened line, stopping to pick up a shiny object half buried in ash. Sunlight flared off the silvery tip of a green-and-scarlet feather.

"Poor Parika," I whispered and gave the feather to Fynda. It pricked more than her finger as she took it from me for, suddenly, she collapsed in tears. Great gashing sobs racked through her as she clutched the feather, moaning, "Mama, mama."

We heard the brook before we saw it: the rippling, tinkling plash of water on stone. We broke into a run, following the music, until we stood on the ravine's smooth-slate ledge. It was as though a giant had plowed a deep furrow through Akiann's scrubby skin, exposing a rocky skeleton of jagged boulders. The cliffs formed a protective barrier on either side of a clear stream that curled through the bottom of the chasm. Silver darts danced on the watery ribbon as we began our descent. Although some rocks were firmly rooted, others tottered precariously. I moved cautiously. The others pushed ahead, impatient at the water's promise.

"Even with night eyes, I don't see how you managed this in the dark," Garan said, rubbing a skinned knee with a scraped hand.

"Me neither," Fynda replied. "I don't remember ever falling once. It all seemed so easy then. Ouch!" A loose rock gave way, wedging her foot between two others. It took the three of us to pry it free. She limped the rest of the way down, each step forcing a grimace to her face.

At last we reached the brook. I immersed my scab-streaked arm and watched the bloody slashes fade and disappear. Then I removed Fynda's shoe and led her into the water. She exhaled with relief as the swelling melted away. Tentatively, she jiggled her foot then stomped and splashed with both feet before peeling off her clothes and dropping into waters that vaporized her remaining bruises. Garan, Yhoshi and I followed. We took long, thirsty gulps that sated our gnawing hunger then sat in the middle of the shallow stream letting it bubble over and around us, basking in the calming mix of warm suns and cool water.

"I could stay here forever," Garan sighed next morning. We each lay on a flat, gray slab by the burbling water, staring up at flyks that swooped and darted in a giddy ballet.

"Me too," I said. We hadn't planned to sleep on the rocks. The stone had looked backbreakingly hard. But we soon discovered it to have the slight spring of packed straw and quickly succumbed to the spell of Alanda's lullaby.

I rolled over and lowered my face into the stream, letting the water wash over my lips, cheeks and eyes before lapping up its coolness. Reluctantly, I sat up.

Garan turned his head lazily toward me. "One more day?" he asked hopefully.

"Several more," I replied. A contented smile stole across his face. Yhoshi's eyebrows shot up. "In Alanda's company," I continued, "but not lazing about like overstuffed grondii."

For four bright, cloudless days we hiked north along the ravine's edge, climbing down to the brook to drink and sleep. For four days the landscape never altered. The Plains of Akiann seemed determined to continue forever. On the fifth morning, hints of green poked through the brittle grasses and rocky banks began to surrender to flowering meadows. By evening, Alanda's youthful tumble had matured to a broad, stately progress that did nothing to dilute her healing powers.

"Where is everyone, I wonder?" Yhoshi asked. He and I watched the velvet blackness swallow Aygra and B'na's dying embers.

"What do you mean?"

"All we ever see are soldiers."

"I'm glad we're not seeing anyone," Garan said. He and Fynda had struck off in search of food after failing to catch any fish in the river. Now, Fynda flopped by my side as Garan released an armload of fruit-laden souk branches. Yhoshi plucked a handful of berries and popped them, one at a time, into his mouth.

"I know, Garan. But it's odd, isn't it?" I asked. "Sometimes I worry that all that's left of Q'ntana are Fvorag and his men."

"And us," Fynda added.

"And us." I paused and gazed up into the moonless sky. "Do you think we're too late?"

"For what?"

"For M'nor," I said.

"What does she want with us?" Fynda asked.

"She waits for us," I said, my eyes following Alanda's straight northerly course, straining for a hint of light.

"She waits for story," a voice deep within me whispered.

"She waits for story," I murmured. I closed eyes, mind and heart to all but the silver glow I sensed just below the water line on the farthest horizon. Fynda, Yhoshi and Garan no longer existed. Only the light, a light I couldn't see but knew. I spread my fingers and reached out as if to touch it, as if to renew some ancient bond between us, and then the words came, unbidden as always.

"There was a land," I said slowly, enunciating each vowel and consonant as though trying to make myself understood to a newcomer to the language. "There was a land, a sandy sea that rolled from horizon to horizon in undulating waves that formed, unformed and reformed in the rippling winds. An oasis stood at its center, the sole constant in this ever-changing, never-changing landscape. Ringed by palms whose swaying fronds moderated the brutal heat and held back the desert's gritty, blinding rages, the oasis was the only haven in a merciless wasteland.

"One man lived alone in this oasis. His name was Kyri, though he had long ago forgotten it. He had forgotten much: how and when he had arrived, where he had come from, his age. One loses track with only the suns and stars to mark the passing of one identical day into the next. He had forgotten his age but felt old, and the face that gazed up at him each day from the spring looked as beaten as the sand-pocked stones that edged the oasis.

"One morning, no reflection greeted Kyri from the spring. He stared and stared and stared. He walked away and returned. He walked around the spring. But whenever he looked in, from wherever he looked in, he saw nothing but clouds sailing between palms across the desert sky. He smashed his fist into the water. He jumped in and climbed out again. But once the water stilled, no face gazed back at him.

"'I must be dreaming,' he spoke aloud and pinched his arm until it throbbed. Still, no reflection. Not certain what else to do, Kyri lost himself in the limited busyness of his daily routine: preparing and eating his morning meal of grapes and coconut milk, tidying his simple shelter, circling the oasis in one direction for his morning walk and in the other for his afternoon walk; then nap, another meal of fruit, another walk, another night's sleep.

"'If it was a dream, I'm surely awake now,' he said next morning, trying to ignore the greenish purple blotches that still colored his arm. And so he returned to the spring. But his reflection did not. Nor did it the next day, or the next. After four days of this he grew angry. After seven, he grew fearful. That night he dreamed. He didn't recall ever having dreamed before, though of course he had. So vivid was it, he could have been awake. Yet he knew he was not. As though watching images paint themselves across canvas, he saw the oasis — all of it, from the tops of the palms to the bubbling bed of the spring. He saw it with eyes that were not his, with eyes that knew nothing of a man named Kyri.

"'I don't exist,' he wailed as he leapt from his sleeping mat and raced to the spring. At first he didn't dare look into the water's mirrored surface. When at last he did, through eyes open but a slit, relief washed over him. A face looked back. As he opened his eyes wider, relief drained away. A face looked back, but not his face. He touched his hand to his cheek. The reflected figure aped his actions. He felt a coarse, grizzled beard and leathery skin. He saw a smooth, youthful chin and laughing eyes.

"'Why do you mock me?' he cried.

"'I do not,' the face in the spring replied. 'How can I mock you when I am you?'

"Kyri didn't understand. 'What do you want of me?' he whispered, averting his gaze.

"'You must go.'

"'Go where? There is nowhere to go.' Kyri pointed beyond the fringe of palms. 'I will die out there.'

"'Stay and you are already dead.'

"A gust of wind slapped through, erasing the reflection and choking him with the grit of a rising sandstorm. Kyri stood in stunned silence as eddies of dust whirled around him.

"'Now,' the wind urged. 'Now.'

"Barely aware of his actions, Kyri ran to his shelter and wrapped himself in cloaks and shrouds leaving only his eyes uncovered though shielded by an overhang of drapery. Thus protected, he shouldered his way through the sand-filled air to the edge of the oasis, to an arch formed by two adjacent palms. Here, long before memory, he had passed into the oasis. Spitting out the coarse grains that blew into his mouth, he stood uncertainly before this threshold. He turned back but saw nothing. Ahead, the palm arch grew fainter.

"'Now,' the palms moaned.

"'Now,' the sand rasped.

"'Now,' Kyri whispered, and stepped through the arch."

I said nothing after that, and my silence filled the night. It dimmed the light that had gained in strength through my telling, a light we all saw. It shimmered tentatively just beneath the river's rippling surface.

"What happens next?" Fynda asked.

"I don't know," I breathed hoarsely.

"You must know," Garan cried. "If you don't, you must continue until you find out, until we all find out."

"I don't know that I can." I surprised even myself with this admission. I had never left a story unfinished. Even with those I didn't know, I always continued, word by word, until they spoke their ending to me. This time should be no different. Yet it was. I was desperately tired. "Maybe after I've slept," I said.

"No," Garan insisted. "Now."

Now. Wind and sand spoke through Garan, urging me as they had urged Kyri.

"Hush, Garan," Fynda said. She dropped her hands into the river and touched them to my eyes. I felt the water's healing coolness.

"Won't you try?" she said. "We all need to know what happens next."

"Even M'nor," Yhoshi whispered. Ahead, a distant light twinkled encouragingly.

"Very well," I sighed. I held the light within me as I closed my eyes and continued.

"Kyri stepped across the threshold into a billowing veil of dust. It blew and blew and blew, scraping his skin, even through his layers of cloak. He saw nothing but sand, felt nothing but sand. Then, with a single, violent burst, the wind swept the sand away. The desert had vanished. Kyri spun around. The oasis had vanished, and daylight with it.

"As his eyes adjusted to the dark, Kyri found himself at the gates of a castle in that final moment before dawn. Silence hung in the air for an instant then collapsed as a chorus of warbles, twitters and cheeps sang out in day-greeting prayer. Soft bows of orange, yellow and white shot into the sky, illuminating the castle's pink stone.

"The castle stood at the top of a road that wound up the highest hill in a rolling swell of thick woods and quilted farmland. It sprawled lazily over the hilltop yet possessed an eye-pleasing symmetry. Kyri counted seven turreted towers, each flying a multicolored pennant. He counted seven but knew there were more by the tips of other pennants fluttering just beyond these. For all its candy-pink stone, the castle presented a formidable aspect. From a broad, deep moat rose sheer walls topped with crenelated battlements. A pair of massive towers, punched through with arrow slits, flanked a raised drawbridge hewn from a single slab of red wood. At the bottom of the hill, the winding road passed alongside a river that speared the landscape. A small ferry pushed off from the roadside quay as the full light of morning broke through.

"'Where am I?' Kyri wondered. But before he could begin to imagine a reply, he heard stirrings from within. A rooster crowed — a bit late, he thought wryly — as the general hubbub of morning activity filtered up and over the castle walls.

"'Who goes there?' a sentry shouted down.

"Kyri didn't know what to answer. Who was he? He gazed into the moat. A familiar reflection greeted him. The youthful face smiled. Kyri touched his lips. He smiled too. Did one of those laughing eyes wink at him? He knelt for a closer look just as a swan glided past, shattering the image into a kaleidoscope of color and light.

"'Friend or foe?' the sentry called. Next to the sentry, a woman hoisted the castle standard. Even before the wind caught it, Kyri knew what he would see: a flying eagle emblazoned on a scarlet rose. A second flag rose from the other tower. He knew it would be a silver sphere floating on a midnight field. It was.

"'Friend,' he replied.

"The sentry raised a telescope to his eye and focused it on Kyri. 'By the Lady and all that's sacred,' he exclaimed, 'it's the prince! It's the prince, come home to Castle Rose at last!'"

Like Kyri, I knew what I would see before I saw it. I opened my eyes to a giant arc of incandescence emerging from distant waters. The arc ascended, swelling into a half-circle then into a glowing orb that fired the river in a rippling column of silver. No one spoke. No one moved. No one breathed. Only M'nor lived, her milky beam reaching toward us, flooding into the darkest folds of our being, filling our hearts with her song. Yes, she sang. Like distant sleigh bells, her music tinkled gently through the night, carried on a soft whisper of wind. I strained to hear. We all did, craning our necks to bring our ears closer to the source of this hypnotic, minor-key melody, willing our hearts to stop beating so we could make out the words.

> Mir M'nor m'ranna
> M'ranna ma Mir

Over and over the refrain repeated, spiraling from a faint, sweet solo into a soaring complex of harmonies. It was as though the entire universe joined M'nor in song. The chorus rose as she did, swelled as she did, filling the night with music as she filled it with light.

When she reached the apex of her night's crossing, she hung there for a moment as the music surged to new heights. Then, as she began her descent along the river's path, the choir thinned until M'nor sang alone. Only then did we hear our own voices and realize that we too had been singing — singing words we didn't understand to a melody we didn't know.

> Mir M'nor m'ranna
> M'ranna ma Mir

Our voices dissolved into the night. I turned to follow M'nor's passage into Alanda's southern waters, but my eyes grew heavy. I yawned, then yawned again, struggling to stay awake. But it was as though the same force that drew M'nor toward her watery bed also pressed my eyelids together. The last thing I saw before seeing nothing at all was Yhoshi, Fynda and Garan, asleep where they sat.

Once again, darkness turns to light as M'nor begins her night journey. She is not alone. The Lady Gwna sits on her crest, clothed in a pale blue cloak that shimmers with moonlight. The strange words of M'nor's song float over me and I struggle to decipher them.
Mir M'nor m'ranna
M'ranna ma Mir
"What does it mean?" I ask.
Over M'nor's music, the Lady Gwna sings:
"Remember this song, the song of your heart
"The song of the moon's ascent
"You know the song, Toshar. Listen with your heart not with your ears, and its meaning will be clear."
Remember this song, the song of your heart
The song of the moon's ascent
Remember this song, the song of your heart
The song of the moon's —

"Sirs, madam. Please!"

A high-pitched voice insinuates itself into my dream. It's a peculiar melding, and for a moment the increasingly frantic entreaty seems to come from the Lady Gwna's lips.

"Oh, my heavenly days. Sirs, madam. Please!"
I opened my eyes a slit. A diminutive man, round-faced and stocky, paced nervously in and out of my field of vision. Fat, red suspenders hung loosely from his shoulders, clipped to skintight pantaloons that rasped as he walked. "Won't you wake up? Sirs, madam. Please." He stopped in front of Yhoshi, reached out as if to jiggle him awake, then thought the better of it. He shook his head and resumed pacing.
Beyond him, moored to a post jutting out of the water, floated a small blue-and-white barge, bare but for a tiny, flat-roofed cabin amidships. From atop the cabin, two flags fluttered from a single mast. My eyes jerked open. They were the Castle Rose standards, and though in the story I had seen it only from a distance, through Kyri's eyes, this was that ferry. It bobbed at one end of a wooden quay. I sat at the other, Yhoshi, Fynda and Garan still asleep

next to me. In the gathering light of dawn I could just make out the contours of a hill crowned by a sprawling castle. At that instant, the suns broke through the horizon, burning off the castle's purple shadows and coloring it a sublime, luminescent pink.

"Oh, my heavenly days," said the ferryman, shaking his head once more. He reached the end of the quay, peered into his boat, then swiveled around. His eyes lit on me. "Oh, my," he exclaimed. "Oh my, oh my, oh my. You're awake at last." He lunged toward me, stopping only when his nose was a hair's breadth from mine. "Please," he said, "wake your companions and let us be on our way. I should have departed before suns-rise, and look." He gesticulated wildly at Aygra and B'na, now in full view. "Even at double-stroke, I shall never make up the lost time. Never. Oh, my heavenly days. Wake them, please," he urged. "And on this of all days. Hurry. We must set off at once."

"Set off?" I asked. "Where for?"

"Where for?" The ferryman's arm launched into a manic spin as his voice rose a full octave. "Where for? Where for? Where for? For Castle Rose, of course." His arm stopped in mid-twirl. "Is that not why you wait here on the quay?" He narrowed his eyes and threw me what I took for his sternest look. "It would be a cruel prank indeed if you set out to sleep here knowing I must by law stop for any who wait at Alanda's quays."

The effect was so comical I struggled not to laugh. "Forgive me," I said, half-covering my mouth. "We travel from distant lands and do not know your customs." I chose not to add that there had been no quay beneath us when we had fallen asleep.

"Oh, my heavenly days." The ferryman ran to his boat, began to untie it, shook his head, nodded his head, then shook it again, before resecuring the boat and running back to me. "Oh, my," he said. "Oh my, oh my, oh my." He repeated this exhortation at an increasingly piercing pitch as he dashed indecisively between me and the boat. The commotion finally roused Yhoshi, Garan and Fynda.

"What the —" Yhoshi exclaimed.

"What, indeed," the ferryman muttered as he hopped into the boat and tried to push off with his oar.

"What's happened?" Fynda asked. "Where are we?" She looked up toward the castle then back toward me, her eyes wide with disbelief. When I didn't respond, she nudged Garan and pointed. "Look," she said.

"Wait," I called to the ferryman.

"He's not going anywhere," Yhoshi said to me as the ferryman pushed and pushed and pushed, not realizing his boat was still moored to the pole.

"I am indeed going somewhere," the ferryman countered. He cast a disdainful look at Yhoshi and pushed some more.

I pointed to the crest of the hill. "Is that Castle Rose?" I asked.

The ferryman stopped pushing. "Is that Castle Rose?" he repeated. He reached for the pole to steady himself, dropping the oar into the river. He cursed and leaned over to retrieve it. Too far.

We each grabbed an end of the oar and I pulled the ferryman to shore. He climbed onto the quay, shaking himself like a dog. "Is that Castle Rose? Is that Castle Rose? Is that Castle Rose?"

"Is it?" Garan asked.

"Of course it is. What else would it be?" He looked at me suspiciously. "Who are you that you don't know Castle Rose?"

"Travelers," I said, "from afar. We do seek passage, if you'll take us."

The ferryman scrutinized each of us in turn, as though seeing us for the first time. Satisfied, he untied the boat, climbed in and motioned to us. "Come aboard, then, and be quick with you."

I stepped forward then stopped. "Only —"

"Only what? Only what? Only what?" the ferryman shrieked. "Only what? Have you any idea how late I am? And on this of all days. Only what?"

"We have no coin to pay for the trip."

"No coin?" The ferryman stumbled backward, laughing so hard he couldn't get up again. "No c-c-c-coin?" he sputtered. "No one pays for this ferry, young man. Oh, my heavenly days. What a thought..." Finally, he stood, brushed himself off and picked up the oar. "Well, come aboard and let's be off. No coin," he giggled. "Imagine that. Wait 'til the missus hears."

True Heart of Q'ntana

Seventeen

Fynda gazed dreamily up toward the castle as we climbed the winding road from the ferry dock. With its pink walls and rainbow pennants framed in misty haze, Castle Rose could well have emerged from dream...or story.

"It's just as you described it, Toshar," she said. "How did you know?"

"I didn't. I don't." I shook my head in wonder, no less awestruck than she.

We stopped before the lowered drawbridge and looked back at the river, the barge a distant speck. It hadn't quite carried us to the castle quay when the ferryman, still giggling, noticed the position of the suns. He sobered instantly.

"Oh my heavenly days," he said. "Look at the time...and on this of all days." He barely touched prow to pier before pushing off again, leaving us to scramble ashore as best we could. We stopped at the lowered drawbridge. Yhoshi looked warily across and scanned the castle walls. "Are you sure it's safe?" he asked.

"No," I said, "but it makes no difference." I stepped confidently onto the broad, single plank, certain that whatever lay on the other side would aid us in our quest.

Yhoshi pushed ahead of me, clutching the hilt of his dagger. "Then I'll go first," he said. "You don't have a weapon anymore."

Instinctively, I reached for O'ric's knife and felt nothing. A chill of loneliness shivered through me. All that had accompanied me out of Pre Tena'aa was gone: Oriccan, my ivory moon pendant, even Rykka and Ta'ar.

"Are you coming, Toshar?" Fynda touched my arm. I hadn't realized I'd stopped. I smiled wistfully and took her hand. We passed under the darkened archway of the main tower and toward a central courtyard. At the inner threshold, a sentry, his back toward us, leaned against the stone wall, more intent on the flurry of activity within than threats from without. The courtyard was a massive field of cobble bound by a delicate three-story colonnade of arched galleries. In one corner stood a trestle table replete with breakfast meats and foaming tankards. In another, musicians sat in a circle of wooden stools tuning their harps, lyres and flutes. Everywhere in between, people and creatures of all shapes and sizes scurried about, stringing up cream-and-scarlet bunting, hanging eagle and rose banners, hammering together planks and setting up benches. Many whistled or sang. Others either stopped to watch the jugglers, acrobats and minstrels who circulated through the crowd or stepped aside to avoid the children, who raced among workers, ladders and scaffolding, nearly toppling several.

The sentry turned as we approached. "Quite a scene, eh?" He chuckled but eyed us closely. Yhoshi stared back suspiciously. "The last time there was this much excitement around here must have been…" His eyes darted to the top of his head as a gang of shrieking youngsters bulldozed past and onto the drawbridge. "Why, I was no older than they are. And look at me now." Tufts of white hair pushed out from under his helmet. Though strong, his face was etched with wrinkles and scars.

"That little one there." He waved to a young girl crouching under the refreshment table with her friends. "She's my great-great-granddaughter." Meeting Yhoshi's gaze, he said, "You think I'm too old for guard duty, don't you?" Yhoshi opened his mouth to protest. "No, no. I know you do. You're right. My guard days have long passed, but the young men are needed for all that climbing and clattering in there. He gestured toward the battery of workers. It's been many a season since Castle Rose needed true guards. I'm here more to keep an eye on the little ones." Stepping into the courtyard, he retrieved a purple candy stick from under his tunic. The young girl raced over. He knelt as she plucked it from his hand and pecked his cheek. He rose, turning his attention back to us. "Good news must travel speedily if you've come as far as you have so quickly."

"How do you know where we come from?" Yhoshi asked edgily.

He studied us again, more openly. "Your faces are suns-darkened, and your clothes, what remains of them, are not like ours."

I blushed. It had been so long since we had seen anyone but soldiers, I had forgotten how dirty and bedraggled we looked. "Excuse our appearance," I said, "we've traveled a long way."

"A long, hard way," Garan added.

"You spoke of good news?" I asked.

"Is it Prince Kyri's return?" asked Fynda.

"That and more," the sentry replied. "What a celebration it will be: feasting, festing, fireworks…all day and through the night. We've waited long years for this. Long years." He gazed off into a distant past, lingered there for a moment, then returned to the present. "But we never expected strangers to want to celebrate with us. You're welcome, of course."

"We've come not for the festivities but to see the prince," I said, surprised by my words. "We must meet with him as soon as possible. Today."

Disbelief clouded his face. "Don't you know?" he asked. "Isn't that why you're here?" I stared back blankly. "It's King Kyri you will see." My eyes widened. "But not today. Certainly not today, of all days. He's to be crowned this very suns-merge."

"*King* Kyri?" Garan asked. "King of what? Isn't this part of Q'ntana?"

"It is and it isn't," the sentry replied. "Fvorag calls this the Province of Pyra'aa. We call it the Kingdom of Alanda." He traced a white gash that scarred his left cheek from the bridge of his nose to his jawbone. "The battle that determined that compromise also gave me this. I'm lucky to still have my eye...to still have my head."

"I've never seen Alanda on any maps," Yhoshi said.

"Nor will you," the sentry said, "so long as Fvorag's mapmakers draw them."

"Alanda...named for the river?" I asked.

"Each named for the other," he replied, "so long ago that no one knows which came first."

"What's this compromise?" Yhoshi asked.

The sentry smiled ironically. "We let Fvorag think he's king — as long as neither he nor his men set foot across the river. It was Fvorag the Elder and Fortas, Kyri's father and king until today, who negotiated this fiction. It was that or continue fighting a war that had begun long before either was born, one neither could win."

"I see," I said. But I didn't. Why had I never learned this?

The sentry slapped his hand against his helmet. "But I'm rude," he cried. "I am Kronan, young Kyri's uncle and godfather. You are...?"

"Toshar," I said, "and these are my companions." I completed the introductions. "We travel north on an urgent mission. We didn't know about the coronation. Will it be long do you think, before Kyri can see us?"

Kronan's smile broadened. "Stay and celebrate with us and I'll wield what influence I can to see that you meet with my nephew as soon in the coming days as possible."

The need to speak with Kyri had lodged in my head, but so had the desire to speed toward M'nor's aching call.

"Thank you, Kronan, but we daren't linger."

"As you wish," he said. "At least let me outfit you with food and fresh clothing." Before I could respond he hurried into the crowded courtyard. I looked back toward the drawbridge.

"I know that look," Yhoshi said to Fynda and Garan. "His mind is made up."

"Is it?" Fynda asked. I shrugged. "If your story carried us inside itself to this place, it wasn't an accident. I believe that. Don't you?" I said nothing. "Isn't that why you asked to see Kyri?" It was, and yet... "And if there's no way to see Kyri until tomorrow or beyond, I believe that's no accident either."

I caught a glimpse of the river as the suns glinted off its mirrored surface. Fynda followed my gaze. "Still," she sighed, "if you decide to leave, I'll go with you."

"Me too," said Yhoshi. "But I think you should accept Kronan's offer. We've traveled long and hard, you and I, since leaving Pre Tena'aa. A day's rest, even two, would recharge us. We'd make better time because of it. And..." He hesitated and dropped his eyes to the cobblestones. "There's something to what Fynda says," he mumbled quickly.

I smiled. "Another mutiny? Garan?"

Garan shifted nervously from foot to foot, avoiding my gaze. "I don't pretend that the prospect of a coronation feast and down-filled bed don't tempt me. But that's not why I stay" — he raised his eyes to meet mine — "whatever you decide. Something in your story last night told me we must meet this prince. When it was only a story, I could dismiss it. Now..." He paused. "You once told me to follow my heart, and that's what I mean to do. I also ask you to stay, but for selfish reasons."

I watched my friends watch me, saw the love in their eyes as they patiently awaited my decision. They were more than friends now, and if my story held that much power for them, I needed to look again within myself to find its power for me. Only by staying in Alanda and living out the story could I do that.

"We stay."

Garan breathed out a relieved grin. Fynda squeezed my hand. Yhoshi dove into the crowd, resurfacing moments later with Kronan.

"I thought you might change your mind," Kronan said. He clapped his hands twice and four young pages appeared at his side. One, a red-haired boy with cheeks awash with freckles, latched onto my elbow and propelled me through the courtyard. We crossed into the castle, along an endless corridor carpeted in midnight blue and lined with tapestries, up five flights of winding stairs and, finally, to a heavy oak door. He opened it and motioned me into a turreted bedchamber.

"I'm sorry for this," he said, "but there was no time to prepare anything more." What more could be there be? In the middle of its pink-stone floor, a hot bath, fragrant with oils, steamed invitingly. Next to it stood a low table set with warm breads and cool fruit slices. A cloud of down comforters blanketed the ample four-poster, its canopy a lacy confection of white tulle. Laid out on the bed were three complete outfits of clothing.

"I must go now, to help prepare for the coronation. But if you need anything, anything at all, one pull" — he tugged on an ornate piece of needlework that hung by the bed — "will summon me."

"Thank you," I said, "but I can't imagine needing anything else. What's your name?"

"Miknos, sir." He bowed. "My sister Sorros and brothers Artos and Simmos are looking after your friends."

I smiled and reached out to shake his hand. "Please, no 'sir.' My friends call me Toshar and I hope you'll be among them. Won't you stay? There's so much I want to ask."

Miknos bowed again, grinning shyly. "Thank you, sir...Toshar. Another time, maybe, but not on this —"

"Of all days." I laughed and after a moment's confusion, he joined with me.

When Miknos left, I retrieved the kolai from my pocket. It was warm. I held it in my hand for a moment and placed it on the mantel. Then I peeled off my tattered clothes and flung them into the fire, little caring whether the new ones fit. As I lowered myself into the bath, scented steam rose from the water, eddied around me and soaked into my pores. With a deep, contented sigh, I closed my eyes.

Next I knew, Miknos was gently shaking me awake. I had no memory of quitting bath for bed and was barely conscious of being eased into the finest of the three outfits: black leggings flecked with silver and a powder-blue tunic.

We met Yhoshi, Fynda and Garan — as magnificently attired as I — as we entered the Grand Court. What a transformation. The morning's labors had created a dazzling mélange of pomp and color. Yellow rose petals carpeted the cobblestones, filling the air with their bouquet. More petals, these crimson, climbed three concentric steps to a circular dais that thrust out from the colonnade. At each balustrade stood livery-clad heralds, silver trumpets pressed to their lips. Brilliant pennons hung from each instrument, matching the banners that dressed the pink stone throughout the courtyard. Rows of wooden benches curved around the dais and overflowed out onto the drawbridge and beyond — all packed tightly with buzzing Alandans dressed in their holiday best.

Miknos, Sorros, Artos and Simmos showed us to our seats — in the front row, to my surprise. Next to me, a young woman watched the dais fixedly. She was my age, maybe a year or two younger, and her hair, pinned up with strands of sparkling diamonds and rubies, shone gold as the suns. She flashed me a quick smile then returned her gaze to the platform. Separated from her by an empty chair sat a white-bearded elder whose cloud-like fringe ringed a pale, shiny pate. Their names came to me as I sat with them: she, Dafna; he, Dyffyth. Before I could find out more, a blazing fanfare heralded the emergence of three men from the shadows of the colonnade.

All eyes rested on the first, none more devotedly than those of the girl at my side. A heavy gold crown fringed with scarlet velveteen and studded with flashing sapphires rested on the old king's head. His face could have been Kronan's — gentle, with eyes that sparked the same blue fire as did the jewels in his crown. A silver torque encircled his throat. Suspended from his neck was an orb of creamiest pearl, which hung at the end of a chain of large, ebony links. A snowy mane melded into the ermine cape that trailed far behind him. Peeking through the cape in front were emerald leggings and a tunic of finely linked mail. Each of his fingers bore several rings and each of these held a delicately cut stone that flamed colored lightning as he moved. Only when the procession halted in front of the platform and the king motioned us to sit did I look behind him. I expected to recognize Kyri and I did. But when the figure behind him stepped forward, I gasped.

"It's O'ric," I whispered loudly, poking Yhoshi. There was no time to say more. O'ric raised his arms to the sky and began to speak.

"As the suns unite in crossing the heavens, so do the generations unite before moving apart. This is an ancient rite rarely celebrated, for it is rare that a living king steps aside in favor of his heir. So rare is it that few alive know it. I am honored to be one of them and to have been asked by your esteemed Dyffyth" — he acknowledged the old man — "to take his rightful place before you today."

Sorros and Miknos climbed onto the dais, one from either side, each bearing a white garment draped over an outstretched arm. Artos and Simmos followed behind, carrying lit torches to a stone-circled pyre around which the platform had been built. They threw their torches into the pyre, which erupted in flame, then joined their siblings.

"As Aygra the father meets B'na the son, so Fortas meets Kyri one final time as father-king and prince-son." Kyri knelt before his father then rose into Fortas's embrace as the two suns merged overhead. They separated with the suns and O'ric stepped between them.

"By the ancient laws of succession that rule these lands, I call on Fortas, king, and Kyri, first-born, to relinquish all that they are in order to become all they are destined to be." Slowly and with great dignity, Fortas unclasped his silver cape and passed it to Artos, who staggered under its weight. Then piece by piece, he removed it all, handing each item to the pages assembled around him. Across the platform, Kyri stripped off his princely robes. Soon Kyri stood naked and Fortas bore only his crown. Inhaling deeply, Fortas removed the crown and passed it to O'ric.

"From father to son, from one eagle king to the next," O'ric said, placing the crown on Kyri's head. Artos and the other pages began to dress Kyri in his father's regalia. From the corner of my eye I saw Sorros lead Fortas, now clad in a simple, white robe, to the empty seat next to Dafna. O'ric stood aside while Kyri slowly took on the aspect of his father. But for the prince's smooth face and red hair, they were the same man.

"As the two suns become one in the heavens, so father and son, king and prince, become one on earth," O'ric intoned. Kyri strode to the center of the dais and stood in solemn silence as O'ric continued. "Succession is not sameness, nor is continuity. Just as B'na must separate from Aygra to follow his own path, so must Kyri separate from Fortas and let go all that encumbers him to the old reign."

Once again, Kyri began to shed all that he wore, letting each piece fall to the ground. When he stood naked but for the crown, O'ric placed each item in turn atop the burning pyre, chanting, "The past is passed. We let it go." He repeated the mantra with each addition to the flames, and soon all in the Grand Court found ourselves chanting it with him: "The past is passed. We let it go."

When only the crown remained, Kyri handed it to O'ric. He held it aloft as sunlight danced off the sapphires, then silently added it to the pyre. We saw it for a moment, its gold blazing with reflected fire, before the flames leapt up and devoured it. "The past is passed," O'ric said one last time and turned to Kyri. "Now you are ready to chart your own way as king of this ancient land."

Miknos held out the white robe and Kyri stepped into it. O'ric then placed an unadorned circlet of white gold on Kyri's head and a simple gold torque around his neck. "Long may Alanda prosper through your wisdom. Long may she remain a light in times of darkness. Long may you reign in mercy, sagacity and love." They both faced forward.

"Long live the king!" O'ric shouted. "Long live King Kyri!"

"Long live the king!" we thundered.

Dafna leapt to her feet. "Long live King Kyri!" she sang out, her pale cheeks flushed with excitement. An explosion of cheers and whistles echoed through the courtyard until Kyri raised his arms to still them.

"My friends," he said, now alone on the dais, "I did not expect to become king today. I did not expect to be welcomed back with the warmth and love all have shown me, especially you, my most forgiving and generous father." He climbed down from the dais and over to the old king. Kneeling, he took his father's right hand and raised it to his lips.

Fortas pushed Kyri's hand away. "Rise, my son," he said. "You do me too much honor. It is I who need bow to you, for I am now but one of many loyal subjects."

Kyri placed his hand on his father's shoulder to prevent him from kneeling. "No, father, as long as you live and I am king, you shall not kneel before me. You are not my subject. You are my most loving and beloved father, ever my lord." The crowd erupted and Fortas acknowledged the cheers with obvious discomfort. As they stood side by side in their simple garments of kingship past and kingship emergent, the resemblance between them was even more striking.

A lone voice rose above the commotion, chanting, "Fortas, Fortas. Fortas, king." Soon the call spread, surging through the courtyard until even the stones seemed to join the refrain.

Fortas's jaw clenched and unclenched to the rhythm of the chant. "You see what your homage has wrought?" he hissed through a forced smile. Dafna sat forward and stroked first his hand then Kyri's. "You do me great honor," he called out in a voice that silenced the crowd, "but I am no longer king, nor will be evermore."

A chorus of no's rang through the courtyard.

Fortas shook his head. "You honor me with your continuing love. You will honor me more by transferring it to my son, your new king. I have words to say, father to son, words I would have you all hear." Only the pennants flicking from the corner turrets broke the hush. As he looked into his son's eyes, at the momentary panic that flashed across them, his features softened.

"Do not bow to me, my son. I stand here as the past, and you must never worship the past. Honor me as your father, as a simple subject who is no more meritorious than any of these good people. Honor me most by living *your* reign, by learning the lessons I could not. You called me 'my lord.' The past is not your lord. Set your sights on the future, my son, my king. Set your sights on the future by seeing to the present. Don't, I beg, let your vision linger longingly on the past. Let it go, my son. Let it all go." He embraced Kyri then held him at arm's length before releasing him. "Let me go," he added, so softly that only those seated nearby heard. Then he touched Dafna's cheek and, not looking back, walked through the archway and out of the castle. All eyes followed him, Kyri's first among them.

With Fortas gone, all eyes now fell upon Kyri, judging him, weighing each word and act. Dafna watched him intensely. "My friends," he said quietly, "the ritual speaks true. The past is passed and, with however much distress, we let it go. I let it go."

He strode up to the dais. "The future begins today. This moment. I have much to prove to you to earn your love and trust." His voice rose until it washed over the courtyard and into the sky. "But earn it I will."

A testing silence still reigned. He continued, speaking softly. "None of you is my subject." A wave of confused murmurs burbled around us. "I am yours. I am your servant and together we serve Alanda, today and forever." Heads nodded. Kyri's voice cut through the rising buzz of approval. "There is but one way to mark a new beginning: with a feast. The castle gates are open to all. Long live Alanda."

"Long live Alanda," we called back.

"Long live Alanda," he shouted again.

"Long live Alanda," we roared, even louder.

"Long live Alanda...." He paused. "True heart of Q'ntana."

For a full minute no one moved or spoke. It was as though everyone waited for the demons unleashed by that last cry to destroy them all. Then, as one, the crowd lobbed volley after volley of cheers at him until the stones beneath us shook with anticipation.

"True heart of Q'ntana," I whispered. "We're home."

Eighteen

The feasting continued through the day and long into the night. Tray after tray of roasted meats, succulent fruits and savory delicacies flowed in an unending stream from the castle's cavernous kitchens, as did bronze rivers of ale foaming up over the lids of pewter tankards. On the dais, tireless fiddlers sawed reel after jig after trot as Alandans swirled, spun and flung themselves from partner to partner in fevered revelry. The merrymaking extended beyond courtyard, castle walls and moat and out onto the lawns that sloped down to the river. There, jugglers tossed flaming daggers, colored balls and each other, musicians blew, bleated and strummed, and young soldiers — men and women alike — jousted in public displays of horsemanship and swordplay. While adults danced, picnicked or strolled along the riverbank, children made their own fun. They dove into the moat and chased the swans, hopped up the castle road in one-legged races and tore through corridors and along battlements in a never ending whirl. Eventually, most ended up at the ale table, where they stole quick swigs and scurried off, unaware of the foam mustaches that betrayed them. Once darkness fell, exploding spiders burst through the sky, their glittering limbs painting a shifting palette of hues on the blackened night.

I tried to enjoy myself. Maybe I tried too hard. Maybe I didn't try hard enough. My mind leapt beyond this night, beyond Castle Rose and to the next turning in the road, and to the turnings after that. What lay ahead? Whatever it was, it worried me. I roamed the castle and its grounds, pretending to bask in the revelry. In fact, I searched for Kyri and O'ric, hoping to pull one or the other aside to plan the future. I never found O'ric and only once saw Kyri, Dafna on his arm, surveying the celebration from under a third-story arch. But by the time I swam through the sea of dancers, up the stairs and along the corridor, they had moved on. I leaned over the balustrade and glumly watched the festivities. Now and again, I glimpsed a familiar face as the dancing swept it into the amber flicker of torch light. There was Yhoshi. He cut a fine figure in his white-ruffed terra cotta tunic as he swung breathlessly from one outstretched arm to the next in a snaking necklace of shifting partners. Was that the ferryman, his red suspenders flapping as he flung himself into the buxom embrace of a well-padded matron? His missus? She pitched him to the next link in the fluid chain and opened her arms to Garan, who flew at her, his single tuft of hair manically askew.

"Come, Toshar. Come dance with me." I hadn't heard Fynda's approach. She stood next to me, eyes bright, cheeks bela red, firelight glinting off the tiny gold sequins sewn into spirals on her emerald gown. A turquoise comb pinned her hair up, but dance-loosened strands dangled over her brow. She brushed them aside as she spoke. "Won't you dance, even with me?"

I continued to scan the crowd below and shook my head. "Not with the Lady Gwna herself," I said. "I must find O'ric. Something terrible is going to happen here. I just know it. If only I could talk to him, or to Kyri."

Fynda rested her elbows on the stone rail and her chin on her hands. "If disaster is coming," she said, "this may be Kyri's last night of cheer. Let him have it." She tugged my hand. "Come, share it with him — and me. Open your heart to some laughter."

I forced a smile and shook my head. "Go back down and laugh enough for both of us. I'll watch from here for a while then go to bed."

It was seven days before Kyri sent for us — mornings of late, lingering lie-ins, breakfasting on aromatic broth and steaming bread; days of meandering strolls, lazy picnics and floating daydreams on river rafts; nights of clear velvet shot through with starry plumes. It was just the restorative Yhoshi had predicted, once I released myself into it. Each meal, each swim, each walk, each sleep washed away more of my dread, though it was six days before I stopped inquiring after O'ric and wondering when the king would call for us. Vacant smiles were all that greeted my queries. Even the four pages, who continued to see to our needs, remained politely guarded. And the ferryman, who we often encountered by the river, could manage little more than, "Oh, my heavenly days," before vaulting into his barge and hurriedly sailing off.

When the summons finally came, it burst into my still-darkened room in the person of Miknos, who shook me awake, poured me into the camouflage shades of a traveling outfit and led me through a maze of sleeping corridors to a pair of mighty copper doors. Fynda, Yhoshi and Garan, propelled by Sorros, Artos and Simmos, joined us moments later. Etched into the doors, which rose the height of four men, were square panels depicting scenes from every corner of Q'ntana. A circle in the center spanned both doors. Within it stood Castle Rose, eagle standard flying from its central tower, the whole watched over by a smiling moon. Miknos tapped a complex sequence involving a half-dozen panels, then laid his right palm on the moon. The doors swung open. Inside, at the head of a massive oval table of polished pearl, sat Kyri, flanked by O'ric and Dyffyth. An immense brick fireplace, flames groping greedily up the chimney, framed them.

"Come, my friends. Come." Kyri beckoned us in, at the same time signaling a trio of servants who bustled in behind us bearing trays of food and drink. "I've waited impatiently for this moment." I must have betrayed my surprise, for he grinned boyishly. "I would have missed my own coronation feast to talk to you. But wiser heads urged patience.

He signaled for the pages and servants to retreat. When the doors swiveled shut behind them, Kyri continued. "O'ric has told me all about your journey," he said. "This is good, for we have a lot to discuss and little time."

"Little time?" Garan asked anxiously. His gaze shifted from Kyri to O'ric to me.

"Yes," O'ric replied. "I have allowed you all the time I dared."

"What do you mean?" I asked.

"Your journey and Kyri's words have provoked much. Even if I believed you could spare a further delay, this would not be a secure place to spend it. Alanda is no longer safe from Fvorag's wrath."

"What about the treaty?" Yhoshi asked.

Dyffyth glanced up from the papers that had been occupying him. His eyes, the color of the flames behind him, seemed to burn all the more intensely for the parchment translucence of his skin. "The treaty is dead," he said, then returned his gaze to his papers. It was the first and last time I heard him speak.

"Fvorag will surely try to punish us now," Kyri explained. "Even if he doesn't, I am king now. I can't sit by idly while he terrorizes Q'ntana. Better to be destroyed than to watch truth be destroyed all around us."

Garan leapt up. "If we're the cause of your danger," he exclaimed, "we must stay and help you fight." Dyffyth stared into Garan's face with such fiery eyes that he blushed and turned away. "Mustn't we?"

I said nothing, torn by conflicting desires to stay and leave.

"The time to fight will come," O'ric said. "The time to part is now." Pain streaked Garan's face. I thought he would explode. "You will see Alanda again," O'ric said. "But your MoonQuest is the only way to insure that there remains an Alanda to be seen.

Rays of early morning light slanted through leaded panes on either side of the table. They formed a cross of beams that met over a mirror-polished obsidian chalice at the table's center. As the crossed beams shifted away from the cup, O'ric pulled it toward him with the crook of his staff.

"This wine from Alanda's ancient and holy vineyards has been consecrated this day by Aygra and B'na, whose union reminds us of the oneness of M'nor." He handed the cup to Kyri. "We drink from it now to bind ourselves to M'nor and to this land she has not forgotten."

Kyri cradled the chalice lovingly before drinking from it and passing it on. It came to me last. I inhaled the fruity vapors then drank, leaving some wine at the bottom, as was the custom. When I tried to return the cup to O'ric he refused it.

"The final sip will be taken by M'nor, in the right and perfect moment. Until that time, you must keep this chalice, The Nayr." As he spoke its name, bolts of emerald, ruby and sapphire sparked from it then ignited it. The Nayr flamed for a moment, brighter than the fire in the grate, then returned to its burnished blackness.

"I can't," I said, remembering the fate of O'ric's knife. "It's too valuable."

"You can and must," replied O'ric. "It's value lies not in its aspect but how it serves. It will serve you when the time comes."

We would leave, then, and soon. Questions raced through my head. Sheaves and sheaves of them, and I feared the answers would remain behind us, here in the castle. I longed to know more of Kyri and Alanda, more of the state of Q'ntana...of Pre Tena'aa...of Eulisha and the other bards. Before I could open my mouth to ask, O'ric pierced me with a knowing look that touched off a tingling though still-ineffable dream memory. With mental fingers I tried to reach back into the night and touch the images, but they eluded my grasp. I let out a silent cry of frustration. The memory was there, but it hid behind a veil of darkness I couldn't penetrate. All I could recall was Eulisha's presence...or was it her absence? I shook my head, trying to clear the tendrils masking my mind's eye.

"You have the answers you seek, Toshar," O'ric said. "They are not clear now, but they will come." He stood and bade me take the cup and follow him to the window, where a rainbow of sunlight poured through the cut glass and into the chalice. "Look inside, into the cup, into what remains of the wine."

As I did, a flood of light exposed a dream-memory that nearly dissolved again in the cascade of tears it triggered.

A rolling thunderclap of hooves shakes the ground as wave after wave of black-shirts, black masks and black mounts surges through the black night.

Roaring...crashing...booming...louder...louder...louder...

I cover my ears to muffle the sound.

The only light sparks off mirrored sword blades, slashing, slashing, slashing until blood sheathes them in sticky darkness. My hands press more tightly still against my ears, trying to deaden the slaughterhouse shrieks, against my mouth, trying to stifle my own screams. I hear it all, see it all...know it all.

Eulisha is dead. Gwill'm is dead. Those of his people not slain are swept back to the capital as slaves. The other bards escape. Zakk leads them to safety. They owe their lives to him and name him Elderbard. But they don't see what I see. I see Zakk and a masked officer. Together. Laughing together. They plan the raid, the slaughter.

I see...I see...a younger officer, a younger Zakk...another meeting, another time. I see myself sneaking out after Zakk. It's late. Everyone sleeps. It's a game, like hide-and-seek. Zakk slips out to hide. I seek. Only he doesn't know I seek. He tiptoes out, his head jerking left to right, left to right. Furtive. Secretive. No one must know. But I know. What do I know?

I tiptoe after him, past the chamber where my parents sleep, through the cookery, where a dog dream-whimpers from his bed by the stove, past the hut where Eulisha sleeps, past all the bards...past and through and past. Distant past. Past trees that no longer stand. Into dreams long ago buried.

Zakk creeps through our village-in-hiding, up the wooded slopes that rise behind it, light-footed as an antelope. Where does he go? I grin. I will know. No one else will know, but I will know. I'm aware of each crackling twig, each nayla howl, each whir of flot-wings as we climb higher and higher. To the top of the mountain. I know these slopes. I've explored here often. But never over the mountain. It's dangerous to come this far. Dangerous and forbidden. I hesitate. Zakk continues. Should I follow? I look back. I've come too far not to follow. I no longer hear him. Have I lost him? No, I sense movement ahead. Coming toward me! I leap behind a tree trunk just as a man creeps past. He's all in black and I can barely see him. A soldier! The night swallows him.

I look for Zakk but see nothing. Fear slithers over me. Have we been discovered? Again? Will we have to flee? Again?

I crouch, frozen in place. I don't know whether to run back and wake my father, stay and warn Zakk or... Movement again. Zakk. Relief floods through me. I step out to intercept him, then stop.

"There you are, Holgg. I was halfway down the mountain looking for you. You're late."

"I'm here. I'm here." Zakk and the black-shirt are so near I can almost touch them from where I stand. I hold my breath and try to disappear into a mound of dead leaves.

"Well then, what does the king say?"

"That you are as clever as Bo'Rá K'n himself," Holgg chuckles.

"Does he ratify my plan? Do we proceed?"

"He says it is not yet time."

Zakk paces away then turns back. "Not yet time?" he asks angrily. "The time is ideal. How much longer must we wait?"

"Until the king decides the time is right."

"Until Bo'Rá K'n tells the king the time is right."

"Whatever." Holgg shrugs. "I know my orders and I know yours." His voice rises. "Shall I tell the king you dispute them?"

I feel the heat of rising tempers and shrink deeper into the leaves.

"He's a fool," Zakk breathes, then clamps his mouth shut. Holgg says nothing. Silence. Can they hear my heart pounding? I don't understand what's happening. I'm afraid to understand what's happening.

"Be patient," Holgg says at last. "You will be Elderbard at the king's right hand. You have the king's word."

"And what's that worth?"

Holgg's voice is gruff. "You've come too far to question it now, bard. Are you with me or do I wipe out the lot of you this night. That's my choice. What's yours?"

"Easy, Holgg." Zakk's manner reverts to its familiar charm. Before this moment I have never seen beneath it. For the first time, he frightens me. "Of course I'm with you. Only a fool would cross the king, and neither of us is a fool."

"As long as you know that."

"I do. But..."

"But what? I must get back before suns-rise."

"What of my brother? He grows dangerous."

"Agreed. The plan you set out is already in motion. Leave it with me and your hands will be clean."

I gasp. My hand rushes to my mouth, to push back the sound that has escaped.

"What was that?" Holgg draws his dagger and steps toward the tree. If I reach around it I can touch the tip of its blade. Panicked, I seek an escape. There is none.

"Just a k'nrah nesting in the leaves," Zakk replies. But he too looks around warily. "What else could it be?"

"Someone up to no good, that's what." Holgg is almost upon me.

"Just a k'nrah," Zakk repeats.

"Then its pelt will make a good hat for winter." With that, Holgg plunges his dagger into the mound of leaves.

"No," I cry, leaping out from my hiding place.

With a roar that drives leaves down from the trees, Zakk pulls me toward him. "What's this?" he bellows. I gag at his sour breath and cower, covering my face.

"You know this boy?"

Zakk rips my hands from my face and spins me around. "My brother's son," *he spits. "Toshar."*

"If this is a ruse, if this boy is here with your knowledge…"

"Don't be a fool." Zakk grips my left shoulder so tightly I fear the bone will *snap.*

"You had better not be play-acting, bard," Holgg says through clenched teeth, *his dagger still at the ready.*

"Nor you, boy," Zakk hisses.

"More than your brother is dangerous," Holgg says. "Your whole family is a *threat. If I had my way —"*

"I know. But you don't, no more than I."

Holgg presses his dagger to my throat. "He will have heard everything. He *must be killed."*

With his free hand, Zakk pushes Holgg away. "And force us to a new hiding *place? That will ruin our plan. Leave him to me."*

"He'll talk."

"Not when I'm through with him."

"He must not live."

"You are as big a fool as the king," Zakk mutters under his breath. Aloud, he *says with that charm I know now to be false, "He's a bigger threat to me than to* *you. I promise I'll take care of him, my way. Leave him to me." Holgg grunts. "The* *suns will soon be up. Go now. You needn't fear him. He won't talk. I promise."*

Holgg slices his dagger through the air in front of my nose. "Next time," he *spits, "you won't be so lucky."*

Zakk holds me still until Holgg's last crunching footstep fades into the night. *For a moment, all I sense is Zakk's chest, expanding and contracting against my* *back. Then he spins me around with such force my shoulder blade wrenches from* *my body. It's dark. No stars pierce the canopy of leaves. But Zakk's fury flares* *through the night and I see his face clearly, more clearly than ever before. His* *eyes are slits of icy hatred. His lips curl into a malevolent sneer. A tiny stream of* *spittle drips down from the corner of his mouth. Without tearing his gaze from my* *face, he snaps a branch from the tree. I hear it whistle, hear the crack of wood on* *fabric, never on flesh. Over and over I hear the stinging smack until it becomes* *one continuous, deafening burst of thunder. I must be flinching, but after the first* *or tenth or twentieth lash, I feel nothing. I bite my lip, willing the noise to stop,* *trying to hold back tears of fear not pain. I will not cry, I repeat. I keep wanting* *to die, waiting to die. But I'm not even bleeding. Zakk says nothing, just raises* *his arm again and again in a blinding, unremitting blur, the branch whining* *through the air before it smacks down one more time — on my legs, on my back,* *on my chest, on my arms, on my backside. Limb upon limb. It never stops, never* *stops, never stops, never stops…*

The pain...it's as though my body is experiencing it for the first time. I flinch, stagger, let go what I'm holding. A cup?

A hand reaches out to steady me. I blink and the images fall away like shards of shattered mirror. The spell is broken.

"Quick," O'ric said, thrusting the cup to my lips," drink the wine down. It will fix the memory in your heart." The others pushed toward me, but O'ric held them off.

Tears coursed down my cheeks. "Was it all true?"

"That and more," O'ric nodded and led me back to the table.

"Was what true?" Yhoshi asked.

Fynda reached for my arm. "Are you all right?" She turned to O'ric. "Is he all right?"

"It's Zakk," Garan said fiercely. "I know it is."

"Zakk," I said weakly. "I knew, O'ric. I knew it all. How could I know and do nothing?"

O'ric wrapped his arm around me and my tears soaked his sleeve. "You knew but did not know. Zakk planted a thicket of brambles between you and your knowing. There was no way through, until now."

"Now that it's too late," I sobbed.

"It is never too late."

"But Eulisha...Gwill'm..."

"Their time had come to an end. Yours is beginning."

Kyri yanked insistently on a bell pull by the fireplace. "I'll send for more wine," he said.

I swallowed my tears and touched the rim of The Nayr. "No, I'm all right. It's best I tell you what I saw while I remember it."

"With that sip of wine you will remember it always, for better or ill," O'ric said. I sank into my seat and let my head drop into my hands. O'ric motioned to Miknos, who hovered uncertainly in the doorway. "Fetch something stronger than wine, but be quick about it." Miknos turned to go. "Wait. Are the horses and provisions ready?"

Miknos nodded. "In the rear court as his majesty ordered. Everything is ready."

O'ric touched my left shoulder and I felt the reawakened pain of Zakk's long-ago grip fade. "Meet us in the rear courtyard with a flask of spirits," he said to Miknos. "Our travelers depart directly."

One Out of Time

Nineteen

My weakness fled the moment I saw what awaited me in the rear court. Breaking free of O'ric's support and brushing away Miknos's flask, I flung myself at Rykka. Yhoshi followed close behind and threw his arms around Ta'ar.

"I knew I'd see you again," I cried, stroking the lightning bolt that streaked down Rykka's nose. She shook her head and cobalt sparks flashed from her mane.

"They turned up yesterday," Kyri said. "Dafna found them grazing outside the castle walls." As he spoke her name, Dafna entered the court leading a chestnut mare and mahogany stallion. This morning her loose hair cascaded to her waist, rippling over a powder blue dress embroidered with a pattern of moon and stars.

"Have you met my sister, Toshar?" Kyri asked. Dafna smiled and her green eyes deepened as for an instant they locked with mine. His sister? For all my inner knowing, I had labeled her his queen-to-be. I stammered a reply then blushed. Kyri ignored my discomfort.

"These are yours for as long as you need them," he said as Dafna presented the mare to Fynda and stallion to Garan. "Corem," he said to Fynda "my favorite." Fynda smiled shyly and her face glowed with pleasure. "And for you, Garan, Merek. I know he will serve you well on your journey."

Garan crossed his arms and set his mouth in a pout. "I'm not going," he said. "I'm sorry, Toshar, but for the first time since Kemet, I feel at home. My place is here now, and I intend to stay and defend it..." He faced Kyri. "If you'll have me."

"Prithi knows I would welcome your courage here, Garan. But what about your companions? What about your MoonQuest?"

Grief threatened to crack Garan's composure. He looked longingly at Kyri. "If you command me to go..."

"I command nothing, Garan. You're a man of free will. As for me, though, I trust O'ric when he says it's a time for parting." Garan's face fell. "Just as I trust him when he says you'll be back."

In the end, Garan chose to continue with us. I was glad but understood his sorrow. I too felt Alanda's pull. But leave we did, and in short order.

"Remember the power of The Four As One," O'ric said as we guided our pack-laden mounts into the tunnel that was the only exit from the rear court. He offered no other guidance, no sense of what lay ahead. The power of The Four. At least we still numbered four.

Garan remained silent as we rode through the long tunnel. When we emerged he gazed back wistfully. We all did. But Castle Rose was nowhere in sight. Even the opening through which we had just passed melted into the hillside behind us. Garan's eyes glistened and I noticed a new softness about him. The Garan I recalled from my childhood and the Garan I had reencountered at Horusha merged in new ways. Some of his creases and wrinkles had smoothed over. Others seemed less furrowed. A few more tufts of hair had sprouted from the top of his head, which now seemed in cleaner proportion to the rest of his body. Had we all changed? Yhoshi's face was firmer, more manly, and not only from shaving off his boyish beard and mustache. It exuded a strength and maturity that flowed outward, from beneath his skin. Fynda, too, looked calmer, more assured...more joyful. The hardness had melted from her face, revealing a beauty that surprised me with its intensity.

What about me? What did I look like? When we next stopped at a stream, I peered curiously at my reflection. My hair was longer now, pulled away from my face in a ponytail secured with a pyynch'n stem. Unlike Yhoshi, I had freed my beard to grow and it added a wisdom to my face that my eyes reaffirmed. Those eyes, jet black as my hair and beard, gazed into me with a depth of knowingness my mind could not begin to grasp. What did I know? At that moment, only that the Toshar of Pre Tena'aa was a stranger I had left behind. Who now filled this wiser-seeming body? No answer emerged from the water. I didn't know this Toshar any better than I had known the other.

Rykka led us into a meadow dotted with buttercups still sparkling with morning dew, and northward toward a silvery glint of water. The suns rose higher as galleon-shaped clouds sailed by on a westerly breeze. For all the ground we covered, the water remained far distant, farther than it had appeared when we first set out. Then, Yhoshi had estimated a half-day's travel at most to reach it. Now, as we descended the steep slope of a granite steppe, I could see the visual tricks the landscape had played. The band of light had vanished behind a thick veil of green, itself separated from us by a dry, rusty canyon. When some time later we reached the lip of the canyon, we paused, contemplating the narrow trail that plunged down one cliff and scaled up the other. We could navigate the trail on foot or detour eastward to a vine-lashed bridge that swayed drunkenly over the canyon in the middle distance.

"It doesn't look very sturdy," Fynda said doubtfully. "Look how it swings in the wind."

Garan stared across the canyon then sniffed the air. "There is no wind," he said, his first words since leaving Castle Rose.

If not the wind... We strained for a closer look. Soldiers. Soldiers on horseback. A snakelike column of black that thrust across the bridge and curled in our direction. Had they spotted us?

"Quick," said Yhoshi, "into the canyon." We dismounted and pulled the horses as quickly as we dared down the steep grade. Rocky outcrops jutted out all around us, but none offered enough concealment.

We were running out of time. The first thunder of hoofbeats drummed toward us.

"In here," Yhoshi urged. He guided Ta'ar under a protruding table rock and we followed.

Silence. Had the soldiers ridden off? Did they camp nearby? We waited in impotent frustration and fear. Finally, Yhoshi and I climbed back up. We moved cautiously, testing each surface before placing any weight upon it. If King's Men were still about, we didn't want falling rocks seizing their attention.

King's Men were still about. We heard them as we hid under a ledge near the top.

"See anything? ... Neither do I. ... I was told they would come this way." That voice. I knew that voice, and I knew the face that went with it. Holgg's threatening leer, still fresh from this morning's rekindled memory, flashed before me. How had he known to look here for us? Were there spies in Alanda? Or did Zakk's power extend beyond my pendant.

A heavy footfall thudded overhead. Another voice, a different voice: "With all the men we have, sir, we could conduct a thorough search down there."

"I should have killed him when I had the chance," Holgg muttered.

"Pardon, sir?"

"Nothing. A search is pointless. We don't know if they're here and hiding or have come and gone." Holgg's voice dropped to a confidential hush. "All these men — it's too cumbersome. I said from the start it was a mistake. How can we surprise anyone with a mounted battalion of one hundred? 'There are only four,' I said. 'Let me take ten of my best men and swiftest horses.' You don't know what he's like when his mind's made up. 'Ten men couldn't capture them when they were two,' he said. What does he know? He wasn't there, and he isn't here." He paused. "What's that?"

A third voice spoke, too quietly for us to hear.

"Brilliant, Vix," Holgg replied. "It will keep most of the men busy while the three of us and five others — you pick them, Vix — ride after them. I'm sure they're already well ahead."

The voices trailed and when all was silent, we crept back to the others.

"What if one of us acts as a decoy to distract their attention?" Yhoshi asked. "That might give the others time to get away."

"Might," I said. "It's a desperate idea."

Garan looked anxiously down the canyon. "Aren't we desperate?" he asked.

"I don't like the idea of separating. Whatever power we have is in remaining together." Yet what other choice did we have? Shouted orders blew toward us in a gust of wind that seemed to pull time away with it as it breathed past. If we didn't do something...

"Remember the power of The Four." I heard O'ric's voice as though he stood next to me. But how to exercise it against a such a threat? I thrust my hands into my pockets, ready to surrender to Yhoshi's plan, though I knew it to be hopeless. My hand touched cool marble. Red veins throbbed warmly through it. I withdrew the kolai and held it in my open palm.

"It saved us once before," I said.

"And didn't, once," Yhoshi said.

Fynda pulled out her kolai. "We have nothing to lose."

"Nothing but time," said Yhoshi.

Nothing but time. Boots and falling rocks clattered toward us from above. Four polished stones stared up at me from four outstretched hands. Could these inert pieces of marble truly help? If we took the time to try, there would be no time for Yhoshi's plan. Fynda reached for my hand. I pulled back. Why did I still doubt? "Do you really think a diversion could work?" I asked Yhoshi.

"No guarantees," he said. Never any guarantees. I craved certainty, but there was none. Still unsure, I accepted Fynda's hand, completing the circle. Power surged through me, diluting my fear. The power of The Four As One. O'ric was right.

"Now what?" Garan whispered.

"Wait," I said. I pulled my hands free and rummaged in Rykka's saddlebag. The others opened their eyes. The thud of heavy boots drew nearer.

"Hurry," urged Garan.

I returned to the circle carrying The Nayr, into which I had poured a small quantity of wine. "We need to call on all the things of power we have,"

I said. I lifted the cup over my head and called out as loudly as I dared, "I summon the power of The Nayr, the power of the kolai and the power of The Four as One to guide us through this danger." We each sipped from the cup and I placed it in the center of the circle. "Now," I said. "Now, we're ready."

Eyes closed, I strained against my fear, trying to focus only on stilling the commotion I heard outside, felt inside. The sound dulled for an instant and then a voice burst through.

"There! Under that rock."

Under that rock...under that rock...under that rock...

The echo faded into an eerie silence split by the caw of a crow high overhead.

I opened my eyes and a rush of despair flooded through me. Nothing had changed. No miracle had transported us to safety. Now what?

Yhoshi sat still as the stone around us. "Listen," he whispered.

"To what?" I asked. "There's nothing to hear."

"Exactly." He stepped out from the rock's shelter. "Come," he said. "Look."

Garan followed first. "At what?" he asked.

I scanned the canyon and along the cliff top. "At the soldiers who aren't there," I said, incredulously. Something else was different. More than the silence. More than the absence of soldiers. The crow cawed by again, a black speck against the cloud-studded sky.

"Suns!" Garan burst out. He jumped up and down, waving his arms excitedly, tripping over his words. "Look," he finally sputtered. "Up." I did and with a start saw what he saw. The positions of the suns had altered. Backward.

"Time has shifted," I whispered. "There are no soldiers because they aren't here yet."

For a moment no one spoke. It didn't seem possible. Yet there were the suns, where they had no right being. And where were the soldiers?

Bards of old declared that time does not follow the trajectory of an arrow pulled from its bowstring. To them it is a spiral of misty tendrils with no fixed boundaries, where ages past and future curve alongside the present, sometimes overlapping, sometimes traveling side-by-side with no contact. The suns, they taught, may move quickly across the skies for one man, yet move not at all for another. Those were teachings of another era, near-forgotten teachings that had never touched my experience until this MoonQuest. Now, again, I had encountered time's fluidity as it doubled back on itself, for us but not for Holgg's troops.

The truth of it took some moments to digest. When it had, I whooped with relieved delight and pulled Fynda into a boisterous jig, the dance we never danced at Castle Rose. Yhoshi and Garan joined in and to the bemusement of the horses we whirled and twirled and spun — as freely as we could in the little space we had — until we collapsed in a laughing, panting heap on the ground.

"We're safe!" Garan hollered into the canyon, which pitched his words back at us again and again.

"Shhh," I said, suddenly, soberly. How much time had we gained? Or how little? "The soldiers may be near enough to hear," I whispered. "They could arrive at any moment."

"Then let's get out of here before they do," Yhoshi said. He called to Ta'ar and began down the canyon trail.

"Wait," I said. "The Nayr." I turned around, then around again. But for a fading purple ring, the rock surface was bare. The chalice was gone. First O'ric's dagger, now his cup. "I'm surprised I haven't lost the kolai," I berated myself silently, then thrust my hand into my pocket to make sure I still had it. Had I needed to use the cup? Could we have saved ourselves without sacrificing it? What would O'ric say? That there were no answers didn't stop me from repeating the questions until my head ached.

Twenty

Time had shifted, but it didn't stand still. The suns continued their celestial progress as though nothing had altered. Perhaps for them, nothing had. For us, still dazed by the power of the kolai to tinker with the reality we had long taken for granted, something more than our perception of time had changed. As we descended deeper into the the canyon, cautiously guiding Rykka, Ta'ar, Corem and Merek over and around giant boulders jagged with knifepoint shards, we paused frequently to study the sky. So well had we memorized the suns' previous positions that the slightest variation in their course would have attracted our notice. But Aygra and B'na, oblivious to our scrutiny, remained true to their trajectory. They moved together then apart as morning melted into afternoon into dusk. And we moved as quickly as we dared, never certain when time might present us with the missing battalion. Twilight found us climbing the opposite face of the canyon, tired but determined to make our way to the top and into the forest before stopping for the night.

Twilight...that time of half shadows when even night eyes can't be certain what they see...

Fynda saw him first — or thought she did, for one moment the dark bundle was a cluster of rocks stacked against a larger bundle. The next, it was a pile of dark clothing. The next... Fynda gasped. Her free hand clutched at her throat as the pile of clothes tried vainly to lift itself up.

"Who goes there?" it called in a voice strained and tight.

Knife drawn, Yhoshi thrust Ta'ar's reins into Garan's startled face and lunged toward the crumpled body. "I've waited a long time for this," he hissed, his blade-tip aimed into the black-shirt's mouth.

"No, Yhoshi. Wait." I hastened toward them. "He's hurt."

"He'll be more than hurt when I'm through with him."

"Who are you, soldier? What are you doing here?" I asked. The soldier moved his face away from Yhoshi's knife, but Yhoshi's knife followed. "Let him answer, Yhoshi."

"Why? He'll only lie." But he grudgingly moved his blade free of the soldier's mouth.

"Why do you lie in wait for us?"

"I lie in wait for no one," he replied, "unless it's for the crow of death to pick at my bones." He winced as he tried to sit up. "My leg, I think it's broken. I took a bad fall. When they saw I couldn't move, they took my horse and rode off."

"Who? When?"

"My fellow soldiers."

"That's awful." Compassion overrode fear as Fynda rushed to his side.

His shoulders rose and fell in a painful half-shrug. "I would have done the same."

"Oh." Fynda recoiled.

Yhoshi pressed his blade closer to the soldier's face. "Let me find out what he knows."

"So you can kill me? I'm not afraid to die. I was trained to die — to kill and to die. You don't frighten me." He pushed Yhoshi's hand away and turned to me. "This one frightens me."

"I do?"

"You're the one we were seeking. They still seek you, wherever they are. Until now, all I knew was that you were a traitor and must be stopped. Now I see into your eyes and know that whatever you are, you won't be stopped. *I* can't stop you," he said for Yhoshi's benefit. "I'm not sure even King Fvorag could stop you now."

"Why do you say that?"

He half-shrugged again. "I don't know."

"Is that why I frighten you?"

"No," the soldier laughed. "King's Men don't frighten, or give up, that easily." He coughed, and blood sputtered from his mouth. "No, I'm frightened by what I see in your eyes." I looked away. "It's too late. I've seen it."

"What?" I whispered.

"Power, but that's not what frightens me." He paused, trying to understand his own thoughts. "It's your blindness." He nodded, satisfied with his cleverness. "That's what it is — your blindness to your own power. That's what frightens me." He paused again. "It would frighten you too if you weren't so blind," he added with a trace of scorn. Another cough thrust itself up through his chest, a painful, wracking wheeze that shook his body. When it subsided, he flicked his hands dismissively. "Now you know all I know. Go where you must. I can't stop you. Go and leave me to die."

"Enough," Yhoshi roared. "I don't know what he's on about, but he's a soldier, a black-shirt, one of Fvorag's finest. This is a ruse, a trap." He seized the soldier's shoulders and shook them violently. "Where are they?" he shouted. "Where are the others? Where's the ambush?"

With a single touch on his arm, I stilled him.

"But —"

"He wants to die. You help him by bringing that moment closer."

"Well spoken, bard." The soldier spoke, but it was not his voice. This voice was clear, undistorted by pain.

My eyes met his. Though night had fallen, light flickered deep within them. I caught the light and held it. As I did, I saw beyond this one soldier and into a vast universe of light. The light poured through and around him, a golden glow that illuminated the truth of the soldier's words. My power. My blindness. My fear. Slowly the light faded. There was more to this man than his uniform, more to him than his allegiance, more to him than his darkness.

"You will not kill him, Yhoshi. Whatever was done to you was not his doing. You and I will bind his leg and make him comfortable. In the morning we'll get him to the top. From there, I don't know. He can't come with us, but we can't leave him to die. For now, though... Fynda, take Garan up to the forest and gather some firewood, and something for a splint, if you can find it."

"No!" Garan's voice shattered the shocked silence that greeted my decision. "No," he whispered. "Please, Toshar, no. It's too dangerous. What if Yhoshi's right? What if it is an ambush? I can't be captured again. I can't be tortured again. I've borne all I can bear. I can't bear anymore. I can't, Toshar. I can't." Tears coursed along the furrows that scored his face and he trembled with fevered panic.

"Do you trust me, oldest friend?"

Garan nodded. "It's not you I distrust. It's him." He pointed a trembling finger at the shadowy hulk, which now, again, resembled a pile of stones.

"If you trust me, you must trust him. There is no other way."

"I'm frightened," Garan whispered.

"Me too," I confessed, "but I trust what I saw in his eyes — just as Eulisha trusted what Zakk would not when we first encountered Heraff. Go with Fynda. This is right, I know it."

My faith, so steady now, wavered through this MoonQuest like a candle flame in the breeze. At this moment, the wind had stilled and trust came easily. In the next, who could tell?

Reluctantly, Garan let Fynda lead him past the soldier and up the cliff path. They blended almost instantly into a darkness so complete it swallowed not only sight but sound. After a time, I heard no breath, not even my own.

The fire changed all that. The fire changed everything. When its flickering glow illuminated the scene, we found ourselves alone. It was as though flesh and bone had evaporated and the uniform that had hung from them had collapsed in on itself. Yhoshi said nothing, but I knew what he thought. My certainty wavered. Had it been a trap? Were we now in danger because of what I thought I'd seen?

"We'll have to leave right away," Yhoshi said. "Fynda can lead."

Fynda nodded. Mutely, she untied Corem and began up the path, slowing as she passed the soldier's place. Then, with a sharp intake of breath, she stopped. "I-I think you'd better come here."

The uniform was gone. In its place lay a white cape glittering with gold. "I knew it," I whispered. "That was no ordinary soldier."

Garan edged forward. "Are you sure?"

Yhoshi snorted. "He came back for his clothes and snuck off to warn the others. I knew it was a trap."

I picked up the cape. Firelight glinted off its satiny surface. "What about this?"

"I don't know. Maybe he was sitting on it. I still say it was a trap and we need to get away."

"No. We need to stay." I laid the cape back on the ground, retrieved a blanket from Rykka's saddle bag and returned to the fire.

"What for?" Garan followed behind me. "I trust you, I think, but this place... I just want to be gone from here." His eyes darted from shadowy crack to crevice, as if expecting the soldier to reemerge. "What for?" he repeated.

I wrapped myself in the blanket and said nothing. There was nothing to say. I knew what I knew. After some confused hesitation, the others joined me. Only then did an answer to Garan's question make itself known.

"For me." From beyond the fire's flicker we heard the soldier's voice, once again clear and free of pain.

Yhoshi stiffened and unsheathed his knife. Garan paled and inched away.

"I knew you'd be back," I said.

"Good. Then I did not underestimate you." A stranger strode into the light. He stood four or five heads above us. He wore the white-and-gold cape, but in an instant it had dissolved, leaving a black caftan so dark it merged with the night. Only his hands and face were visible, had substance.

"That was an act of love," he said to me. "There are so few nowadays. I know."

I raised my eyes to the Stranger. "No," I replied sadly, "if I had truly believed you to be a soldier, that would have been love. But I acted with mercy only when I knew you were no soldier."

"But I was," the Stranger said. His shape and demeanor shifted and for an instant the soldier again sat before us in a painful heap. "You saw beyond the uniform, beyond the flesh. You caught a glimpse of what you all see now."

"Who are you?" I whispered. "What are you?"

"I am all that was, is and will be. I am the Stranger you loved on the road. I am here to remind you that without love, your MoonQuest cannot succeed. The Return has been joined, but without love..." He shrugged.

No one spoke for some minutes. Instead, we watched the flames dance against the dark. Each saw a different face take shape in the heart of the fire, a face that spoke to us of other times, more joyful times, more loving times — times past and times yet to come.

"Mama," Fynda moaned as face faded back to flame.

"What is it, my child?" the Stranger asked.

"What is love?"

"Love is everything. Love is the trees that shed their leaves in fall, stand proudly in their nakedness through winter and blossom into luxuriance through spring and into summer.

"Love is Aygra and B'na, that wake with joy each morning, ready to embark on a new journey across the heavens, that die in a flaming pyre each night, content in the knowledge that they will be reborn. Love is M'nor, whose light still burns behind her tears, who shows herself to those who love, to those who trust, to those who follow. Love is the stars, who form patterns in the night sky to guide us.

"Love is the birds, who soar effortlessly on the wind, scattering feathers over the land to remind us of our freedom. Love is Q'ntana, that, battered and bruised though she be, continues to nurture us, provide for us and shelter us through the seasons.

"Love is Prithi, the One who created all, who loves and lives in each of us — past, present and future. Love, my friends, is life."

"Your words are poetry," Garan said. "But I've written poetry, and I know it can mask as much as it reveals. You say love is everything. Have you looked at my face, at my body?" Garan leapt to his feet and posed in angry caricature. "Love did not do this to me. Hatred did. Cruelty did. Malice did."

"Fear did," the Stranger whispered.

Garan ignored him. "How can love be everything in a land that permits this?" He dropped back to his haunches and searched the fire for the loving face of moments before. "If loves rules all, why the need for a MoonQuest?"

"Ah," the Stranger replied, "I never said loves rules all. You're right, Garan. If love were king and queen, we would need no quests. Once, when love did rule..." The Stranger's voice dropped off as a light of wistful wonder filled his face, until a crow's screeching caw wrenched him to the moment. "But, no. That crow is right, as are you. Love is all but rules little here. Instead, you are ruled by a despot whose fear has banished love from his heart. But love will return. You saw it this night. You see it in each other."

He turned to me. "Do you know my name?" I shook my head. "No, your power of naming is not yet at its zenith. That time comes. In that moment, you will know the king by his truth name, the true name long ago renounced by Fvorag, by his father and grandfather, and by all the Fvorags back to the very first. You will know it in an instant and it will double your power...treble it. For a truth name is bestowed by Prithi and can no more be shed in life than can skin and bone. You will know his truth name in the ancient tongue and you will feel it deep within your body. And when you are called to act from that feeling, know that you act from love, from the love of Prithi, from the love of Q'ntana, from the love of M'nor...even from the love of Fvorag."

Prithi, Q'ntana and M'nor, yes. But Fvorag? "How can I love the king after all the killing and cruelty, after all he has done to those I have loved... to those I love?"

The Stranger opened his arms, which expanded in length and breadth until they seemed to embrace the night. "Love not the acts but the flesh, bone and soul that are of Prithi, as are you, as is all of Creation. Despise Fvorag and you despise a part of yourself. For we are all One in Prithi."

"I don't know..." I mumbled.

"I do know," Yhoshi barked. "I know what has been done in Fvorag's name. I've witnessed it and I can't forget what I've seen. And what I can't forget, I won't forgive. And as for love..." He aimed his knife at a misshapen rowan that knotted arthritically from the ground twenty paces away. "If that were his heart — no, his eye, for he has no heart." The knife flew through the flickering firelight and shuddered into the trunk with angry force.

"Your aim is as true as your heart needs be." Yhoshi rose to retrieve his weapon. He sat down again by the fire and scored savage gashes into the earth.

"No one has asked you to forget, Yhoshi son of Yhosha. It is your duty to remember — your duty as a son and brother, your duty as a Messenger, your duty as one who walks this earth. It may be your duty to kill too, if your act is not one of heartless vengeance. Yet even as you kill, you must love, you must forgive. For if you cannot forgive the Fvorags of this land, you cannot forgive yourself. And until you forgive yourself, you will never love from the depths of your innermost being."

"That's where our stories come from, isn't it?" Fynda asked shyly.

"Yes, child. That is where stories come from. Your stories, my stories, M'nor's stories...which are all one in this Oneness that exists only to be loved." The Stranger looked from face to face around the circle. Fynda's was quietly thoughtful, her eyes focused on the dancing flames in the fire pit. Garan stared into the dark, his face unreadable through the hieroglyphs of his torture. Yhoshi glared in stubborn defiance and continued to slash at the earth with his knife. My eyes met the Stranger's, calling out in troubled confusion.

"You will come to understand, young Elderbard-to-be," he replied to my soundless questioning. "Understanding, like love, cannot be forced. It comes when it is ready. When you are ready."

"Like stories," I whispered.

"Like stories." The Stranger smiled and nodded. "Love, too, is story — the stories we live, breathe and share, the stories whose words fire the universe with light, whose light restores M'nor, whose love heals Q'ntana. Tell us a story now, Toshar. Tell us a story of love."

I gazed into the fire. "I can tell you only the story the fire tells me, whatever it be."

"If it's a story of truth, it will be a story of love, whatever it be."

I placed my hand on my heart, closed my eyes and listened. And as I listened, in love, the words came.

"Once upon a time there was a young king, an inexperienced, reluctant king. While his peers chased peacocks across castle lawns, he met with ministers and made decisions that shaped lives, that altered the course of history. He liked neither the decisions nor those who pressed him to make them. They called themselves counselors and advisers, these nobles who sat around his massive council table. They were kind and solicitous to young Kumar, even deferential. But for all that, or perhaps because of all that, they always got what they wanted. And Kumar, well, Kumar got nothing.

"'How did he get to be king?' you ask. Had he no parents? Of course he had. Kings don't appear like magic, though many were the days when this king would have preferred a replacement to turn up just that way. How did he become king? His father died in battle and his mother died of a broken heart. There was a sister, much older than he. She could have been crowned queen in his place and would have been, but she had long ago married another king in a land far distant.

"No, Kumar was to be king or there would be no king. And that would never do. No king would plunge the kingdom into chaos, or so his ministers — who had also been his father's — warned. And so Kumar was crowned, this youth with no experience of kingship. And so he ruled, with no knowledge of statecraft. And the land survived, though it didn't thrive. The ministers thrived. Their wealth and power swelled until they threatened to exceed the king's.

"And day faded into night, blossomed into day and faded into night again. And thus the seasons passed one into the other and the king matured, but in years alone. It seemed life would continue this way forever, or at least until the king married and produced an heir.

"Among them, the ministers had many fine daughters, granddaughters, nieces and cousins of childbearing years, creatures of elegance and refinement, perfect mothers and wives all — or so their sponsors insisted. At first, they tried to decide among themselves which to present to the king.

"'If we agree on one,' they said, 'he cannot refuse.' But they could not or would not agree, for none trusted a father- or mother-in-law-designate to share the inevitable spoils of increased power with the others. In this, they were wise. For none would have shared, although none spoke this aloud.

"As his ministers argued among themselves with mounting bitterness and accusation, they increasingly left Kumar unchaperoned, unattended, unsupervised and undirected. It was a brief respite, for when negotiations over the in-law of choice collapsed, Kumar's short-lived peace was replaced by a cacophony of fathers and daughters, mothers and daughters, uncles and aunts with nieces in tow and grandparents whose knees bounced with girl-infants barely out of swaddling — a never ending parade of impossible choices, presented, for the first time in Kumar's monarchical career, without ministerial unanimity. Under normal circumstances, the young king would have collapsed in tearful confusion at this lack of clear counsel, but something had shifted during that short-lived holiday from self-serving ministerial direction. Something had happened.

"Silence had happened.

"Full days of it.

"Those first days — nay, those first hours — had left Kumar anxious and confused, struggling to replace the councils and audiences, the staged walkabouts, pointless ceremonies and meaningless lessons. And so those first hours of those first days passed slowly — barely seemed to pass at all. Young Kumar paced, ate, paced some more, called in his servants only to dismiss them moments later, then ate and paced some more.

"'What am I to do?' he cried. No one answered. And so he ate and paced yet more. He paced indoors, up and down long, endless corridors. He paced outdoors, along the battlements and through the castle's vast grounds. He paced across soft, spongy meadowland, under the shady canopy created by ancient groves and along the banks of sparkling streams. He paced, but saw nothing. He read, but the words bounced nervously, incomprehensibly around the page. He strummed his dulcimer, but the strings twanged dully and without melody.

"When three days had passed in like fashion, with no sign of a single minister to tell him what to do, he summoned Pasha, an elderly manservant who had served his father, and his before him. 'Send for my ministers,' he cried.

"'But Highness —'

"'At once, Pasha.'

"'But —'

"'Speak no buts. I must convene a council, immediately.'

"Through eyes rheumy with age and disease yet clear with vision, Pasha regarded the monarch who had once been his charge with deep compassion. 'Highness,' he said slowly, his eyes never straying from Kumar's, 'your ministers have left strict orders not to be disturbed. Not by anyone. On pain of death.'

"Kumar hesitated in confusion. 'Surely, Pasha, that cannot include me. It cannot and must not. I am king.'

"Pasha said nothing.

"'Aren't I?' he whispered.

"Pasha's eyes could no longer meet the king's. They dropped to the cold slate floor.

"'Thank you Pasha,' Kumar sighed. 'You may go.'

"Pasha raised his eyes and blinked away a tear. His mouth opened then closed again in silence. He would speak. He would but could not. He knew his place. He bowed and retreated, leaving Kumar alone in his lonely emptiness.

"The remaining hours of that day crawled by. Kumar attempted to fill them, but whatever the activity, it left him profoundly unsatisfied and whatever the company, it left him profoundly lonely.

"That night he dreamed, a dream like no other he had experienced. In it he found himself again pacing through the castle when he came upon an unfamiliar corridor. Curious, as he believed he knew every stone and brick of this place that had always been home, he stepped across the threshold.

"'What is this?' he asked aloud. 'There are no doors.' And there were none, only curving walls of polished black stone, masked every twenty paces by an abstract tapestry shot through with bolts of vibrant color. As he followed the corridor's gentle spiral, he took to peering behind the tapestries, thinking they might obscure the doors that every other castle corridor possessed. But the walls behind the tapestries were as smooth and unbroken as the walls between them. And so he continued his mysterious journey through this mystifying hall. He walked, it seemed for hours — for days, perhaps — encountering no one, hearing nothing but his own footsteps as they clacked on the bare, stone floor, seeing nothing but blank wall and formless tapestry as he followed the corridor's ever-tightening curves.

"And then he saw it: a single door of heavy-planked oak beyond the final curve at the very end of the corridor. As he approached it, he noticed a spiraled pattern etched deeply into the aged wood. The door had neither handle, knob nor lock. But when he traced his finger along the spiral's route into its heart, the door swung open. The room beyond the portal was dark and no light spilled in from the corridor. Kumar couldn't see what awaited him, but he stepped into it nonetheless, drawn by some inexplicable force, by some undeniable desire. The door swung shut behind him.

"Kumar stood still, waiting for his eyes to adjust to the dark, waiting to discern at least vague shadows. But strain as he would, there was no adjustment, no discernment. The blackness that surrounded him was so complete he might have been blind. He was barely aware of his body, of his feet on the floor, so thick and impenetrable was the darkness. He was barely aware of his breath, of his heartbeat, so thick and impenetrable was the darkness.

"The waking Kumar would have wept in terror. The sleeping Kumar experienced neither panic nor fear. Instead, this heavy blanket of black enveloped him in an unfamiliar calm, enfolded him in hitherto unknown peace. He felt as though he floated, free of body, free of the burden of kingship, free of all physical and worldly encumbrances. His mind drained itself of all thought, all memory, all words. It too seemed to float away. Nothing remained. But in that nothingness was everything. In that nothingness was all his kingdom and all the kingdoms of this and other worlds — past, present and future. In possessing no time, this nothingness encompassed all time that ever was or ever would be. This nothingness was Prithi and all the gods, M'nor and all the planets, Aris and all the stars, Pasha, his ministers and all the sentient beings that had ever existed and ever would. This nothingness was All. And All was One.

"If it was possible to feel at once humbled and exalted, powerless and omnipotent, that's how Kumar felt. And that feeling remained with him when he opened his eyes from the dark of sleep and dream into the dawning light of familiar bed and bedchamber.

"That morning heralded the procession of brides-designate. The parade of girls and women of all ages, shapes and sizes lasted all that day and well into the next, filling the vast audience chamber. Through it, Kumar said nothing. Through all the wheedling and cajoling, all the flattery and foolishness, Kumar smiled and nodded but said nothing. When he was bored, which was often, he reentered his dream and felt that same empowered well-being wash over him once again. It was then he smiled and nodded, not at the senseless spectacle unfolding interminably before him, but at the nocturnal gift that lingered lovingly deep within his innermost being. Only when the last ministers had marched the last of their marriageable relatives before him did Kumar speak. The voice was new to him, but he knew it to be his.

"'I have decided,' he announced. Like a wave rolling in from the sea, the assembled throng leaned toward him as one. Even as he spoke those three words with confidence and certainty, he didn't know what that decision was. As he opened his mouth to continue, he cast his eyes around the room and saw into his ministers' hearts for the first time. In that instant he knew what he had always known but never known. He knew the truth — their truth, to be sure. But, more importantly, he knew his own truth. And for the first time, not only in his kingship but in his life, he spoke it.

"'I will marry—' he began, and the hush in the chamber deepened as all breathing but his stopped, '—none of these.' Not only did the breathing resume, but after a moment's shocked speechlessness, so did the frenzied babel. Ministers rushed forward, encircling his throne, barking to be heard over the pandemonium, shrilling to drown out their rivals for royal relative-to-be. When the noise reached an explosive pitch, Kumar rose from his throne with such unexpected grace, dignity and power that all shouts ceased in mid-syllable.

"'I have made a further decision,' he said quietly, so quietly that his subjects again leaned forward as one to hear, yet so lovingly that there was no mistaking his words and no argument once they were spoken.

"His decree issued, the chamber emptied in resigned silence until only Kumar and Pasha remained — Kumar still standing in front of his throne, Pasha at the door. No words were needed, for in Pasha's smile he saw all the old man saw, and he smiled back. Pasha bowed and retreated, and Kumar settled back onto his throne. He cast his eyes approvingly around the vast emptiness that surrounded him, nodded his head and smiled. 'Now,' he said aloud. 'Now, I am king.'"

When I opened my eyes, the fire had dimmed to a wavering glow and the faint light it shed revealed that I too was alone. Yhoshi, Fynda and Garan slept, curled into a single, slumbering ball. The Stranger was gone.

Twenty-One

The thick forest we had spotted the previous day greeted us when we reached the cliff top early the next morning. It offered no clear trail, only an overgrown track that so twisted and curved in on itself, it seemed we rode in circles.

"I don't know how we can keep north through this," Yhoshi said after we had ridden for much of the day.

"Are we lost?" Fynda asked.

I didn't know. I didn't trust the track, but without being able to see the suns, I knew no other way to proceed. Rykka pulled impatiently. I tugged lightly on her reins and whispered soothingly into her ear. She pulled again, sniffing the air and snorting softly. This time I loosed my hold and she stepped off the track.

"I think she's found another path," I said. Whether she stalked an ancient route or blazed a new one, she pushed effortlessly through the thick woods. The others followed close behind. She broke into a trot then a canter, and the crackle of four sets of hooves over dead leaves and brittle twigs scattered dense clouds of birds that rose around us in bursts of angry screeching. Deeper and deeper we burrowed into ancient, pristine forest, weaving among massive pyynch'n that Prithi must have planted here at the dawn of time.

Now Rykka galloped, faster and faster still, until she seemed to glide, her hooves barely touching the ground. All I saw was a blur of brown and green as she gained more speed.

"To-o-o-o-o-sha-a-a-a-r." Was someone calling? Or was it the rush of wind past my ears?

"The others," I reminded Rykka. "Don't forget the others." But Rykka moved faster. Ever faster — faster than light, faster than time.

Still faster she flew. Rising. Flying.

The blur around me lightened, brightened, whitened, but remained a blur. I forced myself to look down and saw a receding green-black mass. I leaned into Rykka's mane.

"Where are we, Rykka? Where are you taking me?"

Rykka whickered and continued her swift ascent into the opalescent glow. In time it dimmed and smoked, deepening first to gold, then to orange and purple. With each shift, Rykka's color shifted too, blending so fully with the surrounding light that at times she seemed to vanish altogether. Purple darkened to indigo, the indigo of night, I realized as we began to descend and decelerate.

Rykka was now white — luminescent, star-like, her own constellation in a firmament of flickering light. We dropped gently past winking stars. Toward what? Nothing but inky blackness lay below. We sailed toward it, leaving stars behind.

As we fell a lone white light rose to meet us. A familiar tang brushed against my lips and tongue, curled up my nose. Salt. The white light drew closer and closer until with a soft, skidding splash, we merged with it.

Rykka stood on the water's surface, her mane a cascade of feathery light. Wonderstruck, I sat in the enveloping blackness, hypnotized by the gentle plash of waves against her legs. How long did I sit there? Long enough for Aris to move in the sky.

"Where are we, Rykka? Why have you brought me here?" Rykka whinnied, pawing the water. Her reflection, clear the moment before, rippled into an abstract wash of alabaster, then vanished. She shook her head then pointed her nose to a silvery glow that ruffled the water directly ahead. After a moment, a gleaming disc broke through the surface with a laughing splash. It rose majestically until, giant and whole, it cast aside the night. All I saw was an endless plain of water. And M'nor. I gasped. I had never seen her so large, so full. So near. She hovered just above the water's surface, letting the waves reach up to kiss her, then resumed her ascent.

"Mir M'nor," I heard a voice, my voice, say. This time I knew what it meant. Mir M'nor. The Sea of M'nor. The Seat of M'nor, where all journeys begin and end. "Sing to M'nor," I heard myself say. "Accompany her birth this night. Sing...sing...sing..." I felt a melody break through my lips — strange, haunting, familiar.

Mir M'nor m'ranna
M'nor m'ranna ma Mir
Mir M'nor m'ranna
M'nor m'ranna ma Mir

I still didn't understand the words, yet I felt their meaning, their celebration of the joy and pain of birth. M'nor soared, not shrinking with the distance, until she filled the sky.

"Tell *me* a story," I whispered when the song faded of its own accord.

"You are my story," I felt rather than heard. "You hear it as you live it. You tell it as you live it. Live it truly and so will I. Live it truly for Alanda, for all Q'ntana."

Before I could respond, Rykka pushed up onto her hind legs and with an enormous leap, passed through a moonbeam and into the dark, empty sky that lay beyond it. We rose swiftly through and above the stars and into a blur of early morning light, whose pale blue coloring Rykka again assumed. As we flew over the arc formed by the rising suns, Rykka began her descent. Before I knew it, we were once again in the forest. She slowed to a gallop, a canter, a trot, a slow walk and then stopped.

"Wait for us. You're going too fast. Wait for us." The distant chorus drew nearer. Rykka turned around as Yhoshi, Garan and Fynda crashed through the brush and stopped before us.

Once again, time had revealed its elusive nature. Worlds might have been created and destroyed in the few minutes I was out of sight. A world had been created, within me, a world of imagination and hope. I felt recharged by the experience, by the knowledge that M'nor awaited us, by the certainty that we would reach her in time.

"I wish I could have been there with you," Fynda sighed when I finished my story.

"You will be," I said. "I'm sure Mir M'nor is where we're going."

"Where is it?" she asked.

"I don't know. I don't know that anyone knows. Garan?"

Garan steepled his fingers together in thought. "It's funny that I never noticed it before," he said after a while.

"What?"

"I can't think of a single song or story about Mir M'nor where someone has actually been there."

"Until now," Fynda said, her eyes on me.

"I'm still not sure how we get there," I said.

"Rykka got you there once," Garan said. "She will again."

Rykka had been snuffling among the decaying twigs and leaves, rooting out rare clumps of green to feed on. She raised her head at the sound of her name and stomped her front hooves. It was time to move on.

I let her guide us and she ambled at a more comfortable pace that carried us onto a wider, less secluded path whose dense thickets thinned as we continued forward. First, single shafts of sun burst through the leafy interstices of the forest roof, spotlighting now a ruby thrush, now the mossy stocking pulled up over the base of a rotting tree trunk. As the canopy lightened, multiple rays pushed through, dappling everything in motion-filled flickers of light and shadow. Kyrrels and k'nrahs, no longer alarmed by our intrusion, emerged from hiding and resumed their business. Above us, angry screeches softened to musical chirps and whistles. The forest resonated with a playful joy uncommon in Q'ntana, one we had rarely witnessed through our travels.

The respite was short-lived. Fitful frenzy soon displaced spirited exuberance. Nayla darted blindly into the middle of the road then froze. Herds of korak vaulted past us, their eyes white with terror, trampling those k'nrah that hadn't tangled themselves among the horses' legs. It was all we could do to keep moving.

Rykka and Ta'ar remained calm, but the heightened tension infected Corem and Merek, who shied then reared, nearly throwing Fynda and Garan.

I urged Rykka forward but a swarm of flot swooped and screamed at us, forcing us to a halt. We tried to shoo them away but that only increased their agitation as wings flapped, slapped and whirred around us. When they began to peck at us, we buried our faces.

Then, as quickly as they came, they fled in a cacophony of squealing, screeching squawks.

Silence descended on the forest. Unnatural silence. Not even the leaves rustled. I opened my eyes. Not a single creature was about. They had all gone the way of the korak, back into the deepest part of the forest. Overhead, Aygra and B'na vanished behind a single dark shadow. It dropped toward us, dove toward us.

With a shrill, piercing caw, an immense span of black wings ripped through the air. It grazed the treetops, blotting out the sky and plunging the forest into night. It passed and the suns reappeared, but only for an instant. Again, the crow hurtled past, lower this time, its steel-like wings slicing away the topmost limbs of the trees in its path. Each time it returned, it shaved yet more as it moved nearer. On the fourth fly-past it hovered over us, its wings thrashing out an icy wind that chilled the color from the remaining leaves before blowing them to the ground in a shower of dull, ghostly brown.

"Caw. Caw. Ca-a-a-a-a-w-w-w-w." The crow thrust its oily beak through the stripped limbs. Rykka and Ta'ar shifted tensely but stood their ground. Corem and Merek whinnied, tried to bolt. I felt panicked eyes on me as mine remained fixed on the crow.

Through the tumult, I heard a long-ago voice, crystalline in its present-moment clarity.

All Bo'Rá K'n's power emanates from a single source. Refuse your fear its power and your mastery will rival his.

The Lady Gwna's face hovered before mine, bracing me for what I knew I had to do. I swallowed hard, took a deep breath and gripped Rykka's mane.

"Are you through your tantrum?" I asked the crow in a voice that startled me with its calm.

The crow thrashed its wings, trying to slash through the thick columns of wood, all that remained of surrounding trees.

"I know you, Bo'Rá K'n," I said. "I will always know you now, whatever your face, whatever your voice. I know you and I know that you are powerless against me. Go back where you came from. Frighten Fvorag if you can. Frighten Holgg and Zakk if you can. You don't frighten me. You can't frighten me." Gently, I urged Rykka forward. "Let's go. M'nor is waiting for us."

The crow made a final, stabbing thrust through the naked trees before dissolving into a tight ball of smoky cinder that spiraled into the sky, leaving a tail of soot that turned, focused and, like an arrow, aimed right for me.

Despite Rykka's footwork, the arrow found me, coating me in an icy ash that chilled me to my soul. I tried to clean myself off but couldn't move, apart from the currents of trembling that shuddered through me. I clutched at Rykka's mane.

"Wonderful," Garan said, slapping me on the back. "I always knew you had it in you."

"I-I-I don't know where it came from," I stammered through a staccato of chattering teeth.

"What does it matter? It's gone now," Garan said.

"N-n-no. The w-w-words. It all just c-c-came." I looked up through the trees, half-expecting to see the crow's menacing red eyes. "And now it's g-g-gone." Was it sweat or tears that soaked my face? It didn't matter. Nothing mattered.

"What's wrong?" Fynda's eyes peered anxiously into mine. My eyes closed and she was gone. Everything was gone. I felt other hands unclench my fingers and help me down as sentence snatches flitted through my consciousness.

"...must be feverish..."

"...his hands...like fire..."

"...water..."

Wetness touched my lips and dribbled down my chin. Coolness bathed my face. I tried to open my mouth to speak, my eyes to see. They wouldn't obey. "What are you saying?" I wanted to ask. But I couldn't feel my tongue in my mouth.

My mouth. I can't feel my mouth! A flash of panic and then...I feel nothing...hear nothing...know nothing...

I'm falling...sinking...floating...breathing cool, damp air. Now, no air...no sound...no light. Everything is black...dark...empty.

Nothing.

And then, something. The faintest riffle of air. A light, feather touch. It's there, then gone. There again, enfolding me, cushioning me...embracing me. Am I still falling? Everything is so dark...impenetrably dark. Everything? No, nothing.

And then, something. A distant flicker. It wavers and gutters as it draws closer, grows larger. A hand cups the flame from behind. The light is nearly upon me, dancing atop a yellow taper. No, gold. No, blue. No, red. The colors dance as the flame pirouettes. Now the taper is white, as white as the halo of hair behind it, as white as the robe emerging from shadow.

"Do you know me, Toshar?" *a woman's voice issues gently from the flame.* Toshar. *I know that name from...from somewhere. Where?* "Do you know me?" *the flame repeats, now in a man's voice, equally gentle.*

"You are fire," *I say.* "But who is Toshar?"

"Who is Toshar?" *The voice is male and female, neither and both.*

"I can't remember. Does it matter?"

"You are Toshar." *The hand falls away and, with it, the shadow, revealing an ancient face etched with wrinkles. Candle flames dance in eyes as black as the blackness that surrounds us. It's a woman, long white hair flowing freely over her naked breasts. No, a man, his chest buried under a snowy beard. The face is male and female, neither and both.* "You are Toshar MoonQuester. I am Toshar Ko'lar. We are one, you and I. One out of time."

It makes no sense, yet I understand in a way that surpasses understanding. I reach out to touch the apparition, but there is nothing to reach out with. I have no body.

"What am I?" *I whisper.* "Where am I?"

"You are here and not here, everywhere and nowhere. You are dream, you are reality. You are light, you are dark. This place, too, is all that...and none of it."

"I don't understand," *I said.*

"You will...in time. Why have you summoned me, MoonQuester?"

"I, summoned you?"

"Forgive me. I forget. It was so long ago."

"What was?"

"This encounter, this marriage of past, present and future into the eternal now."

"You confuse me."

"Do you remember nothing? Nothing of Q'ntana? Nothing of M'nor? Nothing of Bo'Rá K'n?"

Memory's door opens a crack. I pull it shut with a cry of pain.

"Was it truly that bad?" he asks, more to himself than to me, as his image begins to dissolve.

"Where are you going?" I cry.

"If you do not know yourself in me..."

"...then do you know me?" Holding the candle is a wrinkled crone, leaning on a walking stick. Behind her, beyond an archway and through a misty, fluttering light, sits a steaming teapot atop a three-legged table.

"Come," she says. She releases the candle, which hovers in the air unassisted, and extends her hand to me. I see another hand — mine? — take it and follow her across the threshold. "Perhaps some tea will reawaken your self-fullness."

"Grandmother?"

"Come," she says, "sit on your favorite pillow and drink from your favorite mug." I cup my hand around the familiar piece of clay. Its green chevron shimmers luminously against my skin. I raise the mug and feel the steam bathe my eyes. As the sweet heat touches my lips and slides down my throat, I remember. I remember it all.

"Oh, Grandmother. I'm so frightened."

"I know, child." Her voice is the cool evening breeze that sweeps away a scorching summer day.

"But why? Why did I feel no fear then only to feel it now?" I start to tremble.

Eulisha refills my mug. "Drink this," she says. "It will restore the balance." Her eyes never leave me. "Do you understand yet who greeted you when you reached this world between worlds?" I shake my head. "You will be Elderbard, son of my son. What you saw was you, in the time to come."

"But she...I mean he...that is, both...I mean, which?"

Eulisha's smile fails to ease my confusion. "He and she," she explains. "A union of all the qualities, masculine and feminine, resides in the truest of bards."

"Will I...I mean, how...?"

"No," she laughs, "you will not appear that way to the world, no more than do I." Her voice grows serious. "Look at me closely. Look at me with the eyes of a bard, with the eyes of Toshar, Elderbard-to-be."

I shut my eyes and reopen them. As I stare through the violet of Eulisha's eyes, her face shifts subtly — a masculine jaw, firmer mouth, cheeks sprinkled with the salt-and-pepper stubble of a day's growth. It lasts only an instant, then the familiar features return. There is so little difference, and yet...

"And yet we are one, as will you be when your time comes." She gazes at me, her eyes boring through skin, bone and blood, then smiles. "And come it does. You ask why you fear once the fearful has passed."

"Yes, grandmother."

She lifts her mug and takes a first sip of tea. "Know first, child, that you needn't understand everything, that mystery is among life's greatest gifts." Setting her cup on the table, she takes my hands in hers. They are like velour — soft, smooth, warm. "You fear your strength. You fear your power. You fear your fearlessness. You fear the future because you cannot see where it will lead and you fear what you cannot imagine.

"You have glimpsed what may lie ahead. But you are only now building the foundation of that future. If you continue to build, stone by heavy stone, you and that Elderbard will meet again. If you continue to follow the path that is yours alone to follow, you will be that sage, the greatest sage in the time of Q'ntana's greatest king, under the gaze of a grateful moon. If not... If not, then who can say?" She gestures to the door. "It is time for you to return to your friends. They worry and there is much traveling before you reach The Mir. Much traveling..."

As I stand, Eulisha's image fades. "Wait," I cry. I reach out but my hand passes through her as through a cloud. "What of my fear? I'm still frightened."

Only the candle and Eulisha's voice remain. "Walk with your fear. Walk through your fear. Walk on...into the promise."

The candle recedes and darkness returns. Everything is black...dark... empty...

Nothing.

And then, something. Voices. Familiar voices.

"...breathing regularly again...skin cooler..."

"...more water...raise his head..."

"...hear me?..."

"...speak...Toshar...one word...?"

Slowly, black turns gray turns cloudy and the mist dissipates.

Leaves. A thick curtain of leaves, framing a face that peers anxiously into mine.

"Ro'an?" A hand pressed down on my shoulder as I tried to sit up. It was another dream. It had to be.

The eyes that embraced mine were thick forests of wood-flecked green. Beneath the surface color, I recognized a deep pool of liquid crystal that cradled a single, sacred flame. The face had changed. The fire had not.

"No, cousin," Ro'an said. "This is no dream."

Twenty-Two

Ro'an. More older brother than cousin, Ro'an had shared my early childhood in Kemet. We shared everything — our toys, our books, our secrets, our fears. For a time we even shared Garan.

Ro'an's parents, Fyran and Lorh, had vanished soon after my father did. Zakk branded them traitors, gone over to the king's side. But Ro'an refused to believe it. Taking nothing but the clothes on his back, he left one night to seek out the truth. I never saw him again. Until I opened my eyes to those eyes.

When Fynda, out seeking herbs for a tonic that would counteract the effects of the ash, had chanced upon Ro'an, they danced a wary dance around each other, neither prepared to reveal anything of themselves. Only when she learned that Ro'an possessed healing lore did she risk bringing him to where I lay. It was his skill that ended my fever.

"Must I finish it?" I asked as I sat up. "I'm okay now."

"All of it," Ro'an insisted.

I forced it down, screwing up my face in disgust as I swallowed the last of the tonic. I shuddered.

"Ugh. Why do herbs always taste so bad?"

"They don't. But where you were...that ash...you needed something uncommonly strong to bring you back. You'll be fine now."

"It was almost worth drinking that to see you again." I smiled. "I thought you were dead."

"And I, you."

We sat around the flat-topped stove in the center of his hut, tucked into a clearing not far from my encounter with Bo'Rá K'n. We sat on the floor because he had but a single chair, pushed against a plank table by the sole window, its pane clouded with steam from a simmering stew. The table was empty but for a clay bowl and plate and an oil lamp.

"Do you know about Zakk?" he asked. The look in my eye must have been all the answer he needed, for Ro'an continued without waiting for my reply.

"It didn't take me long to suspect that he had something to do with my parents' death," Ro'an explained. "I hurried back to Kemet to warn you but it had been razed. I assumed Zakk's treachery had claimed you too."

"We fled," I said. "Zakk insisted."

"I roamed from place to place until I came to the Forest of Avedan and happened on this abandoned hut. I've been here ever since — however long that has been — with only birds and trees to hear my songs." He shook his head sadly. "That is what it means to be a bard in these times."

Ro'an crawled under the table and lifted a loose floorboard. "Thank Prithi for my books." He hauled out six hefty, leather-bound volumes.

"Books? But how—?"

"This is where I found them, along with a supply of quills and writing paper. They have taught me much about plants, herbs and other medicines."

Yhoshi looked around with new interest. "This hut belonged to a Believer," he said.

"I know more than that," Ro'an said. "I know the name she took for herself: M'naben, Daughter of the Moon. And I know something of her fate." He lit the oil lamp and the light cast shadows under his high cheekbones. His face was hollower and more angular than I remembered, softened only by the fine brush of auburn hair that fell over brow and ears. He carried the lamp to the doorway, where it illuminated M'naben's ugly, ghostly remains.

"It can't have been an easy death," he said. "The floor was dark with blood when I first saw it. She was either tortured or brutally murdered here. Or both. Every day I expect the King's Men to return for me."

"Then why don't you leave?" Fynda asked.

"To go where? No place in Q'ntana is safe." He rose and stirred the stew.

While we ate, I told Ro'an our story, weaving its disparate threads together in ways that surprised even me. I urged Fynda, Garan and Yhoshi to contribute, but they sat quietly as the day carried with it what little light seeped into the hut.

"...and when the crow had gone," I said, "I fell into a fearful darkness, as deep as the night that will soon envelop us."

They waited, but I spoke no more. At last Ro'an said softly, "I too saw the crow, but I flung myself onto my pallet, pulled the covering over my head and waited until noise, wind and shadow abated. Had I known its power, I might never have emerged. You have much courage, Toshar. More than I."

"You went in search of your parents," I whispered.

"That was a long time ago." The flickering light picked out a single tear at the tip of Ro'an's lashes. It hung there, a glistening dewdrop, then fell onto his cheek and slid away. Another silence filled the room, broken only by a flot's distant scream and the answering wail of a faraway nayla.

"We'd best get some rest," I said finally. "We've lost the better part of a day here and we'll need to make an early start in the morning. Will you guide us through your forest, Ro'an? Will you join us on our MoonQuest?"

"A day?" Garan shouted. His eyes bulged as though ready to burst from their sockets. "A *day*?!"

"We've been with Ro'an the better part of three days, Toshar," Yhoshi said gently.

Three days. How could that be? "Tell me you jest. Fynda, tell me they jest."

"There's been no chance to tell you how sick you were," she said, "and how long you remained beyond our reach."

I looked incredulously from one face to the next, my eyes finally resting on Ro'an's.

"It is indeed three days since the crow flew through," he said. "Whatever you experienced, cousin, took three days."

"Experienced?"

"Come, Toshar," Ro'an said. "I may be a coward, but I have enough bardic sight to know that you experienced more than empty darkness."

"Toshar?" Fynda touched my arm.

Was it shame or modesty that had kept my visions private? It no longer mattered. We traveled this road together — Fynda, Yhoshi, Garan and I — and I had no right to conceal any part of it from them.

"If any surviving bard merits the honor, it's you," Ro'an said when I finished. "I envy you. It isn't worthy, but I do."

"I don't know that I want to be Elderbard," I said. "I don't know that I want the burden."

"The blessing, you mean," he said, "but it's not that I envy. It's your gift of vision and story."

"I don't know... I didn't choose this."

"Didn't you?" His eyes bathed my face with their searching fire. "Remember the teachings, cousin. There is always a choice."

Ro'an spoke true. I chose to undertake this journey and I, not Eulisha, not O'ric, not even Zakk, would determine my fate. The choice lay in my hands, in my heart. Panic seized me and then dissipated. Somehow, all was well.

We slept peacefully that night in Ro'an's cabin, and the three nights following under the trees on our way through the forest.

"Here Avedan ends," Ro'an said as light began to fade on the fourth day, "as must our time together." He gestured toward a gentle, wavelike slope. "Beyond that ridge lies Pre Vilda'aa, a rough country inhabited by rough folk."

"And beyond it?" I asked.

"Nothing, if Vilda'aa legends are true. They call it the end of the known world."

I followed his finger and looked past it, beyond the horizon. "Then that's where we shall find Mir M'nor," I said with a certainty I neither understood nor questioned.

Ro'an strained to see what I knew, yet seeing, I knew, nothing. He turned to me, defeat in his eyes. "I hope so, cousin," he said.

I allowed him time to swallow his disappointment, then asked, "Do you know the Vilda'aa?"

He nodded. "They come to me for medicine, as they did to M'naben before me. It's a great honor, for they distrust strangers. Mention my name when you encounter them. It may earn you a friendlier reception. They call me Coro Ta'aa, Healing One. To them, M'naben was also Coro Ta'aa. Their language makes no distinction between genders." He slipped off Rykka, who had carried us both. "And now it's time to part."

I dismounted after him. "Are you sure you won't travel with us?" I asked.

He gazed ahead, out to Pre Vilda'aa, then behind us, back into the forest. "I am," he said. "My place is not with you. I lack the courage to journey beyond the end of the known world." He raised his hand to silence me. "It's true. More important, you are The Four Who See, not the Five."

I looked at his sandals, nearly worn through to his feet. "It will be a long walk back..."

"The forest is gentle to those who know her ways," he said. "Her carpet is soft and she will nurture me as she has done these many years." He caressed the textured bark of an oak then removed his sandals. His pale, bony feet disappeared into the thick, loamy pile. "It's a long walk, but not as long as our ride has been. This slim body can slip through narrower paths than can five on horseback."

He embraced Yhoshi, Fynda and Garan, then turned to me. "Will I see you again?" he asked.

In his eyes I saw the answer — a violent, bloody answer, one I wished not to see. Saying nothing, I opened my arms to him and we clasped each other tightly. I didn't want to let go, but he pulled himself free and prodded me toward Rykka. "I can have no wisdom to offer you," he said. "Your wisdom lies far deeper than mine. Travel in the light of Prithi, cousin, and bring M'nor back to us all."

Twenty-Three

Fynda woke first. It was her favorite time, that stately transformation from dark to day, and she often preferred to greet it alone. In her days at the inn, she had treasured this dawn ritual. It was the only time truly hers, the only time free of innkeeping drudgery, the only time she she could almost remember her mother, almost forget her father. This dawn, a single word stuck to her tongue like a fly to flypaper. It wriggled and flailed, refusing to die and let her in peace: *q'wanda*. To her it was another early morning shred of meaninglessness. To me, it was the surviving glint of a nighttime vision, the footprint left by a dreamwalker.

"Then why do I remember nothing, not even that I've dreamed?" Fynda asked as we breakfasted by a mirror-faced pond. "You keep saying that Tikkan send night stories to teach and guide us. But what use are they if they take them back before we wake?"

"They don't take back the dream," Garan said, "only the memory and, then, only sometimes."

"You always talk about Na'an and the dreams she sends you, Toshar. They're always so full, so clear. So knowing."

I laughed. "Only the ones that are. The others... I've had my share of q'wandas too, you know."

"What do you do with yours?"

"I try to remember my father's words when I complained as you do: 'Patience and trust. The answers will come...if you let them...when they're ready for you...when you're ready for them.' Are you ready for them, Fynda?"

"I've so wanted to dream —" Fynda corrected herself before I could, "— to *remember* my dreams. My reward has been one q'wanda after another." She spelled it in the earth with her finger and underlined it once, then again. Her eyes lit up. "A place," she cried. "It's a place!"

I smiled. "You see? Patience and trust." I watched her study the word scratched into the ground. "Close your eyes," I said when at last she looked up. "Can you see anything of this place in your mind's eye?"

Fynda screwed her eyes shut, twisting her face so tightly that the blood throbbed through bulging veins in her temple.

"Don't try so hard. Just let it come as it it comes, when it's ready...when you're ready. *Are* you ready?"

Fynda relaxed her face, but the vein that crossed her left temple still pulsed fiercely. After a few minutes she blinked her eyes open, then, crying out in pain shut them again, more tightly than before.

"What is it, Fynda?" Garan asked. "What's wrong? What have you seen?"

She squeezed her eyes tighter still and clenched her fists until they were white. "Oh, my eye! It's as though someone plunged a knife into it."

"Which eye?" I asked.

"My left."

"What did you see?" asked Garan.

"Nothing for all that," she moaned in anguished frustration.

"Nothing?" I asked softly.

"Not really," she whispered. "A flash of light so bright it blinded me, so bright that when I open my eyes even to this dim light —" she opened them a slit then shut them with a gasp "— the pain is unbearable. What's happened? What has this dream, this q'wanda, done to me?" She clawed at her face, as though trying to rake her eye from its socket. Gasping for breath, she collapsed onto the ground, into a fetal ball. "I don't want to die," she whimpered. "I don't want to die."

Gently, I cradled her head onto my lap, rubbed my hands briskly until they were hot, then rested one on each temple. "Can I tell you a story?" Fynda shrugged. "This isn't a story plucked from Prithi knows where. It's a story about me, about my eyes, about my vision." As my eyes fell shut, the dark carried me back to to Pre Tena'aa, back to the womb-like warmth of Eulisha's chamber.

It's the end of another lesson with Eulisha, another sacred time of learning through story, of seeing through dream. We sit, as always, on the floor, the wooden three-legged table between us, its full-moon surface partly obscured by teapot and bowls.

"My eyes hurt." I press and rub the heels of my palm into my brow.

"Both eyes?"

"No, my left."

Eulisha nods knowingly. "Your inner-vision eye. It's being reawakened from a long sleep. It's no surprise it aches. You're asking much of it all of a sudden after having asked little of it for so long."

"What should I do?" I continue the massage, though it affords no relief, then drop my hand over the aching eye.

"Nothing. Honor it. Thank it. Respect it. But don't shut it. Don't run from it. Don't run from the pain, from the pain of what you might see...of what you will see."

"What will I see, Grandmother?"

Eulisha gazes into my left eye, the deep violet of her iris pouring into the coal black of mine. As her gaze penetrates behind and beyond the fragile membrane, I see my eye in hers, its color lightened. It fades first to gray then brightens to yellow, deepens to gold, fires to red, then relaxes to burgundy, green, blue, orange, violet and white before darkening back to gray and black, a new black — not coal's brittle lifelessness, but a liquid pool of infinite depth that carries me far into my soul, that embraces many hundreds of lives and spans many thousands of years, past and future.

"What will you see? Tell me first what you experienced as I looked into your eye."

If words exist to describe the visions that flashed before me, I don't yet know them. If words exist to describe the sensations that surged through me, these too are beyond my ken. I look blankly, helplessly, wordlessly at Eulisha.

"Now you understand why there is no answer to your question. No answer in words. There need not be when you've already tasted the answer in your own sights and senses."

I half-smile and half-nod as she touches her left palm to my left temple. Heat radiates into my face, into my body. This isn't a new feeling. Eulisha often applies her healing touch and I know well the soft warmth of her hands, the silky smoothness of the one part of her aging body free of wrinkles. I know too the contrasting coolness of her rings when she presses her hands into my flesh. I know this as I know her breath, as I know my own.

For the first time, though, energy travels not one way but two. Not only does the pressure ease on my eye but something strange from within streaks from my eye into Eulisha's hand. A strange...a strange..."power" is the only word to describe it, but it's a word I shrink from. I jerk my head free and look away, unable to meet Eulisha's eyes.

"No!" she thunders. Taking my head in her hands, she forces my gaze into hers. Her herb-scented breath mingles with mine. "If you want to heal, you mustn't run. If you want to feel, you mustn't turn away. It's your strength you turn from, your power you flee."

I struggle to keep my eyes trained on hers. But my gaze wavers. I see too much, fear too much. In an instant the force of her eyes pulls mine back like a magnet.

"But Zakk says—"

"I know what Zakk says. He is more than your uncle. He is my son. That Prithi should send me such a son." She shakes her head in bewilderment then breathes out a chuckle. "Prithi's reasons are for Prithi alone to know. There are reasons for Zakk's place in my life and Myrrym's." She caresses my face then drops her hands to her lap. "And there are reasons for his place in yours. I know his ways are not mine, Toshar. I cannot change that."

"But Grandmother," I implore.

"I cannot."

My pleading gaze hardens into anger. "I don't understand," I rage, tears cascading down my face, my left eye throbbing mercilessly. "You're Elderbard. If you know that what he teaches me isn't...if you know..."

Eulisha shakes her head. "It is Prithi's will that I not interfere yet, and so it is mine. And so it must be yours."

"No!" I can barely contain my fury. "If that's Prithi's will, then Prithi is a... Prithi is a... Prithi is no better than Zakk... no better than Fvorag!"

"Perhaps not. They are both Prithi's creations, as are you and I. In their own way, without even knowing it, they carry out Prithi's will, just as do you and I."

"But —"

"We are here to learn, Toshar. All of us. That is Prithi's will. That is Prithi's gift to us. Here, drink this." She pours out a bowl of tea and pushes it toward me. Sinuous vapors dance into my face, dissolving my rage. "I am glad to see you angry," she says at last. "In order to see what you see, you must first feel what you feel, however ugly or dangerous. Remember that when you're with Zakk. Remember that when you leave this place."

"Leave?" My left eye twitches uncomfortably. Without thinking, I cover it with my right hand.

"You know you will leave, will choose to leave. You know it because you have seen it. Yet you refuse to trust what you have seen." Gently, she pulls my hand from my face. Trust, Toshar," she says tenderly. "Trust what you see. Trust what you know. Trust what you know to be true. With that trust — in yourself and in Prithi — you will always be safe."

I touched my hands to Fynda's eyes. "Your eyes too are powerful, more powerful than you know. You too can see what others refuse to see. Honor that power, Fynda, that power that Prithi gifted you. Honor and trust it. Trust it with all your heart, and your eyes will never ache in the light nor go blind in the dark." I let my hands slide away from her eyes and down her face. "How do they feel now?"

Slowly she blinked them open and sat up. She looked directly into B'na's new-day light, closed her eyes, then gazed into Aygra's brighter fire. Her smile broadened. "I trust *you*, Toshar."

"That's not good enough, not unless it comes first from a place of trust in your deepest self. I might let you down one day. Any of us might. That's true for me as much as for any of you." I took both her hands in mine. "Now, Fynda, are you ready to tell us about q'wanda?"

"I'm frightened," she whispered. "I don't want to die."

"Dreams aren't bad things, Fynda."

Fynda pulled her right hand free and twirled strands of hair around her index finger, tightening it until her fingertip turned blue and she gasped in unexpected pain. "Aren't they?" She shook her finger loose, freed her other hand and rubbed the strangling mark left by her hair.

"What was q'wanda? Tell me about it."

"Q'wanda," she said in a voice stripped of emotion, "was a wall, a giant brick wall so long I couldn't see around it, so tall I couldn't see over it, so slippery I couldn't climb it. When I turned around to go back the way I'd come, it surrounded me. I couldn't go back. I couldn't go forward. I was stuck. That was q'wanda. That's all there was. That's all I remember."

"You know what lies beyond the wall, don't you, Fynda?" I prompted.

"I-I can't."

I draped my arm around her shoulder and pulled her to me. "I think you must."

She planted both hands on the ground where she sat, where she had slept. "Here," she said. "Beyond the wall was here, this place, last night."

"And...?" Fynda shook her head.

"Free it, Fynda. Free it so it can free you."

"It-it was about my fath— About Crozon." She coughed chokingly, as if something had grabbed her by the throat. She jerked her head, trying to shake free.

"What is it, little one?" Garan asked.

Fynda looked at him in startled horror. "How...? How...?" She studied him closely, letting her eyes follow all the creases and folds of his skin. "How did you know to call me that?" Tears coursed down her cheeks. "Only my mother called me that. Only my mother..." Her voice drifted off as she looked out toward the water. After a moment, she stood, her back to us, her face to the water.

"The dream," she started, "was about my father." Her voice was ice, and I shivered as its chill shot through me. "He raped me," she said simply. "There was more to the dream, but that's what it was about."

She said nothing more for some minutes, then began to shake. "He raped me, again and again and again. It was night and we were here. Right here. Last night. You were all asleep. I was asleep. Then I woke with a start when I felt something heavy fall on top of me. It felt leaden, limp, like a sack of potatoes...rotting potatoes that were soft and putrid. I tried to scream but a hand clamped over my mouth, over my nose. I couldn't breathe. I could only open my eyes and stare into the night, into the one night I wished I lacked night vision. I didn't want to see the face that stared back at me, the eyes that bulged greedily, the beard that curled and scratched like a thousand wormy bristles." She paused, inhaling deeply.

"It was your father, Crozon," Yhoshi said.

"It was Crozon, my father." She swiveled her head to meet Yhoshi's sympathetic gaze then jerked it away. "I heard my blouse rip open and felt his other hand on my breast. Softly at first, just a light brush, a whisper of gentleness that vanished in an instant. The hand pressed down on my breast then squeezed and squeezed and squeezed, wringing the life out of me, wringing the spirit out of me. First one breast, then the other, until I knew my breasts were purple with bruises.

"'Take them!' I wanted to cry. 'You've touched them, soiled them. I don't want them anymore. Cut them off and take them.' But I couldn't say it. I couldn't say anything through his dirty hand, the one covering my mouth, stifling my breath. Then I felt him grope at my leggings, tear at my leggings... all the while he lay on top of me, a dead weight over my deadening body. My leggings were open, ripped open like the rest of me. I felt his fingers down there, jagged fingernails cutting at my flesh. I couldn't cry out. I couldn't breath. Even had my mouth been free, I couldn't have spoken. My tongue was numb. My throat was raw."

Fynda's hands leapt to her throat, clutching chokingly. The next words rasped out tightly. "Then he fumbled with his trousers, unbuttoned his fly. And I felt him... felt him...enter me, ram into me like a dagger piercing flesh." One hand dropped to her groin. A faint sigh issued from her lips. "He thrust and he thrust and he thrust until it felt as though he had thrust right through me, as though he had impaled me."

Both hands dropped to her sides. Her shoulders slumped impotently. She turned back to face us, to face the dead fire pit, its blackened, brittle stumps laying in a bed of lifeless ash, as lifeless as her voice when she continued. "He might as well have impaled me," she said. "When he was through in the front, he flipped me over like a tosti on the grill and pressed my face into the mud while he plunged into me from the rear. Then he turned me over again, flipping me back and forth over and over until I lost consciousness."

She stood, still as the air, saying nothing, her eyes drained of light, her face drained of color, her body drained of will. "And then I woke up," she said as coldly as she had begun. For an instant, fire burnt through the ice cloud in her eyes, which glared accusingly into mine. "I never wanted to dream. I never want to dream again. I don't want your dreams," she spat. "Your dreams are garbage. I don't need them. I won't have them. I won't."

"You mustn't say that, Fynda," I replied softly. I rose and moved toward her. She thrust both arms out against me and stepped back.

"Stay away from me — all of you," she cried angrily. "If not for you, if not for this MoonQuest, I wouldn't have dreamed this dream, any dream. I wouldn't have seen what I saw. I wouldn't have felt what I felt. What I feel. My breasts still feel bruised and dirty." She ripped open her blouse. "Here," she cried, "take them! I don't want them anymore. They're not mine anymore."

As she reached for the knife at her belt, Garan scooped his jacket from the ground and flew to Fynda's side. He draped it over her and the rage died into a whimper.

"If not for this MoonQuest, what you dreamed might eventually have happened," he said.

"But it did happen," she whispered. "It must have. I still feel his hands all over my body. I still feel the pain of his...of his..." She fell sobbing into Garan's arms. She sobbed tears that rose from every pore and cell and spilled out through eyes that grew redder and redder, down cheeks that washed oceans of grief onto her clothes and Garan's, until no more tears remained.

"I hate him," she breathed. She whispered it again, a little louder, and then again, her whisper swelling into a throaty growl then a piercing shriek. "I hate him!" Her body writhed and twisted, trying to shake off his essence, his taint. Her hips gyrated, her head rolled, her eyes ballooned from their sockets, as she continued her dance of freedom.

She didn't undress. Her clothes fell away. Once naked, she turned and danced into the pond, scooping up handfuls of water, slapping and slopping it all over her, rubbing her hands down arms and legs, over breasts and genitals, cleansing the pollution from her body, from her soul. The writhing and splashing continued, her fiery hair flailing from left to right, from back to front. Now it streamed down her back, now it masked her eyes, nose, mouth and neck, reaching down to her navel. Then, in a single, fluid dive, she disappeared into the water. Strands of red floated in view for a moment, then they too vanished. No air bubbles boiled up. No underwater movement disturbed the glassy surface.

Garan held his breath with her. When he could hold it no longer, he exhaled in a sighing gust. "I'm going in after her," he cried. "She'll drown."

"No." I pulled him back to shore. "Let her be. She needs this." I looked from Garan and Yhoshi to my reflection in the water. "We all do."

"I too dreamed about my father," Garan said. "It's the first dream I've remembered since...since Kemet." He fidgeted nervously with a blade of grass. He yanked it from the ground, then another and a third and began to braid them into a tiny plait.

Fynda shivered and edged closer to the rekindled fire.

"No, Fynda. It wasn't like your dream...not at all like your dream."

"What was he like, in the dream?" I asked.

"Like me," Garan said, touching his face. "Like this. At least that's how he was when I first saw him. He looked just like me — ugly, deformed, misshapen. In the dream, I'm a little boy, a perfect little boy, looking, I suppose, just as I did back then. My father comes into my room and stares at me...stares hard at me, his eyes large and round and blue." Garan looked up to the sky. "Pale blue, just like the sky this morning. His eyes were the only part of him I recognized. I looked at him, stared back at him, in fear and horror, my hand covering my mouth, my knuckle wedged into my mouth to stop me from screaming. I was afraid. I'm afraid when I think back on it, when I see the image again in my mind's eye.

"'Dadú?' I cry out finally. 'What has happened to you Dadú?'

"He looks back at me sadly, wisely, lovingly, his eyes widening until they fill his face. And as they do, the deformity clears and he looks as he has always looked. But only for an instant. It happens so quickly that I'm not even sure I saw what I saw.

"'Don't go,' I cry. 'Come back!' But he just stands there, silently staring at me, accusing me with his eyes, with those eyes." Garan fell silent. He began to braid all the plaited blades into a single rope.

"What was he accusing you of?" I asked.

"Fear," Garan replied in a barely audible whisper. 'Your fear has done this to me,' he says. 'Only you can undo it. Come...' I take his hand. It feels both raw and scaly. He leads me out of the room, out of the house and into a tunnel. It's black as Horusha's, but two pale beams of blue light project from his eyes and light our way to a spiral staircase descending deep into the ground. Deeper and deeper we bore, deeper and deeper, until my legs ache and I can barely drop them down another step.

"'I can't, Dadú,' I cry. 'I've gone as far as I can.'

"'A little farther, Gara,' he says. That's what he used to call me, Gara. And his voice is so warm and filled with so much love that I bite my lip and follow. At last we come to a heavy oak door with a keyhole set in a heavy iron plate.

"'Now we'll just slip through the keyhole to the other side,' he says and dissolves into a pale blue vaporous swirl that sails effortlessly through the keyhole.

"'Wait for me!' I cry. But it's too late. He's gone. I push at the door. It won't give. I struggle with the massive knob. It won't turn. I beat my hands against the door, but its weight is so much greater than mine that little sound emerges.

"'Dadú,' I shriek. 'Come back for me, Dadú.' My voice bounces off the clammy stone and into my own ears and I know no sound will penetrate this barrier. When my shouts fade to whimpers and my pounding to impotent scrapes, I remember the keyhole. Dropping to my knees I peer through to the other side. There is my father, my Dadú, looking every bit as handsome as he'd always been — ruddy complexion, shiny, black hair, smiling mouth. He laughs, bouncing a young boy on his knee. Me."

"You?" Fynda asked.

"I was as confused as you at first. Dadú sits next to a fireplace. An enormous blaze dances in the grate. Over the mantel hangs a giant, egg-shaped mirror. In its reflection I see the other side of the door, the door that keeps me from him. I call out for him to open the door, to let me through. No sound emerges. I stick three fingers into the keyhole — it's that big — hoping to attract his attention. But the door is too thick, and my fingers don't reach out the other side. Again I peer through. Again I see the mirror. Only this time I see only the keyhole reflected back, a single blue eye staring longingly through it. As I stare and stare and stare, the reflected keyhole expands, enough that I can see clearly through to the other side."

"So you climbed through?" Yhoshi asked.

Garan shook his head sadly. "On my side, the keyhole remained big enough for three fingers. Nothing more. But through the mirror, I could see one eye, then two, then a face, than an entire body." Garan looked down at the thick knot of grass he had created. He pulled out his dagger and slashed it to shreds.

"What did you see?" I asked gently, already sensing his response.

Garan gazed slowly around the circle, his eyes resting at last on his crabbed and scaly hands. He lifted one and touched it to his face, to the single tear that fell from a sky-blue eye. "You're looking at it," he said.

"Oh, Garan," Fynda murmured, for the moment forgetting her nightmare. She took his hands in hers and rubbed them. "What happened then?"

Garan pulled his hands free. He brushed his fingers against her cheek then covered his eyes. "I couldn't look," he said. "I didn't want to see. I kept willing myself to wake up, for I knew at that moment it was a dream. But the dreamwalkers wouldn't release me.

"Slowly, I spread my fingers and peek through the cracks. Like this." Two pinpoints of blue light poked through the dark crevices between his fingers. "The oak door is gone. In its place stand heavy, wooden bars locked into place by the same keyhole. The room is as it was. Sunbeams stream through windows on each side, crossing in the center of the room, where a man sits, bouncing a young girl on one knee, a young boy on the other. He sings to them, a song about M'nor, about this MoonQuest. I hear the words but can't make them out, however hard I try. And I do try, straining to distinguish words I should be able to understand."

"Your father?" Yhoshi asked.

"No. No one I know. Not at first. His eyes are like my father's, but different. His face is older, but familiar.

"Who was he?" Fynda asked, her eyes wide with wonder.

Garan ignored the question. "The mirror still hangs over the mantel and through it I still see myself as you see me now, in all my hideousness, trapped in that dark, damp place, locked behind that impenetrable barricade. My eyes move from my reflection to the man in the room. He's filled with such joy, I with such pain. Back and forth my eyes travel. Back and forth, forth and back. The more I gaze from my reflection to this familiar stranger, the less strange and more familiar he grows. Until in an explosive flash of vision, I know him. I know his name and everything about him."

"Well, who was he?" Fynda cried impatiently.

"Alas, when the flash passed, he was gone. All that remained was me, as I was in the dream, as I am now, trapped in that place, trapped in this body."

"And the other man?"

"I no longer knew his story, but I still knew his name."

"Well?" Fynda grabbed his arm, but Garan pulled it free and turned away.

"Ryolan Ò Garan," he whispered.

No one spoke. Only the squeaking chatter of a flock of passing flot broke the silence. The birds soared past then circled back, their black-tipped orange wings motionless as they glided toward the water then breaking into a fluttering, splashing whir as they skimmed its surface.

"You're lucky," he said to Fynda, his back still toward her. "The water cleansed away your nightmare. It can do nothing for mine."

"Are you so sure?" I asked.

"Yes," he replied, turning his back on the pond.

No one spoke for a time. Fynda and Garan had returned to their dreams and sat gazing off into seeming nothingness. Yhoshi's eyes remained locked to the earth in an unblinking stare.

"I had a dream too," he whispered at last. "The first I ever remember having." As softly as he spoke, his voice and words pulled Fynda and Garan from their reveries.

"What did you dream about?" I asked.

"I'd rather not say."

"Come, Yhoshi," Garan said. "Don't be coy."

"I'm not being coy. It's not something I want to talk about...to anyone."

Garan turned on him angrily. "After all we've lived through together, we're not 'anyone.' Aren't we on this MoonQuest together? You all keep reminding me that I'm one of the Four. Well, so are you, Yhoshi. Doesn't that mean anything to you?"

Yhoshi glared back. "This is different."

"What can you possibly say that's more intimate than what Fynda and I have shared?"

"Let him do as he pleases," Fynda said. She stood and waded back into the water. "I'm hungry. Will you help me try for some fish, Garan?"

"Thank you, Fynda," Yhoshi said icily. "I'm glad someone understands."

She turned back to face him with angry eyes that belied the calm of her voice. "I didn't say I understood. It just isn't worth arguing about."

"You're wrong, Fynda." Garan stabbed a finger at Yhoshi. "Toshar has shared his dreams and visions. He shares them every day. Fynda and I have shared our nightmares. What have you shared of yourself? You sit there, this golden boy, this little cherub, with no feelings, no emotions, no pain..."

Yhoshi grabbed Garan's finger and yanked Garan toward him, until they were nose to nose. "What do you know of my feelings, my emotions, my pain?" He released the finger and Garan tumbled back.

"Just my point," he grumbled, brushing himself off. "We travel together, we four. We do more than travel together. We quest together. How will we find M'nor? How will we know what to do when we do find her? Only by being one in our deepest hearts. That's what I say. What do you say?" Yhoshi turned away. "What do you say, Toshar?" Garan asked.

I saw the pleading look in Yhoshi's eyes that Garan in his anger missed. "Dear friend," I said tenderly, meeting Yhoshi's anxious gaze, "behind Garan's anger lies an important truth. You know it, don't you?"

Yhoshi nodded, a barely perceptible twitch. He hugged his arms over his chest, squeezing them until they bruised. His shoulders hunched then tensed. "You don't understand," he whispered, "it's different. What you dreamed last night didn't really happen. What I dreamed did. It happened just as I dreamed it. Exactly as I dreamed it.

"Every thrust, slash, shriek, jeer and taunt: It was all as it happened. I didn't want to live it the first time. I didn't want to live it again last night. I don't want to live it a third time —" his voice rose and his finger stabbed back at Garan — "just to satisfy his curiosity."

I guided Yhoshi's finger back into his lap. "You know it's not that at all, don't you?"

Yhoshi slumped in defeat. "Yes," he murmured, "I know that." He sat silently for some minutes, staring bitterly into the distance, struggling with the images that jerked into his consciousness. He shook his head to clear them and fastened his gaze on me.

"I told you," he said at last, without emotion, "of how I became a Messenger, of how I returned to my village to find it empty and razed, to find that the black-shirts had been through, destroying everything, leaving no one." I nodded. "I told you that I followed their bloody trail to the capital where I found my family...their heads...on the Wall of Traitors." I nodded again. "That last part is true. I did see their heads on the wall." He paused, swallowing hard.

"I didn't tell you —" he rasped. "I couldn't tell you all I really saw. How they got there. I couldn't." He inhaled deeply. "There was something in it of Garan's experience with Fvorag and his torturers. There was something in it of Fynda's nightmare. But it was mine. Is mine. I witnessed it and tried to forget it. I witnessed it and tried to die. Now I've witnessed it again. In a dream just as brutal as the original."

Compassion poured from Garan's and Fynda's eyes, but Yhoshi kept his eyes fixed on mine.

"In the dream, as in life, I'm climbing through thick forest, up a mountain slope. The forest is lush and green and I can still smell the rains that washed through last night. It's a magical place and I spend as much time here as I can. This is where I learned my woodlore, just from being here. As I approach the mountaintop clearing where our tiny village sits, where our cell of Believers has hidden since before I was born, I hear shouting. Though we've never been raided, I've been taught caution. I fall to the ground and crawl closer.

"I see billows of black smoke, smell burning flesh. Shouts become shrieks, howls, wails. I recognize no voices, make out no words. I haven't crested the mountain so I don't see anything. Not yet.

"I slither closer, though part of me wants to run away. Closer to the smoke. Closer to the screams. I hide behind the dreaming rock, my favorite place next to the forest. It's not white like it used to be. It's sooty from the fires.

"Even behind the rock I'm still high enough that I can see into the village. Into what was the village. Just about every building is on fire, surrounded by King's Men who won't let the people inside get out. The screams get louder. The smells get worse. A child is pushed through a window and collapses on the ground, wailing in pain. I can't tell who it is or whether it's a boy or girl because it's a writhing mass of fire. Even before it's dead, the soldiers laugh and kick it back into the house.

"Our house is still standing. The door is shut. But where are my parents? My sister? All I see are burning buildings, burning bodies, jeering soldiers.

"Then the door opens and my father, mother and sister, Saffie, come out. I want to run to them but I clutch at the rock to hold myself in check. I want to call to them but I cover my mouth.

"Behind them, prodding Saffie with a saber, struts a soldier, no older than I am. He jabs her with the saber and when she turns I see pinpricks of blood staining her shift. He herds them to another soldier and asks him a question I can't hear. But the answer, a grinning nod, sparks a hideous leer. Two more soldiers step forward. One grabs my father, the other grabs Saffie. The young one shoves my mother to the ground. He shoves her to the ground, and —"

Yhoshi's mouth clamped shut. When he opened it he was gasping for breath. "I can't," he whimpered. "You know what happens next. If you don't, imagine the worst then make it more brutal still. Do I have to speak it, Toshar? Do I?"

"It will be better for you if you can. But say only the words that come. Trust that. Trust yourself. Trust us."

Again, Yhoshi inhaled deeply. His body trembled as he exhaled a dragon-fire spew of rage. "He pushes her to the ground, rips off her clothes and rapes her. That whoring snot-nosed— He rapes her. In front of my father, in front of my sister."

He gulped down a breath then roared, "In front of me!" He thundered to his feet, stomped, kicked up earth, slashed at tree limbs.

"Oh, Yhoshi..."

"Shut up, Fynda. I'm not finished. *He* wasn't finished.

"When he's done, he kicks her to her feet and slashes his mark on her chest. A big, bloody X. Not his name so I could find him, that illiterate pig. An X. An *X*!"

His voice deepened to a growl. "I saw his face, though. He took off his mask so she would see him before she died, before he killed her.

"If only he had killed her then. But, no, that wouldn't have been torture enough. What he did to my mother, he did to Saffie." He spun to face Garan.

"He fucked her, Garan. He fucked her! He was so proud of himself, flaunting his erection. If I ever find the him, I'll slice it right off, but not before I've slashed my name into it so he knows who I am."

Tears coursed down Yhoshi's cheeks in a salty torrent. Mucous dripped from his nose, onto his lips, into his mouth, off his chin and into the earth.

"When he was through with Saffie, the other soldiers took turns. I don't know how many. I stopped counting after ten." His voice dropped to a whisper. "She was only twelve, for Prithi's sake." He swallowed hard.

"Then they slit her throat. Not 'they.' He. That sadistic little nothing, who thinks he's something because he has a uniform and a saber. He kills her then he kills my mother. He slices off their heads and throws their bodies into the fire."

Yhoshi slumped to the ground and buried his head in his hands, sobbing deep, gashing sobs that wrenched his body in jerky spasms.

"There's more, Yhoshi, isn't there?" I asked when the shaking subsided.

"My father," he said, "they made him watch it all. It took seven men to hold him, and then..."

"And then?"

Yhoshi set his jaw and continued with cold rage. "And then they did the same thing to him."

He closed his eyes, squeezing them shut, squeezing the nightmare from them. "In the dream," he said, "I screamed. I screamed and screamed and screamed until my throat was raw and bleeding, until I had no voice."

"And in life?"

"I bit my knuckles until they were raw and bleeding. I bit them to keep from screaming. I bit them to hold back the rage. I bit them because I didn't know what else to do. I should have done something," he whispered. "I should have gone in there."

"What could you have done?" Garan asked. "Nothing. That's what. All you could do was stay alive."

"What for!?" Yhoshi shrieked, startling the flock of white-feathered gannus that floated near shore. The birds took flight in an angry, braying flurry. "How could I live with that memory? I couldn't then. I still can't. That's why I became a Messenger."

"So soldiers could kill you too."

Yhoshi barely moved his head as he nodded *yes*.

"Yet you're still alive."

"I still can't live with the memory, with the nightmare."

A flutter of snowy fluff floated into Yhoshi's lap from the gannus circling overhead.

"It will be easier now," I said.

Yhoshi's eyes fired cannons of fury. "How can you say that?" he bellowed. "I'll never forget. Never. Never. Never."

"I never said you would. I said the memory will be easier to bear." I met his gaze and returned his fire of rage with the fire of love. "It will be easier to bear because you don't bear it alone. Garan's anger wasn't directed at you, Yhoshi, but at Bo'Rá K'n, at the silence.

"Unless we tell our stories, unless we share our stories, the land will not heal and M'nor will be lost to Q'ntana forever. This is your story — one of your stories. Telling it as you did is part of The MoonQuest, part of The Return. It *is* The Return. Sharing your dreams — remembering your dreams and sharing them, sharing them as you did, as Fynda and Garan did — that's what will carry us to M'nor, that's what will restore her light, to us as to all Q'ntana. Do you understand now?"

Yhoshi nodded. Tears still trickled down his face. He wiped them away with the back of his hand. "Thank you," he whispered through a weak smile.

Garan shuffled closer to Yhoshi and put an arm around his shoulder. "I'm sorry," he said. "I was horrible to goad you like that. Toshar was too kind. I *was* angry at you. But I understand, Yhoshi. Now I understand."

"No, Garan. You were right to say what you said. I had to tell it. I didn't want to, but I had to." He shook his head sadly. "It was eating at me, but I couldn't let it out. Who could I tell?"

"Until now," Fynda said softly.

"Until now," he let Fynda take his hand. "It was a monster, as bad as that boy in his black uniform. The more I held it inside, the more it ate at me. If I hadn't let it out it would have killed me and that soldier's work would have been complete."

Yhoshi's smile broadened, but it was veiled in melancholy. "I think I can live now. It won't be easy. But you're right, Toshar. It will be easier."

"I hesitate to ask for more than you've already given," Garan began, "but..."

"But what? I've told you the worst of it. Ask what you need to know."

"I don't need to know this, but I would like to." He paused, trying to frame his query as benignly as possible. "In that whole cell of Believers, why was your family singled out for such brutality? Or did others experience the same...the same...atrocities?"

"No, you're right. They were singled out. We were singled out." He gazed into the distance and a contented smile played at his lips as his memory carried him back to happier times. "My father was village chief," he explained proudly. "It was he who had gathered this cell together and found this village site hidden in the hills. He was a wise man, a gentle man. A courageous man. He could fight if necessary, but he was no warrior. He would not have styled himself a bard, would never have permitted anyone to call him Elderbard, but that's what he was to our village — a teller of tales, a singer of songs, a leader of men...king and Ko'lar in his own tiny realm. Until..." He shook his head, clearing the painful sadness.

"Do you know what happened, how they were betrayed?" Garan asked.

"Do you know how your family was betrayed? Or Toshar his? Does any of us know how we're being betrayed? There are spies everywhere, Garan," he said bitterly. "For all we know those gannus are agents of Fvorag and will race back to him to tell him where we are."

"Not those lovely birds," Fynda cried.

"Even them. It's possible. No human, no animal, no tree, no rock, no blade of grass, can be above suspicion. I saw too many betrayals in my time as Messenger, betrayals that can't be explained any other way."

I stroked the mossy ground then touched my cheek. "We're right to be cautious, Yhoshi, but not to mistrust."

"But —"

"I can barely imagine what you've seen and experienced. But mistrust has deformed Q'ntana, twisting it until lies are truth and truth is a lie, embedding it with layers of fear so thick even M'nor's light can't pierce through. It's the same infection that held you back from sharing your story. It has spread so subtly we don't even see it. Yet it's there. And it must be stopped. We must stop it and begin again."

The gannus stilled their squawking, spread their ample, silver-speckled wings and glided back to the water. They swam in slow, lazy circles, pausing twice in each circuit to bathe their downy faces and broad, black beaks in the comforting warmth of the suns. We watched them in silence until they took to the air again, watched as their broad wings carried them north, into Pre Vilda'aa.

To the End of the Known World

Twenty-Four

The past lay behind us — a billowing expanse of green now flecked with the emerging rust of death. It swelled into the distance, back to the ravine's wavering slash. Ahead, from the top of this half-mountain, narrow trails zigzagged down a steep escarpment to a lush wilderness crisscrossed by ribbons of suns-bleached platinum. Beyond Pre Vilda'aa, a thin line of silvery blue shimmered on the horizon. To thc Vilda'aa it marked the end of the known world. To me it promised a new beginning.

That this new beginning would not arrive easily became quickly apparent. Surging toward us from east, west and south were waves of mounted men, a black tide that would drown us if it could. Confident that a massed battalion could never penetrate Pre Vilda'aa's steamy, untamed jungle, we plunged down the escarpment, leaving behind Mir M'nor's distant promise.

Our confidence was premature. Two masked soldiers, lances crossed, stood grimly at the bottom of the trail, flanked by knotted growth. From the rear, I heard their colleagues navigating toward us.

"Charge them!" Yhoshi yelled and spurred Ta'ar forward. The startled soldiers tried to hold their ground a moment too long. I shuddered as bones snapped under Ta'ar's merciless advance. She pressed on, and we after her, then lurched to a halt before a tangle of thick vines, low-slung limbs and exposed roots. We dismounted and slowly picked our way through until we reached a shallow river. Back on horseback, we splashed along the winding waterway, slowly at first, then picking up speed as the riverbed smoothed from loose rock to sand.

As the way cleared for us, it also cleared for the King's Men, who bounded toward us from the rear. Even had we the will to leave Corem and Merek behind, there was no time to stop. On we raced, as fast as our slowest horse would allow. But the soldiers' shouts grew louder. Louder. Louder.

I looked back — into the spray. Four soldiers — no six — flew toward us. Gaining. Shouting. Gaining.

The creek veered to the right, removing us from the soldiers' vision for an instant. A sharp jog to the left, then to the right, then to the left again. Up front, Yhoshi scanned the riverbank. His head pivoted shore to shore, ahead, then back toward the rest of us and the soldiers. Shore to shore, ahead, then back. Shore to shore, ahead, then back. It took some minutes before I realized what he sought: an opening into the jungle that would let us disappear from the river during one of those windows of invisibility. I searched too. Nothing.

I looked back. The gap narrowed. If the soldiers gained much more ground, Yhoshi's plan wouldn't work. Wait...an opening. I called to Yhoshi, but he didn't hear me over splashing water and shouting soldiers. Yelling. Yelling. Louder. Louder.

I looked back. More soldiers had joined the six. I counted nine. The lead horse rode within a few lengths of me. Yhoshi shouted. Watery tumult drowned his words. Another jog in the creek ahead. Rykka picked up speed but wouldn't pass Corem and Merek.

I looked back again. The nearest black-shirt fell from his horse. His companions pushed toward us. A second soldier toppled. What was happening? With a startled whinny Rykka reared to a stop. Arrayed before us, blocking our passage, stood column after column of androgynous beings, every bare patch of their ebony skin streaked with slashes of white dye, their thin lips turned down into scowls. Vilda'aa.

The first line stood knee-deep in the water. Behind it loomed a second then a third, astride purple korak that rose up from the water on their haunches. Some Vilda'aa held blowpipes to their mouths. Others readied longbows. In the next instant, as the remaining soldiers reined in to a halt behind us, yet more korak-mounted Vilda'aa vaulted out from the shore to surround them.

The lead soldier reached for his sword, preparing to charge through. An arrow whistled over our heads and lodged in his shoulder. He dropped it. Cursing, he pulled the arrow free and waved it angrily at the Vilda'aa warriors. "You dare?" he bellowed. "You dare attack *your* King's Men?"

A blow dart whistled by. It pierced the back of his hand. First his hand then his entire body went numb and he tumbled into the water.

A rush of splashing hoofbeats signaled the arrival of more soldiers. Another company of nine, this one led by Holgg. The Vilda'aa let him push to the front of his ranks then closed in around them. Holgg cursed when he realized he couldn't reach us.

"Hello, Holgg," I called. "How's my uncle?"

He glared at me across a forest of bows. "You'll see for yourself soon enough," he growled.

A volley of high-pitched squeaks issued from the tallest of the Vilda'aa. She wore a headdress of sapphire plumes, each crowned with a burst of crimson. The same feathers decorated her white korak, which hopped through the Vilda'aa lines toward Holgg as she continued her tirade, jabbing bony fingers at the soldiers. Other Vilda'aa chimed in, arguing loudly among themselves.

Garan watched them with intense concentration, his brow even more furrowed than usual. "I think they're discussing whether to turn us over to the soldiers, kill us or take us back with them," he whispered. "If I understand right, one says they should boil the lot of us and have a feast."

Fynda shuddered.

"I had forgotten your knack for languages," I said. "Do you think you can communicate with them?"

"I'll try." Garan screwed up his face and listened. "What do you want me to say?" he asked.

I thought for a moment. "Offer our compliments to the leader. That's the one on the white korak, I think. Say that we bring greetings from Coro Ta'aa, that we come in friendship, that we seek safe passage through their land. Make that 'their beautiful land.' Say that we beg not to be handed over to these soldiers. Say that —"

"Hold on, Toshar. That's enough for a start." Garan cleared his throat then spoke haltingly, his tone calibrated to a higher pitch.

The leader aborted a shrill argument with Holgg, one in which neither seemed to understand the other, and swiveled around, ignoring his barrage of epithets. She half-smiled at Garan, revealing zanga green teeth, then burst into rapid-fire discourse, all the while gesticulating wildly.

Garan shook his head in frustration. She stopped mid-sentence. "Ga-ran," he said, stretching each syllable. He pointed to himself, then introduced each of us.

"Fara," she replied. Her smile broadened with delight. She stuck a fuchsia tongue out at us then smiled again.

Holgg reached for his sword and tried to force his way through. "Tell it to let us go," he roared, "and you with us, or it will have the king and his army to answer to. Tell it that."

Fara bared her teeth and raised her arm. In an instant, every longbow and blowpipe was primed. Holgg glared angrily and held back. Fara dropped her arm, barked a command, then turned back to Garan, enunciating very slowly. She pointed to Holgg.

"Molk Fara," Garan translated, not meeting Holgg's stare, "asks that you surrender your weapons."

Holgg kicked at the Vilda'aa boy who reached up for his sword. Fara hissed, again raised her arm and waited as the young warrior picked himself out of the water and tried again. Holgg slashed at him. Pink hand severed from ebony wrist in a geyser of blood that soaked into the black of Holgg's uniform and his horse's coat. Fara roared, drew a circle in the air and the soldier next to Holgg tumbled into the creek, his body a pincushion for Vilda'aa darts and arrows.

"She says she'll pick you off one by one until you do as she says," Garan said, looking at Holgg's feet. "She says it won't take long."

Holgg glared at Garan then at the mass of Vilda'aa arrayed against him. "Do it," he grunted. "Drop your weapons." Then to Fara, "You'll pay for this. Very soon." He looked back, trying to see beyond the bend in the creek, trying to listen for the soldiers I knew couldn't be far behind.

To Garan, he roared, "Tell it that we *will* take you, even if we have to torture and kill everyone to do it." He fixed Garan with a fierce stare. "Starting with you." He smiled cruelly. "Again."

Fara shrugged and turned her back on him. Garan, clearly shaken, finally delivered my request to Fara. She smiled and again stuck out her tongue before responding.

"We're welcome to stay in Pre Vilda'aa as long as we wish," Garan said, "but she says there is nothing beyond here. The world ends, she says, when these lands do."

"Tell her —" I began, but Holgg cut me off.

"Tell *it* this," he snorted. "Tell it that unless it releases you into my custody, this land will be overrun with soldiers by nightfall. Tell it that the king's will will not be denied, not by the likes of such creatures."

Fara nudged her korak through Vilda'aa lines until it stood nose-to-nose with Holgg's horse. She waited until all was still, then spoke quietly, her voice bristling with contempt.

"You have two choices," Garan translated, looking directly at Holgg for the first time. "Leave as you came, under escort, promising never to return. Or stay and be killed." I could hear the wicked grin in his voice. "'You'll make a fine stew', she says."

Holgg's face reddened. "I'll be back for you," he snarled at Garan. He turned to Fara and spat in her face. "There are more where we come from. There always are."

Without waiting for Garan's translation, Fara called out an order. As she raised her arm and circled it over her head, an arrow and dart whizzed past us. The first killed the soldier next to Holgg, the second felled Holgg's horse, pitching him into the water. Cursing, he reached with dripping hand for his dead colleague's horse. But one of Fara's warriors was already leading it away to a chorus of high-pitched titters. Sloshing forward to the next horse, he jerked the soldier off and mounted. "You'll pay for this," he shouted.

"No," Fara said, "it is you who will pay if you cross into our lands again." She spoke clearly, in our tongue. Turning to Garan, she smiled mischievously. "Yours is such an ugly language," she said. "Such a pity."

Twenty-Five

Fara and I watched stars wink knowingly through a near-invisible frame of trees. Ours were the only eyes still open at this hour. One by one, Garan, Yhoshi, Fynda and the half-dozen Vilda'aa warriors who accompanied us had followed Aygra and B'na into sleep. Even the horses dozed. Now, rumbling snores competed with the crickety-squeak of waking insects — the only sounds in the sultry, starry jungle night.

What did the stars see that I couldn't? What could they tell me if only I knew how to hear? We were so near to Mir M'nor, to the beginning of the end and the end of the beginning. Would we know what to do when we arrived? I offered a silent prayer to the milky wash of stars and to the moon that still hid her face. No answer came. The answer would come. I knew it would. But would it come in time?

The crack of stone on stone and a white spark-turned-flame interrupted my reverie. Fara had lit her pipe and a fragrant aroma filled the air — sandalwood with a hint of cherry.

"It is still dark in Q'ntana, is it not?" she asked.

"As dark as it has ever been," I replied.

"That is what the Coro Ta'aa told me. She...you say 'she'?" I nodded. "He. She. That is what I find most difficult about you goniga'aa, you strangers-from-beyond-the-cliff. To us, there is no he-word, no she-word. All living things are 'omm.' It is simpler, I think, and more respectful."

"I think you're right," I said.

"The first Coro Ta'aa, omm you call M'naben. I visited her many times in Q'ntana. I will never set my foot back in that place again. It is evil. The land itself is evil."

How could I disagree? My homeland had torn my parents from me, slain my grandmother, taken from me all I knew and loved. It was an evil place, a cruel, malevolent land. At moments like this it seemed beyond redemption and my MoonQuest hopeless folly. I opened my mouth to say so. But the words that emerged were others. They came from the stars, who spoke at last.

"The land mourns, Fara, for all the blood that soaks into it. The land weeps, for all the hatred that desecrates it. The land rages, for all the malignance that grinds into it. But the land is not evil, Fara. M'nor smiled on Q'ntana once. She will again."

Fara poked at the dead coals. An ember sparked then died. "The first Coro Ta'aa spoke the same," she said. "I am not so sure."

"M'naben spoke wisely."

"She taught me your dialect. Do I speak well?"

"Very. Why didn't you speak it to Holgg?"

"Few of my people speak it. It is not right that others should not know what is said. I don't mind that goniga'aa like that Holgg think I am stupid. It frees their tongues to say what they would otherwise not say." Her face broke into a green, toothy grin. "It is useful."

With a twig she emptied the pipe bowl of its ashy residue then refilled it from a tiny fur pouch. Once again, she struck flint against stone and lit the pipe. A new aroma — lemon sage — wafted toward me. She puffed once and passed me the pipe.

"We see few goniga'aa here we can call friend," she said. "It is the custom to share second pipe, the pipe of friendship, with honored guests." The slender ebony stem and blond bowl, both delicately carved with circles and spirals, came from a single limb. Berakka. I had only seen this two-tone wood once before, on a pendant that had belonged to Eyla, Eulisha's father and Elderbard before her. My mother had been wearing it when the q'eenah swallowed her.

I inhaled, choked, coughed up smoke. Fara laughed and pounded my back. "Let smoke find its way down," she said. "Open your lungs and become the smoke. Become the fire."

I closed my eyes and imagined myself a plume of smoke that braided and mingled with the burning tobacco. Warm, woody air swirled freely through me. Its breath became my breath; its spirit, my spirit. When it was ready to leave, I let it go, and part of me seemed to float away with it.

"Now you are no longer goniga'aa," Fara pronounced. "Now you are Vilda'aa."

I drank down a few gulps of night air before responding. Still moist, it was cooler now. It was as though the lemon sage had expelled the day's stifling humidity.

"I am honored," I said, "but I have no gift to match yours."

Fara bristled. "Guests do not offer gifts. That is host's duty." She drew heavily on the pipe, breathing out her moment of outrage. Four, more tranquil puffs followed. After each she blew a perfect circle-cloud of smoke. When the last had dissolved into the night, she asked, "Can your journey to the end of the known world truly heal Q'ntana?"

"I can't know for certain," I said. "But I must go and see."

"Yes," she said thoughtfully, "For Q'ntana's sake." She inhaled deeply, igniting the orange ember that glowed from the pipe bowl. She exhaled, sighing, then looked past me, back toward the escarpment. "The cliff has guarded us well. We are good here."

"Are you? Holgg and his thugs will be back."

Fara spit into the dying embers. The sizzle of her saliva lasted for only an instant before being swallowed up by the silence.

"That's what I say to those— What do you call them?"

"Thugs."

"Yes. Thugs."

"It's too late for spitting, Fara. The change has already happened."

"What change? What do you mean?" She looked into the darkness as though expecting my answer to come from there.

"I think you know" I replied gently, pulling her gaze back to mine. "Do you still tell stories around the fire? Do you still sing of the Vilda'aa who came before you? Do you still dream of the Vilda'aa yet to come?"

"Once upon a time..." Fara struggled for words then stopped, shaking her head in frustration. Tears coursed down her face, driving ebony rivers through the white dye that streaked her cheeks.

"Then Q'ntana's sickness has already spread," I said. "The cliffs have not held it back."

"You are right, Toshar Vilda'aa." Fara wiped her cheeks, smudging white into gray. "There is one gift, if you can," she whispered so quietly I could barely hear. "You must finish your MoonQuest. You must stop the sickness. Vilda'aa need it too."

Daybreak saw us once more on the move. Fara hurried us awake and onto our horses. We breakfasted as we rode — dry, leathery koya that Fara and her warriors wolfed down with noisy rclish. Their tastes were not ours. Nor their teeth. We chewed and chewed and chewed the tough, stick-like root willing it to soften enough to swallow, if only to avoid its bitter flavor. But it was food, and we didn't know when we would eat again. Fara led, striding confidently through the jungle. Her warriors walked behind us, pointed ears tuned to every sound. As the suns neared union, she stopped.

"You must leave horses now if you wish to continue safely," she said. Ahead, the tangle closed in. We dismounted and scanned in vain for the way ahead. "There is always a way," she said. "Pre Vilda'aa teems with invisible roads." She clicked her tongue and four warriors stepped up to the horses.

"No!" Fynda cried. She stood between Corem and the warrior, pushing his hands away when he tried to touch the horse. "We can't just leave them here, in the middle of nowhere."

"This is not nowhere," Fara snapped. "This is Pre Vilda'aa. Where you go is nowhere." She clicked her tongue again and the warrior stepped back. "I am sorry for your horses, but there is no way they can accompany you. We will care for them and hold them for your return." She eyed me closely. "You will return," she said. "There is no other way back."

I said nothing. We would not return. There would be no Pre Vilda'aa to return to. Rykka and Ta'ar would find us as they had before. As for Corem and Merek... Fynda stroked Corem's nose and whispered in her ear. "She knows," I thought. "Even if she doesn't know she knows." Garan, too, nuzzled Merek with a wistful finality.

Fara watched with mounting impatience as first Yhoshi then the rest of us riffled through our saddlebags, transferring supplies to our backpacks. "No-no, no-no, no-no," she shouted. "No room for packs. Barely room for you. You must take nothing, nothing at all. Fill your pockets and no more. Pre Vilda'aa will shelter you. Pre Vilda'aa will feed you. As for this Mir, that is between you and omm."

Fara saw openings in the dense greenery where we saw none. Every few minutes she stopped at what seemed an impasse, turned full circle, pondered, then stepped into another jungle tunnel. We crawled after her, thorns, burs and bristles snagging our clothing, snarling our hair, slashing our faces. Now and again, she disappeared altogether. When I called after her, she reappeared, pink hands gesturing us through a fresh aperture and into another maze of rabbit holes, each more cramped and constricted than the last. Each scratchier than the last. Although the suns rarely penetrated, the gloomy shade offered little respite from the muggy swelter.

We crept on. A buttery snake slithered onto Garan's head. He shrieked, flailing blindly at it, until Yhoshi flicked it off.

"I don't see why we couldn't have made better time by water, with our horses," Garan whimpered. "One of these rivers must lead out of here."

"They all do," Fara said. She stopped and once again scrutinized an apparent dead end. "The river is one way, but it is not right way. This is the way I must lead you, so this is the way you must travel."

She paused, ears alert. "Listen," she whispered. First nothing but splashes cut through the viscous air. Then, voices. Men's voices. Soldier's voices. My body tensed as the splashing drew near. Too near.

Fara gestured toward the sound. "River way is just beyond," she said, "but we are safe. Even if they knew to find us here, they could not reach us."

I didn't feel safe. The soldiers spoke as if they stood next to me.

"We've killed everyone we've found, sir." Holgg's voice. "A score."

"Is that all? What about those you haven't found? I want them dead. Kill them all." I hadn't thought it possible to hate a voice more than I hated Zakk's. But from those three words, spit out in clipped tones accompanied, I felt sure, by a sneer, I knew I'd been wrong. Who was he?

"The others must be hiding in the bush," Holgg replied. "I can't see how. You can't push an arm in there without it coming out scratched and scraped."

"I don't care if you're cut to ribbons. I don't care if you chop down the whole jungle. I want these people put down." His voice seethed with loathing. "Burn them out. Turn all this and everyone in it into ash. There's your answer."

As Yhoshi fidgeted impotently with his dagger, a warrior directed his blowpipe toward the voices. Fara shook her head.

"We can't, sir," Holgg said. "The vegetation is too green." Fara nodded.

"You're full of excuses, aren't you, Holgg? Then smoke them out."

"No, sir. I mean, yes, sir."

"Kill them. All but their leader. I want that one alive, so I can kill him myself."

"You mean the bard, sir?"

"What?"

"The bard, sir. Is that who you want?

No response. The silence lasted so long I began to think I had imagined the conversation. "You forget yourself, soldier," he replied at last. "There are no bards."

"Of course not, sir."

"You forget yourself and remind me of your incompetence. That boy, the one you call 'bard.' You've been chasing him how long?" Holgg didn't answer. "Do you ignore me, soldier?" he roared.

"No, sir. I don't know, sir. Too long, sir." I couldn't help but take pleasure at hearing Holgg humiliated, even as I knew it would serve only to heighten his cruelty.

"If I had more men..."

"First you whine that I've sent you out with too many. Now you have too few? You have what you have. Do you understand me, Holgg?'"

"I think so, sir. Yes, sir."

"If you don't, there's another who will."

"Yes, sir."

"There's always room for another head on the Wall of Traitors, Holgg. Do I make myself clear?"

"Yes, sir."

"Then do it. Now."

A moment's silence then splashing hooves receded into the distance. Fara said nothing at first. Using leaves from a nearby shrub, she bandaged the worst of our cuts. But her thoughts were elsewhere. When she spoke it was to her warriors and in her own tongue, with a rapidity Garan couldn't follow. Their faces, expressionless until now, looked grim. They nodded and vanished into the undergrowth.

"They go to warn others," she said quietly.

Yhoshi still fingered his dagger. "Why didn't you let the warriors kill them?" he asked.

Fara stared through the thicket as though she could see right to the river, and beyond. "Maybe it was mistake. Maybe it was right. It is too late now." She turned back to us. "If they go the way I think, they will be ambushed before they reach their men. If not..." She shrugged. "It is in Prithi's hands."

"I'm sorry, Fara," I said. "We have brought this to you. I wish..." I paused, not sure what to wish. "I wish there had been another way."

"Had there been another way, Toshar-Vilda'aa, we would not be sitting here this day. This is the road Prithi has set for us. This is the road we must walk."

"It's a hard road," Fynda said, "and so unfair."

"Others might have been harder," Fara said. Her copper eyes pooled with tears. "I would cry for Vilda'aa. I would cry for all the life these goniga'aa strip from my lands. I would cry," she wiped her eyes clear, "but there is no time. I will mourn later, if I am cursed enough to survive." Her dry eyes bore into mine. "Your gift," she said, "becomes more precious than ever."

The burden of her hopes pressed into me, exposing the roots of my fear. I didn't know what to say. I felt sure I would fail her, fail everyone, and no one more than myself.

Her fingers brushed my cheek. Her skin was rough, but her touch gentle. "Do not fear," she said, touching my cheek. "You will do what you must. I will do what I must. That is the only way." Her nose and ears quivered like a k'nrah's. She sniffed, sniffed again. I smelled it too. Smoke. "They have begun their slaughter," she said. "The ambush has failed."

Fara burrowed deeper and deeper into the jungle, trying to outrun the smoke. We struggled to keep up with her as thin curls licked at our heels and twined around us. Although we saw no fire, distant crackling reminded us that more than jungle heat drenched our clothes with sweat. I had no sense of time's passage. The suns offered no clues. When not cloaked by plaits of vine and limb, they vanished behind rolling billows of white smoke.

"How much farther?" Garan asked wearily.

"Do not speak," Fara said. "Save your breath for breathing. We will get there when we get there." Would we have breath left when we did? Smoky tendrils insinuated into the dark passage, strangling us in their suffocating grip. Fara slowed to let us catch up with her.

"Faster," she said. "You must go faster. This is a race smoke must not win." But it was winning. A dense, choking river gushed past, as though glad to find a clear route through the tangle.

"I can't," Fynda cried. Tears streamed from bloodshot eyes. "I can't move," she gagged. "I can't breathe."

"You can," Fara said. Her pursed lips opened into a rare smile of encouragement that collapsed into a fit of coughing. She tore a yellow frond from the ivy twining a nearby tree and popped it into her mouth. Then she passed one to each of us. As we chewed, the coughing subsided, and we resumed our progress, crawling with one hand on the ground, the other clearing the branches that blocked our path. Only once did Fara's step falter. She stopped, glanced left to right and back. She turned her head again, more slowly, then again, more slowly still, as if counting the leaves on each bush, the veins on each leaf. She started forward, then froze. Now she studied the smoke, following its course and contours with her eyes.

"We have reached a crossroads," she said. "One way opens to the sky but travels like a snake. You will be able to stand, but it means two more walking days. The other is quicker, but on it you will be the snake, traveling on your belly through smoke more thick than this."

"For how long?" I asked.

"On the quick path, we reach the end of Pre Vilda'aa, the end of all, before nightfall."

Could we survive more smoke? Could Fynda? Dry, hacking coughs convulsed through her. When the spasms eased, her chest still heaved painfully. She gazed at me helplessly, blinking away smoke. They all did. The ivy fronds could do little against the increasingly acrid air. I looked pleadingly at Fara.

"The decision is yours," she said. "I will lead you either way. But you must decide. Now."

Fynda forced a weak smile. "Either way," she said.

I swallowed hard. "The quick route," I said, "There's more danger in delay. For your people and for mine."

For mine? How can I speak of "my" people? I am not King. I am not Elderbard. I may never be Elderbard. I don't want to be Elderbard.

Yes, I do.

I do? I can't think that. An Elderbard speaks for his people. How can I speak for anyone? How do I dare? What if I make a wrong choice? What if I've just made a wrong choice? We can't survive more smoke. Fynda can't. Hear how she coughs, how they all cough. Could a delay be worse than this?

I open my mouth. "I've changed my mind," I say. No one notices. I say it again. "I've changed my mind." Still, they slither ahead on their bellies behind Fara, paying me no heed. I'm on my belly too. Breathing in smoke. Coughing out smoke. Nothing but smoke. I'm alone in the smoke. Smoke that blows at me from S'kala's fiery nostrils and molds itself into familiar faces — Zakk, Holgg, Miknos... Not Miknos! Images that form, unform, reform. Another face. A stranger. Dark, drooping mustache forcing a lipless mouth into a permanent scowl.

"Burn them out," it says — again and again and again. "Burn them out." I look away from the mouth, up a pinched face to hooded eyes. "That boy," the eyes say, "seize him...seize him...seize him..."

I look up again to escape those words, past coarse black brows that meet over a bulbous nose, coarse black brows that merge with shiny black hair over an unseen forehead. Something else shines on that head, shines with a flash. It's gone. He's gone.

Another form emerges from the smoke: a trunkless head that hovers in front of mine. A green face with empty, red-ringed eye sockets. The mouth opens, opens wide in a silent, gaping laugh. Wider and wider it stretches until the blackness inside devours the whole head. The smoky mouth moves closer. Closer. Constricts my throat. Crushes my chest. Tightens my stomach as it loosens my bowel. The mouth enters my mouth and I taste sooty bile. I gag, shrink back. But the mouth moves with me, gains on me. Is set to devour me.

"You are nothing," I hear myself whisper. The mouth suspends its advance. "You are nothing," I repeat, more loudly. The mouth begins to shrink in on itself. "I do fear you," I say. "I wish I didn't, but I do." The vacuum wavers uncertainly. "But my fear will not stop me, Bo'Rá K'n. You will not win."

I step forward, toward it, into it. "You cannot win."

The mouth dissolves into formless smoke. I feel a flame ignite within me, a white fire that flushes through me, from me, around me, smokelessly burning off the blinding smoke. I see a light ahead, a bluish-silver light through the thinning weave of branches. A faint, salty tang tickles my lips. I'm no longer crawling. I'm standing, wonderstruck by the shimmering turquoise halo sea that frames Fara's silhouette.

"We are here," she says, "at the end of my lands, at the end of the known world."

Twenty-Six

ara stood before an arched opening in the trees, her face a mixture of longing and confusion. Beyond her, smooth sea and empty sky merged seamlessly in an infinite palette of deep blue. Seven earthen steps descended from our leafy threshold to a narrow strand of pink beach. I moved to pass through the portal, but Fara held onto my arm.

"I go no further," she said. "I hear the cries of my people and must return. I cannot see how this emptiness will save anything, but I turn my trust to you and Prithi to make it so. However." Turning her back on the calming vista, she flashed a quick, uneasy grin and disappeared into the billowing smoke.

Garan look after her anxiously. "How will we get back?" he asked.

"Not that way," I said. "Come, there's no time to lose."

Again, I stepped toward the threshold. Again, I was pulled back. An angry burst of smoke encircled Fynda. She grabbed my arm and collapsed, coughing up blood and phlegm. Tears coursed down her cheeks. "I can't," she gasped.

"You must," I said. Wheezing ourselves, Yhoshi, Garan and I half-carried, half-dragged Fynda to the portal. "You have to walk through on you own," I said. "There's no other way." She stood, but her legs crumpled beneath her. We helped her up. Again, she collapsed. Once more, with the smoke denser than ever, she pulled herself up and flung herself across the threshold.

No smoke followed us through. Here, clean, salty mist enfolded us in a healing embrace that cleared our lungs and cleansed our pores. Fynda inhaled, smiled tentatively, inhaled again, then with a whoop of joy, leapt onto the beach and into the water, leaving behind a trail of sooty clothes. Yhoshi, Garan and I stripped and bounded in after her. Laughing, jumping, splashing, we swam, chased the surf and dove for spiral shells that glinted luminously on the sandy ocean floor.

When we finally chanced to look back, the view stunned us into silence. Jungle and portal were gone, replaced by more sea and sky. Gone too was the beach, and with it our clothing. My heart sank. The kolai. Had I now lost these too? The only solid ground in this endless wash of blue was a rocky, low-lying spit. Foam-flecked waves lapped playfully against its sides, sending up vaporous fountains that met and mingled in midair before settling on the narrow, north-pointing finger. We clambered onto it and there were our kolai, dry despite the mist. They sat in a close circle, their red veins glowing through the polished black marble.

From atop the spit we could no more see where this land form began than where it ended. This was more than the end of the known world. This was a vast emptiness, though not a frightening one. Nor were we alone in it. Flying fish currahed past as they vaulted from one side of the spit to the other, carried by feathered wings that fanned out from tapered, scale-wrapped torsos. Feathers and scales shimmered violet, lemon, green and red in the air then shifted to turquoise when they touched water, blending with the sea as they sank beneath its surface. In the distance, large, whale-like creatures, shiny with sleek, russet pelts spouted watery columns, forcing flocks of creamy doves to break formation around the steaming geysers. The brilliant, silver-tinged light that washed around us seemed to filter up from the sea not down from the sky, where neither suns shone nor clouds sailed. Warm air balanced the cool wetness of the spit as we walked single file along the slippery stone, clutching our kolai. Even the salt that soon dusted our lips and skin neither stung nor parched.

"It's incredible," Yhoshi said. "I couldn't have imagined so much water in one place. Is this Mir M'nor?"

"I don't know," I replied. "It was dark..."

"My father talked about a place like this once," Garan said. "Once upon a time... He said I would see it one day. Maybe it is The Mir..."

"What else did he say?" I pressed.

Garan shook his head. "Until this moment I had no memory of it. And now, as soon as I try to say it, the words dissolve on my tongue."

"Even when I was little, you never talked about your family."

"There was nothing to say. Like Yhoshi, mine was a family of Believers. Like you, Toshar, they were taken from me. I learned your father's courage when he took me in as an orphan. I lost it somewhere in Horusha's labyrinth. In between, I taught you what little I knew." A dove perched on his shoulder and he stroked it tenderly, exchanging soft throaty coos with it.

"As for this place, I don't know what to say," he said glumly. "As for my father's story..." He shrugged.

"The stories will return as we live them," I said. We walked on in a silence broken only by the sounds of the sea. Ahead, the spit rose to a mossy hillock — a good place to rest, I thought. A closer look revealed it to be scaly green slate. From the top, we scanned the horizon for land, for an end to the spit. Nothing. Nothing but that invisible line where sea and sky became one. Garan's brooding melancholy spread as we contemplated our endless walk to nowhere. How long could we keep walking? How long could we continue without food or water?

"I know there's no choice but to go on," Fynda said, "but I wish I knew where we were going."

"And when we'll get there," Yhoshi added.

I nodded but said nothing. I had no answers.

Something did. "Seven days and seven nights, don't you know," it said. A fleshy, mud-colored head poked out from the front of the hill, which rose slightly on the four webbed feet that appeared on each side. "I've been expecting you," the creature said, "and you're right on schedule. Perhaps even a bit early. But that's fine, just fine." He twisted his head around as far as he could, then gave up. "I can't see you up there, but it feels like four. I was told to expect four. You are four, aren't you?

"Oh, I know all about you," he continued before I could reply. "All about you. Are you comfortable?" He stretched his head out and around even farther, but his single eye still couldn't see us. "I'll try to make this as smooth as I can, but my legs are stiff — from the damp. Silly, I know, but there it is. Hold on tight, now." He rose slowly to his full height and with painful effort pushed himself into the water. As he paddled away, two giant waves crossed over and swallowed the spit. It never reappeared.

"Yes," he continued, prattling nonstop, "seven days and seven nights. Are you comfortable? You never said. My, my, but you're a quiet group. Or am I talking too much? She says I talk a lot, but she's never said it was too much. But you aren't her. No, that you're not. Hello? Are you still up there? Of course you are. I feel your weight. No, don't apologize. I don't mind, especially in the water. Swimming's easier than walking these days. My legs, don't you know. It's been a long while since I've carried anyone over to her. A long while. Though I can't remember whether it was a long while ago or a long while to come. No matter. Are you comfortable? You never said."

"Yes, thank you," I injected before he could pursue his monologue. "But who are you and where are you taking us?"

"Didn't I say? How rude you must think me. Are there no tartarucas where you come from? That's what I am. A tartaruca. Pryma: That's who I am. Pryma, messenger to M'nor. That's where we're heading, of course. 'Bring them to me,' she said. 'No dilly-dallying.' She knows me. I like to dilly-dally, to stop here and there, now and again. Even with no dilly-dallying it will take seven days and seven nights, don't you know. Not that you'll notice."

We sat in expectant silence, ready to leap in with questions. But Pryma never paused, not even for breath. He just chattered on until, lulled by his voice and the water's rhythm, we fell into a lazy doze. When we awoke, sea and sky had faded to a charcoal haze and Pryma's soliloquy had dissolved into a haunting, wordless melody. He hummed softly and, without realizing it, we hummed along as we lay on his back watching color drain from the sky. I knew this song of M'nor's. I had sung it before. Yet when the last light retreated and took Pryma's humming with it, we stopped too, as though, suddenly, we no longer knew the melody.

Pryma slowed then ceased his paddling. We floated, rocking gently with the breath-like heave of the sea. "We're here," he announced.

"I thought it was going to take seven days and seven nights," Yhoshi said.

"It did. What you didn't sleep through you sang through. And now we're here."

"Where is here?" I asked.

"Here. Open your eyes. Open your minds. Open your hearts. And you will see." At first we saw nothing, not even each other. No stars hung from the ink-black sky. Then a ruby beam from Pryma's eye cut eerily into the night, touching down on a single circle of sea that remained fixed as he paddled toward it.

"You have sung the song. Now it is time to speak the story." He spoke so softly I could barely distinguish his words from the soft susurrus of waves. "I must leave you now," he said, sinking slowly. The red light vanished, plunging us into darkness.

"We're going to drown," Garan said dreamily.

"Can you see anything at all, Fynda?" Yhoshi asked nervously. "Solid land to swim to?"

"There's nothing to see," I said.

Water sloshed around my legs. I was strangely calm, as was Garan. "I can't really swim, you know," he said, not at all concerned by the water that now rose to our shoulders.

"Stand up quickly and link hands," I said, but these were Pryma's words not mine. As we did, we stopped sinking and slowly floated back to ankle-depth.

"Now what?" Yhoshi asked.

"We have sung the song," I said. "Now it is time to speak the story."

"What story?" Fynda asked. What story, indeed? I closed my eyes in search of the words then opened them again, for the dark within and the dark without were the same.

"Trust," an inner voice prompted. "Trust and listen." Was it Pryma's? Na'an's? The Lady Gwna's? It blended elements of all of them but was none of them. It was my voice — calm, purposeful, strong. "Speak what you see," it said. "Speak what your heart bids. Speak what you have always known." What I have always known...

I focused all my being and listened — to the water's murmur, the wind's whisper, the night's silence. They all spoke and I repeated their wisdom, making it my own. "It is not a long story," I said, "but a true one. Truest of the true." Garan squeezed my hand encouragingly. "It begins with a moon and will end with a moon. In between is the story we speak from our hearts, the story each speaks in turn until The Return is complete. Only then can the land be healed.

"From that first moon until this night of no moon, a land was created and destroyed, a kingdom of light fell into darkness, a sea of joyful tears turned bitter in sorrow. It is for us to restore that light.

"As we tell M'nor's story, we tell our own. As M'nor rebirths through that telling, so do we. As we do, so does Q'ntana. That is The MoonQuest. That is The Return." I took a deep breath. My part was done. "Fynda," I said, "I pass the story to you."

Sweat greased her palm. Her pulse quickened. "I-I don't know any stories. I don't know anything."

"You know more than you know, which is all you need to know." I heard the voice emerge from the dark. It was Fynda's voice, though not a voice I had ever heard. "Listen to the words that speak through your heart. Repeat what they say. Be still and listen."

"I-I —" She fought for air and shuddered uncontrollably.

"Breathe. Breathe deeply and fully of sea-salt air. Breathe." Fynda inhaled, taking in the living moisture that enveloped us, then exhaled — a long, deliberate breath. Her palms dried and her heart's pounding stilled. When she spoke, it was in this new voice — clear as crystal, light as gossamer, strong as iron.

"Once— Once upon a time, when M'nor was young and joyful, Q'ntana was the land of magic and light that its name signifies in the language of our ancestors. It was in this language that bards sang their legends, spoke with dragons and taught their young. As all lived these songs and stories, all prospered: the people, the light and the land.

"Then from the black heart of one dreamwalker, darkness spread to every heart. Stories ceased. Dreams ended. Singing stilled. The kingdom of Bo'Rá K'n and Fvorag arose in this land of bards. Of no bards. Of no light.

"From that place of no light, a new kingdom arose, ruled from a new capital when the ancient heart of Q'ntana refused to surrender. It refuses still. It awaits The Return."

A white light, deep in the water beneath us, inched upward almost imperceptibly as Fynda spoke. Its dim wavering glow illuminated the faces around the circle. Fynda's was the brightest, radiating an inner power that shone through her skin. Yhoshi's face was tight, as though worrying through a difficult dilemma. A smile played on Garan's lips, his eyes still unfocused and tranced. "And what do I look like?" I wondered again.

"Light," Fynda said, as if in response. "A light from within that pushes its way out. But it is a struggle...the struggle for Alanda." Frowning, she strove to continue. No words came, until at last she said, "Garan, I pass the story to you."

Garan's smile broadened as the underwater light drew nearer. "Bards will sing again," he said. "They will return from beyond the endless seas that cradle Q'ntana. They open their eyes even now."

As though an invisible lamplighter strode through the sky, first one star then another blinked alight, until an infinity of eyes smiled down on us through the velvet night. Garan gasped at the power of his words.

After a moment's startled silence, he continued. "They open them for Prithi but not yet for Q'ntana." His voice darkened. "Prithi watches but does not interfere. Prithi watches the stars and Prithi watches Alanda. Prithi watches...and waits." He paused again. He too struggled to speak on, but could do no more than pass the story to Yhoshi. Meanwhile, the underwater light continued to rise.

"I don't know any stories," Yhoshi began.

"You know many stories, Yhoshi, son of Yhosha," a voice sang. "It's time, Yhoshi. Time to remember what you know, to speak what you see, to share the dream. Look to the light, Yhoshi."

"I—" Yhoshi hesitated, confused. His mouth moved noiselessly as he groped for words that would not come. Then his eyes caught the reflection of the ever-approaching sea-light and his face relaxed. "I know no stories—" His eyes closed and started to twitch. "But I will tell you what I see... A battle. The battle for Alanda and Q'ntana. For M'nor. The final battle. It's happening now, in this moment. I see it...

"A black flood surges toward Alanda, washes up against Castle Rose. Wave after wave. Again and again. From all sides. But Castle Rose stands and sunlit pennants fly defiance from its towers."

A look of horror scarred his face. "No. I see a single, fire-blackened rag hanging limply from a single turret. Blood and soot smear crumbling walls. Wait…

"The image shifts back. Now I see Castle Rose undamaged… Now I see a desolate shell. Back and forth, back and forth, back and forth. My head hurts with it." His voice was agitated.

"Which is the truth?" He opened his eyes. "Which is the truth?" he asked again. "Toshar?"

"Toshar." The voice that spoke my name this second time was not Yhoshi's. It was a woman's, muffled, a delicate bell swaddled in wools. "Look up," she said. Directly above our circle, in line with the still-rising light, was a dark patch no stars had penetrated. Slowly, traces of opalescence burned away the blackness. Weak at first, they gained strength as they pushed through. The more light was revealed, the quicker the remaining blackness dissipated, until M'nor shone through: clear, radiant, whole.

"Welcome," she trilled in carillon chime. "You have answered my summons and I, yours. Your words have melted the blackness around me and dried my tears. For that I thank you."

"Then Castle Rose has won?" Yhoshi asked.

"Though I shine for you who have opened your hearts to me, I cannot yet shine for all Q'ntana. Yhoshi has seen it and spoken it. You all have. The final battle awaits a victor."

Yhoshi swallowed hard. I had never seen him this nervous. "May I ask a question?" he asked.

"Of course, Yhoshi-warrior. I am here for you as I am for all who listen, trust and follow."

"You say I know, but I don't. Which is the truth?"

"Wisely and boldly asked," she replied. "The truth has yet to be written. It hangs, waiting — but not forever. Before another day passes Prithi will carve it into the earth. Then it will be fixed for all time." We held our breath. Even the waves had stilled. "At this moment, Alanda fights the armies of he who calls himself king. Many die — on both sides. This is the final battle. There is no longer room for truce. One side must prevail."

"But which?" Yhoshi blurted.

M'nor's light dimmed. "What do you see now, Yhoshi-warrior?" she asked.

Yhoshi closed his eyes. We waited.

"What do you see?" she repeated.

"The image doesn't change," he said. "I want it to change."

"It will not. See, all of you." Suspended in the beam that linked M'nor with the underwater light was a wavery likeness of Castle Rose — a blackened shell, reeking of death and lost hope. "That is the truth that emerges from this moment. That is the truth Prithi will carve if this moment lingers unaltered."

I thought I would explode with anger. Where was the meaning in our journey if Q'ntana was doomed. "Has all we've endured been for naught?" I shouted up at her.

"No, young bard," she answered gently. "Nothing is ever for naught. Nor has your quest reached its end, unless you will it so. Do you?"

"No," we cried fiercely.

"Regardless of the peril?"

"Regardless of the peril."

"Then know this: There is no end to the quest for those who choose to live the journey." She regained her former luster, bathing us in a radiant aura. "Now the time has come for The Nayr."

Shame flooded through me. I dropped my gaze. "I-I don't have it," I stammered. "I-I lost it." My folly had condemned Q'ntana. Tears cascaded down my face dropping like rain into the water.

"You did not lose it, young bard. You sent it back to me, as I now send it back to you." I looked up and felt her warmth dry my eyes. "Do you know its story?" I shook my head. "This chalice was forged at the beginning of time by Prithi, who gave it to the dragon Kumba at Q'ntana's birth. Kumba poured himself into it and gave me life. He will do it again once you have returned The Nayr to its rightful place in Castle Rose."

"What about the battle?" Yhoshi asked.

"You will have to win that first."

"How?"

"You will know how."

"But how do we get back to the castle?" Fynda asked.

"You have your kolai?" We nodded. "Then fling them into the center of your circle, into the light."

We unlinked hands and immediately began to sink. I had been certain that M'nor would keep us afloat. We grabbed for each other and once again bobbed to the surface.

"You do not trust," M'nor said. Disappointment shaded her voice. "You must either trust or abandon the quest. The choice is yours, but time is short."

"What will happen?" Fynda asked. She inclined her head toward Garan. "He can't swim, you know."

"You either trust or you do not," M'nor stated. "There is no halfway in between."

"I trust," Garan shouted. He pulled his hands free. Again, we began to sink. Water lapped at our shins as we aimed for the light. The stones hissed then fizzed as they hit water and disappeared. It seemed we were destined to follow them. Water splashed around our knees, our thighs, our waist. Fynda and Yhoshi clutched at my hands. I shook them off.

"No," I said. "What will be will be." I was no longer afraid. Warm and womb-like, the water massaged me and I relaxed into it, even as it rose up my chest, past my neck, mouth, ears, eyes... I held my breath until I could hold it no longer. And then something solid beneath my feet pushed me back up. When it broke the water's surface, I saw that we stood on a black marble disc veined with red: the Kol Kolai, the Table of Prophecy. In the center sat The Nayr, aglow with the same fiery light I had seen at Castle Rose. Brighter and brighter it blazed until it engulfed us in a blinding white brilliance.

When the light faded, M'nor and the night were gone. We stood on pink sand, in a circle around the cup. On one side of the narrow beach, Mir M'nor glistened into infinity. On the other, ugly billows of smoke shrouded the sky over Pre Vilda'aa.

The Final Battle

Twenty-Seven

The truth would be written before another day passed. M'nor had said it.

"We must get to Alanda," I cried. But how? The table might have carried us this far, but Mir M'nor had claimed it. I picked up The Nayr. Its light warmed my face but offered no answers.

"Even if we could get there in time, we have no way to fight," Yhoshi said gloomily. "No clothes, no horses, no weapons. We have nothing."

"Won't Kyri be able to give us all that?" Fynda asked.

"We don't know if he's still alive," Yhoshi replied. My blood turned to ice and all color drained from my face.

"You didn't see the battle, Toshar. Bloody...merciless...men with no armor...women fighting with sticks...even children. We can't count on Alanda to arm us."

Garan walked to the water's edge, shaking his head. When he turned to face us, he barely resembled the deformed, light-starved creature of Horusha. Whatever transformation was moving through him had nearly completed the job. A thick brush of hair sprouted wildly from a brow nearly free of furrows. All over his body, his skin had lost its creases and folds. They had smoothed and filled, pumping out sunken chest and scrawny legs until his head and torso no longer met as mismatched strangers. "Listen to you," he said, jabbing his finger into the air. "Do you think M'nor would send us into battle unprepared? Trust. Didn't she repeat that word again and again?"

True. But standing naked and impotent while Q'ntana burned made trust hard to touch. Yet now, more than ever, we needed that trust.

"Garan is right," I said. My words disappeared in the roar of an immense breaker. It thundered in from the sea, knocking Garan to the ground. Its curling, froth-lipped crest thrust toward and past us, licked against the seven steps, then charged back, carrying much of the beach with it. When the wave had receded, Garan sat up and rubbed the water from his eyes. He half-stood, noticed something in the sand and began to pick at it.

"Come quick," he called. "Look!" The retreating breaker had bared a double column of massive, claw-tipped prints, each half as long as Garan himself and cast indelibly in the sand as though in stone. He smiled with satisfaction. "Dragon prints," he said. "There's your answer."

An answer, perhaps. But one that raised yet more questions. These belonged to no ordinary dragon. With six claws on its left feet and four on its right, they could only belong to Kumba. I watched the surf erase our prints but leave the dragon's intact. Its trail began where we stood and followed the water line into the distance.

"I thought M'nor said Kumba lived a long time ago," Yhoshi argued.

"She didn't say he died a long time ago," I said. "Besides, these aren't fresh prints."

"What does it mean, Toshar?" Fynda asked. "Is it good or bad?"

But I was already sprinting ahead on Kumba's trail, chalice in hand. The others broke into an enthusiastic run behind me. We followed the tracks far along the beach and around the curving edge of its crescent, leaving behind Pre Vilda'aa's smoky plumes. Gray cliffs on our right paled to white then crystal. As they soared higher, their jagged fingers thrusting into the sky, they angled sharply toward the water until sea and glass met in a slender, towering pyramid whose zenith flared with light. The prints disappeared through a tall, triangular opening, folded invisibly into the glass.

We stepped inside. Fynda shielded her eyes against the brilliant sparkle. But for the prints in the sand, still wet from the receding wave, there would have been no way forward or back, only a blinding mirage of reflecting glass. The tracks led and we followed, along a labyrinthine passage that carried us, finally, to a stone chamber, pink as Castle Rose. From there, the trail took us into another chamber, then another, each redder and darker than the last. Now, Fynda led, her night-seeing eyes focused on the sandy floor. Another chamber, then another and one more still. Then Fynda stopped, dropped to her knees and scrabbled in the sand.

"That's it," she said. "There are no more." Her voice echoed eerily against rocks only she could see.

"There has to be," Yhoshi said. He poked blindly at the ground. "They can't just end like that."

"Well, they do," she insisted. "I'm standing in the last one." As we joined her in this fossil-like print, a faint light glowed from the chalice, revealing red, roughhewn walls, so dark they first seemed black. Angled, they rose to meet somewhere in the shadowy heights. Fynda was right. No prints extended beyond this one. Where would they have led? There was nothing beyond this chamber, nothing but blank stone.

No one suggested returning. We all knew that if the sea had cleared Kumba's trail to lead us here, there was a reason. Nor could anyone but Fynda explore the space. As soon as any us stepped from the dragon print, the cup's glow extinguished. And so we stood, peering out from our crater at the center of this dimly lit chamber, until Garan's hand accidentally brushed against the cup. The light brightened at his touch.

"Touch the cup," he said, "all of us, together." The moment we did, The Nayr exploded in brilliant flame that caressed our hands with gentle warmth. An instant later, platinum light swirled out from it in an ever-broadening spiral that so transfixed us we didn't immediately notice the changes it wrought. On each wall, now a deep, rich-hued scarlet, hung a sword of dazzling white steel, a scabbard studded with emeralds in double-chevron pattern, a jewel-handled dagger that was Oriccan's twin and a shield emblazoned with a flying eagle and scarlet rose — all of the same luminous alloy as the cup itself. No longer naked, we each wore sturdy battle dress, M'nor's standard stitched over our hearts.

"The Arms of K'varr," I whispered reverently.

We placed the cup at our feet and stepped gingerly from the crater, afraid the light would fade and take this miracle with it. The light didn't fade, nor did the armor.

"Here are your weapons, Yhoshi," I cried exultantly. "Are they worthy?" Too awed to answer, Yhoshi lifted down one of the swords, hypnotized by its terrible beauty.

One dagger drew me to it. I touched it and knew it to be Oriccan. Then I hefted its companion sword and shield, absorbing strength and power that seemed molded to my hand, my body. Although the weapons appeared outwardly identical, each exerted a unique pull. And each sword blade flared in a shaft of colored light, but only when wielded by the hand meant for it. Yhoshi's and mine matched Ta'ar and Rykka. Fynda's was emerald, Garan's gold.

"It's a perfect fit," Garan marveled as he admired his outfit, "even for this misshapen body."

"Not so misshapen as you think," I said. Garan raised his eyebrows. He actually had eyebrows now. "You almost look normal. Older," I joked, "but normal." We laughed and raised our four swords in salute, touching them tip to tip. A rapid-burst of sparks flashed through the chamber accompanied by booming, rock-shattering thunderclaps. When it ended an instant later, cave, ocean and beach were gone.

We stood in a copse on a low hill overlooking a vast plain black with King's Men, a raging sea of death that surged up against the base of Castle Rose Mount. A clammy chill crawled up my spine, devouring the exhilaration we had felt moments before.

"What hope do we have against that?" Garan asked.

Yhoshi shook his head in defeat. "This is worse than I saw."

Ashen, Garan's face furrowed in worry. As his features wavered between the Garan of Horusha and the Garan of Mir M'nor, I saw Yhoshi's vision as it flickered between victory and defeat.

"Listen to you!" Fynda exclaimed. "M'nor said it was up to us. She said we could do it."

"But—" Garan started.

Fynda took his hand. "I told a story, Garan. To M'nor. Me, Fynda. I'm no one. Nothing. And *I* helped dry M'nor's tears. She shone for me, Garan. For all of us. That was bigger than what's down there. I know it doesn't look that way. But it is. I know it is." She turned to me and raised her sword. "Isn't it, Toshar? Isn't it?"

Tentatively, I raised my sword to meet hers. As I did, a wave of confidence flooded up my arm and through my body. "Fynda's right," I cried. "What hope do we have? The hope that carried us here. We are warriors for M'nor and Alanda. We bear the Arms of K'varr. We *will* make a difference."

Smiling weakly, Garan touched his sword to mine. Yhoshi, energized by Fynda's speech, added his. In that moment our blades glowed with our individual colors as our eyes lit with renewed strength. A polite cough interrupted the ritual and we spun around, swords at the ready.

"No, please, it's only us," Artos said. "We've come to take you back to the castle." He stood with Sorros at the entrance to the copse, looking small against the giant trees, and I remembered Miknos's face in the swirling smoke of Pre Vilda'aa. My trust had its limits.

As Yhoshi disarmed them, I moved toward Artos, my sword level with his neck. "How did you find us?"

"The king sent us," Sorros said in a small voice.

"Which king?"

"King Kyri," Artos replied.

I scanned the trees for movement. Seeing none, I turned my gaze back to the pages. "Where's your brother? Where's Miknos?"

Artos wouldn't meet my eyes. He stared at his feet, shuffling them awkwardly. His sister burst into tears. Putting her arm around Sorros, Fynda asked, "What is it? You can tell us."

"He...he...he..."

"He's dead," Artos mumbled. "By the king's hand. My brother, a traitor. I still can't believe it." He raised his eyes to mine and tears rolled down his cheeks. "I'm sorry," he whispered.

Kyri himself met us atop Castle Rose's highest tower. He smiled and hugged us, but his smile was weary and his embrace weak. A swatch of dried blood stained his bandaged left arm. Though our reunion was sweet, his news was bitter. In only two days of fighting, Kyri's troops had been pushed back to the castle wall, their every thrust repelled by Fvorag's superior numbers. Wave after wave of black death had cut down not only trained Alandan soldiers, but the farmers, shopkeepers, women and children Yhoshi had seen in his vision.

"These men know no honor," Kyri said with barely concealed disgust. "They kept constant guard over the battlefield last night and wouldn't let us gather our dead. Today, they trample ours and theirs into the mud. As do we: There are so many, there's no way to avoid it. As for them, I think they take pleasure in it."

Kronan came up behind us, Dafna at his side. Fresh scars gashed his face. "You give them too much credit for feeling, your majesty," he muttered.

"Perhaps, uncle, but I don't want to become like them. The battle has already turned crueler than I thought possible. I wish there was another way..."

"This is no time for wishing," Kronan said. "I need a decision. Do we retreat into the castle or try to hold our ground?"

Kyri looked over the battlefield and grimaced. The slaughter had intensified. For every slain black-shirt, two more took his place. No one replaced slain Alandans. "You've been closer to the fighting today, uncle. What do you say?"

Kronan's face was grim. "Unless we retreat," he said, "everyone loyal to Alanda will be closer to the land by nightfall, with his face pushed into it by a black-gloved fist. Retreat will buy us five days, time perhaps for a miracle."

I drew my sword and pointed it toward the brooding mass that shrouded the suns. Its blue light cut through the clouds to reveal a slender, blade-shape slice of sky. "Your miracle is here," I said. "In these swords." Fynda, Yhoshi and Garan's blades met mine, sparking a flash of white light. The display failed to impress Kronan.

"You are wise and true," he said kindly, "but you are no soldier."

"And you are no bard," I snapped. "Retreat and we are lost." I turned to Kyri. "There's no time to tell you what we've seen and how we know it to be true. You must trust." I saw the struggle in his eyes. Every logical fiber in his being told him to heed Kronan, the soldier. Were I him, I would.

"What does O'ric say?" I asked.

"No one has been able to find him to ask," Kyri replied wearily.

"Ask Dyffyth," Fynda suggested.

"He has died," I said before Kyri could respond.

Kyri nodded. "It happened early yesterday, before the suns had risen, just as Fvorag launched his attack. Bless Dyffyth. He foresaw it all, to the hour of their coming, and guided us through seven days of preparation. Without this miracle, there would be no next step to decide."

Platinum sparks leapt from our sword tips as Yhoshi, Fynda, Garan and I touched blades again. "Then trust this miracle, and the one that brought us here. We must not retreat. We must hold on through this day and into the night."

"And then?" Kyri asked.

"That's as far as I can see."

Kyri again studied the battlefield. A lull in the fighting had created a surreal tableau of blood, mud and severed limbs. The smell of death hung silently over it all. "Give me a moment," he said. He walked slowly away, deep in troubled thought. When he returned, grim determination had displaced tormented uncertainty.

"I am decided," he announced, "and what I say is law. We will fight one more day — and survive." He turned to Kronan. "See that my horse and armor are prepared at once. I return to lead the charge."

Dafna touched his bandage. "But Kyri, your arm..."

"No buts, Dafna. If we are all to die, then I will die at the head of my people, not hidden away in this castle." He embraced her and stroked her hair.

"Then I will fight too," she said, pulling free. Kyri nodded sadly. As she disappeared into the castle, I wondered if I would ever see her alive again. Kronan followed her, then stopped at the head of the stairs. He looked back inquiringly.

"Yes, uncle," Kyri said, "prepare their horses. These four ride at my side."

Twenty-Eight

We charged across the drawbridge in V formation, Kyri at the head astride a magnificent snowy stallion eager to lead us into battle. I followed to his right on Rykka, Yhoshi to his left on Ta'ar. Behind us Fynda and Garan rode mounts that matched the colors of their blades — emerald for her, gold for him.

As we emerged from the castle, enfolded in a subtle shaft of light and flush with courage, the gory bloodletting stilled for an instant, as though frozen on an artist's canvas. When it resumed, more barbarous than ever, a new spirit had awakened in the ragged Alandans, who flung themselves at the King's Men with renewed vigor and hope.

Of the four of us, only Yhoshi had known serious fighting before, but nothing, not even his vision, could have prepared him for the savage ferocity of Fvorag's army. As for me, that initial burst of fearlessness melted quickly into terror. That too dissolved almost immediately. There was no time for it.

Within seconds our formation collapsed and I was on my own, fending off the merciless thrusts of men bigger, stronger and more ruthless than I. But if I didn't know how to maneuver through a battlefield, Rykka did. And if my arms lacked experience in violent combat, sword and shield did not. I let them take charge of both offense and defense, and together we cut down scores of black-shirts within minutes of entering the fray. Time slowed after that first, dizzying sally. Every gesture, every breath, every twitch, seemed to last hours as all around me moved in a lingering, stately dance of death.

Rykka springs up in a graceful jeté...sails over a sea of slaughter...glides down next to a black-shirt. ... The soldier pushes his lance toward Kyri's back. ... "Kyri-i-i-i..." The sound emerges tortoise-like from my throat. ... Kyri can't see this threat for others...can't hear my cry over others. ... My sword lifts...slices down on the soldier's arm...severs it from his shoulder. ... His mouth distends in pain. ... He tumbles from his saddle...ground into the mud by his riderless mount.

Each time the sword raised my arm, it taught me how to wield it myself. And the more confidence I gained, the quicker time moved, accelerating gradually then blindingly to a whizzing blur. Aygra and B'na moved together then apart as more black-clad bodies littered the field. More Alandans too, and I wondered if our ranks would die off before our time did. But thoughts distracted me, and I couldn't afford distraction. Too much swirled around me, too much that demanded response.

Now, Kyri needed assistance. Now, Dafna. Now an Alandan picked himself up from the blood-sodden ground next to me. His horse had been cut out from under him. I pulled him up onto Rykka until, with a sword thrust and a kick, I could a free a black stallion for him. How could I move so rapidly, so expertly? There was no time to analyze, only to act and react. And so I did.

Aygra and B'na sat at opposite ends of the sky before I permitted myself a quick scan across the battlefield's lengthening shadow. Had our numbers stabilized? Were we no longer losing? Kronan's smiling thumbs-up confirmed it.

That gesture was his last. In that same instant, a black-shirt's outstretched sword severed his still-smiling head from his neck.

I urged Rykka after the man. But she tugged me in a different direction. Reluctantly, I let her take the lead. Seconds later, we landed at Fynda's side as a soldier vaulted onto her horse. He tightened his arm around her neck and pressed a dagger to her eye. For the first time that day, neither Rykka nor my sword leapt into action. I was paralyzed. Grinning malevolently, the soldier stabbed spurred heels into the horse's flanks and raced away. I watched helplessly, unable to move. Then, Garan flew past and the whoosh of his backdraft revived me. I tore after him and caught up just as he sailed over Fynda and her captor. The distraction enabled Yhoshi to emerge from nowhere and thrust his sword into the soldier's back. He toppled, dragging Fynda to the ground with him. She threw him off, leapt onto her horse and in an instant, the three riders vanished into the sea of fighting.

Inadequacy washed over me. Why had I been unable to act? I glanced anxiously around, afraid to again expose my ineptitude. What I saw charged me back into action. Storming ahead was the soldier who had slain Kronan.

"Now!" I bellowed. With a single leap, Rykka carried me to his side, dancing out of his way as he lunged at me. Blade clanged against blade, shooting sparks high into the late afternoon sky.

Once again, time slows and the battle around me dissolves into an unfocused blur. All I know is this one burly soldier, his masked face always in shadow.

We cross swords for what seems hours, days. Neither gains advantage. My arm aches and the sword's weight pulls at my shoulder. It's heavy...so heavy. I can barely lift it. How long can I go on?

Now, the suns abandon us, scraping a bloody scar across the sky. Now, it too vanishes.

My arm lifts and swings, lifts and swings, the sword seeing what my eyes cannot. The automatic thrust-and-shield continues into the night.

My eyes can't pierce the dark, but they pierce the truth: We have made it to the end of the day. Alanda will survive. I will survive, if only I can fell this one horseman.

My blade begins to glow, casting a dim blue light on my adversary. Who is he? They all dress the same, these King's Men — black shirts, black gloves, black masks. Nothing to distinguish rank. Nothing to distinguish king from commoner. The sword-light brightens and I see his face, for the first time.

I know that face, that bushy mustache that droops down either side of an indelible scowl. I've seen it before. But where? And then I know, and the knowledge drives a fresh burst of strength through me, enough to immobilize his sword.

"You are Fvorag."

"King Fvorag to you, boy," he hissed, barely opening his mouth. He pushed hard against my sword.

"No king of mine," I shouted, pushing back with equal strength.

"No matter. Dead men don't need kings."

"What about dead kings?"

"You're the one who will die tonight, last-of-the-bards."

"Not before I see you dead."

"We'll see what you're able to see in the morning from the Wall of Traitors. You and all your traitor friends. You'll die as your father died, as the bards before and since have died. Pity it must be quick." He broke free of my sword-lock and maneuvered his horse to thrust again. Rykka sidestepped clear then turned, freeing me to level my sword at his neck.

"You call yourself Fvorag," I retorted. "I call you by your truth name: Ynos." And then time, which had slowed and quickened, quickened and slowed, stopped. Fvorag-Ynos loomed before me, his sword upraised, ready to strike.

"Now!" a voice commanded. Mine? I didn't stop to question. Letting my shield fall, I grasped my sword with both hands and swung with all the strength I possessed. Like Kronan's before it, Fvorag-Ynos's head rolled to the ground. It wasn't smiling.

The Nayr was. From a battlement high atop the castle it glowed, brighter and brighter until it burst into flame and its light flooded the battlefield, revealing dead bodies, splayed and distended. Severed limbs sank into blood-soaked mud. Riderless horses and horseless riders wandered in dazed circles. I swallowed back the vomit that rose to my throat. Yet the butchery barely entered my consciousness. I stared at my sword, at the blood that scarred its glow in dark splotches. I tried to fit it back into its scabbard, but my hand shook too violently. My arm tumbled to my side and my fist unclenched. But the sword held to my hand. Every cell in my body quaked as hot liquid scored my cheeks, blurring the circle of smiles that surrounded me. Whose were they? I didn't know. All I knew were the retching sobs that heaved up from a place deeper than I had ever been. I dropped my head into Rykka's mane, letting her soft, silky down soak up my tears.

It was over.

Twenty-Nine

I longed for peaceful oblivion that night. But it eluded me. Vividly and with its gore intact, the battle played over and over in an endless loop that whirred before my eyes whether I woke or slept. Snatches of sound from outside my window merged surreally with these nightmare visions, so that I saw trunkless heads bobbing over the wounded, free-floating arms gathering the dead and headless trunks preparing the castle grounds for victory celebrations. On the final turn of the loop, the head that tumbled to the ground from Fvorag-Ynos's body puffed out, blocking my view of the battlefield beyond. Its green face leered mockingly from empty, red-ringed sockets. Then, a formless black mass pushed it up, up, up, until it sat atop a towering, black-cloaked figure. All the while it laughed — a grotesque cackling caw that grew louder and louder, exploding finally in a deafening blast that jarred me awake.

Trembling, I pulled back my soaking bedclothes and padded to the window. I peered through a crack in the heavy, velour drapes and gazed into the night darkness. Where was Bo'Rá K'n? A cool breeze rustled through and I shivered, still wet with perspiration. Stripping off my nightclothes, I wrapped myself in a dry blanket and curled into the window seat. My eyes drifted shut.

Na'an stands before me, resplendent in her shimmering, gossamer. Silently, she pulls back the curtains. Moonlight rushes into the room. M'nor smiles and says nothing. My eyes follow Na'an's arm as she extends it out the window. Silver-tinted serenity rules the vista before me. This is not the battlefield of my nightmare — waking or sleeping. Fresh, red earth soaks up the blood. No bodies litter this giant farmer's field waiting to be sown.

My gaze returns to M'nor, hovering bright and full as she did over her great northern sea. Her smile beckons, seeming to embrace all Q'ntana, as slowly, softly, joyously she begins to sing.

As I stare up, transfixed by her radiance, I too sing — the same melody we have sung together before. Her voice is confident, jubilant, triumphant — as is mine. The words come back to me, those words in a language older than Q'ntana itself.

> *Mir M'nor m'ranna*
> *M'ranna ma Mir*
> *Mir M'nor m'ranna*
> *M'ranna ma Mir*

The words remain strange, but their essence is clear, and I repeat them again and again, in a voice I barely recognize, so ripe, vibrant and assured is it. The louder I sing, the fuller and brighter M'nor grows, until her light exceeds even that of the two suns. Suddenly, I'm aware of other voices, a symphony of song that soars around me. I pause for an instant to feel the music, then rejoin the exultant chorale, my voice mightier than ever.

I awoke to brilliant sunlight and the music of carpentry. Zinging saws and rat-a-tat hammers mingled with laughing chatter as platforms, benches, tables and flagpoles took shape beneath my window. All signs of battle had vanished. The farmer's field of my dreams had been sown — with saplings and flowers, banners and bunting. Along fresh gravel paths, Alandans, some bandaged and limping, hummed and whistled as they prepared for festivities that must surpass Kyri's coronation. As the melodies filtered up, I realized they were one. It was M'nor's song. Had they dreamed it too?

And then I recalled my nightmare and Bo'Rá K'n. How safe was M'nor? How safe were any of us if his shadow could still stalk the land? I splashed water on my face, trying to clear his ghoulish grin from my mind's eye. How could we celebrate when Bo'Rá K'n still lived?

"Even a bard cannot understand everything." O'ric's face looked into mine from the looking glass over the washstand.

My glad smile faded as quickly as it had formed. "Where were you when we needed you?" I asked angrily.

"You didn't need me, Toshar," he replied softly.

"You abandoned us! "

"A people must fight its own battles. I did what I could, as did you. That's all anyone can."

"But you can do anything," I said stubbornly.

"It is not so. Nor would I want it to be." His reflected eyes never left mine.

"I don't understand."

"I say it again: Even a bard cannot understand everything."

"I understand that you deserted Kyri when he needed you most."

"A king must make his own choice between general and Elderbard. It is not for me to intervene."

"Elderbard? Surely, in Dyffyth's absence that is you." O'ric emitted one of his rare laughs — a short burst, then silence. He shook his head. "If not you, then who?"

"Who else do you see before you?" he asked gently. Dark eyes older than mine stared back at me from the mirror and I turned from them in fear.

"So soon?" I whispered.

"The number of your years means nothing. It is how you have spent them that has value. It is what they have taught you, what they have earned you, that matters."

Slowly, I turned back to the mirror. My sleep-tousled hair and pouting mouth stripped more years from those few I already had. "I am to be Elderbard, then, because there is no other living bard."

O'ric placed his clawed hands on my shoulders. "You see a youth's face but overlook a sage's eyes." He touched a taloned finger to the mirror. "Look into those eyes — yours, not mine — and say what you see."

I forced my gaze away from O'ric's and into ancient pools of liquid coal. "I see an old man," I said, "the old man of my vision. The old man who is Elderbard." I paused. "The old man who is me."

"What does he say, Toshar?"

"His lips move but I can't hear anything." I pressed my face closer to the mirror until the image blurred, until his face and mine merged. "'It is time,' he says. 'It is over and begins anew.' He's fading." I blinked. "He's gone." I turned to face O'ric and felt his fiery breath on my cheek. "Then it's true. I am already Elderbard."

"In all but Naming, my son."

Thirty

Yhoshi, Fynda, Garan and I stood with all of Alanda by the river that bore its name. No sound broke the silent dusk as the fallen Alandans, shrouded in white cotton, were laid on five funeral barges. When the sky's final fiery streaks ebbed to black, Kyri stepped forward in the modest white robe and simple coronet of his young kingship. With his torch, the only light in this lightless night, he ignited each barge in turn and launched it into the river. No one moved until the current pulled the last of the flaming pyres over the horizon. Only then did Kyri speak.

"Our heroes have passed from this world to the next. May their lives carry as much meaning there as they did here." Raising the torch into the night, he turned away from the water to face his people. "May this flame that has sped them on their journey also light ours. Let the torchbearers approach."

Few in the crowd did not carry an unlit torch. One by one they filed past Kyri, firing their torches from his, then proceeded in a snaking queue up toward the castle grounds. Garan, Fynda, Yhoshi and I were the last. It was the first time we stood alone with Kyri since the battle.

"I've had no chance to thank you," he said, embracing each of us in turn. We stood in a ring of fire, Kyri at the center. "There's no honor great enough to offer heroes such as you."

"Toshar is the hero," Fynda said. "He killed Fvorag." Yhoshi and Garan nodded.

"If it couldn't be me," Garan said, "I'm glad it was you."

I didn't know how to reply. I felt strangely distant from the battle and from the journey that had preceded it, as though they had happened to someone else. "I'm no hero," I said. "I did what I had to do — nothing more. It is M'nor you must honor."

When we reached the battlefield, now a living garden illuminated by hundreds of flaring torches, a thunderous cheer echoed through the night, bearing us to the foot of the dais in a surge of love. Shyly, Yhoshi took Fynda's hand. She smiled. They stood on one side, Garan and Dafna on the other, as Kyri and I climbed the six steps to join O'ric. The Nayr sat on a white-clothed table behind him.

"Once more I return," O'ric called out over the still-cheering throng, "to preside over singular rituals. No precedent exists for this ceremony — no precedent for the rededication of a kingship already crowned and no precedent for the Naming of an Elderbard by other than a living Elderbard. That we create new rituals for this day is fitting, for today, in the heart of this ancient and eternal capital, we reestablish Q'ntana as a single, indivisible realm."

He stepped behind the table and cupped his hands over the chalice. As one, the torches extinguished, plunging us into darkness. O'ric then lifted the chalice. It glowed with white brilliance in his hand. "This chalice, this Nayr, is older than the land itself. It is the grail of light that restores your land to you and consecrates your leaders." He raised it over his head and shouted, "Let the people name their king."

"Kyri!" they roared back.

"Let the people name their Elderbard."

"Toshar!" Dafna's voice rose above the others.

"Kyri, heir to Fortas, and Toshar, heir to Eulisha, do you swear allegiance to Q'ntana, to Aygra and B'na that light her by day, to M'nor that lights her by night and to Prithi that lights her always?"

Kyri stepped to the front of the dais. "I do."

I swallowed hard. In a flash, I saw myself the day O'ric arrived in Pre Tena'aa. I barely remembered the boy I felt then, any more than I knew the Elderbard I was to be. The Elderbard I already was. "I do," I said. My voice rang through the night.

"Then take this Grail of Nayr, each of you in turn, and drink from its light that you too may radiate wisdom, mercy, compassion and love."

A perplexed look briefly crossed Kyri's face as he lifted it to his lips. He drank, and for a moment his whole body glowed. Then O'ric passed the grail to me and I understood Kyri's puzzlement. It was empty of anything but light. As I sipped from it, I felt an abiding warmth slide down my throat and fill my heart.

"Long may you both serve Q'ntana in peace," O'ric said. As he clasped The Nayr in both hands — six fingers on his left hand, four on his right — and held it up to the sky, it burst into flame. Its light flowed up his arms and suffused his body, which flickered and wavered like a candle flame. After a minute, the light returned to the grail — taking O'ric with it.

Only The Nayr remained, suspended in midair, glowing brighter than ever.

Kyri looked at me in confusion. His eyes asked, "What do we do now?" For once, I knew and trusted the answer: nothing. We waited — all Alanda waited — in awed, breathless silence. And then a small, silver disc emerged from the grail. It rose swiftly, ballooning as it climbed into the midheaven, a glowing orb that filled the sky with joyful song and cast its light over all Q'ntana.

Epilogue

I never saw O'ric again, but I saw M'nor often. I see her now, beaming across my parchment, massaging my tired hands. Soon, she will go to her rest and I to mine, free to rejoin my companions and my Dafna, free to continue my journey in other realms. Na'an spoke true this night. The time had come to fix the story in ink. My story, my time. Now, it is done. I have written through the night and filled the oceans of emptiness that caused me so much dread once upon a time.

Once upon a time... We speak these words freely now, all of us — for we are all bards in Q'ntana. We have all remembered in the light what we gave up to the dark, and our words nourish M'nor as she nurtures us.

As for Bo'Rá K'n, I never saw him again either. Yet I know he still lives. That knowing pricked at my joy for many years. Na'an would not answer when I asked how to erase his shadow. And I asked often, refusing to trust her silence. I learned in time that Bo'Rá K'n cannot die, as Na'an cannot, as M'nor cannot. He lies in wait just beyond the next turning, in that land of unknowingness where fear always lurks, that same land where M'nor burns most brightly, when we open our hearts to her. For it is through his darkness that she shines. Without his scowl, her smile could not endure. I repeat this truth, though I do not welcome it.

O'ric was right. There is much even an Elderbard cannot understand. Perhaps the eyes that succeed these will see. Perhaps the heart that succeeds this one will accept. Whether in this world or the next, they will not cease trying. That is the journey. That is the quest.

Visit these Web Sites

for...

- *More LightLines products*
- *Free newsletters*
- *More about Mark David, including touring/event schedules & contact info*

www.lightlinesmedia.com
www.markdavidgerson.com
www.markdavidgerson.blogspot.com

Order Form

ONLINE ORDERS: www.themoonquest.com. PayPal or credit cards only

FAX ORDERS: 978-268-7304. Please fax this form. Credit card orders only

PHONE ORDERS: 800-369-4506. Credit card orders only

MAIL ORDERS: LightLines Media (Orders) • 223 N. Guadalupe St., #171 • Santa Fe, NM 87501

——————— copies of The MoonQuest @ US $16.00   US $ ———————

SUBTOTAL   **US $** ———————

Gross receipts tax (NM only) @ 7.625%   US $ ———————

Shipping (subject to change)
US/Can US$2/order + $3.75/bk • Int'l $4/order + $6.25/bk   US $ ———————

TOTAL   **US $** ———————

Name ———————————————————————————————

Shipping Address ————————————————————————————

City ———————————— State/Prov —————— Zip/Postal Code ————

Phone Number(s) ——————————————————————————

E-Mail Address ————————————————————————————

PAYMENT INFORMATION

Payment by check, money order, MasterCard, Visa, Discover, AmEx or PayPal. We apologize to our non-U.S. customers but all checks and money orders must be remitted in U.S. funds; checks must be drawn on a U.S. bank.

Check number ——— Check amount ———Card # ——————————

Card type ——— Exp date——— Security code (back of card; front if AmEx) ———

Name on card ————————————————————————————

Billing address ———————————————————————————

City———————————— State/Prov —————— Zip/Postal Code ————

Signature ———————————————————————————